THE
GOOD
DIAMOND

Also by Skye Kathleen Moody

Fiction

Medusa
K Falls
Rain Dance
Blue Poppy
Wildcrafters
Habitat

Nonfiction (as Kathy Kahn)

Hillbilly Women
Fruits of Our Labor

THE
GOOD
DIAMOND

Skye Kathleen Moody

St. Martin's Minotaur
New York

www.minotaurbooks.com

Library of Congress Cataloging-in-Publication Data

Moody, Skye Kathleen.
   The good diamond / Skye Kathleen Moody.—1st St. Martin's Minotaur ed.
      p.   cm.
   ISBN 0-312-32415-4
   EAN 978-0312-32415-5
   1. Diamond, Venus (Fictitious character)—Fiction.   2. Government investigators—Fiction.   3. Women environmentalists—Fiction.
4. Animals—Treatment—Fiction.   5. Northwest, Pacific—Fiction.
6. Diamond smuggling—Fiction.   7. Black bear—Fiction.   I. Title.

PS3563.O5538G66   2004
813'.54—dc22
                                              2004042801

First Edition: August 2004

10 9 8 7 6 5 4 3 2 1

For G. M. Ford
Who knew?

PART ONE

On the night Big Jim Hardy died, a thick crust of ice blanketed the length and breadth of Lac de Lune, reflecting a blue incandescence stolen from the waxing moon. Nearing midnight, stars exploded across the sky, the moon looming on the horizon, stars like diamonds, dazzling gems of the Universe, that only the Universe could wholly possess. The land and its lakes lay frozen now, dormant beneath winter's icy mantle. On Lac de Lune, a serpentine scar of tire tracks wound across the frozen surface, lit by moon rays casting across the lake and the frozen eskers beyond. Those eskers, long sinuous streams of gravel, now burrowed beneath winter's mantle, embodying gems of their own, there for the plucking by a human hand.

Twenty miles west-southwest of Lac de Lune, six individuals clad in white survival suits and driving white snowmobiles moved swiftly across the ice road, heading east, invisible against the barren white landscape. The sky's cavity swallowed up the sound of the vehicles' engines and though they hardly needed headlights beneath this moonlit, starlit sky they used halogen beams, the better to spot ice-dwelling creatures or other potential obstructions on their path to glory. For ultimately, these six believed they were destined for greatness. Each knew in his heart that great nations are built only upon great risk, and more often than not, on bloodshed.

Sure enough, the lead driver's halogen beam surprised a polar bear and her two cubs feeding in a fish hole. Startled by the intrusion, the ungainly cubs scampered off across the tundra as the adult bounded forward to attack the intruders. But the snowmobiles swiftly outdistanced the polar bear, leaving her ranting in their wake. A few more kilometers across the ice, and the lights from Zone Mine's headquarters appeared on the horizon. The lead driver signaled the others to cut their engines and the snowmobiles fell silent.

Surrounded by this frozen beauty, a soul might experience the quick thrill of God's wonders, and yet Big Jim Hardy was blind to the Creator's panorama outside Zone Mine's headquarters. Big Jim was too busy indoors, preparing for, if not the most important, the most rewarding moment of his long and eclectic career. Like the name he went by up in the Northwest Territories, Big Jim Hardy was a large and simple man, with no especially outstanding features other than his formidable girth and the particular shape of his nose, a broad isosceles, as wide as it was long, a protuberance that set the folks in Yellowknife to wondering about Jim Hardy's origins. No one had ever seen a nose quite like Big Jim's. He never talked much, never told anyone where he came from, he just showed up in Yellowknife one day a little over three years ago and, like every other diamond prospector, registered his staked claims at the provincial clerk's office. Almost as soon as he'd staked his first claim, rumors began flying. Big Jim Hardy was working undercover for De Beers. Big Jim Hardy was working undercover for AKG, or for Rosy Blue, or Parecles, for one of the big diamond companies, anyway, trying to

confuse other prospectors by pretending he'd discovered diamond pipes up as far north as Lac de Lune. Or maybe he
worked for the native people, from whose land the big mines
had pulled billions of dollars' worth of diamonds since the
early 1990s. Big Jim Hardy this and Big Jim Hardy that. But
Yellowknife's rumormongers had never garnered Big Jim's interest, and they were all so far off base he could only laugh at
the absurdity of their speculations. And too, Big Jim was far
too busy prospecting. That was part of what he'd come north
to do and that was mostly what he had done every day, seven
days a week, 365 days a year, for three years now.

Until ten weeks ago, when Big Jim's strong work ethic
had finally paid off. The story first got going around Yellowknife: Big Jim Hardy had hit a rich new diamond-yielding
pipe up at Lac de Lune, and he had immediately dropped a
thick cloak of secrecy over his operations. All anyone in the
capital of the Northwest Territories knew for sure was that
Big Jim Hardy had just hired four new security guards, giving
Zone Mine a total of twelve, and he had sworn them and
every other Zone employee to utter secrecy. The fact was,
most of Zone's employees, drillers and pullers and sorters of
rough diamonds, knew nothing more than the general public
about what was going on at Zone Mine. Last January, when
activity at Zone had picked up, and Big Jim had hired the extra security guards, he flew in more mine workers and equipment and drove a drill rig across the winter road to Site 3 on
Lac de Lune. The rig sat now on the frozen lake, its drill running night and day in a race against springtime and melting
ice, driving deep into the earth beneath the lakebed where
riches beyond anyone's wildest imagination waited to be
plucked. That was the word going around Yellowknife.

Other prospectors flew over Lac de Lune, to spy on the
activity up there, to see which of Big Jim's several stakes had
turned up G10 kimberlite, the first foretoken of a diamond
pipe, to determine if he'd really found a pipe at Site 3, and
was actually drilling out rough. Whoever got there first and
staked the adjacent land might get as lucky as Big Jim appar-

ently had. Since January, Big Jim's geologist, Karen Crandall, had seen De Beers's sleek new Cessna flying low over Zone territory, especially over Site 3 on Lac de Lune.

And then Big Jim Hardy broke the news publicly announcing he had discovered the largest blue-green diamond ever mined from the Earth. Big Jim named the 384-carat rough diamond the "Lac de Lune," and when news shot out of Yellowknife, as news like this can never be kept for long, the Lac de Lune made headlines worldwide. No such fabulous stone had ever been pulled from Canada's flourishing diamond mines. And the size and intensity of the Lac de Lune's rare glacial color instantly sent awe and wonderstruck scheming through the international diamond trade. In Antwerp, London, New York, Gaborone, and Johannesburg, diamond brokers lusted for the rare stone and sent their representatives to call on Big Jim Hardy. They wanted to inspect the diamond in its rough state, study the color and clarity for themselves, determine what flaws might impede the cleaving of the stone. But he turned them all away. Big Jim had his own plan for the Lac de Lune.

In his office at Zone Mine headquarters, Big Jim moved quickly, lumbering around the room, lurching from the computer to the walk-in vault and back again to the computer as he prepared for a fast departure under cover of night. In the office with him was his geologist Karen Crandall, whom he trusted implicitly, who had been at Jim's side when he had pulled the baseball-sized rough diamond out of the slurry. Now, on this winter's night, the task at hand was emptying Zone's vault of all its uncut rough stones, some forty million dollars' worth of excellent-quality rough, packing them into a body belt which Jim would wear around his torso, taking care of last-minute e-mails, double-checking his airline flight schedule, and paying the security guards a bonus to keep the mines safe from intruders until his return. This may have been the last task he intended to complete before locking up the mine's offices and heading by bush plane into Yellowknife, airline tickets to Vancouver and New York City in his jacket pocket. Crandall would fly along as far as Vancouver, and by the time the news got around town—for inevitably one of the guards would leak it, the startling revelation of Big Jim's secret departure with the famous stone—Crandall would be winging her way to Antwerp, leading anyone lusting after the Lac de Lune on a wild-goose chase. Meanwhile Big Jim would be flying to his final destination, carrying the stone he had named the Lac de Lune because it matched the color of the lake's water in springtime.

Jim was carefully laying out stacks of cash bonus money for the security guards when he heard a man shout and then gunfire outside Zone's office building. Dousing the indoor lights, Jim peered out the office window. Across the compound's moon-swept yard, he saw the sign ZONE MINE, LTD. NO TRESPASSING, at the entrance to the drill housing. He saw the guardhouse tower, but no sign of the guards. Then he looked down, beneath the tower, where searchlights flooded the mining company's entrance, and saw two bodies slumped where they had fallen after being shot off the tower catwalk. Nathan Mwangi and Lamar Atkins, his two best guards. Jim reached into his holster and drew out his Italian Beretta. Fifteen rounds might be enough. Sweat drenched his brow as he placed a call on his cell phone to the Yellowknife Mounties. He reached Royal Canadian Mounted Police headquarters and was reporting the assault when he heard more shots, this time closer, just outside the office entrance. Jim edged back up to the window and looked out. Ten feet from the office entrance lay the lifeless body of another security guard, Jack Purdy, blood gushing from his mouth. Purdy's watch partner, Jeff O'Neil, was bending over him, checking vital signs, but there were none, and Jeff reached down and closed Jack Purdy's eyes. Then came footsteps thudding across the ice, another security guard, moving swiftly around the building's corner to the front entrance, to see what the shooting was all about. A second shot cracked through the air and then a third, and now a volley of gunfire, and Jim saw both men fall just outside the office door. Then voices, and now thudding footsteps moving closer to the door. In the distance, more gunfire, coming from the towers at the mine's entrance.

No way help would arrive in time. No way.

Now they were trying to break down the office door. Jim reached up and caressed the leather pouch that hung around his neck, his heart pumping fast, in rhythm to the noise of a battering ram against the last obstacle between them and him—the door. Another few jolts and they would be in. Crandall, filling the last of the canvas pouches with rough, quickly strapped the canvas belt onto Jim's waist, then ran into the open vault to hide. Jim figured he had just enough time left to send one brief e-mail. He turned to his computer, typed the message, and pressed send.

Big Jim planted himself against the office's north wall, his back to the open vault door, his spine pressing against the safe's locking mechanism. If he had to close the door on Karen, she could get out later by employing the interior escape mechanism. Hardy turned around and saw Crandall hovering in a corner.

"You'll be okay, Karen," he said, and she believed him.

If the intruders had gotten this far onto the mining company's property, they had certainly killed all six security guards. Then in one crashing blow, the battering ram broke through. Jim spread his legs and aimed his gun at the door, clicked off the safety latch and held the weapon with both hands, his grip as steady as anyone's could be facing down the ruthless unknown. He didn't want to be a hero and he hoped like hell the Mounties would haul ass.

He could hear their voices, and then the battering took up again, now with earnest intention. He knew what they were after, and he knew if he just surrendered it to them his life and Karen's might be spared. But some things are worth dying for, and Hardy would risk his life for the magnificent Lac de Lune. And the secret he had lived with for ten years.

The Lac de Lune, all 384 carats, lay heavy against his chest in the pouch secured around his neck by a leather cord. Since he had first held the stone in his hands, he had kept it close to his body, protecting it from the lustful eyes of fellow miners and big-time thieves. After one public showing for the news media, for no other reason than to protect the gem from greedy interlopers, he had kept its whereabouts a secret from all but Crandall. And he had kept his plans to travel with the gem a secret from all but four individuals. Four of his twelve security guards. And now it came to him that one of them had betrayed him.

The battering ram had finally made a sizable hole in the outer door, the intruders now in the insulated gear room, then the ram punched through the inner door, and now Big Jim Hardy faced his masked killers, and though he fired off a shot, a near miss, and two more that missed their targets, he didn't stand a chance. He was cut down by a single blast to his chest, and slumped over onto the floor.

Lying in a pool of his own blood, Big Jim felt the terrible jerk of the leather cord at his neck, and heard the cord snap softly as it broke, and then he felt the weight of the Lac de Lune lifted off his body. He felt the belt loaded with diamond rough yanked off his waist. From where he lay, through the dimming sight of his failing eyes, he saw a thief's hand holding the Lac de Lune high against the overhead light. He heard the thieves exclaim, heard Crandall arguing with them, and then he heard them hurrying out into the long winter's night, Crandall yelling for help as they dragged her away, and though he tried to stop them, he could not even stanch the bleeding from his chest wound, could only lie helpless in the fatal flow. Light-headed, his consciousness slipping, he had only enough energy left to dip a weakened finger into his own blood and scrawl two words on the wall:

Venus Diamond.

CHAPTER TWO

Zone Mine

Dawn.
Sergeant Roland Mackenzie of the Royal Canadian
Mounted Police's Integrated Border Enforcement Team had
seen plenty of murder victims in his thirty years on the job,
but this was the first time he had seen evidence in the form of
words the victim had written in his own blood shortly before
expiring. Mackenzie noted the bloody script on the plywood
wall of Zone Mine's office, and marveled at how a man so
drained of blood had managed to write in neat flowing cursive. At Mackenzie's feet lay the corpse, a huge crumpled co-
coon of the man whom he had known only slightly, a man
whose reputation for secrecy had dwarfed every other diamond prospector in the Northwest Territories, a loner, an
enigma, a man everyone knew as Big Jim Hardy, the sneakiest
damn diamond prospector in Canada. And lately, the most
famous. Mackenzie knelt beside the corpse and touched Big
Jim's throat.

Mackenzie's underling, for that's how he thought of her,

Officer Sandra Benton, stood at the entrance to Zone Diamond Mine headquarters, looking in at Big Jim's corpse. She hadn't yet stepped inside the building, not out of fear or loathing, but in order to guard the scene from defilement by intruders. At her back, on the snow-covered tundra surrounding the company's prefab headquarters, a crowd of perhaps two dozen mining employees milled about restlessly beneath a single overhead spotlight illuminating the building's entrance, wanting to know what was going on in the office and what had happened to Karen Crandall, Big Jim Hardy's geologist. Some local ham radio operator had picked up a frantic call from Jim Hardy's cell phone, Hardy pleading for help from the RCMP. And word spread fast. Something had happened here before the first shift had arrived, and the employees knew it must have involved the Lac de Lune.

Officer Benton proffered her back to the crowd, her broad frame blocking their view of the gear room and, farther inside, the office. Behind her, several officers tried calming the crowd, keeping them at bay. Moments earlier, an RCMP helicopter had delivered Mackenzie and Benton into Zone Mine, and now another chopper arrived, blades clattering, then whirring to a slow spin as it put down on the hard ice. What Officer Benton called the mortuary bird. Big Jim's call for help had come at 3:05 A.M. Now it was 4:15 A.M. on this exceptionally warm winter morning, warm being defined as anything above thirty below zero, and the temperature was twenty-six below zero, warm enough that Sergeant Mackenzie had said to Officer Benton on the way up to Zone Mine, "Spring is coming. I can feel it in my knees." Now Officer Benton stood in the outer doorway, her front side warmed by the office heating system, her backside freezing from the cold outdoors. Spring, indeed. And so when Sergeant Mackenzie ordered Officer Benton to shut the outer door and come inside, she grinned smugly and quipped, "What's the matter, Sergeant? Such nice spring weather out there."

Mackenzie ignored Benton's rude taunt. The flesh at Big Jim's throat felt cold to the touch. And Mackenzie noticed a deep abrasion on the skin at the base of the neck near the collarbone, a deep red chafed line, as if a cord or string had been drawn taut there, cutting into the flesh.

Mackenzie looked up at Benton. "He's gone. And so's the Lac de Lune."

"Oh, lordy," exclaimed Benton. "Lordy, lordy."

"Weird thing, though."

"What's that, Sergeant?"

Mackenzie examined the corpse. "Abrasions across his midsection."

Benton shrugged. "Where they yanked his waist pouch off. Everyone in Yellowknife knew about that. Besides, a lot of the miners wear those things filled with their best rough."

"You'd think they wouldn't care so much about the smaller rough. You'd think they'd just grab the Lac de Lune and let the other stones go. Since they'd be in a real hurry."

"His waist pack must've held a gazillion dollars' worth of rough. Can't say I wouldn't be tempted myself."

Mackenzie gestured with his chin at the wall. "But he left us one hell of a damn clue."

Benton followed Mackenzie's gaze to the wall and read aloud the two words written in blood. " 'Venus Diamond,' " she said. "Why do you suppose he wrote those two words in particular?"

Mackenzie shrugged. How the hell would he know what Big Jim Hardy was thinking as he lay bleeding to death? Mackenzie said, "Maybe it's the name of another diamond. How the hell would I know what it means?"

"I never heard of such a diamond. I've heard of the Hope diamond. And the De Beers Millennium Star. But never the Venus Diamond." Benton drew forward and peered at the corpse. "He still looks powerful," she quipped. "Even dead. He looks invulnerable."

"Well, he wasn't. And you can start taking pictures. Then let's do a complete video of the office, the building's exterior, and the guard towers. When you've finished, collect the surveillance cameras. Maybe we'll get lucky."

"We'll be up here all day," Benton complained. "I had a dinner date for tonight. I'll bet my badge we won't get back in time."

"You're a Mountie, Benton. Get used to it."

While Officer Benton photographed the scene, Mackenzie scoured the office for evidence. The bullet had entered Big Jim's chest but had not exited. Big Jim's Beretta lay by his side. Mackenzie checked its cartridge. He'd fired three times before he went down. Still, no blood spatters except those up close and personal by Big Jim's corpse.

The office door had been rammed open, not a difficult task in a prefab structure. Apparently, Big Jim had placed his faith in the small army of security guards who kept watch around the clock on the building's perimeter, and in the towers at the mine's entrance. The night shift were all dead now, like Big Jim. Yellowknife, where the murdered guards had left families behind to come up to work for Zone, would reel with disbelief and mourning. Six fine citizens gunned down while protecting someone else's diamonds.

Big Jim mustn't have worried much about forced entry into Zone's headquarters, or he would have made a building of stronger stuff. But like Officer Benton had said, whenever Hardy left his office, he emptied his vault, took all his diamonds with him, in the canvas bag belt attached around his middle. And, of course, the Lac de Lune, secured in a pouch around his neck. He never took chances.

Mackenzie noted the vault in the rear wall of the office, its door wide open, more foreboding than welcoming. Feeling slightly foolish, he drew his weapon and stepped inside the vault. It was empty except for a small stack of papers lying on a shelf. Mackenzie looked them over. Stake claims. He saw nothing else in a vault the size of his ex-wife's walk-in closet. He tucked his gun back in its holster, and to be certain he hadn't missed anything, pulled a flashlight off his belt and leveled its beam at the vault's corners. Aha. He stooped over and picked up a thin strip of fabric. Violet satin ribbon, the kind women tie in their hair. Nothing else visible, but he'd have the vault and the whole damn office scoured for fingerprints and DNA.

Either the intruders took Crandall hostage, or she was one of them.

As if reading his thoughts, Benton peered out from behind the camera. "Must have been some sort of inside job. And several intruders. Big Jim could've handled one, or even two guys easily. And the gunfight outside? Would've taken at least four or five guys with weapons to fight off Hardy's security guards."

Mackenzie grunted in agreement. He wished Benton wouldn't intrude on his ruminations.

The Lac de Lune had generated lots of excitement, Mackenzie knew. The pandemonium had started about three weeks earlier, after the news broke about Big Jim's discovery of the world's largest rough diamond exactly the color of a glacial lake. Suddenly Yellowknife had been flooded with diamond brokers from all over the world vying for a look at the stone, drooling at the chance to get their hands on it. But Hardy was having none of them. To appease the raving media, Mackenzie recalled, Big Jim had displayed the stone for them to photograph, but he'd refused to show the stone again until after he had it cleaved and polished. Just who would cleave the stone and where this transformation was to take place was apparently a secret Big Jim Hardy shared with no one, except perhaps with Karen Crandall. So rumors had spread around Yellowknife, of thieves arriving from all corners of the world, planning to steal the Lac de Lune from Big Jim Hardy.

A sergeant in the RCMP's joint Canadian–U.S. border patrol unit, the Integrated Border Enforcement Team, Mackenzie had been assigned to the Yellowknife beat because both governments hoped that the lure of the Lac de Lune might attract some of the world's most notorious diamond smugglers, some of the same criminals who smuggled weapons and drugs across international borders. Mackenzie had asked for the assignment; having seniority, he got it. He'd been in Yellowknife three weeks before the robbers hit Zone Mines.

Mackenzie had heard people in Yellowknife saying Big Jim was behaving stranger than usual, saying he had hired on the new security guards and had sworn them and everyone else to secrecy over where exactly the gem had been pulled from the ground beneath Lac de Lune. Some said it was at Site 3, but others claimed Big Jim had discovered a new pipe down at the southernmost end of the lake, that Site 3 was a ruse, a red herring to throw the competition off the pipe trail. And then lately, a rumor about Karen Crandall turned out true. Crandall had moved out of her little apartment in Yellowknife and was living up at the mine.

Benton had finished the stills, ready to shoot the video. She had been trained in forensic evidence and she knew what to capture on her digital format equipment. Switching cameras, she said, "Six guards and Big Jim make seven murders. And then what happened to Crandall? Was she even present when the killers burst in? Where's Crandall now? Hell, she might have been one of them."

Mackenzie looked down at the little strip of violet satin ribbon. Karen Crandall's? He shrugged and said, "I don't know. They maybe had a thing going, Crandall and Big Jim. Maybe it was about love, not diamonds."

"I'll tell you something about Big Jim Hardy," said Officer Benton, breaking into Mackenzie's ruminations yet again. "He's been seen at the registry these past few days, staking new claims left and right. Pat Hogan, you know, the registrar? He was in Bud's the other night and he'd had a few too many. I heard Pat Hogan tell some others he thought Big Jim was going crazy. The claims, see, he was staking claims all over hell and gone, in a confusing geographical pattern so no other prospector could figure out if he'd found a new pipe, or even the exact location where it might be. And I'll say one other thing, too. It's not just me, but everyone seems to have noticed how lately Karen Crandall's become really secretive and tight-lipped. Not like her at all." Benton frowned. "What's that in your hand?"

"A ribbon."

Benton squinted at Mackenzie's hand, at the length of violet ribbon. "She wore ribbons in her hair."

"Crandall?"

"Yup. She was a real girlie girl. Shoulda seen her the other night down at Bud's. She had a dress on, a tight lacy thing, made her look like a whore. High heels and those fishnet stockings. She had her face made up so heavy you could hardly recognize her. Some folks even said it wasn't her at all. But I knew it was her. Crandall. She didn't talk to anybody, just swiveled into Bud's and up to the bar. She handed Bud something that looked like a small camera and then swiveled her ass back out the door. Hell, I'd recognize that snooty bitch anywhere."

Mackenzie wished Officer Benton would just shut up and finish shooting the videos. But she kept rambling on as he checked in desk drawers and cupboards for anything resembling a clue to what had happened here just a few hours ago. Besides the dead man's body, nothing had been touched. Not the stake claims. Even the computer system, an elaborate setup, hadn't been taken.

He said to Benton, "A competitor would have taken the computer system. At least, one hard drive."

Benton agreed. "I'm betting it's big-time thieves. Really big-time. Professionals. After the Lac de Lune. Maybe your unit was right to send you up here. And all along, I've been thinking you had some ulterior motive for moving up to Yellowknife. You really are after smugglers, aren't you?"

They'd bring the stake claims and the computer, and of course the piece of violet ribbon, into headquarters for evidence. Maybe the computer would reveal something. But secretive as the man was, Mackenzie bet the files would tell them less than zero. Still, it was worth a look and he'd be shirking his duties to ignore it.

Diamond lust had apparently brought Big Jim Hardy's enemies to the Northwest Territories. But now as Mackenzie finished scrutinizing the scene of the murder, he wondered where Big Jim had come from and what secrets his past history might hold. Once again Officer Benton interrupted Mackenzie's silent ponderings.

"He might have named it after someone he knew."

"What? Named what?"

"The diamond. Maybe he had changed the name from Lac de Lune. Maybe he named it the Venus Diamond after the goddess. Or maybe some chick."

Mackenzie drew a long deep breath. He despised working with Officer Benton. She talked more than she should and always thought she knew more than he did, and he a veteran. He wished she would get pregnant, as she was constantly threatening to do, and leave the Mounties for good.

CHAPTER THREE

To Mackenzie's utter astonishment, Big Jim Hardy's computer had delivered a bonanza of data, some of it potentially incriminating. First, Mackenzie was able to verify the employment of the dead security guards, six men whose families soon would come to claim their bodies from the morgue: Lamar Atkins, Rocky Dyer, Jeff O'Neil, Nathan Mwangi (a West African transplant), Jack Purdy, and Peter Stanhope. All locals, except Mwangi, who had arrived in the Territories the previous summer from Gaborone. Each of the victims would be autopsied before the bodies were turned over to their families. Mwangi had no family in the Territories. His body would likely be shipped to relatives. If they could find any. Mackenzie made a note to check on Mwangi's background.

The bonanza: RCMP's computer nerds had captured enough information off the hard drive to implicate an individual by the name of Venus Diamond. Mackenzie got on the phone to Interpol. Within an hour, Interpol had located two Venus Diamonds and guaranteed if any other individuals named Venus Diamond had ever existed they were now dead. Of the two living, one was a ninety-seven-year-old retired bordello madam in Amsterdam; the other was a United States Fish and Wildlife undercover agent, located in Washington State. Mackenzie took less than a minute to decide which Venus Diamond to go after. Furthermore, he had taken a scrap of paper from Hardy's corpse before it was removed from the scene of the killings, and on the scrap of paper were written words that pointed directly at the Venus Diamond of Washington State. But even after he received permission to detain her, this Venus Diamond proved hard to pin down.

Quinault Rain Forest
Olympic Peninsula
USA

The bear was a young male adult, *Ursus americanus,* slightly cinnamon colored, and it had gorged over the summer. Now in winter's thrall, it lay sleeping in a hollow Douglas fir trunk deep in the heart of the Kalaloch Rain Forest when Earl Ebert and Kyle Pope's jacklight startled it out of its deep torpor. The bear sprang to life and lunged out of the tree trunk at his attackers. Ebert aimed between the eyes and the bullet struck its target, but the enraged bear fiercely resisted, rising up on its hind legs now, prepared to kill. Ebert fired two more shots before the bear stopped in its tracks, uttered a moaning whine, and crumpled to the forest floor. Ebert and Pope wasted no time slicing the warm carcass open. Ebert reached inside and felt around until he located what he wanted. Using a jack-knife, he severed the organ and yanked it out.

Ebert stood over the bear's carcass, his bloody hands gripping the animal's fresh gall bladder. The size of a large grapefruit, the gall was encased in its slimy green sac, still warm. Ebert held it up like a trophy, or the spoils of a great battle.

"Big as a goddamn basketball," he exaggerated.

Kyle Pope knelt over the carcass, cleaving the paws off the animal's slack limbs. Pope handled an axe deftly, severing each paw with one clean blow. He stuffed the paws inside a plastic trash bag, then stuffed the bag into the Igloo cooler he had brought along just for this purpose. Ebert carefully packed the gall in ice in a separate cooler. They had rigged the coolers to backpacks. Ebert was securing Pope's cooler lid when they heard the bloodhounds moving in.

"Holy shit," said Pope. "They've got us."

"Run," hissed Ebert. "C'mon."

Ebert plunged into the thick forest, and Pope followed. Behind them, shots were fired, warning shots at first, then more serious shots, the bullets zinging off tree trunks near their heads. The sound of dogs barking persuaded them to run faster.

Dawn had announced itself as a thin vapor of illuminated mist creeping through the forest. The team of U.S. Fish and Wildlife agents had fanned out in a semicircular pattern, having lost the poachers on a crooked bend in the old growth section where seven-foot-tall evergreen ferns made a thick crazy-patterned hideaway. All the agents had to go on was the keen scent of the hounds and whatever juju they might summon on a surprise hit. Leading the team, Agent Venus Diamond moved front and center with a greyhound's pace. Up ahead, the bloodhounds howled fiercely as they chased the poachers deeper into the old growth woods.

The agents had been watching Pope and Ebert for six months, but this was their first break, a hot tip from an elderly woman who lived on Highway 99 at the second junction before the Forks town limit. But they had arrived too late to save the bear, and as Venus ran toward the fleeing poachers, she knew her partner Louie Song was now bending over the carcass, attempting identification. As she ran after Pope and Ebert, her usually focused mind strayed. While her body and all her instincts drove her toward her prey, her thoughts had turned from the bear's dead corpse to another death, the death of a little boy, a murder so terrible she had purposely suppressed it in the six months since it had occurred. Until now. Violence triggers memories of violence; the brain filters life events through like events. You never experience closure after the murder of a loved one. Closure is a psychological myth. You grieve, you suffer, you never fully heal, you go on. Because the psyche is hardwired for survival. For a brief moment, Venus Diamond's psyche split in two, between then and now, between two gruesome deaths; both enraged her, neither offering a shred of hope for humankind. And then suddenly, as quickly as the memory came, it evaporated into the heavy sunlit mist and she refocused on the task at hand.

Monstrous ferns enveloped her as she followed the bloodhounds' wails. She had lost sight of her teammates but knew they were in the vicinity, like her, single-mindedly pursuing their prey. And then the hounds wailed and bawled maybe a hundred yards up ahead. As the first shot was fired, the bloodhounds went berserk. One of the dogs must have fallen. Venus drew her handgun and moved forward cautiously until she stood at the brink of a small clearing. On her radio, she spoke to her team members.

"The old Wolford cabin. They're holed up inside. One of the hounds has been hit."

A teammate responded. Eric Sweetwater. "I'm on the north side of the clearing. I can see the cabin from here. But there's no window or door on this side. I can't see them."

"Surround the cabin, but stay behind cover," Venus said, addressing the team. "Sweetwater, they can't see you, either. Move in, but be careful as hell. I'll call for them to surrender. If they don't, I'll give the signal for the team to move in. Everyone got that?"

"What about me?"

That was the rookie, Mandy Kim. She had been instructed to hang back and observe, not to act unless specifically ordered to. Now she was confused. And scared as any rookie enjoying her first detail. Venus said into the radio, "Draw your weapon, Kim. Stay where you are until I tell you to move. Understand?"

"Oh, sure. Yeah."

Venus moved closer to the edge of the clearing, the

hounds now clawing at the cabin's front door. On either side of the old wooden door were two small windows, shuttered from the inside. Venus watched, her eyes focusing on the shutters. One of the shutters moved slightly; she heard it creak and she saw the barrel of a gun appear in the window. The hounds howled beneath the windowsill, the sound of glass clinking, and the window shattering sending them into a frenzy. On the ground near the front door lay the dead bloodhound, Mary Pat. Mary Pat had been the best hound the agency had ever trained. She would be dearly missed.

Taking cover behind a Douglas fir, Venus yelled the first warning. At the sound of her voice, the hounds quit wailing and milled about restlessly, tails poised like antennas.

"Ebert and Pope. You're under arrest. Drop your weapons, raise your hands above your heads, and walk out the door single file. Don't attempt to resist. You are surrounded by U.S. Fish and Wildlife agents. If you attempt to resist, you'll be shot."

Silence. She repeated the warning, her voice strong and clear, and she knew they had heard her. Seconds later, they replied with a spray of gunshots fired from both cabin windows. A bullet struck the Doug fir's trunk, ricocheted into the woods. Venus fired back and signaled the team to move in. Pope and Ebert put up a fight, their gunfire striking one of the agents. Sweetwater. Venus saw him fall, then roll over and rise to his feet and continue shooting. He'd been grazed but stayed in the fight. Venus instructed Mandy Kim to move in and join the fray. The rookie's voice sounded pitifully weak.

"I just can't," Kim said over the radio. "I'm really scared."

Venus grimaced and fired a round at the cabin. She saw one of the men lurch backward. Pope or Ebert, she couldn't tell which. Into the radio she said, "Okay, Kim. Just stay put." Last thing she needed was a scared rookie.

A bullet whizzed past her, barely missing her head. She fired back, moving in, ordering the team to take the cabin. Pope and Ebert weren't ready to surrender. Venus approached the cabin door, her teammates covering her. The thick wood door was braced with iron stays. A battering ram would have trouble opening it. Placing her back against the cabin, she edged toward one of the windows and peered in. Ebert had turned his attention to a bloody wound on his shoulder. Venus signaled the others. Sweetwater came forward and gave her a boost up. Venus fired through the window, taking the already injured Ebert down with another shot. Pope raised his hands and wailed, "Don't shoot, man. I give up, I give up."

Half an hour later, Pope and a seriously wounded Ebert in custody, Venus was riding shotgun in the agency's Humvee, Louie Song at the wheel, when a state patrol car flashed its lights and turned on its sirens.

"Hell, I'm under sixty-five," muttered Louie. "What's the speed limit on Ninety-nine?"

"Thirty-five since the last two curves," Venus said. "Better pull over for Smokey Bear."

The two vehicles pulled over alongside Highway 99, on a soft pine-needle-carpeted shoulder. The patrol car doors opened. The driver stepped out, a Washington State Patrol officer, dressed in the requisite blue uniform. The patrol car's passenger side opened and Venus saw the black boots first, then the black riding trousers, then the red jacket with its brass buttons and fancy braid, and finally the hat, khaki beige with two big dimples in the crown. Another similarly dressed individual stepped out of the rear of the patrol car.

Venus looked at Song and said, "What the hell are Mounties doing in this neck of the woods?"

The thieves had headed west across the barrens, leaving telltale tracks in their wake. They wouldn't have much time before their deed was discovered and a posse put on their trail. Crandall, bound and gagged, had been bundled into protective snow gear and strapped to one of their snowmobiles. When they reached Broken, a deserted miners' way station some twenty miles outside Yellowknife, they ditched the snowmobiles and entered a makeshift hangar where a single engine Otter had been stashed for the getaway. They rolled the plane onto the snow-covered tarmac and scrambled aboard, shoving Crandall into a seat. As they took off from Broken, Crandall counted five men aboard, including the man who piloted the plane. At the mine, she had counted six snowmobiles, and Crandall wondered what had become of the sixth thief.

They flew southwest in the Otter, and landed at Vancouver International Airport. In the airport, they split up, each man negotiating the airport terminal without incident, the geologist Karen Crandall accompanying the lead man, the thief who gave the orders. He'd wired a plastic explosive around her neck to ensure her cooperation. The fact that they hadn't killed her along with Jim puzzled her. Why were they taking her? And where?

Outside the airport, the men took separate taxis to the Blue Horizon Hotel on Robson Street in the heart of Vancouver, where they checked in separately, each paying for his room in cash, and giving shopping and tourism as their reasons for visiting British Columbia, if anyone asked. Crandall was taken to a room with the man they called Ron Fairview, the man she had early on deduced was in charge. She had seen his passport—American.

"Thieves can't trust thieves," Ron Fairview grumbled, tossing his backpack onto the hotel room bed, and Crandall wasn't sure if he spoke to her or himself.

The geologist sat on a chair by the window, her hands and feet tied securely, a gag around her mouth. From listening closely to their conversations over the last several hours, Crandall had a fairly good grasp of their plans. The others would be unpacking in their rooms, preparing to spend four nights and days acting like tourists before they split up for separate flights to Seattle. From Seattle, they would then return to a place they all referred to as the ranch. Crandall tried her best to keep mental notes of everything she heard and saw. Clearly, Fairview was the kingpin of the operation and therefore responsible for taking her hostage. He didn't much like the idea of harming a woman, he had told her when he had tied her to the chair, but when so much was at risk, what choice did he have? He sincerely wished she hadn't been at the mine when they had come for Big Jim Hardy. At least, that's what he told her as he tied her to the hotel chair and put the gag around her mouth. He'd said, "I wish it had been a man. I really do."

They holed up in the hotel, Crandall for the most part tied to the chair and gagged. When the maid came to clean the room, Fairview would take Crandall down the elevator to the hotel dining room, her shackles inside the briefcase he carried. At night, he would tie her to the mattress on one of the two beds in the room, and shackle her to a long chain that snaked across to the bed where he slept. Though she tried desperately, she hadn't yet figured out a way to escape. On the fourth day in the Blue Horizon Hotel, Fairview looked up from a book he was reading and gazed over at the young woman.

Nice-looking kid. Reminded him a bit of his sister, Rhonda. That thick copper hair like a saint's corona. Pale skin, not tall, but sturdy. And those big blue eyes, just like Rhonda's. A real nice-looking girl.

Crandall thought she perceived a twinge of compassion in his eyes.

Fairview hadn't spoken much to her beyond terse inquiries about her appetite, her bodily functions, and sanitary needs. She had never been left alone in the room; when Fairview went out, which he did for several hours each day, one of the men had always been present to guard her. She especially despised the one named Ramie, who looked at her with revolting lust. The room curtains were kept closed at all times. Crandall hadn't seen daylight for four days now, except briefly when Fairview took her down to the dining room, and that was usually at dusk, much to the hotel maids' annoyance. Crandall was beginning to feel a deep depression engulf her spirits, challenging her will to survive.

She tried keeping track of everything. When Fairview went out, when he came back. He always wore baggy trousers and an oversized wool sweater. On the second day, Fairview had opened a briefcase and withdrawn Jim Hardy's canvas belt, poured its contents onto the coffee table and inspected it stone by stone. Then he placed all the rough back into the canvas pouches, placed the belt back inside the briefcase, locked it, stood up, and left the room, the dreaded Ramie replacing him at the door. When Fairview had returned that evening, he came in empty-handed, without the briefcase.

Now Fairview closed the book he had been reading, set it

on a side table, and said, "Maybe you need to use the ladies' room again?"

Crandall shook her head.

"How about a glass of water? You thirsty?"

Crandall nodded and when he brought the water and loosened her gag, she aimed her cornflower-blue eyes at him. He held the glass to her lips and she felt his breath on her face. She said, "Thanks," and he actually smiled at her and commented offhandedly, "A girl gets thirsty."

He hadn't placed the gag back over her mouth. Maybe he forgot, she couldn't tell for sure. She tried an experiment.

"You forgot to put the gag back," she said.

Fairview looked over at her, a look of surprise, maybe even amusement, flickering in his eyes. "So I did," he said. "But you've got to promise not to make any noise, or it goes back on, you got that good and clear?"

He left the gag off after that, after she promised not to yell. She agreed, and he made her a bit more comfortable in the chair. For the next half hour, she followed his every move about the room and she blinked rarely. She worked at appearing calm and unafraid, but of course this was a ruse. Who wouldn't be frightened in her position?

"Anyway," Fairview said to Crandall, "you're not a hostage, really. We're not holding you for ransom. Maybe you'd like a beer or something?"

The woman's eyes flickered.

"Just say if you do."

Crandall didn't speak, but remained still, her eyes watching him intently. Why was he suddenly, after four days of ignoring her, initiating conversation?

For the first time since they had brought Crandall to the hotel, Fairview began to change his clothes in front of her. When he peeled off his shirt, Crandall saw the tattoo on his chest. A flag she didn't recognize. Red, white, and blue vertical stripes, with a strange symbol, something like a snake, overlaid in black. Then the man dropped his baggy trousers and she saw where he had hidden the Lac de Lune, all 384 carats of it.

Clever.

Fairview didn't seem to care if she watched him undressing, nearly naked, revealing a robust physique and too the location of the diamond. He disappeared into the bathroom, was gone for several minutes, and then emerged, clean shaven, his hair neatly combed. He actually looked attractive. Crandall wondered if she would eventually succumb to Stockholm syndrome.

"You've been a good girl the past few days," he told her. "If you promise to be real docile and nice, I'll loosen those cords."

She nodded. Fairview loosened but did not remove the cords around Crandall's wrists and ankles. She felt the blood surge into her extremities. Now he removed the gag entirely from around her neck and mouth and she moved her jaw, trying to loosen it, and she coughed. Fairview poured her another glass of water and brought it to her, held it up to her lips. She drank, swallowed, drank some more, and in a careless twitch of anger, spit it at him. Fairview slapped her face hard.

"Bitch," he cried, as he brushed water off his face and arms.

She said nothing, just stared at him.

"You try that again and this gag goes back on your mouth so tight you won't be able to breathe, understand?"

No response, only a cold blue stare.

CHAPTER FIVE

A knock sounded on the door. Fairview checked through
the peephole and let in the four other thieves, each man
freshly showered and shaven, wearing expensive suits with
ties, gripping small suitcases, the carry-on-luggage kind.

The thief named Ramie looked over at the hostage and
said, "Why the hell is her gag off?"

"She needed some water. She knows better than to
holler."

Ramie didn't like it but Fairview was the boss of the operation and so he didn't argue with him. The men seated themselves variously around the room and Fairview laid out the
next phase of the operation.

Three of the thieves, Louden, Frickey, and Gerard, were
to fly separately to Seattle–Tacoma International Airport and
from there drive rental vehicles to somewhere in Washington
State, which Fairview occasionally referred to alternately as
the ranch and as headquarters. Ramie and Fairview would
follow by car, the girl as their passenger, and join them at the

ranch. They did not say what plans they had for Crandall. Once they arrived at the ranch, Fairview would fly to New York to meet the diamond broker and make the exchange.

Crandall didn't have to wait long to learn what the diamonds were going to buy. Diamonds for weapons. Tanks, guns, ammunition, plastic explosives, bomb-making materials, grenades. Enough armament to outfit a small army. The gist of the conversation implied that these thieves were members of some militant white supremacist organization. But there was something else. The men once or twice had referred to a tube. Crandall knew the colloquialism well. Everyone who worked in the diamond trade knew about the tube, the conduit through which diamonds were smuggled and traded for arms used by guerrilla armies and terrorist organizations. But the diamonds that traveled the tube through North America came from Western and Southern Africa. Blood diamonds mined by African slaves indentured to African guerrilla forces that controlled some of the continent's most lucrative mines. Diamonds in return for supplying weapons to kill innocent people. Canada's diamonds, as far as Crandall knew, and she knew as much as anybody in the trade, were protected from smuggling. Each cut stone was marked with a laser, proof of its Canadian origins. They called a Canada diamond Arctic Ice, or the Good Diamond.

Crandall was worried. These thieves had stolen rough stones, stones not yet marked, not yet identified as Canada rough from Zone Mine. They could sell the rough if they had inside contacts in the diamond trade, including the Lac de Lune.

Crandall heard all of this and for a while she wondered why they allowed her to listen in on their plans. And then it suddenly hit her. Because she wasn't going to live to tell anyone. They were going to kill her.

This afternoon—at least Crandall thought it was afternoon—the men brought out bottles of whiskey and someone found ice and glasses and they began drinking and a couple of them smoked, the smoke making her nauseated. They talked in low voices but fervently. Theirs was a grand scheme, some sort of political coup, she gathered, that would require more bloodshed and sacrifice for their cause. But what cause? It was never stated explicitly, yet all the men seemed to espouse it and to have it clearly imprinted in their minds and hearts. Something about forming a new nation-state that would straddle the present border between Washington and Canada.

After a lingering silence, Ramie said, "So, Fairview, it's been four days now and we haven't had a look at the rock. How 'bout it?"

"Yeah," put in Frickey, "let's see that bastard."

Fairview obliged them, carefully reaching inside the leather pouch strapped to his groin. What he held up for all of them to see was so magnificent that the girl heard their exclamations. She had no need to exclaim. She had seen the Lac de Lune every day for the last six weeks, until her capture, each time Big Jim Hardy took it out of the leather pouch he wore around his neck so that both of them could admire it. This was Jim Hardy's stone, and Karen Crandall had vowed to Big Jim that she would die before she would reveal to anyone where the pipe was located. And yet these men didn't seem interested in the location of the pipe. Maybe they already knew. Maybe they had a spy inside Zone. Maybe these men worked for one of the big diamond brokers, or, God forbid, the De Beers cartel. Anything was possible in the diamond trade.

Fairview wouldn't let the others touch the Lac de Lune, but he held it aloft, rotating it slowly so that they could see its extraordinary shape and size, and he even let each of them peer through the tiny window Crandall had sliced into the rough to study the density of the vivid blue-green color, its quality and evenness, and to analyze the gletz, or tiny crack, the one flaw presenting a dicey challenge, even to the world's best diamond cleavers.

Crandall listened closely as the men exclaimed over the diamond. So far, none of them had mentioned the gletz, a potentially problematic flaw. It would jump out at a trained diamantaire, a flaw so delicate most diamond cutters wouldn't have the nerve to try cleaving the stone. In fact, Crandall knew of only three diamond cutters in the world who were good enough to work this stone successfully. These guys, Fairview and his gang, she concluded, were hired men, professional thieves who probably worked North America's West Coast tube but who knew less about diamonds than they apparently knew about weapons. But who were they working for? Who would claim the Lac de Lune for the price of artillery?

Crandall was twenty-six, a trained geologist graduated from the Canadian Institute of Mines. Her dreams of heading north to work in the Canadian diamond mines had taken her to Yellowknife the day after her graduation, and she had been there since, for nearly a year, all that time working for Big Jim Hardy's Zone Mine. It wasn't her first choice; Big Jim had a reputation as an eccentric and a hard man to work for, but they had instantly connected on some karmic level, maybe because they discovered upon their first meeting that both had lost their parents in tragic accidents. Mutual sorrow had formed a bond between them, and so she had taken his offer of a job and stayed on. It was Karen Crandall who had walked the perimeter of Lac de Lune last August and found K10 on the shore. She instantly suspected the small lake was actually a craton, the cratered top of a diamond pipe, filled over the eons with glacier water. At Karen's suggestion, the moment the lake had frozen solid enough to drive a drill rig over, Jim Hardy had dragged a crane onto the frozen lake and drilled deep down beneath Lac de Lune, deep into the lakebed where, sure enough, they struck a diamond pipe. And out of this pipe had come, in one month's drilling alone, fifty thousand carats of rough, nice hefty chunks worth tens of millions on the international market, even more when cut and polished. But Big Jim wasn't satisfied with the idea of selling his first bonanza as rough. He wanted the whole apple. He had hired a talented Canadian cleaver, a sawyer, and half a dozen cutters. He had supervised the cutting and polishing of the first crop of diamonds himself. He wanted to control his diamonds from the moment he discovered them until they were placed into the retail trade as fabulous gems that brought enormous sums. When the diamond brokers bought from Zone Mine's sight boxes, they bought gems already cut and polished, a tiny Z, invisible to the naked eye, lasered onto each stone to identify it as a Zone gem.

And all this success had come even before Big Jim Hardy had reached into the slurry one winter's morning and pulled out, along with a second bonanza of rough, that enormous blue-green stone. Big Jim and Crandall had shared the euphoria over the find, and had vowed to tell no one, not a soul, where they had found it.

Now as Crandall sat bound to the armchair in Fairview's hotel room, searching her mind for answers, she wondered how these white supremacists had heard of the Lac de Lune and formed their own plan to steal it, to raise money for their cause. Or, had they just planned a diamond heist and happened upon the Lac de Lune? But it wasn't that easy. The thieves would have to know someone in the international diamond trading community, a broker, someone who could feed the distinctive stolen rough through the tube into the legitimate market, where some diamond cutter would be paid a huge sum to cut the Lac de Lune into smaller stones to disguise its origin. Fairview and his men could be working for anyone. Lots of offers had come in for the world's largest blue-green diamond, the pride of the north. Even the Canadian government had tried to buy the stone from Big Jim. These thieves could be working for anyone. Or for themselves.

Fairview said, "Enough already," and put the Lac de Lune back in its pouch and strapped it high on his leg around the groin.

The thief called Ramie said, "We should just keep it, man. Forget that broker."

Then Crandall knew for certain. They had invaded Zone Mine with the intent of capturing the big diamond. The other stones were merely lagniappe. Somebody in the diamond business was behind the theft.

Fairview said, "Don't anybody get greedy here. Remember the cause and remember your honor. The rock goes to the broker. That was the deal. We turn it over and he supplies us with armaments. Whatever happens to the big diamond is none of our business. Our business is taking back the land that belongs to us, creating our nation-state. That's our business and this diamond is only a means to that end. Everyone needs to understand this clearly."

Crandall could feel tension rising in the room, and then the man called Frickey spoke. "When are you gonna kill her?"

Frickey looked directly at Crandall.

Fairview said, "It's not time yet. Ramie and I will take care of that when the time comes."

Crandall couldn't help but hear.

Fifteen minutes later, two of the men departed, leaving Ramie, Gerard, and Fairview, who stayed behind to take care of last-minute business, part of which, apparently, was to kill Karen Crandall. Gerard kept his back to the door. Even if Crandall could break loose of her bindings, she didn't stand a chance against Gerard at the door.

Crandall listened as Fairview made a call on his cell phone. From the number of digits he punched, it must have been an international call, outside Canada, anyway. Soon after he started speaking into the phone, Crandall knew he was speaking to a diamond broker. Fairview had a fair knowledge of the diamond community's vernacular, but the broker was apparently coaching him along.

"Did you receive the package I sent?"

Crandall could hear the other voice come back. "Not yet."

"Well, you should be receiving it soon, within forty-eight hours for sure."

Crandall couldn't make out the rest of the conversation, except for Fairview's final words: "Trust me, we got what your client is after."

Client? Crandall could only surmise that the theft of the Lac de Lune was being handled through a broker for a third party. One of the big guys? De Beers? AKG? Rosy Blue? Hell, maybe even Tiffany. Or a private collector, a sheik or sultan or a spoiled Thai princess. So who wanted the Lac de Lune enough to hire killers like Fairview and his gang?

Fairview's cell phone rang. He listened, then said, "The ranch entrance is half a mile south of the Washington–Canada border. Your deliverymen will see a sign that says LAY-A-DAY FREE-RANGE CHICKEN RANCH. That's it. Exactly three weeks from today. Make it look like farm equipment. And tell your driver not to speed. There's hairpin curves and Johnny Law's all over that two-lane highway."

Ramie had been spread out across the couch and now he stood up and walked across the room toward Crandall. Fairview was still busy on the phone. Gerard, his back still against the door, was perusing an edition of Gideon's Bible. Ramie reached down and put his hand inside Crandall's shirt, found her breast and fondled it. She tried kicking him but her legs were immobilized. She started to spit at him but he slapped her face and then he unzipped his pants and came toward her. Crandall turned her head, her heart racing, her rage as strong as her fear. Ramie moved in and then Crandall heard a soft report. Ramie crumpled to the floor.

Fairview pulled the silencer off his gun and put the gun away. He untied Crandall and said, "I'm sorry as hell he did that to you."

Crandall went into the bathroom and vomited. She removed her clothes and stepped into the shower, standing under the steamy stream of water, filling her mouth with soapy water and spitting it out over and over again. When she came out of the bathroom, Gerard was still guarding the door, Fairview bending over Ramie's corpse, a knife in one hand. Crandall watched in horror as Fairview sliced open the dead man's gut, stuffed the Lac de Lune inside, and then sewed him up with nylon thread.

Fairview looked up at Gerard and said, "Let's clean this place up." Then he turned to Crandall and said, "That was supposed to be you."

Two hours later, in a rented black hearse, Fairview, a disguised Crandall, and Gerard at the wheel, pulled up to the Canada–U.S. border at the truck crossing and queued up for immigration. The immigration officer asked the usual questions, perused their passports, Crandall's a forgery supplied by a friend of Fairview's who lived near the border crossing. The officer checked inside the coffin, and called to an assistant to verify their story: They were bringing the body of Fairview's cousin back to the United States for burial.

The two immigration officials stepped inside their booth, examining some information on a computer screen, conferring privately in low voices. Inside the hearse, Crandall could feel the tension rise, but both Fairview and Gerard appeared calm when the officers approached the driver's window. One officer leaned in and said, "Our records indicate the deceased was female. The body in the coffin is a male."

Fairview spoke up instantly. "It's some mistake. Our cousin is a male. He was accidentally shot on a bear lottery up on the Fraser River. You can check with the funeral home." Fairview reached into his jacket and fished out a business card, handed it to the immigration officer. The officer took the card and went away, entering the booth. He picked up the phone, read the number on the business card, and made the call. On the other end of the line, Frickey's cell phone rang, and from what Fairview could tell of the conversation, Frickey had convinced the immigration officer there must have been a mistake made by whoever entered the information into the Canadian immigration computer system. The officer hung up the phone and returned to the hearse. He took his time deciding. The girl, the only one with a Canadian passport, looked distraught, no doubt about it. And they didn't look like drug smugglers or terrorists or diamond thieves.

They looked like plain folks who had just lost a loved one, taking him home to the family plot.

The officer walked around to the hearse's passenger side, looked in at Crandall. "What relation are you to the deceased man?"

Crandall's lips parted, her heart pounding. She felt Fairview's hand touch her arm.

"Wife," she whispered. "This man's wife."

The officer sighed, handed them their passports, and waved them through into the United States.

CHAPTER SIX

Sergeant Roland Mackenzie of the Royal Canadian Mounted Police's Integrated Border Enforcement Team hadn't spoken more than five curt sentences during the three-hour drive to the U.S.–Canada border at Blaine, Washington. He just sat stiffly in the Washington State patrol car's passenger seat, his back to his prisoner and the young female Mountie named Officer Benton, whose job was apparently to keep the detainee company in the back seat.

From Mackenzie's five curt sentences, U.S. Fish & Wildlife Agent Venus Diamond had deduced that a warrant had been issued in Canada calling for her apprehension as a suspect in a murder investigation in Canada's Northwest Territories, something about evidence on the scene implicating her, and, most disturbing of all, she would not be receiving a much-desired hot shower, change of clothing, and the hot meal she had politely requested, nor permitted one telephone call until after the extradition procedure was completed.

Before loading her into the Washington State patrol car, Sergeant Mackenzie had shown Agents Diamond and Song the warrant issued in Yellowknife, Northwest Territories. The sergeant said, "Your agency has already been informed." Song had asked to accompany Venus, but Mackenzie just chortled and sent him packing. Not without protest; Song nearly decked the Mountie before Officer Benton drew her gun and threatened to shoot him.

Mackenzie helped Venus into the patrol car a bit more gently than he usually handled murder suspects. She seemed such a dainty little thing and he didn't want to risk a brutality complaint. Still, he wondered silently over the subject's small size. If she was one of the killers, she had a lot of guts to face the likes of Big Jim Hardy. And anyway, she had probably paid some thugs to do the job. Still, according to Mackenzie's information, her alibi had more holes than a colander.

Song got belligerent again, so Mackenzie said, "Go ahead, make your call."

Song raised the boss on the phone and shoved his cell phone through the patrol car window to Venus. "What the hell's going on?" she growled into the phone.

Olson, chief of USF&W's regional office said, "Don't blame me. This is Wexler's deal." Wexler was the former director of the U.S. Department of the Interior, now the National Security Council's director of transnational threats, a job that placed Wexler himself on sundry enemies' hit lists.

"What deal? Why am I being shanghaied off to Canada, Olson?"

She heard him sigh. "Look," he said, "all Wexler would tell me is he's returning a favor to a friend in the Canadian Parliament. And he said you'd get the picture soon enough, once you reach Yellowknife."

"Where the hell is Yellowknife anyway?"

"They have polar bears. Now, you are expected to go along nice and cooperative with the RCMP sergeant. Wexler said the RCMP doesn't know dick, but you need to cooperate with them for the time being. That's all I know. You'd better mellow out and play ball with those Mounties, or Wexler will be on your ass. I'm sure he'll elaborate in time. Meanwhile, Diamond, keep your trap shut and behave." Olson hung up.

Mackenzie refused to let Song ride along. He wasn't taking any chances with this case. He was pretty sure he had built a strong case against Agent Diamond. In eighteen short hours, he figured he had compiled enough evidence to hang Venus Diamond by her toenails. Wasn't like American agents were incapable of being corrupted. Especially federal agents, in Mackenzie's mind. Ottawa had granted him permission to take her into custody. He was within his rights and he didn't care to risk complicating the extradition procedure by allowing the suspect to bring along a friend. Suspect? Yes, despite her reputation and nearly spotless criminal record, he felt justified in calling her a murder suspect. Why else would Big Jim Hardy have written her name in his blood as he lay dying? Why else would Big Jim Hardy have sent her an incriminating e-mail deciphered by Mackenzie's computer nerds from Hardy's hard drive? Why else would Hardy have her photograph in his wallet?

They knew each other, that was for sure. It all fit together so smoothly. And something else pointed to the woman he now had in custody, and he could hardly wait to surprise her with it. Mostly, though, Mackenzie just wanted to get this case wrapped up and delivered in the neatest possible package to the provincial prosecutor's office. No kudos, no praise for a job well done, none of that malarkey. Maybe just a fifteen-minute-famer in the *Toronto Globe and Mail* for capturing at least one of the perpetrators of the worst crime the Northwest Territories had ever seen; kudos, even if the big diamond never turned up. But the hell with celebrity. Just a nice fat bonus from the government, enough to finance a small condo in Vancouver overlooking English Bay. A comfortable retirement. Walking the dog through Stanley Park, lying in bed till mid-morning, reading the newspaper and sipping tea. And, most important, writing his memoirs. Mackenzie had much to tell, and when he finally went public, some very inflated heads would roll.

The U.S.–Canadian border at Blaine, Washington, situated near the shore of a shallow saltwater bay, was surrounded on three sides by alternating scrublands and evergreen forests. A Peace Arch marked the border crossing, and in spite of the inviting pristine, manicured gardens and the fraternal proclamations carved into the arch on both nations' sides, the governments didn't suffer fools. No easy border crossing here. Sergeant Mackenzie, however, enjoyed a certain privilege accorded ranking RCMP officers and he and his retinue were granted swift passage into Canada.

On the Canada side of the Peace Arch, an unmarked RCMP vehicle waited, its engine idling. Officer Benton helped Venus into the vehicle's rear seat and then slid in beside her, Benton wearing a vacant stoic expression. Mackenzie slid into the front passenger seat and instructed the driver where to go. Twenty minutes later, they drove onto a military base and out along a wind-whipped tarmac to the edge of a saltwater inlet, where a small Otter seaplane rocked and rolled despite its moorings. Benton held the door for Venus, and when she stepped out of the car onto the tarmac, a strong gust of wind struck her small frame and swept her off her feet. Benton chased her a couple feet, grabbed her arm, and served as an anchor as she led Venus to the Otter and helped her up inside.

"You're no bigger'n my little finger," Benton quipped, but her tone of voice retained its severe official cadence.

Once again Mackenzie rode shotgun, this time beside an RCMP pilot while Benton sat in the Otter's rear compartment with Venus. Someone had packed a cooler with ham sandwiches and root beer. Benton uncuffed Venus, then recuffed one of her wrists to the seat frame, leaving one hand free. Venus ate a mediocre ham sandwich and drank a full bottle of root beer. By the time she had finished her lunch, the Otter had climbed to twenty-five hundred feet and was heading northeast toward the Canadian Rockies.

Five hours later, in pitch darkness, Venus looked out the Otter's window and saw lights twinkling in the distance. The Otter descended, landing smoothly on a lighted tarmac of solid ice. Benton reached behind her seat, fished out a heavy parka, and helped Venus put it on. Twenty minutes later, they were hurrying along a snow-packed sidewalk in the town of Yellowknife, the outdoor air dry, the temperature a balmy thirty below zero, and Venus was glad for the parka's insulation and the hood Benton had pulled up over her head. The arctic air seemed to freeze her lungs and she coughed. How could people live up here in this godforsaken deep freeze?

Inside the RCMP headquarters, the moist heated air warmed Venus's lungs, relieving her discomfort and triggering a strange ennui. Mackenzie sped through the booking procedures as if he could do it blindfolded, then locked her in a sparsely furnished cell and went away. The concrete cell measured ten by ten feet. At one end, a narrow slit of a window confirmed that the world outside was made of something besides gray slab. Peering out, Venus saw a street lamp's glow cast across a snow-covered alley embossed with the deep tracks of four-wheel-drive vehicles. Not a soul in sight; even the rats had gone indoors.

Half an hour passed, then Mackenzie returned with a supper of thick mystery-meat stew and a couple of stale rolls with the heft of hockey pucks. She ate it all and then lay down on the thin mattress atop the cell's cot, grateful for two heavy wool blankets. At this point, all she really cared about was sleep, and her last waking thought was of Ebert's expression when she had shot him.

CHAPTER SEVEN

Morning arrived without daylight. Mackenzie had taken her Swatch when he had booked her, but a neon clock on the wall across from Venus's cell said it was six A.M. and yet when she glanced out the small window she saw a deep blue star-studded sky. Stirring to the sound of Mackenzie's boots clopping down the corridor, she sat up, suddenly alert. She still wore the clothing she'd had on during the poachers' arrest, and it stank of dried sweat. Mackenzie unlocked the cell door and gestured down the corridor where Officer Benton waited with a fresh set of clothing, thermal underwear, subzero arctic gear, and a pair of boots a whole size too large. Benton let her shower in the small prisoner's stall. Hot water and soap brought relief and the fresh clothing felt good. When she preceded Benton into Mackenzie's office, she noticed the sergeant's gaze linger on her a little longer than necessary. She might have looked as good as she felt.

"So what's this all about?" she asked Mackenzie.

"As I told you yesterday, you are being held as a suspect in a murder investigation. Seven murders, to be exact."

Venus whistled. "Let me guess. A diamond robbery."

Mackenzie pursed his lips. "What makes you say that?"

"What else is there to kill over up here?" Venus shrugged. "I heard about it on the news."

Mackenzie sighed and then laid out the scenario, withholding certain details to see if she would inadvertently fill them in later, thus implicating herself, making his job easier. He finished by saying, "The last to die was a diamond prospector by the name of Jim Hardy. The folks up here always called him Big Jim Hardy."

"Big Jim Hardy."

"That's how he was known around here."

"I've never heard of this individual."

Mackenzie smiled confidently. He'd been waiting for this moment of denial. He pushed back from his desk and stood up. "We've added a charge of grand theft."

Venus chuckled. "Oh, yeah? What did I supposedly steal from this prospector? Wait, wait, let me guess. Diamonds."

"Have you ever driven a snowmobile?"

"Nope."

"We found six snowmobile tracks leading into and out of Zone Mine's staked claims area. When we followed them from Zone's guard tower back out to where they came from, they ended abruptly at a spot where one vehicle parted from the others. Five headed west toward Broken. We found the sixth snowmobile abandoned along the ice road where it bordered on the Yellowknife Highway."

"Broken?"

"An outpost. From there, they took a small plane somewhere. My guess is they crossed the international border into Washington State. Maybe you can verify my guess."

"Nope. What happened to the sixth fellow?"

"I thought you could tell me."

"My best guess would be, the sixth individual rode into

Yellowknife. Where else is there to go out here in the wilderness?"

"You'd be surprised. Or maybe not. Maybe you know of some hideouts up in the barrens that even we don't. You could be smarter than all of us put together. Which would make you an excellent smuggler."

Venus stared at Mackenzie until he blinked.

"You ever fly a single-engine Otter?"

"Sure. It's part of my repertoire."

Mackenzie shrugged. She might be this sarcastic by nature. "We have reason to believe that when you and/or your accomplices murdered Jim Hardy, you stole a canvas belt Hardy had strapped around his waist. It was filled with rough diamonds."

"Rough?"

"Diamonds not yet cut and polished. As if you didn't know. Along with the smaller stones, you and your accomplices stole a large, priceless diamond known as the Lac de Lune."

"I've heard about that stone. But I didn't steal it." Her right eye had blurred up again. She shifted in her chair, the better to focus on Mackenzie. "Look here, Sergeant, why don't we just dispense with the charade and you can tell me why I'm really up here on this ice floe."

Mackenzie sucked his cheeks and said, "Why don't you just sign a confession and get this over with?"

"Because I didn't commit these crimes. Anyway, what evidence do you have connecting me to these murders?"

Now Mackenzie couldn't suppress a wide grin. He picked at his fingernails as he listed the evidence off by heart. "First, there's the newspaper article. A story about you written by an Associated Press reporter. We found a clipping of the article in Hardy's wallet when we examined his corpse."

"I don't know the deceased man. I don't know why he'd have any interest in me."

Mackenzie shrugged and stopped playing with his fingernails. He reached out and opened a file folder on his desk. He held the news clipping aloft. It had been folded into neat squares and was yellowed and brittle with age. Mackenzie cleared his throat before he read aloud.

"'NASA Space Mission to Include Butterflies. The U.S. Fish and Wildlife Service announced today that one of their agents would accompany a collection of butterfly larvae on a NASA space launch scheduled for next week. The unidentified agent, who holds a master's degree in lepidopterology, is rumored to be undercover agent Venus Diamond—'"

Venus held up a hand. Mackenzie paused and glanced up at her.

"Spare me the details, Sergeant. Anyway, so what if the guy kept an old clipping about that NASA voyage? A lot of folks were interested in that experiment."

Mackenzie looked at her. "You're famous, aren't you?"

Venus shrugged. "Notoriety's not my thing. I am an undercover agent for the U.S. Department of the Interior, presently assigned to the Fish and Wildlife Service. I like to stay out of sight. My job demands a certain amount of anonymity. And that big blaze of publicity happened several years ago and lasted about as long as one *Seinfeld* episode not counting commercials."

Mackenzie carefully placed the news clipping back in the file folder. A uniformed officer appeared at the door, holding a teapot and two mugs. He blinked a query at Mackenzie. Mackenzie nodded. The officer stepped into the room and set the teapot and mugs on a small table beside Venus's chair. Mackenzie mumbled a "Thanks," and the officer departed.

Venus said, "Shall I pour?"

Mackenzie sensed her lampooning but nodded anyway. He always preferred the woman to serve the tea. Not that he was sexist, at least not in his self-assessment. But tea was a tradition upheld even in the rugged outlands, and in his experience, women always poured the tea, in his family anyway. He watched her pour the tea; when she passed the mug across the desk, he murmured a curt "Thank you."

"Sugar, Sergeant?"

"No. No, thank you."

"How about cream? A spot of cream in your tea?"

Mackenzie held out his mug while she poured cream into the hot tea. He waited until she poured a mugful for herself, then raised his mug in a cursory toast on its way to his lips.

The tea tasted good, strong, black, and hot, the way Venus liked it. "So what other evidence do you have up your bright red sleeve, Sergeant?"

Mackenzie said, "I'm asking the questions, not you." He leaned far back in his chair, as if relaxing, but his eyes glittered like a fervent man carrying out a mission entrusted to him by higher authorities. "You know a woman named Karen Crandall?"

Venus shook her head.

"She's a geologist. Canadian. A bit younger than you. She's twenty-six, to be precise, and you're thirty—"

"I don't need to be told my age, thank you very much."

Mackenzie smirked behind his tea mug.

Ignoring his previous admonition, she asked, "What role does this Karen Crandall play in your little melodrama?"

"This is no joking matter, Agent Diamond. We've had seven murders up here, and the people of Yellowknife are sick with grief, and believe it or not, the safest place for a suspect in this case right now is a jail cell. A lot of families lost their dads and sons and brothers. There's a lot of rage festering in this town."

"Sarcasm retracted, sir. Was that six security guards and Big Jim Hardy, or seven guards plus Jim Hardy?"

Mackenzie sighed and leaned forward. "Seven. We've had seven murders, counting Hardy's. To answer your question regarding Karen Crandall, she worked for Big Jim Hardy. She was Zone's geologist. A Canadian citizen. Came up here to the Territories fresh out of university and went straight to work for Big Jim, whom we suspect was a U.S. citizen, by the way, though we haven't yet found his passport. The mining records suggest that he's an American. In the end, Crandall apparently became his lover. At least, we're fairly certain they were lovers. Does this information jog any memories?"

She shook her head. "Nope."

"Crandall disappeared in the chaos. She was probably one of them. One of yours."

Venus resisted the temptation to roll her eyes. "One of my what?"

"Partners in this crime. We certainly don't think for one moment this operation could have been pulled off without an insider's help."

"Look, Sergeant Mackenzie, I really can't emphasize enough that I have no connection to Big Jim Hardy, to whatever-her-name-is Crandall, or to Zone Mine."

"Karen Crandall."

"Maybe they took her hostage."

Mackenzie set his mug down on the desk and folded his large hands together. "We have certainly considered the possibility. Now, what about the e-mail Jim Hardy sent to you ten days before he was murdered?"

"I never got it."

"So you say."

Venus rubbed her right eye. The blurring had become worse. Maybe a cataract, she thought. Do people get cataracts in their thirties? She pulled her hand away.

"Listen here, Sergeant Mackenzie, and I say this for the last time before you finally level with me as to why I have been snatched up in the jaws of the Canadian justice system and dragged up here to the North Pole. I did not know this Jim Hardy individual and have never received an e-mail from someone using that name. My computer hard drive will verify this, so go for it, check it out. But you'd better have our federal government's permission to pry into their computers."

"We have obtained permission."

"Meanwhile, this tea is a hell of a lot stronger than your evidence. So why don't you release me and start looking for your killers?"

Mackenzie shook his head. "No bail hearing just yet. Want to hear the rest of the evidence?"

"I'm breathless, as you can see."

"Big Jim Hardy had written your name and the address and telephone number of your regional office headquarters on a small piece of paper, also found in his wallet." Mackenzie leaned way back in his chair. "Allow me to offer two more bits of evidence before you go making such a sweeping denial of any involvement in this crime."

Venus sipped her tea and waited as Mackenzie reached into the folder again and withdrew two photographs. He handed the first across the desk. The photo was actually a photocopy of a letter, handwritten in bold flowing cursive. The letter read:

This is to confirm that on the tenth day of January of this year, I, Jim Hardy, discovered on my staked claim at the northern drilled pipe, Site 3, in Lac de Lune a blue-green diamond weighing in the rough 384 carats. The rough stone approximates an oblong shape, slightly narrower at one end. The stone is a clear unusually vivid blue-green color and apparently flawless with the exception of one inclusion, or gletz, close to the stone's center. Inspection with a loupe appears to show a small bubble at the end of the gletz. Otherwise the stone is pristine. In the tradition of the trade, I hereby name my discovery the Lac de Lune. Any other claim against this rough blue-green diamond should be construed as false and as an attempt to steal this priceless stone from its rightful owner. Signed, Jim Hardy (Dated January 2nd of that year.)

Venus handed the artifact back across the desk. Mackenzie wore a smirk.

"I'm telling you for the last time, Sergeant Mackenzie, I don't know this guy. And I don't see how this affidavit or whatever it is implicates me."

Mackenzie tossed a used manila envelope onto the desk. Venus glanced down and read her own name and office address written in the same neat cursive. Mackenzie said, "This article of evidence was taken from inside that envelope. We found it in the victim's jacket pocket. Notice it has postage applied. It was sealed and ready to mail. Addressed to you. At your office."

"I'm telling you, I don't know the chap. Anyway, I don't know about Canada, but in the U.S. opening another individual's mail is a federal offense."

Mackenzie raised an eyebrow and handed her the second photograph. Venus held it out from her eyes slightly, the blur in her right eye still evident. The color photograph showed two words scrawled in red on a hard surface, maybe a wall. The bottom of a windowsill was visible, and the corner of a piece of furniture, possibly a desk. Two words, *Venus Diamond,* were scrawled in approximately the same flowing hand as the cursive in Big Jim Hardy's letter and on the envelope.

Venus set the photograph on Mackenzie's desk. Looking him straight in the eye, she shrugged and showed her empty palms.

Mackenzie snorted, using his own big palms to shove his chair back. He stood up, stretched like he was tired. Maybe he was. He crooked his head, indicating the door.

"A look at him might jog your memory."

They walked side by side down a long corridor, through a warren of offices and into a small crime lab, where they met the province's medical examiner, a stout elderly man with an impossibly cheerful grin. They followed the medical examiner to the deep freeze. Venus hadn't had breakfast yet, just the tea, and was grateful for the empty stomach when the ME rolled open the drawer containing the victim's corpse. Mackenzie watched her expression as she leaned forward and studied the large man's pale bloodless flesh, paying particular attention to his nose.

"Hell," she said after careful scrutiny, "his name's not Jim Hardy. That's Buzz Radke, that son of a bustard."

CHAPTER EIGHT

Parecles & Company
New York, New York

The golden-haired gentleman, thirtyish, in the bespoke
Italian suit cut a sleek figure behind the diamond counter
at Parecles & Company as he waited for a young couple to
reach the biggest decision of their lives. More important
even than their decision to marry, more crucial to their future happiness than their decision about bearing or not bearing offspring, was the decision about the engagement ring.
Mr. Volpe, the golden-haired gentleman, couldn't stress this
enough; a diamond was indeed, forever.

Gordon Volpe was no mere Parecles salesperson; Gordon
Volpe was a diamond expert, a "diamantaire," who sighted
and brokered diamonds in the rough for Parecles's shops. He
sighted and bartered for the very finest gemstones from Parecles's own mining operations, and occasionally, from other
mining companies, such as De Beers, Rosy Blue, KAM, and
AKG. Occasionally, and for certain clients only, Gordon
Volpe visited the Parecles retail shop at Rockefeller Center to
personally advise on purchase of "the stone." As Volpe put it

when comforting an anxious affianced couple, "the greatest investment a man will make in his lifetime."

The young man of today's affianced couple was the son of one of Volpe's A-list clients, a diamond retailer from Houston, to whom Volpe owed a small favor, thus, here he stood behind the counter at Parecles's shop, in the exact spot where he had started out in the business over twenty years ago. Diamond brokers could do worse than starting out at Parecles. Now Volpe regarded the young couple:

He: "I really like the marquise-cut stone, honey. It's so you."

She: "You're just saying that because it's half the price of the emerald cut."

He: (protesting) "Oh, no, not at all. Sweetie, you can have whichever one you want. I just thought that the marquise, being, well, slender and petite like you, would fit your personality better. Really."

She: (not satisfied) "Really? Well, I happen to think that the emerald cut is absolutely me. Emerald cuts are much more elegant than marquise. Besides, Mr. Volpe told me that the emerald stone was hand cleaved, whereas the marquise was ground out of the rough. Isn't that right, Mr. Volpe?" She turned to the expert.

Volpe smiled weakly. "Actually, I stated that while the emerald-cut stone was hand cleaved, so rare these days what with lasers and high-speed saws, the marquise-cut stone was not ground, but sawed from the rough."

"Well, I don't see what difference that makes," began the young man.

His fiancée sighed and looked at the ceiling. "Jeremy, if you will just listen to Mr. Volpe. He just informed us that a hand-cleaved diamond is far rarer than a mechanically carved stone."

"What the hell is the difference anyway?"

Volpe held out a graceful palm for Jeremy, so the purchaser could see the broker's hand held no swindle. "Cleaving is practically a lost art, Mr. Fustic. Only a few master cleavers are practicing in the world today. A cleaved diamond is one that is cut in two from the rough by hand, using hand tools. It takes immense patience to cleave a diamond, immense. When cleaving is practiced, only one of two results is possible. Either the rough stone is cleaved exactly into two pieces, in which case the cleaver, after many anxious hours of studying the stone and calculating its flaws, has succeeded in his goal, or else the cleaved stone shatters, reducing the combined value of its pieces by perhaps millions of dollars."

Jeremy rubbed his five o'clock Val Kilmer. "So why cleave, then? Why not use lasers and guarantee the results?"

"Jeremy!" The fiancée pinched his forearm.

"Ouch."

Gordon Volpe was accustomed to such snappy behavior from affianced couples, their prenuptial nerves tingling like a herpes warning about to explode into full-fledged crisis mode. Volpe wasn't too far removed from his own nuptials to forget his own jangly nerves when Crystal had selected the eight-carat fancy pink flawless for her engagement ring. And even then, Volpe had enjoyed a deep discount on the stone.

"The best diamantaires believe that a hand-cleaved stone results in far superior gems than those cut by mechanized devices." And to allay Jeremy's feelings, he added, "But this marquise cut, albeit cut by a mechanized saw, mind you, is indeed a gorgeous gem, not to be sneezed at, no, not at all."

Miss Emerald harrumphed.

Volpe stepped back a discreet distance from the couple to allow them private negotiating space. In truth, although he was rooting for Miss Emerald, Volpe couldn't give a rat's ass if the two kids walked out of Parecles empty-handed. More important business preyed on his mind, and as if by sheer coincidence, the moment he distanced himself slightly from the quibbling clients, his cell phone vibrated in his jacket pocket.

"If you'll excuse me, I'll just leave you two to your private ruminations," he intoned before turning his back to the couple, walking a few feet along the counter, and pulling out his cell phone.

"So?" was all he said. Volpe wouldn't risk using names, not in Parecles.

Volpe listened to the caller for a moment, then murmured, "Indeed." The hint of a smile crossed his lips. Listened some more, looked around the shop and outside the window facing onto Rockefeller Center, and said, "Excellent." And clicked off, tucking the cell phone back inside his jacket.

Down along the diamond counter, the young couple had apparently reached an impasse, he with his back turned to the counter, she with arms crossed impudently, her lips tight, her sheep's eyes glued to the big emerald-cut flawless white diamond.

Volpe decided to give the couple another few moments to reflect over their investment. Rubbing his elegant hands together, he considered questions of time zones, security precautions, and delivery schedules and then reached again for his cell phone. Just as he was punching in some numbers, a colleague passed by the counter, a pretty young woman named Anastasia, who aspired to become a diamantaire like Volpe.

"Mr. Volpe," purred Anastasia, "you have a visitor." And nodded her stylish bob toward the front of the shop.

Smiling slightly, Volpe replied, "Thanks, Anastasia. Would you mind keeping an eye on my clients for a few minutes?"

"No problem."

Volpe sighed. "Anastasia, how many times need I remind you that in the vast majority of cases, 'no problem' is a rude, lazy, and thoughtless response to gratitude expressed."

Anastasia blushed. "I forgot my manners. Of course, I would be happy to assist your clients."

Volpe nodded once. "That's better, Anastasia. Now, please excuse me."

Gordon Volpe was nothing if not exceedingly polite and well mannered.

The visitor, a dark-skinned man, small in stature, seemingly fragile and sickly, wore a heavy overcoat, and a gray wool scarf wrapped around his neck, concealing the lower half of his face. Still, Volpe recognized the fellow, and knew that he was neither fragile, nor sick, in the physical sense, anyway.

"Good morning, my friend. And how may I assist you?"

The man spoke through the scarf in an undertone that only Volpe could hear.

"I have brought the first installment."

How stupid of Fontana to appear at the shop! Volpe smiled, presenting a calm façade. "Well, well, isn't this fine news." He glanced around the jewelry shop. "But I think our business might be more judiciously conducted elsewhere. Do you know the Starbucks just around the corner from Rockefeller Center?"

The little man nodded gravely.

Volpe read his watch, a fine gleaming gold and platinum Piaget. "Why don't we meet at the Starbucks in, say, twenty minutes? I'm just finishing up with a client."

The little man nodded a second time and then he whispered through the gray wool, "I don't like carrying this around. I'm becoming very anxious, very agitated."

Volpe smiled. "Just twenty minutes more, my friend. And then I'll take possession."

The man slipped outside into the brisk wind and disappeared around the corner.

Volpe sighed and redialed the number into his cell phone.

The number he punched in rang a cell phone on the counter of a scuzzy Newark bar. Into the phone, Volpe said, "Dixon."

Delbert Dixon, Caucasian, aged forty-two, Bard College graduate turned gangster, was one of the Eastern Seaboard's most successful underworld figures. To his merit, he had never been to prison because, although the authorities suspected him of smuggling schemes, they were never able to gather any sound evidence. Because Dixon was way too smart for them, a fact he constantly boasted of to his employees.

Over the past decade, Dixon and his small gang of gunrunners had smuggled enough artillery and ammunition to supply both sides of several African guerrilla wars. You wanted a dozen handheld rocket launchers, a few dozen Uzis, and fourteen Kalashnikovs, Delbert Dixon would find them and deliver them to your front door within forty-eight hours. Hell, Dixon could find you a Russian tank over the Internet and at a bargain price, too. Certain West African guerrilla factions depended upon Delbert Dixon to supply their needs, and what Dixon liked so much about these fellows was they always paid in diamonds, pulled from guerrilla-controlled African mines, glorious white Grade Ds and fancies of every hue, which were easy to convert into U.S. dollars if you knew the right people in the diamond trade. Call it money laundering, but don't try to break this operation unless you're ready for full-scale war.

Trustworthy and discreet, Dixon always came through with the goods. True, he might have had to arrange an execution or two along the way, but Dixon was, above all, a man who delivered on some of the dirtiest jobs in the mysterious world of guerrilla-warfare profiteering. Blood diamonds. And so when Dixon heard the diamond broker's voice on the other end of the line, he smiled, for it could only mean one thing: The Volpe deal was on.

"Yeah, what's up?"

"One week from today," said Volpe. "Do you have the inventory?"

"Yup," said Dixon, a man of even fewer words than Volpe.

"And the address I sent you? And the directions off the interstate?"

"Yeah-up."

"Fine," said Volpe. "Then deliver the inventory, take possession of my goods, and we'll settle up when you return to the neighborhood."

"Will do." Dixon pushed the off button on his cell phone and turned to his two junior partners, Merle Tremaine and

Jack Crumley, who shared barstools nearby. "Well, boys," he
said, "looks like Crumley and me are headed out to the rainy
Pacific Northwest for a spell."

"What about me?" complained Merle Tremaine. "I want
in on some of this action."

Dixon reached out with a grubby hand and patted Merle's
shoulder. "Not to worry, my man. You'll play a critical role
here in New York. Very critical."

This seemed to satisfy Merle. But Crumley had squinched
his face into a worried frown. "Not our territory," protested
Crumley. "We could get into bad trouble fooling around in
someone else's route."

Dixon snapped, "Listen, scumbag, you do what I say or
take a hike. Besides, we're not squirreling in, we're running a
joint operation with the West Coast fellas."

"Now I get it." He didn't, but Crumley needed the work.

Back at Parecles's diamond counter, the young couple, now
embracing, waved as Gordon Volpe approached them, smiling deferentially. The girl pointed to the emerald cut and said,
"He'll take that one."

When Volpe, carrying a sleek black leather briefcase, entered
Starbucks, the place was packed with customers cozying up to
latte ventes, but he immediately spied Carlos Fontana seated in
a corner, hunched over a cup of something steaming, and
scowling fiercely. He had lowered his gray wool scarf, revealing his thin inverted-U-shaped mouth and his pointy chin. As
Volpe approached, Fontana noticed him, and an expression of
great relief crossed his face.

Volpe set his briefcase on the table, unlocked it and
opened it, revealing an empty interior.

"Just drop the package in here," he instructed.

The little man reached inside his heavy overcoat and
brought out an oblong package, the size of a bluefish,

wrapped in newspaper. "It's heavy," he offered, gently lowering it into Volpe's briefcase.

Volpe closed the briefcase, locked it, and reached into his jacket for his wallet. He took out six thousand dollars in cash and handed it to Fontana, who snatched it up and tucked it inside his overcoat.

As Fontana stood to leave, Volpe said, "You haven't finished your, uh, hot chocolate."

But the courier hadn't heard him. He was already at the door.

Volpe hurried to his office in the Luxor Building on West Forty-seventh Street, locked himself in, and opened the briefcase. The package should have been heavy: When he had unrolled the newspaper, he saw the canvas belt and felt its weight. Now, unzipping the belt's long pocket, Volpe poured its contents onto his desk. A little gasp escaped from his lips as he stared down at a small mountain of rough diamonds that, even in their uncut state, sparkled in the sunrays streaming through the window. Volpe plunged both his hands into the fabulous stones.

CHAPTER NINE

Mackenzie said, "So you know him."

Venus stared down into the corpse's face. "I'd recognize that proboscis anywhere."

"Where do you know him from?"

"Buzz Radke was a U.S. federal undercover agent. He worked as an analyst for the National Security Council. His specialty was tracking big-time arms and diamond smugglers. Mostly, his work took him outside the U.S. to Eastern Europe, Ukraine, as I recall, and the United Arab Emirates. Oh, and a place called Trans-Dneiper. Don't ask me to find it on a map. Then, five or six years ago, I was assigned to work with Radke over in northeastern Washington. Radke had documentation that a white supremacist militant group based in Eastern Washington was possibly smuggling diamonds for weapons. NSC thought the group might lead them to some big-time international weapons dealers. Ever hear of the tube?"

Mackenzie's eyes flickered momentarily. "You are referring to the physical path smuggled weapons and diamonds and so forth follow from supplier to client."

"Humans, and exotic animals, too. Numerous pipelines, with arterial connections reaching as far away as West Africa, Antwerp, places like that. One of the big-time operators is based in Ukraine. Interpol has called him the master of tubing. NSC thought this eastern Washington group might be doing business with the Ukrainians and Rwanda and some other diamond-bearing African countries. So they sent Radke to poke around eastern Washington."

Mackenzie pursed his lips. "Why would the NSC need your help? You track poachers. What do you know about arms and diamond smuggling?"

"Maybe not so much, but a lot more than I did before working with Radke." She turned her back on the corpse and Mackenzie shifted his position to face her. She said, "At least one member of said militant group was operating in valuable animal parts, smuggling high-end organs and bones into and out of the U.S. It all travels roughly the same route. As you already know, often diamonds are smuggled to be traded for weapons."

Mackenzie nodded. "I'm somewhat versed on the subject. Although our diamond industry marks their stones so that they can be traced. No diamond leaves Canada without that mark. A broker in the diamond trade would immediately recognize a Canadian stone. All it takes is a loupe and a good eye."

"That's once they've been cut and polished. Not when the stones are still in the rough. Like the Lac de Lune."

Mackenzie stared as if seeing right through her. "So tell me now," he pressed, "why were you partnered with Radke?"

"We often track our suspects along the same tubes. My agency, Interior, partnered me with Radke because I'm familiar with the general path of the tube running from South America up through Latin America and along the U.S. West Coast into Canada. I'm especially familiar with the smugglers

and their conduits operating through Washington State, and I
have a fair knowledge of eastern Washington's hot spots for
smugglers. We spent ten months, nearly a year, working
Radke's leads. We came to a dead end. We never could prove
these guys were anything more than a small community of
racist militants living a sort of survivalist lifestyle. We did
bust one of the group for illegal possession of bear galls, and
the guy went to prison for a year or so, but he never provided
information on their group. They call themselves Ravallah.
As I recall, their cover is chicken ranching."

"Chicken ranching."

"Free range. And, disregarding the poaching charge, we
failed to prove otherwise. On my end, Interior put me back
with F and W on another case. The NSC recalled Buzz, and I
assumed their eastern Washington lead had been a dead end.
They needed Buzz for something else. Buzz just disappeared.
Someone told me he moved to Canada. That's the last I heard
of him."

"So why did you call him a son of a bastard?"

"Bustard. It was a private joke between me and Radke."

"The beak?"

"Something like that."

A short silence, and then Mackenzie said, "Were you
lovers?"

"No."

Mackenzie studied her face, her body language. Was she
lying? "So what about him ticked you off?"

"He owes me three hundred dollars. I loaned it to him to
pay for a gambling debt to some card shark he was trying to
draw information out of. Radke thought the card shark might
be involved with these militants. He never paid me back the
three bills."

"So what was he doing up here prospecting for diamonds?"

Venus grinned. "I'd bet my badge that Radke was back on
the diamonds-for-weapons trade. That he'd found something

that would lead him to the big-time diamond and armaments smugglers. The prospecting was a cover."

"That racket doesn't operate in Canada. That sort of crime occurs between African guerrilla armies and the Eastern European countries and, okay, granted, in the United States. I've never heard of that kind of activity up here in the Territories. As I said, our diamonds are protected against smuggling."

Venus faked confusion. "Then why did the joint border patrol assign you to diamond country?"

Mackenzie had his answer ready. "A favor to the Americans."

"Ah." He might be telling the truth.

Mackenzie said, "You're certain this is your friend?"

"Positive. And I think he was up here on government business."

"Until he discovered the biggest blue-green diamond that ever came out of Canadian ground."

The ME rolled the drawer back into its shelf, shut the door, and fastened the latch. He addressed Mackenzie in a cheerful voice. "We're working fast as we can, Sergeant. We've finished up with the guards, and now this gentleman is our next project."

"When will you have results?"

The ME studied his own fingernails, as if the answer to Mackenzie's inquiry was tattooed on them. Finally, he chirped, "We need a definite ID before we can proceed, Sergeant." Then winked at Mackenzie.

Mackenzie said, "Give me a couple hours, Charlie. We have a U.S. federal agent here in the cooler and she's wasting a bunch of my time."

Charlie looked up, aiming a surprised smile at Venus, then at Mackenzie. "Really? Well, now, doesn't that make the job more interesting?"

Mackenzie escorted Venus back to his office. The same officer who'd brought tea now delivered a hearty breakfast of bacon, eggs, fried potatoes, and sourdough bread. He brought coffee for Venus, but Mackenzie stuck with tea. The officer also brought a copy of the *Toronto Globe and Mail,* the headline blaring, "Lac de Lune Diamond's Whereabouts Still a Mystery. Zone Geologist Remains Missing."

They didn't speak during breakfast, and when they had finished, Mackenzie said, "I've got some other work to attend. Why don't you go back to your little office and think over what you want to say. I'll take your statement this afternoon."

"I have no statement."

"Well, you've got four hours of solitude to think one up. I'll be especially interested in your alibi."

Officer Benton slipped through the door. Mackenzie nodded and Benton sat down, an expectant expression on her face. Like she was all ears.

"I told you, I was camped out in the rain forest spotting a couple poachers."

"And yet, according to statements my officers have taken from your colleagues, none of them saw you for three days or nights, including the night of the raid on Zone Mine and the following night."

"They heard my voice on the radio. They didn't come into the woods until the day I gave the signal. Sure, I was alone. That's how I work best."

Mackenzie snorted. "Well, there's one thing we have in common. I hope the only thing." He sighed. "So you're trying to tell me that you spent those three days and nights camped out in the rain forest spying on some big-game poachers. And I'm supposed to buy the tall tale." He shook his head. "I'm disappointed in you. A person with your experience in the world of crime surely could have arranged a better alibi."

Benton said, "She's right about one thing. You want to catch big game, you've got to camp out like that." She turned to Venus. "I was a veterinarian nurse in my earlier incarnation. I know the hunters' ways." She nodded at Venus. "I buy your story."

"A simple phone call to Wexler at the NSC could clear

this up instantly. I'm telling you, Sergeant Mackenzie, I'm on the level here."

"It all sounds pretty exotic and fantastical to me."

"By the way, Sergeant, what did Radke's e-mail say?"

Mackenzie visibly gloated. "I just might save that for a jury of your Canadian peers. By the way, the ME found a bullet lodged in Big Jim's heart. Forensics is already on it. Maybe this afternoon, we'll know for certain whose gun fired that baby."

Benton stared. "He went forward without a positive ID?"

Mackenzie shot, "Who else could he have been, Officer, but Big Jim Hardy?"

CHAPTER TEN

Lay-A-Day Free-range Chicken Ranch,
North-central Washington

I n winter, a thin sheet of ice crusts over the stark north-
central Washington coulees and nothing grows. The land
God chose as the Eden of the Nation of God's Chosen Soldiers, known to the material world as Company 8, in summer
produces nothing more fecund than dry sagebrush, a few
wispy thorn trees, and unhealthy grape vines incapable of
competing with the lush vineyards of the Canadian Okanogans
to the north. About the only way a man could scratch a living
from this dry sterile earth was to raise chickens, to scatter the
ochre ground with store-bought feed and set the chickens loose
to peck. At market, they were called free-range chickens and
that got a better price, just calling them free range.

But chicken ranching wasn't lucrative enough to support
the Nation of Ravallah, and so the small but growing community had turned to other occupations. Flint Gordy, the nation's ranch foreman, and a soldier in Company 8, worked
the Native American casinos on the side, being a crackerjack

roulette cheater. Ezra Pick drove a long-haul tractor trailer and brought in enough to feed his family and even add a few Ks a month to the aborning nation's coffers. Laura Pick, Ezra's wife, made arts and crafts and sold them at the local fairs and public markets and people bought from her because she made clever things, like little wooden birdhouses in the shapes of churches and even teepees.

In all, the Nation of Ravallah, or Company 8, numbered 236, including adults and children, with three more infants in the communal hopper. Everyone around Pasayten, Washington, knew about the group, but no one had paid them much mind. They weren't troublemakers, didn't proselytize, and when they performed their military maneuvers, they carried them out only on their private lands. They didn't live communally, but their lands stood adjacent to one another, and every chance they got a member of the group would buy up a parcel connecting to their fellow soldiers' properties, lands that spilled across the border into British Columbia, Canada. Some folks called them white racists, some called them anarchists, yet others referred to them as survivalists, but they were all wrong. Company 8 was much more than the sum of these parts. This was a nation-state aborning, on both sides of the U.S.–Canada border, ready to burst forth in an explosion of righteous violence and declare the entire geographical area of north-central Washington and south-central British Columbia the Republic of Ravallah, Land of the Chosen Race. For now, the government of this emerging nation-state was seated on Ron Fairview's property, where chickens pecked through a brittle crust of ice in search of scattered corn kernels.

When Karen Crandall arrived at the Lay-A-Day Chicken Ranch, handcuffed to the passenger-side door, she had to breathe through her mouth the stench was so bad. It wasn't the chicken droppings ever-present along the road to the house, but the stench of Ramie's decomposing corpse in the back of the hearse.

"Just a few more minutes," Fairview said to Crandall. "Then you'll be out in the fresh air."

A woman appeared behind the screen door of the low sprawling ranch house. She waited until the hearse drew close to the house, then opened the screen door and came toward the hearse. She was about thirty, pale as frost. She wore an over-sized knit cardigan and a flower-print dress, and her long black hair fell in two worried braids. Gerard pulled the hearse to a stop near the front porch, turned off the ignition, and stepped out of the vehicle. The woman glanced suspiciously at the girl seated beside Fairview, then Fairview got out of the hearse and the woman threw her arms around him.

The woman helped Crandall out of the car and into the house. No need for handcuffs out here; she wasn't going anywhere far, not on this cold desolate ranchland. Inside, in a tidy living room, a fire blazed in a wood-burning stove and the woman set a chair near it for Crandall to sit and warm herself. The woman's name was Sarah, and she told Crandall she was Fairview's wife. She gave Crandall a cup of hot soup and some fresh baked bread.

Through the window, Crandall saw two pickup trucks pull up and she recognized Frickey get out of one cab and Louden get out of the other. They helped Gerard and Fairview remove Ramie's corpse.

Sarah, watching over Crandall's shoulder, saw Ramie's dead body and exclaimed, "Oh, God, oh, my God. Poor Emily."

Through the window, the two women watched the men carry Ramie's body across the hard ground to a distant barn. Twenty minutes later, the men emerged from the barn, and as they drew nearer the house, Crandall saw Fairview holding the spoils in Jim Hardy's leather pouch. The men came inside the house, into the kitchen where Crandall and Sarah sat by the woodstove. Fairview poured the contents of the canvas bag on the kitchen table and it rolled like a fresh fallen egg. Sarah gasped.

The barn was a large faded red building with a sloping shingled roof. Thirty years ago it had advertised some brand of baking flour, the painted slogan on the roof faded now, and peeling, and as Crandall walked beside Fairview, she tried to focus her attention on the faded ad. Anything to divert her thoughts from what might be coming next.

Fairview said nothing as he led her across the ice-crusted feed yard toward the barn. Fairview's Doberman, named simply Dawg, trotted alongside his master, the dog's tongue wagging, lobbing foamy spit into the air. Overhead, the sky was clear blue and a yellow orb sinking on the horizon must have been the sun and yet no warmth emanated from it. A few scrawny chickens wandered around the yard, braving the wickedly cold temperatures. The sullen hens looked incapable of laying eggs, barely able to survive on the scarce remnants of feed strewn about the yard. Crandall wanted to ask Fairview if now was when he would kill her, but she was too afraid to speak. When they reached the barn, Dawg barked once and wagged his tail. Fairview unlocked a padlock and rolled the huge door open, the rumbling noise sending Dawg into a frenzy of excitement. Dawg ran on ahead into the dim interior.

Daylight spilled into the barn when the door was rolled back. Fairview reached for a light switch, turned on some overhead fluorescents, and then rolled the barn door shut, locking it from the inside. Crandall began trembling.

Fairview, Dawg at his side, led her to the rear of the huge barn where a barred cell had been built into a corner, its floor covered with straw, a single sleeping cot against the wall. No windows, no hope of escape. Fairview unlocked the cell door, opened it, and said, "In there."

Crandall obeyed. What choice did she have? At least Fairview's wife had given her a down-filled microfiber jacket with a hood. At least she wouldn't freeze to death. She had barely stepped inside the cell when Fairview shut the door and locked her in. Without a word, he turned and walked back across the length of the barn, the Doberman accompanying him.

Crandall found her voice. "Hey!" she called out to Fairview.

Dawg whirled around at the sound of her voice and began growling. Fairview stopped walking, reached down and calmed Dawg, then turned around and looked back at his prisoner.

"What's going to happen to me?" Crandall heard the fear in her own voice.

"Sarah will bring you some dinner," Fairview replied curtly. He turned around and continued walking away.

Crandall called out again. "I mean, ultimately. Are you going to kill me?"

Fairview kept walking, as if he hadn't heard her question, or didn't care enough to answer it. When he reached the barn door, he rolled it shut. Crandall could hear the padlock and then the sound of Dawg barking.

Before he left, Fairview had turned off all the overhead lights and Crandall's world had plunged into darkness. Shivering with fear, she groped around, finally locating the cot. She sat on the hard surface and tried to calm down. Crandall had led a fairly adventurous life for a twenty-six-year-old postgrad student. Life in the Northwest Territories, in the area known as the Barrens, was all about survival against the odds. But in the case of the Barrens, the odds against you were mostly nature's harshest elements, and from these, Crandall knew what she needed to survive. None of her adventures, however, had involved killers, being their prisoner, their hostage to kill whenever they decided it was time.

As she sat in the darkness, Crandall lost all her ability to think logically. Now silly, inane melodies began playing in her head, over and over, driving her crazy. In desperation, she began to pray. She had never learned to pray properly; her family was atheist and her only exposure to the concept of One

God was at the wedding of her cousin the previous summer in Alberta. A Catholic wedding, a lot of talk about God, Creator of the Universe, blessing and keeping the union of this man and woman. Crandall had become curious about this One God. She'd read a little about Eastern religions and the Buddha and Vishnu and such. She'd heard about Jesus and the loaves and fishes story. But she'd never taken religious practices seriously. They were for people who needed something to believe in. All her life, Crandall had believed in herself, and in the innate goodness of humankind, and this had been enough. But now, helpless and afraid, Crandall realized she no longer believed in innate goodness, nor in her own ability to save herself. And so she tried to pray.

"If you're there," she prayed silently, "show me."

She must have sat in the darkness for fifteen minutes waiting for God. But no response came, no Great Voice to comfort her, no Presence, nothing. On the edge of despair, Crandall tried one more time. "All right, you son of a bitch, if you really do exist, then you sure as hell better show up now and prove it to me."

In the darkness she lay down on the cot and began weeping. As tears flooded her eyes and rolled down her face, she reached up a hand to wipe them away, and then she realized that she could see her hand.

Light.

Crandall sat up and looked around. She hadn't heard the barn door open. The lights hadn't been turned on. And then she saw it. The window. The tiniest of windows up in the rafters. Through the window shone a beam of sunlight, a strong, steady flow illuminating her surroundings and gradually soothing her frantic nerves. Light suggests hope, which was all Crandall needed now, a shred of hope. Her lips curved into a tiny ironic grin. "Thanks," she said aloud. "You're a peach."

The sunlight lasted just long enough to calm her, relieve the trembling that had overtaken her body, and she was able to fall off to sleep. Somehow, she would survive. She believed this with all her heart, because the light had answered her prayer.

Sometime later, hours maybe, when the moonlight barely lit the barn, she heard the rolling of the barn door. She sat up, startled, her heart thudding in her chest. Now she heard foot-steps crunching softly on the barn's hay-strewn floor. Coming closer. She heard a soft clearing of a throat, a little cough, and then she saw a pool of light move across the barn floor, mov-ing closer, coming toward her. She sat up and placed her feet firmly on the cell floor, pressing the soles of her feet into the floor as if to gain purchase, or strength to resist what was coming. Her body began trembling uncontrollably. This is it, she thought. This is when they kill me.

And now she remembered a prayer. Something she'd learned from a childhood friend, about Mary the Mother of God. "Remember O Most Gracious Mary that never was it known that anyone who fled to your protection, implored your help, or sought your intercession, was left unaided." She struggled to recall the rest of the prayer as the pool of light came closer, the footsteps growing louder, more pronounced. "God help me," she whispered. "If you exist, help me now."

And then she saw the hand holding a flashlight down-ward, its beam creating the pool of light. She saw the silhou-ette of the person holding the flashlight and her breath caught in her throat.

Sarah.

Fairview's wife wore a long wool cape with a hood drawn over her head. She wore gloves and was carrying an object Crandall couldn't make out at first. As Sarah approached the cell, Crandall saw the object was a tray. On the tray, a loaf of bread and a bowl of something. Sarah came forward, set the flashlight and the tray on the floor, and rummaged through a pocket in her cape. Finally she drew out a set of keys, and lo-cating the right key, unlocked the cell door and slipped inside, locking it again behind her. The tray remained on the floor outside the cell.

"How are you faring?" Sarah asked.

Crandall thought she heard compassion in Sarah's question.

"I'm scared," she answered honestly.

Sarah nodded with understanding but offered no words of comfort.

"I've brought you some food. Nothing fancy. Some homemade soup and a fresh loaf of bread. I want you to eat this tonight. Finish the soup and all of the bread. You must do this. It will help you. It will give you strength."

Crandall felt tears welling in her eyes and once again they spilled over on her cheeks and rolled down her face. Sarah sat down on the cot. From her cape she brought out a cotton handkerchief and daubed at Crandall's tears.

"There now," she said. "There now."

Crandall stopped trembling and gradually the tears subsided. Sarah put the handkerchief away and stood up. She walked over to the cell door and for an instant Crandall thought about trying to overpower her, jump her from behind, but just then Sarah turned around and smiled sweetly at her as she unlocked the cell door and slipped outside. In one swift motion, Sarah placed the tray inside the cell and shut the door, then locked it. She picked up the flashlight and, holding it downward, made her way back through the barn. Moments later, Crandall heard the rolling door, and then silence.

Alone again, Crandall stared at the tray of food. She wasn't really hungry. Fear had overcome all desire for food. But Sarah's words hung in the night air, repeating over and over, "I want you to eat this tonight. You must do this. It will help you."

Crandall stood up and walked across the cell. Reaching for the tray, Crandall lifted it and carried it over to the cot. She set it down on the cot and in the dim light stared at the steaming soup for several minutes before picking up the spoon off the tray and dipping it into the cooling broth. She lifted one spoonful to her lips. It smelled fragrant, like fresh vegetables and herbs. She placed the spoon in her mouth, swallowed, and let the warm liquid roll down her throat. It tasted good, like the hearty soups she had made for herself and Jim up in the Barrens. She finished half the bowl of soup and then picked up the small loaf of bread.

It was a dark bread, maybe pumpernickel, and heavy. The loaf appeared to have been baked, then cut, then pushed back together, held by nothing more than its own steamy tack. No knife had been placed on the tray. Certainly they wouldn't trust her with a knife. With her hands, she ripped the loaf in half. A small dark object fell out of the center of the loaf and onto the cot. Crandall stared, her heart racing. What was it? What?

Carefully she reached for the object and, before touching it, leaned forward in the poor light to study it. The object was a small tape recorder. She seized it up, frantically working the buttons until finally the tape began to roll. She heard Sarah's soft voice.

"Keep track of everything that happens," Sarah's voice said. "Start from the beginning and keep your diary up to date. If you need it, I'll bring you more tape. You can hide the recorder in your clothing. They won't touch you again. I promise. My husband would never touch another woman except me. Keep track of everything."

That was all. Crandall clicked off the recorder and tried to gather her thoughts. Why had Sarah brought her a tape recorder? Why hadn't she just unlocked the cell and let her go free? Maybe Sarah knew that Crandall would never get far before being killed by one of the men keeping watch in the yard. But why a tape recorder?

It gave her something to do, something to divert her thoughts from the terrible thing she felt certain was coming. Death. She sat back on the cot, her back against the cold cell wall. She held the tape recorder up to her lips, pressed the record button, and began at the mine, the day Big Jim had discovered the Lac de Lune.

CHAPTER ELEVEN

Yellowknife

"So let me get this perfectly clear," Mackenzie said, scratching his head. "You knew Big Jim Hardy as a fellow named, uh, Buzz Radke. And you say he worked as an undercover agent for the U.S. National Security Agency?"

"Council. National Security Council. He was an analyst, specializing in arms smuggling. Like I said before, one phone call can clear this up," said Venus.

Officer Benton scooted into Mackenzie's office with a fresh pot of tea, set it down on Mackenzie's desk, and scooted out. Venus filled Mackenzie's mug, then hers. Her mug bore a decaled map of the Northwest Territories and the words "Diamond Country." Benton returned, this time bearing a box of tea biscuits. She handed them around, poured herself a mugful of tea, added cream and sugar, and plopped down on a wooden chair that creaked beneath her bulk. Mackenzie nodded, indicating he approved of Benton's sitting in on the interview.

Mackenzie put the call through, and when the NSC director of transnational threats came on the line, Mackenzie placed the phone on conference mode. Venus heard Wexler's familiar gravelly voice say, "We've instructed Agent Diamond to cooperate with you. I hope she isn't causing any problems."

Mackenzie replied, "She's right here, sir. We've had her in custody since yesterday afternoon. We have strong evidence linking her to the crime. You might say she has been cooperating, although I suspect she knows more than she lets on. And she's a complainer."

"Whining about the weather, no doubt."

"Everything. She's a sassy lass."

"Put her on."

"I'm here, sir."

She heard Wexler sigh the way he always did before dropping one of his bombshells. Whatever he was about to say wasn't coming out easily. He cleared his throat, sighed again, and asked, "Are we on a secure line?"

"Of course, sir." Mackenzie, alert now.

"Who is present within hearing distance, Sergeant?"

"Myself, my colleague Officer Benton, and the prisoner, sir."

Wexler cleared his throat and began. "Five years ago, Buzz Radke, an analyst for the National Security Council here in the U.S., went undercover in a joint mission between the Canadian Secret Service and the U.S. NSC. Radke was sent to the Barrens to uncover a ring of diamond smugglers who were mixing West African war diamonds with Canadian rough and selling them on the international market as legitimate Canadian rough."

"War diamonds?" Mackenzie said. "We don't have them here."

Wexler offered an explanation. "You may not think you have war diamonds in Canada, but we're almost certain they are passing through your mines. War diamonds, blood diamonds, whatever you want to call them. I'm referring primarily to diamonds mined in guerrilla-controlled African mines and sold for weapons by various rebel groups fighting internecine battles. We've known for decades that some of the rebels even have their own mines, or else are on friendly terms with mine owners who support their causes. In their own mines, they often use slave labor, and they'd just as soon kill anyone caught stealing a bit of rough."

"You needn't educate me, sir. I am well aware of the existence of war diamonds from Africa. We do not have any here."

Wexler continued. "Five years ago, we received credible evidence that some of these blood diamonds were being mixed with Canada rough and smuggled out of Canada, placed in sight boxes in New York, Antwerp, and London, where they were sold as pure Canada rough. The operation involved smuggling the West African rough through the U.S. into the Northwest Territories. The brokers buying rough diamonds may recognize the African stones, but if they really wanted them, some would just as soon break the law and buy up the inventory, no questions asked. It's a sophisticated scam and everybody in the diamond trade has knowledge of the smuggling. Everyone in the trade knows that diamonds are often traded for weapons. Serious weapons, surface-to-air missiles, tanks in some cases, whole airplane-cargo loads of guns, grenades, and explosives. These are the same bastards buying the Pentagon's surplus bioterrorism lab equipment over the Internet and selling it to our North Korean pals."

"What sort of lab equipment?" Mackenzie, quizzical, apprehensive.

"Radioactive materials. Cesium to name one. Taken out of Ukraine after the Soviet Union fell. The Soviets had huge arsenals of weapons, both conventional and nuclear, stockpiled in Ukraine. When Ukraine became an independent republic, the government fell into chaos. People with access to these stockpiled weapons started grabbing them and selling them for U.S. dollars. A lot of Ukrainians got rich fast. The real pros are still actively exchanging weapons for U.S. dollars and diamonds from both Africa and Canada."

"Officer Benton here, sir. One question. Why wouldn't they just smuggle the African stones straight to the sales points? Why route them through Canada?"

"An excellent question, Officer. Buying and selling war diamonds violates international trading accords. If they're going to be sold on the legitimate market, they have to be disguised as coming from somewhere else."

Mackenzie cut in. "As you no doubt are aware, sir, Canada's mines have processes whereby we track the stone's provenance and mark each stone before it leaves the country. That way a Canada diamond is distinguished from the blood or war diamonds."

"These little lasered-on polar bears and other distinctive logos," put in Benton. "We call Canadian diamonds the good diamond. Because our diamonds aren't tied to guerrilla warfare."

Wexler returned the volley. "But some stones aren't marked while still in the rough. If I'm not mistaken, the mark is made once it has been cut and polished. For that matter, even once the stone is cut and polished, the laser image can be cut and polished off. And provenance can easily be faked."

"I doubt many smugglers are that fastidious," put in Mackenzie.

Wexler continued. "So the African rough is smuggled to Canada and mixed in with Canada rough, and then the stones are cut and polished. Once this has been accomplished, your little polar bear symbol or whatever is lasered onto each diamond. In this finished condition, the African diamonds are virtually indistinguishable from Canadian diamonds."

Mackenzie scoffed. "This all sounds, if you'll pardon my saying so, sir, like a bad James Bond film. Granted, I've heard rumors to the effect, but as far as I'm concerned, it's a lot of shrill paranoia. These rumors are not good for the Canadian diamond trade, I might add."

Wexler continued. "Our sources are reliable. De Beers and Parecles, to name two of the largest diamond brokers in the world, have bought rough Canadian lots on the open market and discovered African stones in the mix."

"Granted, it's easier to identify where the diamond comes from while it is still in the rough," agreed Mackenzie.

Benton nodded. "Yeah, I can possibly see that."

"Both De Beers and Parecles were suspicious, so they compared their lots. They came up with similar mixes and the stones were almost identical in color and clarity. They found a lot of pink, which isn't found in Canada. Of course, it might have come from Brazil, but we're fairly certain these are West African stones, maybe Rwandan or Angolan, smuggled by a guerrilla group, maybe out of Congo, and traded for weapons. So the NSC sent Radke up to the Barrens to check it out. This was over five years ago. Five years and four months to be exact. Radke went pretty deep undercover and we just sort of let him do his thing. We had other priorities. Then we heard a rumor to the effect Radke had discovered some G10 kimberlite, indicating a diamond source, staked some claims of his own, and opened his own mine. Zone Mine. So when the news broke about the Lac de Lune being discovered in a Zone pipe . . . isn't that what they call it, a pipe?"

"Right. A pipe beneath a craton." Mackenzie sipped his tea. His tea mug bore the insignia of the RCMP. His face bore the expression of sheer boredom.

"Then news breaks that a guy named Big Jim Hardy had discovered the Lac de Lune diamond. I saw a photo of him standing beside the diamond. There's no mistaking Radke. So we figured we'd lost Buzz to prospecting. By then, I'd taken over as director of NSC's transnational threats section. I sent Radke a request for his formal resignation. Never received an answer. E-mailed, phoned, tried every which way to reach him but he wasn't communicating. I was on the verge of sending my agents to bring him back to the U.S. when he turns up murdered, the Lac de Lune stolen."

"That's a priceless stone," Mackenzie offered. "There has never been a stone of such color pulled out of Canada's mines.

The assailants also removed a canvas belt off Radke containing several millions of dollars, that's U.S. in smaller stones. Also in the rough."

Wexler said, "How do you know this for certain, Sergeant?"

"Fibers found during the initial autopsy examination indicated that Mr. Hardy, or perhaps I should say Radke, was wearing a wide belt made of canvas. There were welts where something had apparently been ripped off his waist, as well as on his neck. Hardy, or Radke as you call him, always wore the Lac de Lune in a leather pouch that hung from a leather cord around his neck. And everyone up here knows that Hardy never went anywhere without his entire inventory of rough. He always carried that in the canvas belt. And he carried a Beretta at all times."

"Speculation," Venus put in. "Still, it makes sense."

"That the thieves are professionals, we have no doubt. That they cleaned out Radke's inventory, we have no doubt. The question remains, who committed these murders and who now is in possession of the diamonds?"

"Yes, sir." Mackenzie stirred in his chair.

Benton hissed, "He's talking down to us, Sergeant. Like we're idiots." Mackenzie placed a finger to his lips. Benton frowned and recrossed her legs.

Wexler sighed. "Let me make this very simple, Sergeant. One of our analysts has been murdered. Maybe he deserved it, how the hell would I know? He hasn't communicated with us for at least two years. Still, he was on our payroll up till the end, and we have a duty to find out what's going on up there, who killed him."

Mackenzie cleared his throat and said carefully, "This of course is in our jurisdiction, sir, I'm sure you understand that."

"A United States federal agent has been murdered in your jurisdiction, Sergeant. That makes it our business as much as yours. Now, I've already been in touch with Ottawa and cleared this with your superiors. It hasn't escaped my attention, Sergeant, that you are a member of the Integrated Border Enforcement Team and that you had been sent to the Barrens specifically to follow the developments subsequent to Radke's discovery of the big diamond, in hope, so I'm told by your superiors, of nailing a big-time smuggler or two."

Venus glanced sharply at Mackenzie. His cheeks had flushed crimson. Wexler barked, "Contact your minister of justice, Frank Lévesque. We've agreed that you are to stay on the case and that my agent, Venus Diamond, is to work in partnership with you. I suggest that if you haven't already done so, you contact Lévesque in Ottawa."

Venus said, "Sir, Buzz Radke wrote my name in blood—"

"I know all about that." Wexler sounded impatient. "Why the hell do you think I want you on this case? Obviously Radke was trying to communicate with you."

"But sir, I don't know much about this business. It's been years since I worked with Radke. And my job, you know, at Fish and Wildlife? They're real shorthanded right now."

She heard Wexler vent steam over the line. "That's been taken care of. You have been temporarily loaned to the NSC. To me. And stop posing. It's pretentious to think your colleagues can't manage without you."

"Yes, sir." Venus clenched her teeth. Bottom line was, she hated cold weather. Yellowknife in winter was as cold as Siberia.

Mackenzie said, "We haven't yet ascertained Agent Diamond's innocence, and until that time—"

"You're being a prick, Sergeant. Call Lévesque."

Benton's chair squeaked as she rocked forward, a hand covering her mouth, but her eyes blazed and Venus guessed she was cursing behind the hand.

Mackenzie persisted. "Sir, we have other evidence pointing to Agent Diamond as a possible accomplice in this murder. For one thing, we have an e-mail sent to her by the victim."

"We have that communication as well, Sergeant. I have every shred of evidence that you forwarded on to Ottawa, and

I can only presume that you aren't holding any evidence back."

"Of course not." Mackenzie appeared personally offended. "Although—I did remember something just this morning. Possibly relevant, though I couldn't be sure."

"Go on," Wexler said. Venus could hear him tapping something against a hard object. Probably his Waterman pen against his farm-raised teak desk.

"We—by 'we' I mean the Integrated Border Enforcement Team—received some credible reports of a meeting between two possible suspects. One of the guards killed at Zone, a Yellowknife native named Purdy, was operating a failing mine in the Territories. This may explain why he also worked as a guard at Zone. Mr. Purdy was seen meeting with a New York diamond broker in a saloon just weeks prior to the assault at Zone. The broker is apparently known in New York as the King of Forty-seventh Street. A Jewish man. Goldman. Yitzhak Goldman."

Benton's eyes flashed. "Just because he's Jewish, Sergeant—"

Mackenzie glared at her.

Wexler sighed. "You aren't telling us anything new. The evidence so far implies nothing except that Radke was attempting to reestablish communication with Agent Diamond. Possibly in relation to the smuggling operations."

Benton spoke up. "And too she tried to resist apprehension. We had to cuff her to bring her across the border."

"You had better learn to get along," Wexler snapped.

"But sir, she shows no signs of cooperating," complained Mackenzie.

"Hey, I poured your tea, didn't I?"

Benton snickered, stood up, and left the room.

Wexler barked, "There's one more thing. Are you listening?"

"Yes, sir."

"Sir."

"We've received strongly supported intelligence that the

Lac de Lune may actually have been stolen to finance a terrorist operation somewhere on the North American continent. We are not yet able to say in what nation this event is supposed to occur. Our best guess is Latin America. And too there's always the chance the thieves knew Radke, knew he was working undercover. To put it bluntly, if you follow my line of reasoning, we can perhaps surmise that Radke may have been a point man for smuggling war diamonds into Canada and mixing them into his own mine's Canada rough before they were sold. And, this is pure conjecture on my part, Radke might have actually been involved in a scheme that went bad, for him anyway. At the very least, we are positive the assault on Zone Mine could not have been successfully executed without the cooperation of a local."

Mackenzie cleared his throat and said, "That's a lot of conjecture, sir."

"Still, a United States federal agent has been murdered. We want to know why, and by whom. And if Radke's name is leaked to the news media, all of you are fried chicken. Is that clear?"

Mackenzie shook his head. "I'm not ready to trust you yet. Any of you."

"Call Lévesque, Sergeant." Wexler hung up.

CHAPTER TWELVE

Mackenzie leaned back in his chair and stared out the window at the dim evening sky. He didn't speak, just gazed into the bleak outdoors. Venus wondered if he ever thought about Hawaii, about hot sand beaches and hula-hula girls and sunshine and tropical waters warmer than the tea he now sipped. After a while he turned and looked at Venus.

"Okay," he conceded matter-of-factly, "now I've cleared it with Lévesque, so we become a team. But to be perfectly honest, I don't like you one bit and I think you're lying through your teeth. And I'm in charge, remember that, eh."

Venus's mouth curved into a thin smile, just enough to suggest Sergeant Mackenzie should doubt himself. "So now that we're all buddy-buddy, how about showing me the e-mail from Radke?"

Mackenzie sighed and reached into the case file. He fished out a single sheet of paper and handed it across the desk. Venus read Radke's e-mail message addressed to her:

Old pal,
   Free-range chicks. New York: David Goldman. Antwerp: Rubicon. Jo-burg: Haakvig. Watch out for the Russian. Instructions to follow.

   Venus looked up at Mackenzie. "This drivel came off Radke's computer?"
   "Correct. That is, Jim Hardy's. Hell, whatever his name is."
   "Let's agree to refer to him by his real name. Buzz Radke. Okay?"
   Mackenzie nodded tiredly. "What do you make of the message?"
   "I never got it. Must have been lost in cyberspace. And it's another damn puzzle. Radke was the king of codes and riddles. A great analyst but paranoid as hell. He often wrote his reports in riddles. He used to test me with them and it drove me crazy."
   Mackenzie made a face. "So take your best guess. You tell me what it means."
   "Radke often talked about New York, since it's a big diamond center. I remember him saying a lot of smuggled goods that pass through Antwerp and into North American tubes end up in New York where they're sold to the trade." She shook her head. "I don't recognize these individuals' names. Another damn riddle."
   Mackenzie's mouth warped into a triumphant grin. "Allow me to enlighten you, lass."
   "Don't call me lass."
   "Agent Diamond."
   "That's better. Now enlighten me."
   Mackenzie shifted in his chair. "These three individuals, Radke mentions in his e-mail, Goldman, Rubicon, and Haakvig, are famous in the diamond world. Master diamond cutters, they say the best. We hear a lot about their work. Some of our miners send their stones to these fellows,

the difficult stones, the rough stones with imperfections. These require the work of a talented hand." Mackenzie flicked his hand. In the dim light streaming through the window, the gold ring on his pinky finger acquired a deep burnished glow, a fiery halo marking the weakest point in a human hand. Venus would bet her Doc Martens that Mackenzie had just been educated by Officer Benton, who was, after all, a local, more versed in the diamond trade. Mackenzie continued:

"You know how rumors get around. Few weeks ago a rumor spread around Yellowknife, just after Big Jim—okay, Radke—went public with the Lac de Lune. Rumor said Radke had sent exact models of the stone to all three of these diamond cutters, set them up in a competition to see who could successfully cleave the stone without shattering it. See, the Lac de Lune contains a very small imperfection near its center. Dicey business, eh. The wrong cleaver might shatter the stone, thereby causing its value to plunge by millions of dollars."

"U.S. or Canadian?"

"Go to hell."

"Then what happened?"

Mackenzie shrugged. "Far as I know the rumor was true. But then the Zone killings and theft of the stone apparently ended the competition."

"Something's wrong here, Sergeant. Maybe you know something you're holding back, I don't know, but I smell a rotten fish here in Yellowknife."

Mackenzie blew out a long stream of breath. He had to work to stay cool. He obviously despised the thought of working with someone whom he still considered a prime suspect. The muscles at his jawline bulged and quivered. Finally he said, "So what was Radke to you?"

"I already told you."

"Tell me again."

Double-checking her facts.

She went over her story again, finishing with, "Interpol didn't play a big role in the operation, but they cooperated, mainly because we weren't delivering convincing evidence, other than one dubious informant's statement. But we'd used this informant in the past, and frankly, I believed him when he fingered the Lay-A-Day folks."

"The what?" Mackenzie blinked rapidly.

Venus snapped her fingers. "There you go. Lay-A-Day Free-range Chicken Ranch. That's the 'free-range chicks' reference in Radke's message."

"I'm not following you, eh."

"Just let me talk this out. So Radke and I pursued the eastern Washington connection. It was one of those rare cases in which two federal agencies are obliged to cooperate. We actually hit it off and worked well together. We were on the brink of busting them when we reached a dead end. Our informant got cold feet by way of a shotgun blast from someone who didn't want him to talk. We had no other witnesses, and no terribly convincing evidence. Our respective bosses considered it a waste of time. Turned out the subjects are right-wing militants and, according to local gossip around north-central Washington, supposedly planning to build a nation-state right there on the U.S.–Canada border. They have a large compound there, the center being the Lay-A-Day Ranch. In fact, your RCMP border unit worked with us, so I'm surprised you, being an IBET cop, hadn't heard about Lay-A-Day Ranch."

Mackenzie flushed crimson again, a shade Venus didn't trust.

"Like I said already, they raise free-range chickens. Their leader's name is Ron Fairview. Radke and I were convinced Fairview and his fellow militants were smuggling big-time, but we never could put together convincing evidence. The case has been in limbo ever since. Now Radke sends me this message. Why?"

"What about the Russian? What did he mean by that?"

"Your guess is as good as mine, Sergeant."

Crandall had lost count of the days and nights. She didn't know how many had passed since they grabbed her from the mine's office, since they had murdered Big Jim and the guards. When they brought her to the ranch, they'd settled her into the cell in the barn and from then on she had lost track of time. But at least the tape recorder Sarah had smuggled into her cell provided Crandall with something to maintain her sanity, as well as track the passing time. The more she recorded, the more she recalled the smallest of details, some of them puzzling. At this point, what did it matter? She was their prisoner, and she guessed that sooner or later, if she didn't escape, they'd kill her, too. At least recording her memories of events helped pass the time, and in a way, it was therapeutic to get it all out. Twice she had indicated to Sarah that she needed fresh tapes and Sarah had brought them, tucked into loaves of bread. Each time, Sarah hadn't lingered long, her eyes always darting around as if she feared her husband might discover the two women talking, maybe even discover the tape recorder and the tapes. Then what would Fairview do to his wife?

On Sarah's last visit, just this morning, her cape had fallen open and Crandall glimpsed the woman's belly. It was ripe and round.

"You're going to have a baby?" Crandall had taken a chance asking such a personal question.

Sarah nodded, a serene smile crossing her lips. Her soft eyes crinkled at the corners and Crandall thought Sarah looked tired but beautiful. "Maybe a girl this time."

"How many children do you have now?"

"Two. Two young boys."

Crandall nodded. "Nice. I—I wish I could meet them."

Sarah looked away, far off into some invisible distance where something she fervently wished for beckoned on the horizon. "I could bring pictures."

"I love children."

Sarah had set down Crandall's lunch tray and was turning to leave when she thought of something. She turned back to Crandall and said, "Do you have children?"

Crandall shook her head. "Not yet."

Sarah inhaled a deep breath and said, "That's good."

The Barrens,
Northwest Territories

Northern lights shimmered across the midnight sky, throwing a purple and green backdrop behind the ice road. A single snowmobile sped along the road to Zone Mine. Halfway to Lac de Lune, the snowmobile veered east and then south, traveling now at slower speeds, finally coming to a stop on the ice, where the snowmobile's engine was cut.

The driver used binoculars to study the ice field, then drove on a bit farther, at a faster speed now. Making a curve toward the south, the snowmobile slowed slightly but not in time to avoid the collision. Out here in the Barrens, a collision meant only one thing: bear.

The terrible crash sent the snowmobile flying, its driver clinging for dear life. The large bear hadn't been fazed by the collision, in fact had charged the snowmobile in fierce defense of its cubs, who hung in the distance, huddled together.

Sprawled on the ice, the driver reached for a rifle still mounted on the snowmobile's side, already loaded. The female polar bear reared up on her hind legs and rushed forward, her roaring filling the arctic silence. A single dart struck her in her abdomen. She fought the tranquilizer, forging ahead until the anesthesia cut her down not fifteen meters from her assailant. She fell forward, slumping onto the ice, her cubs trembling in terror.

CHAPTER THIRTEEN

Delbert Dixon might rank high on the gunrunning circuit, but he hated the big boys who ran the tube, and the feeling was mutual. Still, they worked together and a certain measure of respect and trust had developed over the years, because time and again Dixon had successfully performed his duties along the smugglers' tube, delivering cargo as it arrived from Odessa or Trans-Dneiper or some other far-off land. Victor Rimsky, the Russian entrepreneur, played a major role in the tube, employing his fleet of cargo planes to smuggle weapons and drugs and sockfuls of diamonds from Siberia that would be traded for planeloads of heroin.

Sometimes Rimsky's cargo planes would land in Newfoundland to take on fuel and Dixon would intercept them there and pull off a cargo-switch routine that had worked like a charm so far. The big boys admired how Dixon pulled off his end of the bargain. Still, no love was lost between them and Dixon. The big boys suspected Dixon of skimming, though he'd never been caught in the act. For Dixon's part, he despised the big boys because they had underpaid and over-worked him more than a few times. For someone as bright as Delbert Dixon, intercepting these cargo shipments and pulling off the switch routine involved a lot of hard labor, mostly performed by Dixon and his longshoremen cronies. Sometimes the cargo would be switched in Newfoundland and placed on an ocean-going container vessel that sailed to certain sleepy ports along the U.S. eastern coastline. Macon, Georgia, was a favorite destination along the East Coast tube. From there, the cargo usually headed to South America, or Latin America, wherever the client requested delivery, and sometimes on to Africa. Delbert himself never actually took part in the offshore shenanigans; he couldn't swim, for one thing. But he worked the shore end, and he paid his boys handsomely, and when one of the longshoremen showed signs of loose-lip syndrome, Delbert's man Merle Tremaine dis-patched the chattermouth in a most unseemly and painful manner, thereby ensuring loyalty from the remaining pirates. Playing in the tube was a risky but lucrative business, al-though not much of a mental challenge for a bright fellow like Delbert Dixon, and his highly polished routine inevitably produced results in record time.

On occasion Dixon had dabbled in Internet purchase and sales of illegal paraphernalia. Not in the usual eBay sense. Dixon worked the Internet by checking out the entire inven-tory being floated on the online auctions, figuring out where they were stashed, and then burglarizing the places, stealing the inventory, and reselling it at his own inflated prices. Thus, Dixon and his pals had managed within two short weeks to put together the inventory diamond broker Gordon Volpe had ordered. The entire inventory, including fifty hand-held rocket launchers, five surface-to-air missiles, and numerous lesser weapons, fit neatly inside one eighteen-wheel semi-trailer container. And so, once Volpe had given the "good to go," Dixon and his lackey, Crumley, struck out for the Wild

West to deliver the goods, traveling a leisurely southern route to avoid Dakota blizzards and such, and stopping at Motel 6s to keep a low profile.

It was on the first morning at the Pennsylvania Turnpike Cafe across the road from Motel 6, where Dixon and his driver, Crumley, were nursing hangovers with Bloody Marys and Dutch pancakes, that Crumley picked up a yellowed weeks-old newspaper, read the headlines, and exclaimed, "Wouldja look at this, for chrissake?" And handed the paper to Dixon.

Delbert Dixon read the headline aloud. " 'Famous 384 Carat Lac de Lune Diamond Stolen from Canadian Diamond Mine. Forty Million (U.S.) in Smaller Stones Also Taken. Thieves Kill Seven, Including Owner, in Assault on Zone Mine.' "

Dixon tossed the newspaper aside. "Hell, I know all about that. It's been all over the news. Where've you been hiding, Crum? Sheesh." Dixon couldn't stand people who weren't up-to-date on world events.

"The part that gets to me," ventured Crumley, rechecking the newspaper's dateline, "is how this diamond mine thingie happened just before Volpe sent us on this job. I mean, Volpe being a diamond broker and all."

Dixon just glared at him, so Crumley shut up and kept reading the story.

Dixon was in one of his moody periods this morning, so Crumley thought he'd back off a little, but when he read further on in the article, he couldn't contain himself and whistled out loud. "Forty million in the small stones alone. Hell, can you imagine what that Lac de Lune boulder is worth?"

Dixon's eyes stared right through Crumley.

"They might've taken a hostage, too," offered Crumley. "A girl geologist. Karen Crandall. Or, it says here, she might be part of the job. I used to know a chick named Crandall. She wouldn't give it up unless you showed her what you had to offer first."

Dixon shook his head in disgust. "Never take hostages. Ever. Stupidest damn thing you can do."

But Delbert Dixon wasn't thinking so much about hostages at that moment. He was putting two and three together and coming up with five and a half. Crumley had a point. Diamonds. A huge MF rock. Thieves would steal them in order to resell them. For what? Money? Weapons? One thing bothered Dixon: Gordon Volpe was a big-time diamond broker. Volpe had instructed Dixon to deliver the weapons and take charge of Volpe's "goods" for the weapons. Dixon was then to be paid a fee for his services by Volpe. What Volpe hadn't been clear about was what sort of "goods" Volpe was to receive—via Dixon—for the delivery. Dixon's imagination might be getting the best of him, but he could feel a hunch coming on, and since it was still a hunch, he didn't bring it up to Crumley at breakfast. Instead, he yanked the newspaper out of Crumley's hands, folded it, and stuffed it in his trousers pocket.

Crumley said, "Damn eggs taste like rubber an' the damn bacon's burnt as hell."

"Shut up," snapped Dixon. "I'm trying to think over here."

Yellowknife

"Let's be honest," Mackenzie offered. "We aren't exactly fond of each another." He stared at Venus, maybe waiting for a response.

Venus stared back. Not wanting honesty between them. Not caring to offer her opinion of him. She thought Mackenzie was a dolt of the first order who had missed the obvious and leaped to conclusions about how things went down with Radke.

"And I don't believe you," Mackenzie added. "I don't care what your boss in Washington, D.C., says, you've got something to hide. Maybe what's his name? Wexler? Maybe even Wexler doesn't know what you're hiding. I'm guessing he's oblivious. Most government officials are. In point of fact, Lévesque has his head up his ass half the time. He has no concept of what happens in the Territories. He's never even visited Yellowknife, so what can he know about how they handle criminal cases up here? What I'm saying is, they're too removed from the scene, and they lack imagination. But I know what you're hiding. And I think I can prove it." He rubbed the back of his neck.

He might be bluffing. Or he might have some piece of evidence he had so far withheld. She said, "You got a kink back there?"

"Yep," replied Mackenzie, apparently grateful for sympathy from any quarter, even a possible murderer. "Don't know what I did to make it sore like this."

"Easy. What you did was have a big knee-jerk reaction to a misleading clue and it pulled your neck out."

Mackenzie didn't smile. "Something's wrong here," he said more to himself than to her. He pondered for a few seconds then shook his head. "It won't work."

"What?"

"Us as a team. How can I work with a suspect?"

"Lévesque told you to drop the charges."

Mackenzie laughed humorlessly. "Politicians make my work harder," he complained. "But sooner or later, I'll come up with the evidence to put this right." He flicked his fingers. "That's all I'm gonna say for now. I've got a hunch, and my hunches are never wrong."

So he wasn't holding anything else back. Except his hunch. All the so-called evidence he had, he'd put forth by now.

"Well, this time your hunch is way off base. I had nothing to do with Radke's murder and if you'd just use your brain instead of trying to tie things up into neat little empty packages maybe we'd make some real progress here."

A knock on Mackenzie's door. "Come in," he growled irritably.

The door opened and a uniformed Mountie Venus didn't recognize entered Mackenzie's office followed by Benton and five other RCMPs. The first Mountie to enter carried lots of scrambled eggs on his shoulders and he was considerably older than the others. They spread out, Benton blocking the door.

Mackenzie stood up. "Inspector Halladay, what a surprise. Are you up from Ottawa on the Zone Mine case?"

Inspector Halladay nodded tersely and said, "Sergeant Mackenzie, I have the unfortunate duty of placing you under arrest for conspiracy and murder in the case of Zone Diamond Mine. Turn around, Sergeant."

Mackenzie's mouth dropped open and at first he was speechless. When he found his voice, he said, "Inspector, what's going on here? Is this some kind of joke?"

"Turn around, Mackenzie, and face the wall."

Mackenzie slowly turned to face the wall the inspector had indicated. Venus watched as Inspector Halladay clipped handcuffs around Mackenzie's wrists and read him his rights. Benton moved into the room and stood beside Venus.

"I knew all along that you were clean," Benton said to Venus beneath the sound of Mackenzie's protests.

"Oh, yeah? Then why did you go along with the program?"

Benton shrugged. "We didn't have enough evidence against Mackenzie at that point. He's my superior. Was. I was in a dicey position, him being a bigwig IBET cop and all."

Halladay and his accompanying officers steered Mackenzie out of the room, Mackenzie still protesting vehemently.

"Mackenzie," Venus called out. At the door, Mackenzie looked back over his shoulder. Venus said, "The cot is uncomfortable as all get out, but the blankets are clean."

When he had been taken away, Benton and two other officers searched Mackenzie's office. Venus watched a Mountie remove Mackenzie's computer and a stack of CDs. Two other Mounties hauled the file cabinet away while Benton searched Mackenzie's desk drawers. She caught Benton's eye.

"How'd you link him to the case?"

Benton grimaced at a rotten apple core she'd pulled from a drawer. "Wasn't easy. We knew an insider was involved. Someone familiar with the terrain, and with what Jim Hardy had stashed in his vault. And where he kept his diamonds."

"Actually, his real name is Buzz Radke."

Benton nodded. "I know. Yeah, Radke. Everyone around here knew him as Big Jim Hardy. It's hard making the mental switch."

Venus stood and walked to the window. Outside, the sky had already darkened to indigo. The streets were practically deserted, only a few vehicles navigating the ice-covered highway. "So how exactly did you finger Mackenzie?" she asked Benton without turning around.

"We had suspected him from the start. He's been seen up at Zone Mine in recent weeks, supposedly on IBET business. He filed a report claiming he had suspicions that two of Zone's security guards were tied to a smuggling ring. Claimed that Hardy—Radke—called him up there to shake out the bad seeds. But then he never pressed charges. We think he was scamming. And then this happened. But since he was running the investigation it's been hard working around him. Ballistics tests were the real clincher. Radke was shot with Mackenzie's personal weapon, a Glock. Also, two of the guards were shot with the same weapon."

"Why would Mackenzie do a dumb thing like use his own gun and leave the ballistic evidence?"

Benton shrugged. "He never registered it. Nothing tied him to the weapon. But I saw it lying on the passenger seat of his car the day he arrived and I asked him about it, so he let me examine it. I took down the serial number and recorded it in my daily report. The Sergeant must've forgotten I knew about the weapon. But there was other evidence besides."

"What evidence?"

Benton sat in Mackenzie's chair, leaned her elbows on the desk. She looked natural there, like she belonged. "Here's how it went down. The thieves came from the outside, from the U.S., we're fairly certain. They needed a local contact to guide them up into the Barrens. They struck a deal with Mackenzie that he couldn't refuse. He became their partner."

"But he's not a local."

Benton smiled. "He was. He's a native of Yellowknife.

Everyone around here knew his family. They were all wiped out in a house fire one winter. Except Roland. He went to Ottawa and joined the RCMP."

"Arson or accidental?"

Benton shrugged. "Who knows? Final call was accidental, but some folks think Roland lit the match. I'm of mixed feelings on that incident. I wasn't even born yet."

"Besides the ballistics, what other evidence points at Mackenzie?"

Benton nodded, smiling. She understood the question but was taking her time answering it. "Besides the ballistics? There was the snowmobile registered to Mackenzie. A personal vehicle, not the department's. The tread marks match those found at the scene, coming and going over the ice road. And then, Forensics, bless their hearts, found a hand-drawn map of the area around Lac de Lune and Zone Mine's headquarters in the storage compartment of Sergeant Mackenzie's snowmobile. They found his fingerprints all over the place, of course, since he led the investigation team when the crime was first discovered. So that wasn't much help."

"What led you to suspect him in the first place?"

Benton placed her chin in her hands and shrugged. She had a broad pale forehead, small eyes, and a tiny little nose that seemed too short for her face. Her lips curved into an ironic grin. "Everyone knew he was nearing retirement. He's nearly fifty-five, so that was a given. His pension wasn't all that much, and he had this dream of moving to Vancouver, buying a condo and living out his retirement in the big city. He often traveled to Vancouver, any chance he got, he'd hop a plane to Vancouver. So as for motive, he needed the money. You can't live in Vancouver on a Mountie's pension, eh? And we'd all noticed him acting out of character in the past couple weeks."

"How so?"

Benton shook her head. "It's hard to describe. He wasn't himself. He was broody and preoccupied and he spent a lot of time outside the office when he should have been on duty. I covered for him numerous times. He'd make excuses like he had a doctor's appointment, or that he was at home fighting a fever, that sort of thing. And whenever he was here at headquarters, I'd say in the last week before the Zone hit, he acted broody, like I said, and preoccupied. Not to mention short-tempered. We all walked on tiptoe around here lately."

Venus sat down across from Benton, Mackenzie's big desk between them. "So the motivation was money?"

Benton nodded. "Pure greed."

"And so far, the hard evidence consists of ballistics and a map of Lac de Lune?"

"So far."

"What about an alibi?"

Benton shook her head. "Mackenzie's a loner. According to his IBET superiors, he's lived alone for twenty years or more. We noticed it up here, too. Once he leaves this office, unless he stops to pick up supplies at the market or his mail at the post office, no one ever sees him. And he took three days off just before the assault on the mine. Vacation days he said he wanted to take before retirement. We've checked thoroughly. No one in Yellowknife saw him during that time."

Venus shrugged. "Maybe you've nailed him."

Benton's lips curved upward again. "We think so. We wouldn't have brought Inspector Halladay all the way from Ottawa unless we were very sure we had enough evidence to support our case." She leaned back in Mackenzie's chair and sighed. She rubbed her small eyes. "God, I'm tired," she said. "Haven't slept in days."

"It comes on when a case is finally wrapped," Venus offered.

Benton nodded, her eyes closed. Then she opened them, looked at Venus, and said, "I'm sorry for what you've been put through. Of course, you're free to go. One of our Mounties can drive you to the airport anytime you're ready."

"Thanks. I'd appreciate the lift."

"There's a flight out to Vancouver at five o'clock this evening. From Vancouver, you could probably catch a late-night flight to the States, be home by midnight. You live in Seattle, don't you?"

"Yes."

"I've been there a few times. Nice city. Real pretty."

"Yeah."

"I'm truly sorry for what happened. It stinks being accused of a crime you didn't commit." She laughed. "But even less fun being caught for one you did commit. Mackenzie can't be very happy right now back there in the holding cell."

"I'd like to see him before I leave."

Benton raised an eyebrow. "Really? Why would you want to do that? The guy almost ruined your life."

"That's why I want to see him one more time."

Benton led Venus down the long corridor and into the holding cell area. A Mountie manned a desk near the same cell Venus had occupied until a few hours ago. Benton told the Mountie to limit the visit to ten minutes. Then Benton shook her hand.

"Once again, I'm truly sorry for what happened to you," she offered.

"Thanks."

Benton patted Venus's shoulder. "If you ever need anything, or need to talk to someone about this, God knows why you would, but if you ever need to contact us, please know that I'm available for whatever it is you need. We made your life miserable and I'd like a chance to make it up to you."

"Thanks again. By the way, who will take over for Mackenzie?"

Benton shrugged. "They'll send a sergeant from some other IBET border post. Probably Vancouver." Her lips tightened into a brief grimace, then she added, "I just hope to hell it's a woman."

After she had gone, Venus walked over to the holding cell. Mackenzie sat on the edge of the cot, the same cot she had spent the previous night on. He looked up when she approached the cell.

"What do you want?" he asked grimly.

"I have something to say to you."

Mackenzie sighed, knowing what was coming. He had put her through hell and now she was going to ream his ass for it. He waved his hands. "Go ahead," he said. "Sock it to me."

She leaned in close to the bars and kept her voice low. "I might not like you much, but you're no killer." Mackenzie looked up, startled. She said, "Keep it down." Mackenzie nodded warily.

"I'm going to find out who killed Radke, and who took the Lac de Lune."

Mackenzie breathed a deep sigh. "You better stay out of this."

"Can't do that."

Mackenzie folded his arms and stared out the tiny cell window.

"A United States federal agent was murdered. My friend was murdered. That's why I can't just walk away."

He looked back at her. "So you're not doing this for me, but for Radke?"

"That's one way of looking at it."

Mackenzie nodded slowly. "Thanks," he said after a long pause. "I do really mean that, eh."

"Give me something to go on."

Mackenzie shook his head. "Wish I could."

"Try real hard."

Mackenzie closed his eyes. After a moment, he sighed, opened his eyes. "Goldman. Yitzhak Goldman."

"The King of Forty-seventh Street?"

Mackenzie nodded. "I've heard his name bandied about among the miners. I gather he's a powerful son of a bitch."

"What evidence links him?"

"No evidence. Just a hunch. An educated guess."

"Based on?"

Mackenzie shut his eyes again. "Just a deep, gnawing hunch."

She spoke the numbers of her cell phone. "Memorize

that," she said. "And call me whenever you think of something."

His eyes teared up.

"Where will they take you?"

He looked up at her. "No idea. They won't keep me here in Yellowknife, that's for sure."

"Why not?"

"Families of some of the murdered guards have vowed to lynch the killers. I'm in danger here. They'll want to save the lynching for after the trial. They're law officers, after all."

Venus nodded. "We'll be in touch."

CHAPTER FOURTEEN

Lay-A-Day Chicken Ranch

Fairview woke before dawn. Frost a quarter-inch thick coated the bedroom windows. The clock said 5:15 A.M., which meant that it was actually 5:00 A.M. Fairview kept all the clocks in the house fifteen minutes ahead, and his wife had learned to live in his imposed time zone. Even the wristwatch Fairview wore was set fifteen minutes ahead, assuring that he would never be late for anything. In recent weeks, punctuality had counted for everything, and Fairview had no intention of resetting the clocks to match the World Atomic Clock at Boulder, Colorado, even after the war was over and the nation-state was established. In fact, he might make it a law in the new Republic of Ravallah that all clocks be set fifteen minutes faster than the World Atomic Clock. Time was relative, an arbitrary system imposed by some legal authority to keep humankind marching to the whims of the people in power. All that would change in the new Republic of Ravallah. But the tube, the tube would remain open and operative.

Sarah, as usual, brought her husband coffee and the

morning paper as he showered and shaved. This ten-year routine had altered only slightly in recent weeks. Sarah was not allowed into the bathroom now when Fairview unstrapped the leather pouch from his body before getting into the shower. So she left the coffee mug and the newspaper outside the bathroom door, knocked twice, and went away. Fairview opened the door a crack, reached out, and retrieved the coffee mug but not the newspaper. This morning, he had no time to read the news and work the crossword. Any time now, the truck would arrive at the compound and its cargo would be unloaded and hidden where no one but Ravallah men would ever find it. And finally, after two weeks of carrying around this great stone, he would turn the diamond over to the man who had planned the whole thing, in exchange for the contents of the truck. He had already delivered the down payment. Volpe had paid off the little courier and taken possession of the smaller stones. This had been verified by a curt telephone call made from a pay phone somewhere, Fairview guessed, in New York City.

As he showered, Fairview kept the leather pouch with the Lac de Lune inside a waterproof container in the shower stall beside him. The stone had never been out of his sight. At night when he slept, Sarah had taken the watch, lying awake beside him, a gun at her side. She made a good wife, and a good mother too to Fairview's two young sons. Now she was pregnant. She claimed the one in her womb was a girl. After this was all over, he might get her pregnant again, have another son, his first son born into the new nation.

When he had shaved and dressed and eaten a bite of breakfast, Fairview walked across the farmyard to the huge red barn that he had built with his own hands. He could see smoke pouring from the chimney at the rear of the barn and so he knew that Sarah had already been out to the barn and awakened the prisoner and built her a fire in the wood-burning stove he had installed at Sarah's insistence. No reason for the prisoner to suffer more than necessary. As he approached the barn, Fairview was aware that he would actually miss the girl. He felt the gun at his side and remembered his duty to his people.

Karen Crandall started when she heard the barn door open. Sitting cross-legged upon her straw mattress, she had been meditating, but was not yet deep enough into a trance to ignore the nerve-shattering rumble of the barn door sliding open. She listened for the sound of footsteps. In two weeks as their prisoner, Crandall had learned to distinguish between Fairview's heavy footsteps and his wife's lighter steps. And always, Sarah would call out when she entered the barn, to let Crandall know who was coming. Crandall had grown used to Sarah's visits, three times a day, lasting only for a few minutes but long enough so she could benefit from the human contact. And Sarah was pleasant and kind, always trying to make Crandall as comfortable as possible under the circumstances. She had brought Crandall sheets and a heavy quilt, plenty of food, mostly dried fruits and nuts, and once a day a loaf of homemade bread and some hearty soup. A makeshift bathroom adjoined Crandall's cell, with a crude toilet and a shallow sink that ran cold water only. Sarah would often bring a bucket and boil some water on the stove that stood just outside of Crandall's reach near the cell. She would bathe in this warm water, luxuriating in the heat and the scent of Sarah's homemade soap. The last thing Sarah would do before she left Crandall in the barn, if she had requested it, was slip a fresh tape cassette to the prisoner, usually as she was talking about other things in case anyone was listening.

"We have to be self-sufficient," Sarah had once told Crandall as she slipped her a fresh tape cassette. "We don't want to depend on anyone but ourselves."

Other than these tidbits, the women had shared little conversation. Fairview had forbidden Sarah to become friendly with the prisoner. Still, an unspoken bond had developed between the two women and so whenever Crandall heard the barn door slide open, she hoped beyond hope that it was Sarah coming.

But it wasn't. Not this time. It was Fairview. She could hear his heavy footfall, the steady rhythm of his pace that reminded her of soldiers marching in movies she'd seen about World War II. And he was a soldier of some kind. He often wore a camouflage uniform and those high-topped black boots, and a scarlet beret. And he had a knife tucked into the belt that held his gun holster. And always there was the gun. Crandall had seen plenty of guns up north in the Territories and they had never particularly bothered her. Fairview's gun was different. Maybe it was the way he kept the palm of his hand resting on the gun's barrel, as if at any moment he might draw it out of its holster and use it on her. Now, as each time before when she heard his distinctive footsteps coming toward her cell, Crandall's heart stuck in her throat. She breathed deeply, trying to calm herself, to prepare for his presence, which always terrified her.

Before Fairview, Crandall had never feared a man. Not even Big Jim Hardy had intimidated her. But Fairview was different. She had seen him kill Ramie in cold blood, and then slice open Ramie's corpse and stuff it with contraband. And she had seen enough of him and heard enough of his political diatribes to know that he was utterly capable of killing her in cold blood.

Which, in fact, was exactly what Fairview was intending to do this morning. As he approached her cell, Fairview thought about how he would kill her. The easiest way would be to order her to face the rear wall of her cell and shoot her at close range, through the heart. No preliminaries, no weeping and wailing and begging for mercy. There was no time for that; the day held much to do. Go in, kill her, place her body in the box that sat ready beside the cell, then get to work. The shipment of armaments would arrive any minute.

Crandall stood up to face him as he approached her cell. She wore a pair of Sarah's jeans and one of Sarah's shirts, and

Fairview couldn't help marveling at how much better they looked on Crandall than they had ever looked on Sarah. Her hair, a tangled mass of copper curls, fell around her head and shoulders radiating the dim light inside the barn, forming a halo around her face. She was scowling expectantly, as if she knew his arrival portended bad news. Fairview had never killed a woman before. This would be a new experience, not pleasant, not in the least.

She spoke first, catching him off guard.

"You're going to kill me, aren't you?" she said matter-of-factly, in spite of the chilling fear she held in her heart.

That struck some nerve in Fairview. He didn't know what to say, so he shrugged and unlocked the cell door, preparing to enter. The girl backed away from him, watching his every move.

"I don't want to die," Crandall said, again matter-of-factly.

Fairview, inside now, relocked the cell door and faced her. She didn't tremble or show any other outward signs of fear, but still, he knew that she was terrified of dying. Who wouldn't be, to die like this? Fairview reached up and scratched the nape of his neck, thinking what to do next.

"I'll make a deal with you," she said suddenly.

"What kind of deal?" He wasn't really interested in what she had to offer, but he was also avoiding the unpleasant task before him.

"I know something about the Lac de Lune that no one else knows. If you let me go, I'll tell you what I know."

Fairview scratched his neck harder. Was she bluffing? Sure sounded like it. He said, "Like what?"

"I'll tell you once you let me out of here. Take me off this ranch, and then I'll tell you, and then you can let me go. You won't regret it, I promise you."

Fairview shook his head slowly. "I know all I need to know."

Crandall said, "It's important that you know. It might save your life. Diamond brokers can be very dangerous."

Fairview made a sound deep in his throat, a sarcastic rattle. He said, "It's not my life you should worry about."

Crandall felt the sweat pouring from her armpits, trickling down her body. She felt her heart in her throat, and she felt faint. "I need to sit down," she said.

Fairview gestured toward the cot. Crandall sat down, her hands gripping the edge of the cot. She breathed deeply a few times, trying to relax enough to think clearly, to buy some more time.

In the distance, a rumbling noise sounded, growing louder. Fairview listened. The truck carrying the shipment. He considered. Should he go out and meet the truck, or should he take care of the girl first? Probably better get the nasty part over with before he got down to business with the gunrunners.

"Stand up," he told Crandall.

"I'm a little weak," she pleaded.

"I said, stand up."

Crandall stood up, her knees trembling.

"Now turn around."

"Please, please, don't do this. Please don't kill me. I don't want to die. I'll do anything you say, just please don't."

"Shut up and turn around."

Crandall turned around, felt tears stream from her eyes, a cold chill run down her spine.

Fairview reached for his gun, drew it, and aimed at Crandall's back. He'd had enough target practice to locate the heart. He clicked the safety off the gun and placed his finger on the trigger.

The sound of gunfire caused Crandall to flinch. But she didn't fall. She heard a dull thud. She turned slowly and saw Fairview slumped on the floor of the barn, blood spurting from a wound in his head. Crandall looked up and saw the gun that had shot Fairview and then she saw the man who held the gun.

"Well, well," the man said cheerfully. "What have we here?"

Overwhelmed with relief, tears pooling in her eyes, Crandall said, "Oh, God, thank you for saving my life. I don't know who you are, but thank you, thank you."

Crandall became animated now, exhilarated. She leaned down and snatched the cell keys off Fairview's belt. She came forward to unlock the cell door. As she did so, the man stepped inside the cell. Crandall thrust out her hand but the man didn't shake it. His right hand still held the gun.

"I'm a geologist," Crandall said, a stream of talk pouring from her. "For Zone Mine. When they robbed the mine, they took me hostage. But you must have known that, to come and save me. You must be the police, right? Or the FBI? I'll bet you're FBI, eh?" Crandall felt like throwing her arms around him in gratitude.

The man stooped down over Fairview's corpse. He searched Fairview's body until he found the leather pouch hidden in the corpse's groin. He told Crandall to remove the dead man's trousers and when she had done so, he snatched the pouch off the corpse.

"That's what he took," said Crandall, "but, you see . . ."

The man felt the shape and heft of the leather pouch. Sure enough felt like a big stone. He said, "The Lac de Lune."

"Yes, but—" Crandall straightened up and faced her savior.

The man shoved the leather pouch down the front of his shirt.

"—this man, Fairview, was so stupid anyway, because the Lac de Lune he stole isn't the real stone. It's a fake. They did all that killing for a fake stone."

"Is that right?" The man who had saved Crandall's life lowered his eyelids slightly. "And how do you know that, young lady?"

She waved her hands excitedly. She was standing less than six feet away from the man who had saved her life. "See, Big Jim knew someone would come after the diamond, sooner or later. So we took precautions."

The man drew air circles with his gun. "So what happened to the real one? The real Lac de Lune?"

"By now the real stone is en route to Venus."

"Venus?" The man frowned.

"Yes, yes, Venus. He sent it to Venus. That's all I know, all he would tell me. I'm thinking it's a woman he knows, by that name. You know? Venus, like the goddess? But he never mentioned her before and never put a last name to it. Just Venus."

She heard herself babbling but her enthusiasm for life had overcome her and she felt exhilarated and didn't care that she could not stop talking. "God, I'm so relieved this is all over. I can't tell you how grateful I am to you. I'm so glad this is finally over."

"How nice for you," said Delbert Dixon, then he shot Crandall through the brain.

PART TWO

CHAPTER FIFTEEN

Antwerp, Belgium

On a cold winter's dawn, diamond cleaver extraordinaire Jean Claud Rubicon rose from his narrow bed in the narrow room where he always slept with a gun under his pillow, his clients' merchandise hidden beneath his mattress. The first sign that the day would not go smoothly was when Rubicon tripped over a box of Canada rough, stubbing his big toe and nearly pitching straight forward out the narrow window that he kept open at all times in spite of winter's chill and the threat of robbers. Rubicon feared no man entering his quarters because below his shop, always on guard, were his two trained-to-kill Dobermans, Kors and Krum. No thief stood a chance against Kors and Krum. Plus, Rubicon was a light sleeper, had to be. His was a dangerous profession. Even if an intruder happened to slip past Kors and Krum, Rubicon could defend himself and his clients' merchandise. He kept the gun loaded and handy at all times.

At seventy-six, Jean Claud Rubicon had been cleaving and

cutting and polishing rare diamonds for sixty years, having learned the profession at his master's knee and carried on a proud Belgian tradition with talent unmatched in all of Antwerp, perhaps in all the world. Thousands of diamonds had passed through Rubicon's unassuming little shop on Treble Lane, and they came and went quietly, the negotiations conducted in hushed voices, the rough stones treated as carefully as if each were as precious as the Hope Diamond. If the truth were known, and it was among a small coterie of the trade, some of the stones that passed through Rubicon's little Antwerp shop belonged to very famous personages. And too, though this fact was never mentioned above a whisper, certain diamond brokers entrusted their illicitly procured booty to Rubicon's hands, for he was a great stonecutter and a discreet man. Diamonds had been brought to him with flaws the size of golf balls, with knots and little gas-filled bubbles so hot that no cutter in his right mind would dare to touch the stone, and yet Rubicon had managed to cleave each stone so expertly that the fewest possible carats of weight were lost in the process. There had been accidents; all diamond cutters experience the mental anguish that arises from cleaving a stone only to have it shatter on a gletz into tiny bits, instantly plummeting in value from millions of dollars to as little as a few thousand. Rubicon had suffered his share of losses during his apprenticeship, but never—ever—since becoming a master.

Jean Claud Rubicon was one of three diamond cleavers in the world qualified to cleave the rough octahedron-shaped Lac de Lune diamond with a minimal loss of carat weight, for, reportedly, the stone contained a thin gletz, or crack, at the end of which was a tiny bubble. One mishap with the cleaver could cause the Grade D fancy diamond to shatter into bits and pieces. His competitors were few, the great masters having died off, leaving Rubicon with the unofficial title of senior master cleaver. And yet, one or two of his competitors, Rubicon had to admit, possessed great talent and the necessary training, not to mention the nerve, to tackle even

the most difficult stones. Still Rubicon held the record for saving the most carats from rough, D Grade stones, and this
made him famous among the world's diamond brokers.

Now, at the height of his powers, Rubicon was preparing
himself for the most important moment of his career. If he
understood the message correctly (how could it possibly be
misinterpreted?), the famous American diamond prospector
Mr. Jim Hardy had handpicked the world's three most talented cleavers to compete for the privilege of cleaving, cutting, and polishing the magnificent Lac de Lune diamond.
Why else would Mr. Hardy have sent him seven simulated
models of the stone to practice on? And although the news of
Mr. Hardy's unfortunate demise and the theft of the Lac de
Lune had reached his ears, Rubicon nonetheless believed that
the competition was still on, and that the stone would eventu-
ally find its way to his shop on Treble Lane in the heart of
Antwerp. Rubicon had several times read the letter Mr.
Hardy had included in the shipment of simulated models:

Dear Mr. Rubicon,
   My name is Jim Hardy. I am the American prospector
who discovered the Lac de Lune diamond up here in
Canada. Enclosed please find seven exact models of the
octahedron-shaped stone in its rough state. You may or
may not be aware that this fabulous blue-green fancy has
been graded D for its purity and intensity of color, and
yet, as you will observe when you study the stone's interior through the small window my geologist made in the
rough, the diamond contains a problematic gletz and a
small bubble. Only an expert like yourself could cleave
this magnificent stone without causing it to shatter and
without losing its best weight value. I have researched
carefully, and have determined that you are one of the
three best diamond cutters in the world.
   My challenge to you, and to your two biggest rivals in
the cleaving trade, is to cleave a model of the Lac de

Lune, taking the problematic inclusion into account and saving the highest possible carat weight. Of course, your two competitors have also received seven simulated models each. Whichever of you succeeds in saving the most carat weight in the models shall be given the privilege of cleaving the real Lac de Lune.

The enclosed models are numbered from 1 to 7, identified by numbers carved into the cement stands to which each stone is attached for your convenience. You will note that the hardness of the models increases with the numbers carved into the cement stands, and you must follow the numerical sequence absolutely, beginning with model number 7 and working up to number 1. Should I learn that you or either of your competitors attempts to cleave the models out of numerical sequence, the culpable party will be eliminated from the competition. Should you decide to accept the challenge, and should you prevail against your competitors, my emissary will deliver the genuine Lac de Lune to you. In fact, soon after I send this letter, the stone will begin its journey to New York, Johannesburg, London, or Antwerp, where it will be kept in a secret location awaiting the outcome of the competition. But, of course, this information is to remain absolutely confidential, and you are under no circumstances to communicate with either of your competitors. For your information, your competitors are Dieter Haakvig in Johannesburg and David Goldman in New York City.

If you decide to decline this challenge, please return the models to me. (I have included a bank draft to cover return shipping expenses.)

I sincerely hope that you will accept this challenge, and I can promise you that if you are selected to cleave the real Lac de Lune, your compensation will amount to a minimum of one million U.S. dollars, considerably more if you manage to retain over eighty percent of the carat weight in one piece.

With respect and admiration for your enormous talent, I remain,

> Sincerely yours,
> James Hardy
> Prospector

Of course, Rubicon had immediately replied in the affirmative. And now, despite news reports of Mr. Hardy's murder and the alleged theft of the Lac de Lune, Rubicon firmly believed he would soon hold that most fabulous diamond in his talented hands. The cloak-and-dagger intrigue infusing the diamond trade honestly bored Rubicon, and he had no desire to speculate or second-guess the location of the real stone or the identity of the person who possessed it. As for his competitors, Dieter Haakvig in Johannesburg wasn't nearly as good as Rubicon at mentally carving the gem from the rough stone, and that young prig David Goldman in New York—Rubicon could only laugh at the absurdity of comparing Goldman to himself. He wasn't worried in the least.

The second omen of a bad day going worse was when Rubicon cut himself shaving. The deep nick bled profusely across the tip of his dimpled chin. Gauze did little to stop the flow of blood and, in the end, Rubicon had to call in the village handkerchief tatter, Francine, who stitched it up with her finest needle, promising nothing worse than a hairline scar.

Rubicon had his usual meager breakfast of a single sausage, a heel of bread, and two cups of thick coffee, and then he set to work. Today, he would cleave the first of the numbered seven simulated models of the Lac de Lune. The late Mr. Hardy had sent, along with the models, a computer-generated three-dimensional photograph of the Lac de Lune, and so he knew not only its shape and size, but where the flaw was located, and how it was situated at the stone's very heart. Now the seven simulated models of the rough stone, mounted with jeweler's cement onto separate pedestals, stood side by side, numbered from one to seven, awaiting Rubicon's expert ministrations. This morning, he would practice cleaving model number seven and he would continue, working on at least one model each day, until he was certain of the correct method to employ on the Lac de Lune.

As he paced around number seven, studying its shape and contours, Rubicon occasionally glanced up at the clock. He was expecting Simon Mehta, a diamond courier for Yitzhak Goldman of New York, for whom Rubicon had just cleaved, cut, and polished a fifty-seven-carat marquise out of a seventy-six-carat rough stone of the clearest, richest pink Rubicon had ever seen. Goldman had told Rubicon the stone came out of a Brazilian alluvial mine, plucked by a *garimpeiro* working for the English diamond firm of Gordon and Goldman. But Gordon and Goldman didn't own a mine in Brazil, Rubicon was sure of that, so they must have bought the diamond from someone else. Or stolen it. The vivid pink marquise beauty was ready and waiting for Simon Mehta, the courier, who should arrive before noon, and so while he waited, Rubicon decided to tackle the first simulated model of the Lac de Lune.

Rubicon felt the familiar tension that preceded a trip to his workbench. Only now it rose in his chest, his breath grew short, and his heart thumped as never before. His lust for the Lac de Lune had nothing to do with money, or power, or greed. It had everything to do with an aging great artist's last chance at glory. Now to work.

A man with such responsibility resting upon his shoulders is inevitably a sensitive soul, a bit temperamental, one might say, given to snits. And so when Rubicon raised his hammer and chisel above model number seven and brought hammer to simulated stone, and the model shattered into tiny bits of dust, the diamond cutter flew into a rage, tearing out some of his hair and even going so far as to smash his television set, a noise that set Kors and Krum to howling. All up and down Treble Lane, shopkeepers and customers heard the diamond cutter's ravings and shivered a little, for Jean Claud Rubicon's fits of pique inevitably preceded the arrival of sinister forces into the normally peaceful neighborhood.

The third bad omen of the day—and it was only ten A.M.

Rubicon pulled himself together, calming his nerves and remembering to breathe slow, deep breaths as his late wife had
always told him whenever he flew into a rage. This helped,
and Rubicon calmed himself enough to take a crack at the
next simulated model. He was studying the model intently,
had just about formed a vision of what the finished stone
should look like and picked up his cleaving tools, when suddenly Kors and Krum started howling again. Rubicon laid
down his tools, stood up wearily, and, cursing aloud, strode
to the open window.

Down below, Simon Mehta stood on the sidewalk across Treble Lane, putting a safe distance between himself and Rubicon's chained Dobermans. Mehta's face contorted into "The
Scream." Rubicon shouted at the dogs and they ceased howling and sat down on their haunches, tongues wagging, their
warm breath steaming into the cold winter air. Mehta called
from across the lane.

"Is it safe now?"

Rubicon motioned for Mehta to come across and then
went down a narrow flight of stairs to let him in. Once in Rubicon's studio, Mehta remarked over the many simulated
models, which, of course, he immediately recognized as repli-
cas of the Lac de Lune.

"So you are one of the chosen three, eh?"

Rubicon snorted. "And why not me?"

Mehta smiled. "Ah, but I am sincere, Jean Claud. You're
the best man. Everyone knows you're the best."

Rubicon murmured a humble response.

Then Mehta's eyes went wide and he spoke in almost a
whisper. "I've heard rumors going around New York that
Gordon Volpe has by some mysterious means acquired the
stone. But of course, rumors only, and only among the trade.
And too, Volpe's reputation is faultless. I can't imagine him in-
dulging in shenanigans, especially when it comes to murder."

Rubicon looked up at Mehta. "Just because Volpe is one

of my clients, you come to me with this gossip? I don't want any trouble. It always makes my arthritis worse."

Mehta waved his hand dismissively. "Not to worry, old man. No one talks to the police. What we know, we know, but it goes no farther than the traders. I'll tell you one thing though, Volpe shouldn't be bragging about getting hold of the stone, even to his wife. You know how word gets around within the trade. You know how many diamantaires would give their big toes for that stone." Mehta shook his head. "No, Volpe should never have told a soul. That could get him killed, and he knows better."

"So that's how word got out? Volpe actually talked about the stone?"

Mehta shrugged. "It's what I've heard, okay? But maybe he didn't actually brag about it. Maybe the wife didn't talk. Maybe somebody was spying on Volpe and figured it out and then, maybe somehow, the leak. To be frank, I'm not exactly sure how the story got out. But you should be careful if you suddenly receive the stone here in your studio. Those two beasts downstairs will never be able to defend you."

Rubicon nodded thoughtfully.

"Well, then," said Mehta, "let's have a look at the pink marquise. Mr. Goldman's client is most anxious to hold it in her hands."

Rubicon got down on his knees, reached under his bed, brought out a cardboard sight box the size and shape of a shoebox, dusted off the top, and opened it. He reached in and brought out a wad of tissue about the size of a small lemon and handed it up to Mehta before slowly rising to his feet. His knees weren't what they used to be.

Mehta carefully unwrapped the tissue, and when he plucked the pink marquise from the center, he held it up against the window light and caught his breath. "Even more vivid pink than before. Rubicon, you're a genius. Now here's a pink lady worthy of a princess."

Rubicon raised his eyebrows. "Ah, so Yitzhak Goldman's client is a royal figure?"

Mehta snickered. "She believes so anyhow. She's really a self-made American billionaire from Oklahoma, you know the kind. Married three times to rich husbands, who all died of heart attacks. They say she's a passionate lover. Now she is engaged to another sucker, and she wants her fiancé to present her with the pink marquise for her birthday gift. She bought it for him to give to her. The fiancé calls the lady his princess. She plans to debut it at a big charity rodeo." Simon Mehta shrugged. "Perhaps in a ring, or maybe a pendant, I don't know how she has finally decided to have the stone mounted. She's flamboyant, though, and Mr. Goldman tells me the stone perfectly matches the gown she plans on wearing. Have you ever attended a rodeo?"

Rubicon immediately lost interest in the tale, disgusted to learn where the fabulous pink marquise would end up. How many times had his brilliant creations ended up in the hands of people who appreciated money and power more than beauty, whose vanity lay at the bottom of their desire for priceless stones? Too many to count.

Rubicon flung out his arm. "I don't care about any of it, I tell you, Simon Mehta, I can't be bothered with frivolous speculations."

Simon Mehta wrapped the stone back up and slipped it into a special pocket sewn inside his overcoat. He took out his wallet and counted out the amount of U.S. dollars his boss owed Rubicon for the work. On this wad alone, Rubicon could comfortably retire, though no artist ever really retires from his work. Rubicon brought out a bottle of Zambuca, six coffee beans, and two glasses. He poured the liqueur into the glasses, placed three beans into each, and handed one to Mehta. They clinked their glasses and drank.

"Once again, my friend, you have done wondrous work," said Mehta, licking the sweet liqueur off his lips. "The pink marquise is astoundingly beautiful."

Rubicon bowed slightly, acknowledging the praise, and said, "If you think that's good work, just wait until you see what I do to the Lac de Lune."

Mehta looked sideways at Rubicon. "Let me offer you some advice, old man, just between you and me. You know how dangerous it is to discuss certain projects. You shouldn't even have discussed the stone with me. In fact, you should have hidden these simulated models so I would have no idea, other than guesswork, that you are one of the chosen three competing for the honor of cleaving this stone. No, no, my friend. As they say, 'Loose lips sink ships,' and in this business, you never know who will stab you in the back at the first opportunity."

"Poof. I'm not afraid of anyone."

Mehta smiled indulgently. "Has it occurred to you, Jean Claud Rubicon, that one of your competitors in the contest for the Lac de Lune is a certain David Goldman?"

"Of course I know who are my competitors. And the other one is that insufferable Boer Dieter Haakvig."

"But think, my friend, think. Do you have any idea who is David Goldman's uncle?"

Rubicon thought this over and then a small twinkle dropped into his eye. "Ah, of course. Yitzhak Goldman. To whom you are delivering the pink stone. Am I right?"

Mehta nodded somewhat gravely. "Keep that in mind, just between you and me, my friend, keep that in mind."

Mehta wasted no more time with small talk, and as Rubicon shut the door behind him and climbed back up the stairs to his studio, he thought finally something good had come of this day. The cash from the pink marquise would secure a comfortable future, and now Rubicon could put his full concentration into the Lac de Lune. At last, the day had taken a turn for the better. Rubicon turned his entire attention to the simulated models.

Simon Mehta walked down Treble Lane, past the handkerchief tatter's shop all the way to the corner, then three blocks farther to the train station. As he walked along the narrow cobblestone streets, he noticed a small, dark-skinned man leaning against a lamppost. The man wore a broad-brimmed hat and an expensive overcoat, much softer and made of better fabric than Mehta's old coat. Simon Mehta decided there and then to purchase a new overcoat first thing when he got home.

At the train station, Mehta purchased a ticket to the airport. Once inside his train compartment, Mehta took out his cell phone and placed a call to Yitzhak Goldman.

"So all is well?" inquired Goldman over a strong clear satellite connection.

"Indeed, sir, you may be assured that the transaction went off as planned."

"And what about the other stone? My nephew is going crazy guessing at how his competitors are faring with their models. I've told him a hundred times now that the stone was stolen right off the dying man's body and has disappeared. Still, David holds out hope."

Simon Mehta couldn't help smirking. "Well, sir, you can tell your nephew that Rubicon has no interest at all in his competitors, and furthermore, he is certain that he'll win."

"But still no sign of the stone?"

"Only the simulated models just like your nephew received."

When he had finished the conversation, Mehta put his cell phone away, leaned back against the comfortable seat cushions, and waited for the train to pull out of the station. Out of habit, he patted the secret pocket in his overcoat, and feeling the little bulge, he smiled.

Soon after the train pulled away from the station, Mehta noticed the dark-skinned man in the lovely overcoat seated in the opposite compartment. After a moment or two, they made eye contact and Simon Mehta nodded genially. The other man stood up and came across the aisle. From his pocket, he removed a silver flask. He unscrewed the top and seemed to take a hefty swig, and then tipping his hat, he said, "You're American, yes?"

Mehta looked up. "Why, yes, indeed I am. And you, sir?"

"Me, too," answered the little man. Holding out his flask, he said, "Shall we drink to it?"

Mehta thought he could use the warmth of a stiff belt. Accepting the flask from the stranger, he placed it to his lips, tilted it, and swallowed. Smooth scotch warmed him inside out. Mehta handed the flask back to the little man, who tucked the flask back in his pocket.

Mehta held out a hand. "Simon Mehta, New York City. And you, sir?"

"Carlos Fontana, originally from Brazil, but now I am an American citizen, and of all coincidences, I too live in New York City."

"Come inside here and join me, Mr. Fontana. There's plenty of room in this compartment for both of us."

CHAPTER SIXTEEN

Dixon watched Crandall slump to the floor of the barn. Searching her body, he found nothing of consequence. When he turned over the mattress on her cot, he found the tape recorder and the microcassettes. The tape recorder was running on record. Dixon shut it off and shoved it into his jacket pocket, along with the dozen or so cassettes.

You never know when a girl will tell a lie. You never know when you might need a fake diamond.

Dixon and Crumley drove the truck to the edge of a field and hid the arms in the place the guards at the ranch's gate had indicated. Dixon had never seen a hiding place quite like this one. From the main house on the ranch, a woman holding a small child in her arms stared out the window, watching them unload. She never came outside, just watched them from the window and held on to the child. He guessed that the woman and the child had heard his gun fire twice. But there wasn't time to kill them. Dixon needed to get out of there with the stone, real or fake, before Fairview's men realized that their leader had been killed.

"You didn't have to kill them," complained Crumley as he drove along the dusty yellow road. "He was going to give us the diamond anyway, in payment."

Dixon shook his head. "You just don't get it, do you, Crumley?"

Crumley shrugged.

Dixon held out an open palm. "It's like this. Fairview might have been scamming us. Maybe he never intended to turn over the diamond to Volpe. Maybe he just wanted the weapons and planned to off Volpe's emissaries." He turned to Crumley. "That would be us."

With a gesture, Crumley allowed as how that might be possible.

"And so when I saw Fairview pull his gun on the girl, I knew we couldn't trust the bastard. If he was gonna kill her, he'd just as soon dick us off, too. You can't trust any of 'em. Not Fairview. Not Volpe. You can't trust anybody, Crum, but yourself."

As they exited the ranch, Crumley at the wheel of the semi, Dixon in the passenger seat, they passed the two security guards at the ranch's gate. The gate was made of wooden timbers, twenty feet high, with a crosspiece wooden sign reading Lay-A-Day Ranch. Several No Trespassing signs were displayed around the entrance, and the entire ranch was surrounded by a cyclone fence with razor wire along the top. A thick grove of trees stood at one side of the entrance, the only foliage visible for acres. Dixon smiled at the guards and waved. The guards apparently hadn't heard the gunshots from the barn and just assumed the men in the semi had unloaded their wares and were taking off. One of the guards actually saluted at Dixon, who saluted back. Down the highway, half a mile away, Dixon looked out the window of the semi's cab and noticed a vehicle driving toward the ranch's entrance, a four-wheel-drive truck. When it came parallel to the semi, Dixon read the words painted on the truck's side:

"Department of the Interior, US Fish & Wildlife Service." A small blond female was driving the truck and she was alone. She turned to look at them and caught Dixon's eye, then looked back at the road and drove on.

"Pull over," said Dixon, and Crumley did. "Turn around," he told Crumley. "Drive back to that curve in the road and wait. Keep the engine running."

Crumley complied with Dixon's order. When they reached the bend in the road, still out of sight of the ranch entrance, Crumley pulled over to the road's shoulder and stopped, engine idling. Dixon stepped down out of the cab, walked toward the ranch, keeping behind the dried thorn bushes and occasional scrub pine, and slipped into the small grove of trees near the entrance. The vehicle with the blond girl driving had stopped at the entrance to the ranch. Both guards had moved up to the driver's-side window and one of them was questioning the woman. The other guard began a slow inspection of the truck, walking around it, his gun drawn. Dixon moved in close enough to hear the conversation.

"Help you, lady?" the first guard asked the woman.

"I'm a federal agent attached to the National Security Council." She showed her credentials.

One of the guards studied her badge.

"Hell, this looks like it was issued this morning." He palmed it off to his partner.

The second guard read the lettering on the badge. "National Security Council. What the hell is that?"

"The government council that oversees investigations into subversive activities."

The guards exchanged a fleeting glance, then the second guard said, "You call chicken ranching subversive, lady?"

The other guard had circled the truck and apparently had found nothing of interest. He leaned against one of the gate timbers and watched his colleague question the woman.

"I'm looking for Ron Fairview."

"What do you want with Fairview?"

"I talk to Fairview and nobody else. You try to stop me

and I'll have a warrant served on you for refusal to cooperate with a government agent. I suggest you call up Fairview and tell him that Agent Venus Diamond is here to see him. He'll remember my name."

Venus? Dixon started at the word. Venus, like the planet. Or the goddess. Diamond? What the hell was going on here?

The first guard said, "Give me a little more. What should I tell Fairview this is about?"

"Tell him it's about the Lac de Lune."

When the guards exchanged glances, Venus hit the gas and crashed through the gate, speeding along the ranch road toward the main compound in the distance. Recovering from their surprise, the guards aimed their weapons to fire at the truck, but Dixon fired first, hitting the bull's eye both times. The guards were already dead when Dixon walked over to where they lay and plugged each one again, just to be sure.

Dixon returned to the semi and said to Crumley, "It's our lucky day."

"Oh, yeah? How so?"

"The girl in the barn said that Big Jim Hardy sent the diamond to Venus. I couldn't figure out what she meant, the planet or what. But now here comes the real Venus. That girl in the truck, that's her name. And she talked about the Lac de Lune."

Crumley wrinkled his forehead. He still didn't get it.

Dixon said, "We'll stay here awhile, wait until she comes out. We'll follow her. We'll keep following her until she leads us to the diamond."

Crumley nodded; now he got it. He reached down, turned off the semi's ignition, and prepared for a long wait.

Venus pulled the truck into a parking spot beside a neatly painted white two-story clapboard farmhouse. Shutting off the ignition, she saw the face of a woman appear at the window. Venus got out of the truck and approached the front porch.

The woman opened the door even before Venus knocked. She was pale, a crop of freckles sprinkled across her nose, and she was thin, except for her swollen belly. Black hair spilled across her shoulders and down her back and the breeze tossed it around in long flyaway strands. She held an infant in her arms, its body resting against her right hip. A second child, a small boy, barely walking, grasped the hem of her skirt, tugging impatiently.

"My name's Venus Diamond. Are you Mrs. Fairview?"

The woman nodded. "I'm Sarah Fairview, yes."

"I'm looking for your husband, Mrs. Fairview."

She shook her head. "He went out. I haven't seen him for several hours. I don't know where he is, but"—she nodded her head to one side—"over there's his car, so I guess he's somewhere on the ranch."

Venus looked around. Several small outbuildings and a run-down chicken coop surrounded the main yard. In the distance stood a red barn, behind the barn, a field of high dry grass that reached back to the horizon where several other buildings, dwellings, perhaps, loomed in silhouette.

"I think he went to the barn." Mrs. Fairview looked almost pleadingly at Venus. "Should I take you there?"

Venus looked at the infant. "Thanks, but I can manage by myself. I'll come back to speak with you before I leave."

"Is . . . is something the matter? Did something happen?"

"I don't know, Mrs. Fairview. I think you should stay in the house, though, for the time being."

"I have two sons. Very young boys." She was trembling now. She turned and went inside the house, shutting the door softly.

Venus walked toward the barn. She shouldn't have come by herself, but when she'd arrived at the county sheriff's headquarters, no one was available right away, and she didn't want to wait. Patience wasn't in her vocabulary. Her lack of patience often interfered with her work, resulting in numerous reprimands. She operated on instinct, moving faster than the enemy. That was her style. This resulted too often in an arrest without sufficient evidence to indict. Still, based on Radke's mention of the ranch, she felt certain he was implicating Ron Fairview as a player in the plot to steal the Lac de Lune. She had convinced a federal judge that Fairview needed to be taken into custody and questioned about the Zone murders and she had the warrant.

A cold dry wind swept across the naked ground, stirring up dust the shade of mustard. Several dozen chickens, too thin for killing, wandered across the yellow ground, pecking listlessly, as if they knew, either way, theirs was a lost cause.

The barn door was rolled back in the open position. Venus stepped inside and immediately felt the familiar tingle of danger travel along her spine. She called out, "Fairview. Ron Fairview, are you in here?"

Silence. Only the sound of the wind blowing through the barn's rafters. She removed her gun from its waist pack, and held it barrel up as she crossed the hay-covered barn floor. From a single skylight, dim, cloud-filtered sunbeams illuminated the barn just enough to see fifteen or twenty feet in front of her. The horse stalls were empty and clean. Along one side of the barn were stacks of empty wooden crates, each stamped with the word "Supplies." She counted the rows and stacks and multiplied. There must have been two hundred crates of "Supplies." Some of the crates were marked with a red star symbol. Others bore the Red Cross symbol stamped on the wood sides.

Beyond the stacks of crates, she saw some iron bars that seemed to form a cage. She walked around the crates and toward the cage slowly, thinking an animal might be kept in it, possibly something dangerous she wouldn't want roused to anger. She called out Fairview's name again. Again, no response. She felt her breath going shallow and once again wished she'd brought someone else along. Her impatience inevitably got her into trouble. But here she was and the urge to turn and run out of the barn overcame her momentarily, and then she remembered Radke, and she went forward toward the cage. In the dim light, she saw that the door to the cage was open, and it seemed unoccupied. She stepped inside, nearly tripping over Crandall's dead body.

Standing on the porch of Sarah and Ron Fairview's house, Venus forced herself to wait until her colleagues arrived before starting to search the house and the ranch. The two guards from the ranch's entrance gate had disappeared. Sarah brought out two straight chairs, inviting Venus to sit. The two women sat down and Venus broke the horrible news. Sarah's wide green eyes flooded with tears.

"He was a good husband," Sarah almost whispered. Her hands rested rigidly in her lap, the fingers clasped tight. "And a good father, too."

Venus wasn't sure what she could say to comfort Sarah without lying. She was overjoyed to see Fairview dead. He'd been a dangerous criminal who had used his charismatic charms to recruit believers into his white-supremacist community. The world was a better place now that Fairview was dead.

The scene inside the barn, the way their bodies lay near each other, side by side, the manner of their execution, suggested the same intruder had shot both Fairview and Crandall. Fairview's body had obviously been searched. A gun with a silencer lay beside his corpse. Loaded, unfired. It was harder to tell with Crandall. Her shirt was buttoned up to her neck, but wasn't tucked into her jeans. The killer might have taken something away. Had Fairview, as Radke had implied, however vaguely, stolen the Lac de Lune?

Sarah dropped her gaze. Her eyes spoke too much of her agony. She had seemed stoic at first, but now Venus noticed her weakening resolve, as if she'd like to be left alone to cry.

"I'm sorry about all this, Mrs. Fairview."

The woman nodded.

"We'll have to search the ranch. It's going to be a zoo around here for the next day or so. Then we'll try to leave you alone. I know this has to be difficult for you."

Sarah nodded. "Unbearable."

"I'm really sorry."

Sarah leaped to her feet and fled into the house. Hearing her sobs, Venus decided to wait on the porch until Sarah recovered her composure, but when sounds of shattering glass emanated from inside, she moved fast into the house, following the sounds to the master bedroom.

Sarah crouched on the carpet surrounded by shards of two pottery bedside lamps and several framed photographs. Glass from a shattered frame lay beneath one of Sarah's hands, and already blood poured from a wound. Venus found a towel in the bathroom, wrapped Sarah's hand, holding pressure against the wound until the bleeding stopped. Sitting back on her heels now, Sarah suddenly grasped her swollen belly and gasped.

"What?"

Sarah looked up at Venus. "She moved. For the first time, she moved."

CHAPTER SEVENTEEN

When Sarah had recovered a little, they went back to the porch. Her wounded hand, cuts bandaged, rested in her lap. She had washed the tears from her face, checked the napping boys, had even brushed her hair, pulling it back and securing it with a comb clip. She had calmed somewhat, Venus noted, and might have enough self-control to talk about what had happened. Venus waited for Sarah to speak first, for Sarah to set the pace, but when she finally spoke, her question came out of nowhere.

"Did you find the tape recorder?"

"What tape recorder, Sarah?"

Sarah bent her head and studied her hands. "I—I felt sorry for the girl. I knew the men, that is, my husband in particular, because he makes all the important decisions, I knew that they would kill her. Ron was on his way to take care of that when he left the house this morning. I knew because he loaded a particular gun and put a silencer on it, he always used it for assassinations. This wasn't the first time, but you probably knew that. I'd never have told you this while he was still alive. But it was wrong what he did. Evil. Unholy."

"Do you follow a particular religion, Sarah?"

Sarah raised her head. "Ron was my religion. Except for all this."

"Tell me about the tape recorder."

Sarah leaned forward over her lap, as if bending her body over her swollen belly, over the child in her womb, could ease the heartache.

"I gave it to her. To the girl. Her name was Karen. Karen Crandall. I felt so sorry for her, and it was all I could think to do, hoping, maybe, I don't really know why, but maybe hoping that it would help her to pass the time."

Sarah looked up. Venus was already halfway across the yard, heading back toward the field and the barn.

The light inside the barn had brightened slightly as the cold sun had risen in the winter sky. The scent of danger prevailed but no longer lay as heavily on the air as when she had first entered the barn and discovered the bodies. She moved quickly past the horse stalls, past the crates of supplies, breaking into a run when she saw the bars of the cage that had been Karen Crandall's last home.

Crandall had fallen backward from the force of the bullet, a straight-on between-the-eyes hit. Her body lay curved as if she had tried to roll over into a fetal position, but she hadn't lived that long. Her copper-gold hair lay spread out beneath her head, glinting like an icon's halo. As Venus had recalled, her shirt was buttoned up tight and untucked over a pair of faded jeans. Venus crouched and began pat-searching the body, but before long she suspected that someone else must have beaten her to it. The killer? One of Fairview's men come over from an adjacent property? Someone had the tape recorder. Unless . . .

She searched Fairview's body with less enthusiasm. Whoever had shot Fairview had already mined his body. Without disturbing the scene, she searched the cage, feeling underneath the thin mattress, checking the corners, feeling underneath the layer of hay that covered the hard dirt floor. Nothing.

Carefully, she unlaced and removed Crandall's sneakers. Crandall's feet were cold underneath her socks. Nothing. She replaced the shoes and tried the same with Fairview's body. No signs of the tape recorder. So the killer had been thorough. Too thorough for an amateur.

Sarah had disappeared from the front porch. Venus walked up the steps, crossed the porch, and knocked on the door. From inside, she heard a child's agitated voice, and an infant's wailing. The children had intuitively understood their mother's grief.

When Sarah opened the door, she was holding the infant, and the toddler stood unsteadily beside his mother, grasping her skirt. The children had been asleep when Venus left for the barn half an hour earlier, and maybe Sarah had appreciated the little time to herself. Now they were awake and demanding all their mother's attention.

Sarah said, "I gave her the tape recorder. It should have been in the barn." And stepped aside to allow Venus into the house.

This time when she entered the house, Venus paid more attention to the condition of the interior. It was sparsely furnished but immaculate, not a speck of dust on the furniture or mirrors, not a stray thread or crumb on the plain, braided rugs. Still carrying the infant, Sarah led Venus into a small living room. The small boy followed, his eyes watching Venus warily, keeping close to his mother's skirts.

Venus had long wondered how a slime-bag like Ron Fairview made his living. It wasn't off these scrawny chickens pecking at the cold earth. Radke's hunches might have proved true; Fairview might have been smuggling. The West Coast tube came up through Colombia and Guatemala, from Central America into Mexico, across the border into Texas, from there into southern California, then up along the interstate highway, through Oregon and up into eastern Washington, the central smuggling hot spot in eastern Washington being Yakima. Yakima had a reputation as the Northwest distribution center for smuggled products, as the northernmost end of the tube before it traveled into Canada. But Radke had always insisted the conduit from Yakima into Canada was the Lay-A-Day Chicken Ranch. From there, the smuggling kingpins fanned out their wares, smuggling some of their cargo across the U.S.–Canada border. Radke had hypothesized that Fairview's community was particularly suited for this work; members of Company 8 held property on both sides of the U.S.–Canada border. Anything could be—and was—smuggled in this tube: humans; heroin refined from poppies grown in South America; armaments; rare animal species, both living and dead; and, rumor had it, diamonds. The smuggling worked both ways and the smugglers were smart and ruthless, rarely caught.

For years, a mysterious kingpin had ruled over the tube in eastern Washington. Radke had believed that was Ron Fairview. But Fairview had been clever and, in the end, Radke had failed to make the case against him. Venus's role had been small but significant; busting Fairview's cohort for poaching bear and selling gall. Even though she had never actually met Ron Fairview, she had learned just enough about Fairview's Company 8 community to conclude that if they weren't smugglers, at least they were neo-Nazi racist militants. And dangerous.

Now, at Sarah's request, Venus sat on Ron Fairview's couch in Ron Fairview's living room and marveled at how such an evil man could live in this tidy home. The little boy raised his arms over his head and pleaded, "Mama." Sarah placed the infant into a small bassinet and turned to the other child, gathering him up into her arms. Already, the infant in the bassinet had fallen asleep. The older boy hugged his mother's neck.

"Good boy," murmured Sarah. "You're my good boy, Jonah."

Jonah smiled and rubbed his cheek against his mother's. Sarah caressed his head, covered in a mass of blond curls. The boy said, "Good Mommy."

Sarah sat down in an overstuffed armchair, placed Jonah on the floor, put her hands over her face, and began to weep.

"Mama," said Jonah, reaching up to her. "Mommy."

"Hey, Jonah," Venus tried.

Jonah ignored her. "Mommy, hold me, Mommy, hold me."

"Hey, Jonah. Look what I can do."

Jonah turned his head and looked at Venus. She pulled a quarter from behind her ear. Did it again. And again. Jonah was fascinated for about twenty seconds, then turned back to his mother, pleading to be held.

Sarah took her hands away from her face, reached down, and picked up Jonah. He hugged her tight, cooing, singing a soft baby tune, a lullaby for his mom.

Sarah bent her head to wipe her tears on the sleeve of her blouse. Venus handed her some tissue, and she whispered thanks.

"Some men drove up," Sarah offered. "In a semi hauling a big trailer, big container. Just before . . . maybe an hour and a half before you came to my door. They unloaded some crates out there in the field." She nodded toward the yard where the chickens pecked the cold ground. "Out beyond the yard. I don't know what was inside the crates." She looked Venus in the eye, as if to show she was being truthful. "I heard my husband call one of the men Dixon. I believe he was the man in charge. Dixon."

"I think I saw their semi on the road, heading away from the ranch. What does Dixon look like?"

Sarah thought for a moment, then sighed. "I'm terrible with descriptions. He's about forty, dark hair, long and slicked back with goop, but some of it fell across his face.

Those dagger sideburns, you know? And on the short side, definitely shorter than Ron . . . was. Ron was five eleven in his bare feet."

"You're very observant. Did you notice anything unusual about him? Any marks or tattoos or scars?"

Sarah shook her head. "I wasn't ever close enough. I just saw him from the window, and once from the front porch when I went out to call Ron about . . . about the men."

"What men?"

Sarah placed Jonah on the couch. The boy protested but she was firm with him and he sat beside her, leaning in close to her side, keeping contact, still whispering the soft lullaby.

"The men of Company Eight. My husband's soldiers." She bent her head. "We aren't a violent community. We only want to be left alone. My husband hated any government interference, and his soldiers felt the same."

"So what about the men this morning?"

"Oh. I received a phone call from one of the wives, a Company Eight wife. She called to say her husband would be late meeting Ron. He'd had a flat or something."

"The men came to the ranch?" Drawing information from her was tedious, but Venus had dealt with newly widowed women before and so went slowly.

"No. That is, I think the meeting was to take place at someone else's farm. Oh, I don't know. I'm so confused."

"Did you notice a license plate on the semi?"

Sarah nodded. "New Jersey."

So it was the same truck Venus had noticed coming into the ranch.

"What does Company Eight mean, Sarah?"

The woman glanced up quickly, then just as quickly shifted her gaze to the window, looking out onto the barren ground.

"I don't know," she said finally. "I just really don't know."

The wind picked up and swept through the compound,

skimming the dry surface of the hardscrabble earth. Dust devils swirled across the yard and the scrawny chickens squawked and scattered. The wind carried the dust devils on a straight trajectory to the barn, where hours after the horrible event evil prevailed. Venus watched a lone chicken scratch the ground near the barn door.

Jonah began whining. Sarah gathered him in her arms and stood up. "He's hungry. Will you excuse me while I feed him?"

Venus waited in the living room, making notes of what Sarah had told her so far, while Sarah made lunch for Jonah. A delivery from back East had occurred just about the time of the murders. Had the men of Company 8 taken away whatever was delivered to Fairview's ranch? Where? She hadn't seen anything resembling a truck convoy on the only highway leading to the ranch, had barely seen another vehicle, besides one or two SUVs, and the semi with the Jersey plates. Maybe another road led out of Fairview's ranch.

When Sarah came back from putting Jonah down for a nap, she was carrying a plate of sandwiches. "I thought you might be hungry, too."

"Thanks. In fact, I am." Venus ate half a sandwich, roast beef and cheddar on homemade bread. Sarah settled back onto the couch, twisting a damp Kleenex tissue with her fingers.

"I'd like to ask you a favor."

Venus set the sandwich on the plate and waited for Sarah Fairview to continue.

"The tape recorder. Please don't mention it to anyone. I beg you to keep that between us."

"Why?"

"Just . . . please. I can't explain it right now."

"I wish I didn't have to ask you all these questions, Mrs. Fairview."

"Sarah, please."

"Okay. Do you mind if I go on?"

Sarah sat up straight and pressed her pale lips together

tightly, and then looked Venus directly in the eye as she had done before. "I've decided that I will tell you whatever I know. I made that decision as soon as the reality of Ron's death sank in. So go ahead. I'm ready."

"You're sure?"

Sarah nodded affirmatively.

Venus said, "Did you ever see the diamond?"

Sarah glanced up in surprise. "You know about it? You know about the diamond?"

"Yes."

Sarah seemed relieved. "So it was real. I could never be sure. My husband never showed it to me. He said it was too dangerous for me to even look at it, that if anything ever happened, I'd have to say that I'd seen it, you know, in a courtroom."

"But he had it?"

"He kept it in a pouch tied to his body at all times. Even when he showered, he kept it in the tub with him. He never let me see it, not a glimpse. I honestly began to wonder if it really existed. So there was such a diamond after all?"

Venus said, "Yes," and then they both heard a knock at the door.

"Sheriff Boyd. Open up."

Venus opened the door.

Sheriff Boyd said, "Two guards dead down near the highway."

The crates in the barn had once held food and emergency medical supplies. Sheriff Boyd inspected the two corpses in the makeshift cell, careful not to disturb evidence. Boyd and his deputies hadn't bothered to wait for the federal agents. Of course, there would be disagreement and haggling over jurisdictional rights. In the end, Venus knew, and Boyd knew too, that the feds would control the case. Boyd finished up around the ranch and returned to the house.

"Bodies stay put until my agents arrive," Venus told him.

Boyd nodded. He knew better than to argue with Venus Diamond. They'd tangled before and Boyd had always lost.

"Sure. They stay put." He turned to Sarah Fairview. "You his wife?"

She nodded gravely.

"I always wondered what his wife would be like."

Venus shot Boyd a dirty look but he missed it altogether.

"What can you tell us about the events that occurred on this ranch today?"

Venus held up a hand. "Whoa, Sheriff. Sarah will give one statement only, when my colleagues arrive. No need to put her through multiple hell."

They heard the helicopter approaching from a distance, its churning blades growing louder. Jonah said, "Airpane." Boyd sat down in a chair to wait.

The FBI agent, metrosexual personified, looked woefully out of place here in rural eastern Washington. He came first up onto the porch, his overcoat flapping around his dress suit. Several forensic specialists followed him. Venus opened the door.

He started to show his ID, but he didn't need to because they already knew each other. Eddie Mixx, the FBI's top West Coast agent. Best of breed. Mixx said, "Thanks for the tip-off."

Venus came back, "Wish we'd pulled this search yesterday. We could have saved the girl's life."

Mixx winced. "Where are the bodies?"

Venus indicated the barn out in the field. Mixx dismissed Boyd and the deputies and went down the porch steps where he was joined by the FBI's forensics team and two hounds. Carrying their equipment, the team tripped across the yard, dodging the pecking chickens, the hounds tagging along, dead set after bigger game than free-range chickens.

A few minutes later, Mixx returned, having left his team to gather evidence and remove the bodies. Sarah held the door to her house open for him. He nodded at her, walked past her into the living room where Venus was seated on the couch. Mixx took out his ID again and introduced himself to Sarah Fairview. When she was satisfied with who he was, she agreed to give her statement. Mixx started a tape recorder rolling. As she answered his questions, Sarah shifted Jonah back and forth on her lap.

"How many people live on this ranch?"

"On the ranch? Six. Counting our family—my husband, our two children, and myself—two security guards."

"Their names?"

"The security guards? John Garvin and Jeff Miller."

"Where exactly do they stay?"

"There's a small cottage out beyond the central compound. You might have noticed it on your right as you were driving onto the ranch."

"I came in by helicopter, Mrs. Fairview."

"Oh. Yes, that's right."

"I saw the building you're talking about. Is that where they live?"

Sarah nodded. "Yes."

"Where are they now, Mrs. Fairview?"

"I have no idea. They had been on guard duty down at the gate. When I heard the gunfire, I called down to the gate, to John Garvin's cell phone. But he didn't answer. I tried several times. I haven't seen either of them all day."

Later, when she wasn't interrupting, Venus would tell Mixx that the two men had been alive and well at the ranch's entrance when she arrived, before Sheriff Boyd found them murdered.

"Mrs. Fairview, can you tell me just exactly how many members of your organization live on or near this ranch where we are now taking this statement?"

Sarah sat silently for a long time.

Mixx waited patiently, picking at his fingernails. Venus wanted to join the forensics team in the barn but had decided that Sarah would feel more comfortable if she stayed with her during Mixx's interrogation.

Finally Sarah spoke. "Counting women and children, including both Canadians and Americans, two hundred thirty-six." She dropped her gaze to the floor. A tear fell from her eye and landed on her forearm. She rubbed it. She said: "Now, it's two hundred thirty-three."

CHAPTER EIGHTEEN

Sarah knew "less than nothing" about the men's business. Sarah knew her husband had been the leader of this community called Company 8. Right now, as she sat here answering this plainclothesman's questions, as she struggled to keep from raging hysterically over Ron's death, she knew word was surely spreading through the tightly knit community, whose ranches and homesteads adjoined one another, and she knew the men of Company 8 would soon rise up and exact their revenge on her husband's killers. They would blame it on the federal government, call it a government conspiracy, and they would go after someone, or some facility, in the federal government to exact revenge.

"My husband's men are capable of doing great damage, both to life and property," she told Agent Mixx. "I know this because many times the elders, I mean Company Eight's leaders, sat around my kitchen table making plans. Occasionally, when I had to go into the kitchen for baby formula or something, I'd hear them talking. I often heard them talk about bombs. How to make them, that sort of talk. And military tanks, and guns, they had a lot of guns, of all different types. I never really saw the weapons but my husband held classes on how to handle them, and"—she pointed out the window— "over there beyond the field, right on the other side of the border, is their target range."

"Who murdered your husband, Mrs. Fairview? And Karen Crandall?"

Sarah bowed her head, her lips moving silently for a moment, and replied, "I have no idea."

"Might you speculate?"

Sarah shook her head. "Honestly, I have no idea. I heard the gunshots, but I didn't dare go out there. I took the children into the back of the house and hid for a while. Then I realized it must have been Ron shooting Karen. Of course, I was wrong."

"What about rivalries inside your community?" Mixx asked. "Was anyone jealous of your husband's position?"

Sarah's eyes flickered, reflecting the cold winter light. She shook her head emphatically. "I know you think one of us did this. Maybe you think I was jealous of my husband and the girl. But that's not true. And no one in Company Eight would think of harming Ron. Every member of this community loved Ron. Including me."

Through the window, Venus saw the forensics team return from the barn and begin loading the helicopter, including the bodies. She signaled Mixx to turn off his tape recorder, and turned to Sarah.

"Do you want to see him?"

Sarah sat stone still, eyes downcast. "No," she said finally. "No, I do not."

Venus went out onto the porch, closing the front door behind her. One of the forensics team was saying, "I hate it when they clean up after themselves."

Mixx appeared on the front porch, a cell phone at his ear. He came down the porch steps and approached the helicopter where Venus waited for him. "The female's fingerprints match the Crandall woman's." He put his cell phone away. "I love this fax phone." He hesitated before saying, "So this means you were right about Radke. He was trying to tell you something about Fairview. Why are you wildlife guys always one step ahead of us?"

So now Mixx believed her. "Like I said, Mixx, this was all about the Lac de Lune. Fairview probably stole it and took Crandall hostage. And then someone else got greedy and took out Fairview and Crandall and made off with the diamond."

She stood facing the forensics team leader, a busty woman whose name was emblazoned on her overalls: "Bonnie." Over Bonnie's right shoulder, Venus could see the barn, and in the distance, the field of tall brown grass swayed in the wind.

"Did you check out behind the barn? In that field?"

Bonnie turned around, looked at the field she indicated. "We had the dogs out there. Nothing."

"What about walking the field? Did we have a team walk the field all the way through?"

Bonnie shook her head. "Too big. We find out someone else is missing, then we'll walk the field. Besides." She pointed. "See that marker on the far side of the field? That's the Canadian border. We can't go beyond that point."

Mixx offered, "Sarah Fairview said she'd seen the semi truck drive off her property on the U.S. side. Assuming the killer or killers arrived and fled in the semi, they fled into U.S. territory, at least initially. Mrs. Fairview doubted any stranger would chance escaping across the border here, although, given the lax security at this marker, she said she couldn't rule it out."

Turning to Mixx, Venus said, "We'll have to call in IBET."

"The joint patrol force?"

"Correct." She shook her head.

"You say 'correct' but shake your head. What's with that?" Mixx asked.

"I was just thinking ironically. This all began with an investigation of the Zone Mine murders up in Northwest Territories. Theft of the Lac de Lune."

"Yeah. So?"

"Chief investigator for the RCMP unit of IBET was the guy they eventually arrested and charged with participating in that assault."

Mixx cocked his head sideways. "Go on."

"Ironic, because if he weren't sitting in a jail cell up in Canada, Mackenzie would be the guy heading IBET's Canadian end of this investigation."

Mixx thought it over. "What are you hiding?"

Venus said, "Pardon?"

"I've known you, what? Twelve years? And in all that time, I never figured out how your brain works. Something about you is real secretive, and every once in a while you say something that seems to come out of left field."

"Or it could be entirely coincidental," she said aloud.

"What?" Mixx frowned.

"Why would an RCMP–IBET officer end up in Northwest Territories investigating the Zone Mine murders?" She looked at Mixx. She said, "I need a favor from the FBI."

"Since when do you need us?" Mixx jabbed at her.

"I need you to background a New York diamond broker named Yitzhak Goldman. Sooner the better."

While Mixx placed a phone call, she stepped around Bonnie and started across the yard.

Mixx yelled, "Where you going?"

She looked back at him. "Take a gander out in the field. Go on, whenever you're ready. I'll wait for the search crew and show them around. Get that Canadian unit in here, too." Mixx climbed into the chopper. Venus watched the bird lift off, bank, and turn southwest toward the Cascades.

The wheat grass in the field had grown five feet tall, summer's proud mane, before it had died to the same ochre color as the ground. The grass swayed somnambulantly, its seedy tips brushing the earth. The ground itself had practically frozen and Venus imagined few creatures survived a winter in this field. Walking the perimeter, she followed alongside a low split-rail fence probably intended to define the property line and perhaps restrict stray chickens from eloping, but not a high, protective fence topped with razor wire as at the ranch's entrance. When she came to a small stone border marker, she stopped and looked around. The field continued on into Canadian territory, ending about fifty yards from the marker, the same split-rail fence defining the field's end. Beyond the fence, on the Canadian side, stood a small red farmhouse set in an adjacent field, and surrounding that field, vineyards. There was no sign of a border patrol on either side of the marker.

The second time she walked the field's perimeter, she moved in about ten yards, focusing on the swaying grasses, looking for anything that might be hiding in there. The third time, she moved closer to the field's center and slowed down her pace. On the western horizon, the sun had sunk halfway behind the Fairview barn, daylight fading fast. Near the field's center, her foot struck something, tripping her. She steadied her balance and hunched down in the grass trying to locate the thing that had tripped her. One last sunray lingering over the barn shone through the grass and she saw something sparkle. On her hands and knees, she crawled over to it and scratched away a thin membrane of hard soil. Gradually it took shape; a circular steel hatch door, bolted shut, the bolts rusted and coated with soil. Big as a missile silo.

"Exactly." Sarah nodded when Venus questioned her about the object in the field. "An old storage site the military used, I think Ron said, for missiles, or for radioactive materials, back when the government owned this land. That's how Ron was able to afford the price of the land. The federal government sold it for practically nothing because of that radioactive field. You really shouldn't go in there. I've never been myself.

Ron has strictly forbidden me and the children from going into the field. He said it's still radioactive, still dangerous."

"You watched the two men carry crates from their truck into this field, right?"

Sarah nodded. "But they must have been meeting someone at the border. I know that sounds improbable, but the Company Eight men cross all the time. A number of our community lives in Canada."

"You think the crates were transferred across the border in broad daylight?"

Sarah shook her head. "I honestly don't know what happened. I could be wrong, even about them going into the field with those crates. I'm just so rattled. Maybe they were carrying crates *out* of the field, I really can't say for sure."

By dusk, the IBET unit arrived, including Mackenzie's colleagues from the Canada side, tight-lipped and clearly hostile about one of their own being charged in the Zone assault. Throughout the night they searched the surrounding ranches and homesteads, but produced little by way of clues. At one nearby homestead, agents seized illegal animal parts, including dried bear gall and rare Russian fox pelts. But at every homestead, the women and children were silent and uncooperative. Venus got a couple hours' sleep on Sarah's living room couch. At seven A.M. Mixx returned, dressed more appropriately this time. Venus and Mixx broke into Fairview's locked office in a small building near the barn, where they found copies of Company 8's printed literature, and removed three computers from a small office on Fairview's ranch. By noon, the case was officially turned over to the National Security Council, the FBI ordered to cooperate fully.

"How the hell did you finesse that?" Mixx complained, staring at his cell phone. His boss had just informed him of the transfer in authority.

"The case actually belongs to a number of agencies. The

joint border patrol unit, U.S. and Canadian Fish and Wildlife both have an interest, since one of the Fairview gang was smuggling animal parts across the border. Bottom line is, Mixx, this was Buzz Radke's case. He'd worked it for years, and I think he was still working it up in the Northwest Territories. And it was Mackenzie's case, before he was arrested. It's my case now."

Mixx shrugged. "I hate these goddamn rural cases anyhow. Give me the Russian Mob on Seattle's waterfront."

"Bright lights, big city."

"Something like that."

At the end of the day, only one decent clue had emerged, but not about who shot Karen Crandall and Ron Fairview. The clue hinted at what was to come: The search of the surrounding ranches and homesteads turned up 148 women and children. Not a single male adult could be found.

The joint border patrol unit packed up and went home. Some women from the community came to care for Sarah and the boys. As Venus was following Mixx out of the house, Sarah called to her. Venus turned around and stepped closer to Sarah. Sarah placed a hand on her arm and whispered, "You won't tell them about the tape recorder, will you?"

"It would help you, Sarah, for them to know."

Sarah shook her head and gripped Venus's arm. "Please don't tell. It's not the government that scares me. It's my neighbors, what they'll do to me and the boys if they find out."

"If it ever has to be raised, I'll tell you first and we'll figure out a way to keep you and the boys safe. You have my word on that."

Sarah placed a thin cold hand against Venus's cheek. Venus flinched at the intimate contact.

"By the way, what does 'Company Eight' mean?"

Sarah smiled into the distance, removed her hand, and said, "I don't know. Honestly, I really don't know."

Crumley drove. Dixon rode shotgun and spent most of the time thinking. Dixon was a thinker. Maybe not Einstein, but a thinker who never acted until he had worked things out in his head in advance. The single exception to this longstanding rule was shooting the girl. But Dixon had had no choice. He certainly had no intention of taking her hostage. She'd be just another stick in the spokes. No, he'd had to kill her. Next, he needed to find out if the rock he'd yanked off Fairview's corpse was the real diamond, the genuine Lac de Lune, or if it was, like the girl said, a fake. If the girl had spoken the truth about the real diamond being sent to Venus Diamond, then Dixon would have to keep an eye on her until the diamond turned up.

There are no coincidences. But there's luck. Dixon smiled to himself at the stroke of luck that had put him at the ranch entrance at the very moment Diamond pulled in driving the government vehicle. Dixon and Crumley hadn't hung around, though. The feds would be swarming all over the ranch and Dixon wanted to be the hell out of Dodge before they discovered the bodies.

And slowly but surely, a plan was forming in Dixon's brain, aided in part by the tape recordings he found on the girl's body. He'd had to search her, after all. She might have been lying about the whole thing. She might have actually been one of Fairview's people, though Dixon doubted that. And when he'd searched her body and found the tape recorder and all the little microcassettes, Dixon felt like he'd turned a double play.

As Crumley held to the speed limit along U.S. 97, heading south from the Lay-A-Day Chicken Ranch, the sun rose high, heating the cab. Crumley switched on the air conditioner. Dixon alternately worked his brain and played the tape recordings the girl had made before he had killed her. She told a fascinating story of adventure in the far north, of how she and a dude named Big Jim Hardy found the now famous Lac de Lune diamond, the biggest blue-green diamond ever pulled out of Canadian ground, worth, according to the news reports, hundreds of millions of dollars. She told how they had hired a glass-casting artist and had carefully fashioned one exact replica of the diamond, in case someone tried to steal it, a very likely scenario, she had added, in the world of diamond traders. The other twenty-one models they'd had made were special acrylic models made for the diamond cutters in New York, Johannesburg, and Antwerp, who were competing to cleave the stone. Practice models, whatever that meant.

"What does 'cleave' mean?"

Crumley took his eyes off the road for a second, looked at Dixon, and pursed his lips. "I gotta think about it."

"Which means you don't know," Dixon snapped irritably. "In diamond lingo, there's a difference between 'cleave' and 'cut.' I gotta get ahold of a dictionary."

"Maybe a thesaurus," suggested Crumley, and Dixon shot him his favorite "ignoramus" look.

"You're talking to a college graduate here, Crum. Don't get smart-ass on me."

The girl hadn't told how she'd managed to get hold of the tape recorder and cassettes. But she had kept meticulous notes, which made sense to Dixon, since she had been a scientist. He was now on the third of twelve tapes the girl had made while in her cell in the Lay-A-Day's barn. She told her story as if she knew she was going to die soon, keeping a day-by-day journal of everything that had happened to her, including the break-in at the mine when she was taken hostage by Fairview, then recounting an awful scene in a hotel room in Vancouver, and then her arrival at the chicken ranch, and how as each day passed, she began to lose faith that she'd be rescued. Her journal ended on the night before she was going to die with a terse comment: "If you exist, God, send me an angel."

Dixon chuckled and Crumley looked inquiringly across the truck's cab.

"Whasup?" Crumley asked. "What's so goddamn funny?"

"I'm an angel."

When they reached the outskirts of Wenatchee, Dixon said, "Follow that road that says 'County Landfill.'" Crumley obliged. Ten minutes later, they came to the garbage dump. Dixon looked around. No other vehicles in sight. "Stop here," he told Crumley.

Crumley stopped. The two men stepped out of the semi. Dixon took out a small travel bag filled with clothing and other necessities. Crumley, following Dixon's instructions, removed his own travel suitcase, then reached into the rear of the cab behind the passenger seat and fished out a can of kerosene. Poured it over the semi. Lit a match and ran like hell. The semi exploded into a ball of fire.

Dixon flipped open his clamshell phone, got the number for the local cab company, and ordered a cab to meet them on the main highway in half an hour. They trudged along the landfill road back toward the highway, Crumley whistling irritatingly the whole way. When they reached the main road, Dixon opened his travel bag and pulled out a change of clothing and told Crumley to do the same. They moved into a grove of scrub pines and changed into one-piece coveralls, then buried their discarded clothing beneath a pine-needle carpet. They came out of the grove and walked up to the highway where it intersected with the landfill road. The highway was a two-lane, and traffic was heavy going both ways. No one seemed to notice the men, though; they just sort of blended into the scenery.

Fifteen minutes later, a bright green taxicab approached from the direction of the city, stopped at the intersection, and put on its blinker before it turned left onto the landfill road. Dixon waved at the driver. The driver pulled over onto the roadside. Dixon slid into the back seat first and then Crumley.

"Bus station," Dixon told the driver.

The driver was a foreigner, maybe Pakistani. He was young and bright-eyed and so talkative that Dixon wanted to shoot him in the head. He wanted to practice his English, he said, and kept asking them questions about pronunciations. Finally Dixon said, "You know what? You talk too damn much for your own good. So shut up and drive." The driver studied the two men in his rearview mirror. A couple of mechanics, or maybe migrant workers. Rude and unfriendly.

Dixon said, "Can't you turn up the heat in here?"

The driver reached down and pushed the heat lever over to high.

"Drive faster, for chrissake, you drive like an old lady."

The driver pushed down on the gas pedal, soon exceeding the speed limit.

Dixon shouted, "Not that fast, goddammit. Keep within the law."

The driver, perspiring now, feeling threatened by his two passengers, complied with Dixon's command. He slowed the taxi down to exactly five miles over the speed limit and kept it there until they reached the city limits. Inside the city limits, he followed the speed limit signs until they reached the bus station.

Dixon paid the driver the exact amount on the meter and said, "Do you remember what we look like?"

The driver thought for a few seconds, then shook his head. "No, sir."

Dixon handed him a one-hundred-dollar bill and said, "Keep it that way."

When the taxi had disappeared around a corner, Crumley said, "Man, I hate the bus."

Dixon laughed. "Not to worry. We're not taking any bus. See, I didn't know the town so I had to give him an address that would more or less be a place that exists in every small American town." Dixon pulled out his clamshell, got information, got the number for the Hertz car rental agent, called Hertz, got directions, and reserved a car.

Hertz was twelve blocks from the bus station. The sun had dropped in the western sky, the air outdoors had turned bitter cold, and Dixon could see his breath come out in thick clouds. He walked with his hands shoved deep into his pockets, wishing like hell that he'd brought gloves or mittens and warmer clothing.

"Shit," said Crumley, "it's colder than a rat's tit out here."

"Shut up, baby butt."

The Hertz reception area had heaters going full blast and a small television set mounted on the wall. While Dixon went up to the counter, Crumley slouched into a plastic molded chair and glanced up at the television screen. A commercial was on, for some local car dealer, the announcer a corn-fed bosomy blonde who all but threatened the audience to get their asses over to Hewling's Pontiac Plantation. Crumley glanced over at Dixon. He was still at the counter. The clerk who had been helping him had gone away somewhere and Dixon was chewing his thumbnail.

On the tube, the noon news began, the top story a quadruple murder in northeastern Washington, up near the Canada border. A man and a woman shot to death on the Lay-A-Day Chicken Ranch belonging to Ron Fairview, leader of the survivalist militant community, Company 8. Fairview was one of the victims. And two of his cronies. And a girl the cops were calling a "person of interest."

Dixon had heard the reporter and, acting nonchalant, turned to watch the screen.

Crumley said, "Jesus" under his breath.

The reporter said that the ranch had been sealed off and was being searched by federal agents with the cooperation of the county sheriff's department. No interviews granted at this time, and one news station's helicopter was diverted from the airspace above the ranch. An all-points search was out for two men who had been seen on Highway 543 turning into the dirt road that led to Fairview's ranch. Witnesses passing in cars could give no description of the men, except that they were Caucasian and driving an eighteen-wheeler, and hauling a full-sized cargo container.

The Hertz clerk returned to the desk and Dixon looked

back at her and flashed a wide grin. The young woman winced slightly.

"I'm sorry, sir, but we don't have a deluxe model available. Not even a mid-sized vehicle. All we've got is an Escort. And only two of them."

"What colors?"

"Let's see." She consulted her computer screen. "One's nirvana glow. The other's, uh, it's called cherry pie."

"I'll take the nirvana glow."

"You know it's purple, sir?"

"I don't give a flying crap what color it is, I won't drive a cherry pie." Dixon slapped a forged driver's license and a credit card on the counter. The clerk took the fake ID and went away, returning shortly with a sheaf of papers, which she asked Dixon to sign. When he had finished, she handed him a wire ring with one key on it.

"It's just outside the left entrance here, Mr. Wilson." She pointed to a set of double doors.

The Barrens,
Northwest Territories

The polar bear lay prone in her cage, slumped against the rear bars, sated from her latest meal of fresh seal meat. Cool air blew across the animal's cage, rippling her fur. She felt the lulling effects of the meal and dropped into a light doze. Captivity had been kind enough to the creature, though her mourning for her cubs had never totally abated and often she would emit great sorrowful moans.

Her captor visited only to feed and water the creature, until one morning, the human arrived bearing the rifle and shot another dart into the polar bear's haunch. She fought less this time, her cubs no longer at peril, and dropped into an artificial ennui, and then eventually a deep slumber.

She didn't witness what happened next, only experienced it.

CHAPTER NINETEEN

Crumley's knees jammed up against the Escort's dashboard and the steering wheel rubbed against his belly. Dixon had picked up a roadmap at the Hertz desk and now he studied it, running one finger along the folds and creases. "Here. Here's where we're going."

Crumley looked over at where Dixon's finger pointed on the map. They were still in the Hertz parking lot, engine idling. "Pick up the interstate, huh?"

"Take it west to Seattle."

"But that takes us way the hell out of our way."

"You think I don't know that? You think I don't know what I'm doing?"

Crumley tilted his head. "Sure, boss, you know what's best. I just wondered, that's all." He steered out of the parking lot onto the interstate entrance.

"Well, it's like this. That truck Agent Diamond was driving said, 'Regional Headquarters, Seattle.' See, she's got to go back there sooner or later."

"Hmmp." Crumley verged onto the interstate.

"If the girl in the barn was telling the truth, she's our target. Venus Diamond. She'll lead us to the genuine Lac de Lune."

Crumley looked over at Dixon. "Maybe we have the real one. Maybe we should just have someone look at it, verify—"

"Oh, yeah and what do you think would happen?"

Crumley shrugged and slowed the car down, being careful not to speed.

"What would happen is, the jeweler or whoever would recognize this rock for what it is. At the very least, he'd know it was a copy, if not the real thing. The Lac de Lune. Nobody around here, not even a jeweler, has seen a diamond this big." Dixon shook his head. "We gotta follow the girl until she leads us to the stone that was sent to her. Then we can take both of them back to New York, have Volpe identify the real stone."

"I thought we were cutting Volpe out of this."

Dixon smiled falsely. Crumley was so dense. "We are, we are," he said reassuringly. "But first we need him to identify the real diamond."

Crumley nodded. "I get it now. Here's the highway."

More than likely, this Venus planned to pick up the diamond at a secretly arranged location, maybe a safe house somewhere. But she was a federal agent, probably too smart to be followed for long. Following her might be a waste of Dixon's time and money, because she'd lead him astray at every turn. Still, he had learned in his long years of criminal activity that coincidences don't just happen. The agent named Venus had shown up and mentioned the diamond only minutes after the girl he'd plugged mentioned her name. Could the dead broad have been lying?

Dixon took the Lac de Lune out of its leather pouch and studied it, holding it up to the windshield and the thin winter light. The stone was spectacular, even in its uncut state. If this was really a fake, it was a damn good replica of the real thing. Even its weight felt right. On his pinky finger, Dixon had a gold ring with three inset diamonds. A flash of sunlight caught the ring's stones and they sparkled, drawing Dixon's attention.

"Goddamn son of a bitch, why didn't I think of this before?"

Crumley said, "Think of what?"

"Just drive and keep your trap shut."

Dixon applied the pinky-ring diamonds to the big stone, where the little window had been cut to see inside. A tiny scratch formed on the stone of his pinky ring.

"Shee-it."

Crumley looked over. Dixon tossed the big stone on the cab floor. "It's a goddamn enigma."

"Shee-it," Crumley echoed Dixon.

"Which means a puzzle, didja know that word, Crum?"

"Huh."

Seattle

Mixx didn't bother phoning ahead. He arrived at Venus's condo at eleven-thirty P.M. and wasn't apologetic about waking her. "Buzz me in, Diamond. It's freezing cold out here and raining cats and hogs."

When he arrived at the door, Mixx was indeed rain soaked. Venus handed him a bath towel, took his drenched outer clothing, jacket, and trousers, tossed them in the clothes dryer, grabbed a couple Heinekins and handed one to Mixx. His shirttails hung down over his long pale legs, almost to his knees. She stifled her amusement, sparing him his dignity.

"I don't drink Heinekin," he said irritably, arranging his shirttails strategically across his lap. "But what the hell." He wanted a glass; he didn't drink from the bottle. Venus, in robe and bare feet, sat across the coffee table from him, sipping from a bottle and waiting for Mixx to explain his nocturnal visit.

"ME just called in the prelims."

Venus nodded and waited for Mixx to continue. Outside rain pelted the high windows and rode them down in sheets.

"Fairview and Crandall were shot by the same weapon. Glock."

"Ho-hum."

"We're tracing it. Why 'ho-hum'?"

Venus shrugged. "Too many Glocks in this world."

Mixx raised both eyebrows, feigning interest in her remark.

"What about the Jersey plates and the individual Sarah heard her husband refer to as Dixon?"

Mixx held up a hand, sipped some more of the beer he never drank, swallowed, then offered, "License plate was traced to a rental agency back East in Newark that rents big equipment." He fished a slip of paper out of his shirt pocket. It was damp, and he opened it carefully before handing it across to her.

"That's the name and phone number of the guy who manages the truck rental concern. He's all yours. I didn't presume to start asking questions. I just said the driver had been stopped on a traffic violation. I didn't use the name. He did."

"Dixon?"

"Uh-huh. He said Dixon had a perfect driving record when he rented the truck. Guy had checked him out. I told him it was no big thing, just a speeding ticket, going seventy in a forty-five-mile-per-hour zone. Said I was just verifying Dixon's story about where he came by the truck."

"Good work. Thanks." Venus set the paper down on the coffee table and waited for Mixx to continue. He didn't. After a while, she tried, "And . . . ?"

Mixx looked at her. "And what?"

"What else? Did you find out what they were delivering to the ranch?" Mixx shook his head.

"What about the King of Forty-seventh Street? You got him backstoried?"

"Oops." Mixx smacked his forehead. "Can I get back to you on that?"

"Something must have been fairly important for you to show up this time of night."

Mixx's face reddened slightly. He tried leaning back on the couch, tried coming off as relaxed, but only looked more sheepish and uptight.

"Spit it out, Mixx."

"Fairview's computer. We turned up some nasty stuff. Maybe tied to illicit business transactions. Our guys are deciphering them right now."

"Nasty like how?"

Mixx scratched the skin beneath his right eye. "You know, sales figures for chickens and other farm products."

"Which you guess are really figures related to contraband."

"Uh-huh."

Venus sighed, went after another greenie. Mixx waved off the offer of seconds. Somebody might detect uncool beer breath. Venus poured her own, drank, and said, "Okay, Eddie, you're trying real hard to spit something out and I'm not clairvoyant."

Mixx blushed. "I, uh, well, I'd like to work this case with you. NSC would go for it, I'm sure."

"Why?"

"Why would they go for it?"

"Don't get me started, Eddie."

He cocked his head, reached out, and picked up the empty green bottle off the coffee table, held it aloft, studying it like it was evidence. "This looks like a big one. I feel like we're on the brink of breaking something truly mega wide open and surprising all the rats in their nest. I want to be part of it." He chuckled dryly, flashed his eyes at her. "Hell, I could be your gofer."

"So long as you can weasel out of the rural aspects."

"Well, yeah."

Venus laughed. "You serious?"

" 'Fraid so."

Venus stood, walked over to the tall windows, and stared out at the rain sheeting down. "And this is why you woke me up?"

"I'm kind of anxious to work on the case. Sorry about waking you up, though. To be honest, I figured you'd be out on the town this time of evening."

She turned to face him. "Mixx, I've been on the road and virtually sleepless for something like ten days now. You really think I'd be out burning up the town?"

Mixx shrugged. "I figured a chick like you . . ."

"Call me a girl, Mixx, or a gal if it makes you feel better. Never, ever, call me a chick. Understand?"

Mixx nodded humbly.

She said, "Ulterior motive?"

He raised his right hand. "Swear to God. Ulterior-free."

"So I'd like to get back to the sweet dream I had going." She left the room, returning a moment later with Mixx's dry outer clothes. Placed them on the couch beside him. Stood, hands on hips, while he pulled on the jacket and trousers.

At the door, Mixx said, "What about 'babe'?"

She shut the door firmly against Mixx's nose.

She was asleep again, deep enough to believe in the orchid garden in Singapore where she and her lover, Reuben, stood together watching an Asian sunset. Reuben had placed an arm around her, drawn her to him, and was on the brink of kissing her when the fiction abruptly morphed into a telephone ringing. And ringing.

It was Sarah Fairview.

"I did think of something else. I hope you don't mind my calling so late."

"Not at all, Sarah. Go ahead."

"My husband was talking to someone on the phone a couple weeks ago. I heard him say the name Volpe. Like the person he was talking to was named Volpe. And I heard him ask Volpe—he didn't use a first name—if he, or she, was in New York at the time."

"Is that all you heard?"

"I'm afraid so. I can only make a guess at this, but I seem to recall a few months ago, Ron had to make a trip to New York. To meet with someone. That was unusual."

"Thanks, Sarah. How are you doing?"

"It's pretty rough. I'm okay, though. One of the women is staying overnight here and helping me out with the boys."

"You don't know where the men went?"

"I give you my word, I haven't the slightest idea where they went off to."

Crumley sat in the purple Escort, pondering the glowing tip of his cigarette. He wished Dixon would finish whatever the hell he was doing, breaking into her pad and searching it, or something crazy like that. Sure, it made sense to follow her, as Dixon said; she'd eventually lead them to the real rock. Since the prospector or whatever she was, the girl Dixon had blown away along with Fairview at the ranch, since she practically swore that the rock was headed to the Venus broad. And her name, Diamond. Crumley thought that an interesting coincidence, but when he had mentioned it to Dixon, Dixon just shot him one of his "ignoramus" looks, so Crumley had determined not to bring that up again. And how, Crumley wondered as he flicked the cigarette butt out the car window and lit another from a yellow Bic, when Crumley had suggested to Dixon that the Venus broad might already have the diamond in her possession, and Dixon had told him to shut the eff up, said he'd already thought of that. Dixon's theory was that the rock was on its way to the girl via a "mystery person." Maybe Dixon was right. He usually was, which was why he got to be boss.

The drive to Seattle had exhausted Crumley. It hadn't helped that the girl's address wasn't listed in the telephone book. Dixon had found six "Diamond" listings, none indicating a "Venus." But Dixon was a lucky son of a gun, and he scored on his first hit: a listing for Bart Diamond.

"Who's calling?" the male voice asked.

"Name's Jimmy Visadomini," said Dixon over the pay phone. "I'm looking for an old pal of mine. Venus Diamond. You any relation?"

"I am her brother, Mr. Visadomini. Why don't you give me a telephone number where she can reach you and I'll try to contact her and ask her to call you back."

"Uh, well, see, that won't work, ya see, 'cause I'm on the road."

"Do you have a cell phone?"

"It's outta juice, and see, I'm only just passing through Seattle on my way to Portland. I'm in a phone booth in a bar but it's closing up right now, so I gotta leave. See, here's the thing. I've come all the way from New York City. Got a load of perishables. I just wanted to drop off a little gift for Venus and say 'hey' for old time's sake. See, we were pals in training school."

"Training school?" The man's voice sounded dubious.

"You know, Fish and Wildlife. We trained together. Hey, man, I'm sorry to bother you like this, maybe I should just forget it, but, you know, Venus and me, we were really tight back then and I just wanted to say 'hey,' like I said, and drop off this little gift."

"All right, all right." The man gave Dixon an address, adding, "I doubt that she's at home, but you can drop off whatever you have with her condo manager. A Mrs. Beasley."

"*Muchas gracias,* man."

"And another thing. This address is not to be given out to anyone else, you understand."

"Hey, no kidding. Same for me, you know? I mean, while I was still working for them." Here Dixon laughed. "Life sure throws a mean curve ball, don't it?" And he hung up.

They drove into the heart of the city, down toward the

saltwater bay, finally locating Venus Diamond's address. An old warehouse that looked to be renovated and turned into fancy condos. Now Dixon was prowling around the place, leaving Crumley to keep watch in the parking lot.

CHAPTER TWENTY

The rain finally stopped and Venus opened the tall windows to catch the cooling breeze. Even in winter, she slept with these windows raised. The windows opened to a wide deck facing out on Western Avenue. Anyone trying to enter through the windows would have to rappel up two stories in full view of the constant foot traffic along the street below. She never feared being awakened in the night by intruders.

After Sarah's call, she couldn't sleep. She took out her notepad and skimmed over her notes, trying to find any reference to a recent link between Buzz Radke and Ron Fairview. She had mentioned Radke's name to Sarah, but Sarah had just shaken her head and said, "I haven't heard that name."

Now the name Volpe was added to the puzzle. On a hunch, she called Manhattan information, asked the computerized operator for the Yellow Page listings of diamond brokers. Asked for the number of a Mr. Volpe, a diamond broker.

"The one on West Forty-seventh Street?" A real voice came on the line.

"That's it."

The operator said, "Hold for the number," and clicked off. Venus wrote the number down.

She thought about Buzz Radke, about his personality, his character traits. Yellowknife in winter held no particular allure. Sure as hell couldn't sleep with windows open. Venus was glad to be out of the place, at least temporarily. The lure of diamonds and riches had apparently been enough for Radke to endure the harsh climate; he'd lasted through five long winters in the Northwest Territories. He'd hit it big, bigger than anyone else in the diamond mining fields, and yet he'd been sent there on an assignment for the U.S. government. The riddle man. The gambler. She had known Radke fairly well, and the idea that he'd fink out on an assignment stuck in her craw. Radke wasn't a crap-out kind of guy. She hadn't argued with Wexler about it. She wished to hell she could sleep, but since she couldn't, she might as well wake up someone else.

Officer Benton answered the phone. Her voice resonated, tight, like a bee caught in a Mason jar. She was wide awake.

"Officer Benton here."

Venus, in bed, propped up against several pillows, a fresh greenie on the side table, asked Benton how the case against Mackenzie was proceeding.

"Pretty much wrapping it up. What's got you so interested at this late hour?"

"Just curious what evidence turned up."

She could hear Benton sigh.

"As you know, at the time of Sergeant Mackenzie's arrest, we had matched bullet casings found at the scene to a personal weapon Mackenzie owned. Additionally, he has so far been unable to account for his whereabouts for a thirty-six-hour period during which time the crimes were committed."

"I remember. Anything since then?"

Benton made a sound in her throat, like a chuckle. "Tons," she said. "Zone Mine surveillance cameras picked up images of the six intruders. They were masked, of course, and dressed in snow gear, but we have a decent enough close-up angle of one of the intruder's hands holding a gun. The clothing matches Sergeant Mackenzie's personal snow gear."

"Who's got the videotape?"

"We do. In our evidence lab."

"Are you having it studied by experts?"

Benton sighed. "Of course. We're not exactly amateurs here, Agent Diamond."

Venus checked her Swatch. Midnight in Seattle. Midnight too in Yellowknife. Benton was on night duty.

"What about the autopsies?"

Benton said, "Nothing we didn't expect. The guards were shot by several different weapons. At least four guns, maybe five. All of them died pretty much instantly. Except Hardy, or I mean, Radke. He held on long enough to write your name in blood. Weird, huh? Why do you suppose he did that?"

"Maybe you can tell me."

Benton laughed. "How would I know? Anyway, these bastards were sharpshooters."

"What else did you find in regard to Sergeant Mackenzie?"

"We found some articles in his home."

"Like what?"

Benton hesitated, then said, "I'm not free to divulge that information. All I can say is the items are directly related to the case."

"Officer Benton, I'm sure I don't need to remind you that this criminal investigation is a joint effort of our respective federal agencies. You are obliged to share."

Benton's breath came heavy across the line. She might be smoking, exhaling. Finally she said, "We found some cut diamonds with Zone Mine markings on them. He had them stashed inside his bed pillow."

"How many is 'some'?"

"Let's just say over two thousand carats altogether. Several hundred stones of varying sizes."

Venus picked up her notebook and wrote down the information Officer Benton had just offered.

"Officer Benton, who's looking at Zone Mine's files?"

"Call me Sandra, please." Benton hesitated, then answered, "Several of us here at headquarters. And if you're asking will we send you copies, the answer is negative. If you want to look at them you'll have to come into headquarters in Yellowknife."

"I might do that. Did you happen to note down the names of the companies that do business with Zone?"

Benton chuckled. "You bet. You know what a sighting is?"

"Not really. Tell me."

Maybe she was anxious to show off her knowledge of the diamond business, or maybe she was actually warming up to Venus. She said, "Most of the mining companies up here hold their sightings in Toronto, but Zone and some of the smaller mining concerns hold sightings right here in Yellowknife, or out at their mines. In the diamond trade, sightings are held every five weeks by the big companies like De Beers. The little guys follow suit, eh? Brokers come from all over the world, Japan, Europe, from everywhere. These broker guys are ultra exclusive, sightings are by invitation only. So the diamond wholesale and retailing companies, the folks lucky enough to be invited, they send their best diamond brokers to the sightings.

"It's really cool how they do it. See, the company, say Big Jim Hardy's company, Zone, selects a collection of rough for each so-called sight box. Then Zone decides who sees which sight box. Normally, a mining company will include its best rough in their biggest clients' boxes. They mix it all up, you know, small diamonds, different colors and grades and shapes in the same box. And they quote a price to each buyer. You take the lesser stuff with the really high-quality stuff. It's a way of evening things out, I guess. You pay or go away, it's that simple. Well, actually, it's not that simple. See, the brokers decide if they'll take what's offered to them in the sight boxes. A broker can haggle some, but not much. Then once an agreement is reached, the sight boxes are locked up in the sellers' safes. The brokers go away, consult with their clients, and come back the following week to pay for and claim the contents of the sight boxes. I see 'em all the time, headed for the airport, headed out of Yellowknife with these briefcases handcuffed to their wrists. It's a very predictable five-week ritual."

"I had understood that Radke was keeping all his rough and was planning to open a cutting-and-polishing shop at Zone's headquarters."

Benton said, "Well, that's partly right. See, Hardy kept out the best rough for himself. He was, like you say, planning to open his own cutting-and-polishing shop. Just hadn't quite got around to it yet. But he sold some of his rough at sightings. I know, because all these brokers, they stay down here in Yellowknife when the big Canadian mines hold sightings. They all hold them around the same time, during the same two- or three-day period. We see the buyers around town, at the hotels and restaurants."

"Wait a minute. I thought you said you found some cut stones from Zone at Mackenzie's place."

"We did. See, Zone had already set up their cutting-and-polishing facilities. Only they hadn't hired a manager, so they hadn't officially opened yet. But they had cut and polished and placed their mark on several hundred stones. That's according to the company's records. Seems to fall right in line with what we've turned up so far."

"Who's on the exclusive Zone list?"

"For the rough?" Benton hesitated, then said, "Tiffany, of course. De Beers has their own operation up here, but they sometimes buy rough from Zone, too. The others are smaller companies, middlemen, independent brokers, that sort of individual. Like I said though, we aren't faxing any of the evidence in this case."

"You sure know a lot about the diamond trade."

Benton laughed. "Everyone up here knows the ins and outs of diamond mining and brokering. It's the Territories' bread and butter. Of course, it helps that I worked summers at a mine while I was in veterinary school, way back in the dark ages."

"Have you got their names? I mean, of Zone's clients."

Benton blew out a puff of air that scratched the phone connection. "It's here somewhere. I can't put my hands on it right now."

"Ever hear of a diamond broker out of New York named Volpe?"

"What name?"

"Volpe." Venus spelled it.

"Maybe, I'm not real sure. But an emergency call just came in. I'll have to ring off here soon."

"Maybe I could call you back tomorrow and you'd give me the names." A statement, not a question.

"Uh, sure. Just don't call before eleven P.M. because I have this damn night shift all week. The daytime duty officer doesn't know squat about the Zone case."

"I'd like to speak to Mackenzie. Can you put me through to the jail?"

"Negative. Sergeant Mackenzie was transferred out of Yellowknife early this morning."

Venus waited for Benton to elaborate. Benton wasn't offering more. Suddenly, drawing information out of her was like pulling hens' teeth. "Please elaborate, Officer Benton," Venus tried.

Benton sighed. "You know that six guards were murdered in the hit on Zone Mine. This isn't just about Big Jim Hardy or whatever his real name was."

"Radke. Buzz Radke."

"Radke, then. Six families up here lost a loved one. There's been talk of a lynching. Late last night, a group made up of some members of these families converged on headquarters here, demanding that we turn Sergeant Mackenzie over to them."

"Frontier justice?"

"You got that right. They even brought the rope. It took

our entire force to fend them off. In the end, they went away, but several of the men promised to come back. So we determined that for the safety of the prisoner, moving him out of the area was advisable."

"Where to?"

"Did we move him?" Benton hesitated again, then said, "Vancouver."

"What's the phone number there?"

"In Vancouver? I don't have it right here in front of me. And I'm fairly busy at the moment. I shouldn't have taken this much time with you. Why don't you call back tomorrow?"

"Why don't you find that phone number right now, Officer Benton. I'll wait on the line."

Benton found the number in under sixty seconds. Reeled it off to Venus. She wrote it down and said, "Who's running the show up there now?"

"You mean, who has taken Sergeant Mackenzie's place? Nothing official yet, but Sergeant Purcell was sent in from Ottawa. As temporary post commander. I have to hang up now, Agent Diamond. Looks like we've got an ATM robbery with injuries. But hey, next time you come up, I'd love to take you to dinner. Just give me a holler." She chuckled. "And don't worry; I'm straight as an arrow."

"How come you quit veterinary nursing?"

Benton chuckled. "Too much blood and gore. Kinda ironic, huh? Where I ended up?"

CHAPTER TWENTY-ONE

Mackenzie sounded groggy, like he'd been sleeping when the phone call came in. "They've got me locked up in solitary, they say for my protection. I haven't been sleeping too well. Feels like a bad nightmare, the whole thing."

Venus said, "I need to ask you a couple questions."

"Go ahead."

"Who were Zone Mine's clients?"

"You mean, who bought Zone's diamonds?"

"Yeah. That's what I mean."

"They were diamond brokers. From all over the world. Actually, I looked at the list when we confiscated Zone's files, but I can't seem to recall the names. I do know that one broker worked for Tiffany, and another for De Beers. Yitzhak Goldman worked for De Beers. But I can't recall any other brokers' names, to be honest. Why don't you ask Officer Benton? She can look it up for you."

"I've already done that. She's too busy at the moment."

"I can sure understand that."

"Ever heard the name Volpe?"

"Not that I can recall. Wait. Maybe. Yes. I think, actually, I saw him in Yellowknife. Recently. Say, in the past couple months. Ask Benton. I'm sure I mentioned him to her. He had this very handsome overcoat. I admired it and pointed it out to Officer Benton. She told me then that his name was Volpe and that he was in Yellowknife trying to meet with Mr. Hardy about the Lac de Lune. Like everyone else. Yes, I'm sure his name was Volpe."

"Okay. I need to ask you something else, Sergeant. A personal question."

"Go ahead."

"The night of the assault on the mine, were you with anyone?"

"I told them in my statement. I was on a three-day holiday. I spent the entire time at my home up on the Naknak River."

"That's not what I asked you. I asked you if you were with anyone."

"I don't need to answer that question."

"If you want me to help you, Sergeant, you need to answer it."

She heard him breathing over the phone. They had a good connection, better than the connection to Yellowknife. Maybe Yellowknife wasn't on the satellite system yet. She waited. She had all night if necessary. Mackenzie was probably allowed only ten or fifteen minutes before a guard would take him back to his cell.

Mackenzie finally said, "It's not relevant."

"The hell it's not relevant. If you have a witness to your whereabouts, we're at least halfway out of the woods. Look, Sergeant, I don't plan on using anything that would harm your case. You need to trust me. If you don't trust me, how the hell do you expect me to help you?"

"Yes, well, just why are you championing me when everyone else is convinced I'm guilty as sin?"

"Look, if I can prove you aren't the so-called inside partner, we'll be a step closer to discovering the truth. And maybe you need reminding, Buzz Radke was my colleague. I want his killers caught. As long as the investigation wastes time on your alleged involvement, we're losing valuable time moving forward. You need to cooperate with me, Sergeant."

"I have an attorney. My attorney has assured me that I'll be out of here on bail within forty-eight hours."

"First off, you're evading my question. Secondly, your attorney apparently hasn't heard about the lynch mob."

"He knows about that. That's why I'm here. That's why they took me out of Yellowknife."

"Don't kid yourself, Sergeant. Those families know where to find you. You're safer in the hole than out on the street. Your attorney must know that."

"All I know is my attorney and the magistrate here are negotiating a bail amount."

"You're fooling yourself. They can't afford to give you up to a lynch mob when they think you can finger your accomplices. Forget bail, Sergeant. And you're still evading my question. This is the last time I'm going to ask you. Was anyone with you during the critical hours?"

"You're a stubborn lass."

"It's not my life that's on the line here, Sergeant. If it were, I'd hope that someone would be just as stubborn for my sake."

Mackenzie cleared his throat and said, "I'd rather not give her name."

"Go on."

"She's . . . she's the wife of one of the security guards who was killed during the assault. The widow."

Venus winced. This did not bode well for Mackenzie. She said, "You were having an affair with this woman?"

"I'm afraid so. She was on the brink of leaving her husband. He was a brutal man. He'd hurt her badly several times. Once, he broke both of her arms—"

Venus heard another voice, a guard telling Mackenzie his time was up. She said, "Give me a name."

"I can't."

"You know it's only a matter of eliminating each widow until we find her."

"I don't want her involved."

"Her husband's dead, Sergeant. What harm could come to her?"

"Her reputation. They might go after her, too, if they find out she and I—"

The guard intervened again, now warning Mackenzie he'd have to hang up.

Venus tried one last time. "That's not good enough, Sergeant. You're hiding something. Maybe about her. If you hide it from me, you can't expect my help. I'm dead serious. I'll get off this phone and I'll get off this case faster than you can say 'jackrabbit.' "

"Eleanor. Eleanor Purdy."

The line went dead.

"Officer Benton."

"Sorry to bother you again, Officer. I had another question."

Benton's long-drawn-out sigh indicated her irritation. "Go ahead."

"I need to contact one of the dead security guards' widows."

"Which one?"

"Mrs. Purdy."

"Eleanor?" Benton sounded surprised. "Why?"

"It's a private matter."

"If I'm going to give out an unlisted phone number of one of our victims, I'll need to know why."

"I think I know her." Benton had to know that she was lying through her teeth. "I wanted to convey my sympathy."

"You wanted to convey your sympathy."

"That's right."

Benton guffawed. "Sympathy? Are you nuts? Eleanor

Purdy must be doing cartwheels to be rid of that monster. He was a sorry-ass SOB. I should know. I had to arrest him on at least four occasions for wife beating. She must be elated."

"Still, I'd like to speak with her. Do you have her phone number?"

"Not readily available." Benton sounded annoyed. "Why don't you call information? Maybe you can wangle it out of them. Like I said a while ago, Agent Diamond, we're busy here. But don't forget that dinner invitation. I'm serious about that." Benton hung up.

The Yellowknife information operator was a real person with a real voice with an East Tennessee accent. She didn't need much time to research the Purdys' number.

"It's an unlisted number. I'm not authorized to give it out."

"What if I told you I was a U.S. federal agent? Working on the Zone Mine assault. Would you give it to me then?"

"You gotta be joking."

"Seriously. I am a United States federal agent, and I'm working with the RCMP on the Zone case. Tell you what, I can give you my badge number and you can check me out. One call to Ottawa will prove my identity."

"I think you better speak to my supervisor."

While she waited for the supervisor, Venus sat down on the edge of the bed. After the second inspection of the ranch, when dusk fell around four-thirty in the afternoon, Venus had accompanied the federal agents back to Seattle, a short but turbulent chopper flight over the Cascades and through a rainstorm. Tomorrow would bring another inspection of Fairview's ranch, this more thorough than the last. Venus might or might not join the search, depending on what she learned from Eleanor Purdy.

The supervisor's name was Lorenz. He wasn't willing to make the call to Ottawa.

"How about this?" offered Venus. "How about I call

Ottawa and report that a Mr. Lorenz of the Yellowknife Telephone Exchange refused to cooperate with a United States federal agent working on the Zone Mine case?"

Silence. Then Lorenz squeaked, "I'll make the call. Hold the line, please."

Five minutes passed. Venus leaned over and massaged her feet. She could almost hear them sigh. While she waited, she divided her thoughts between Sergeant Mackenzie sweating it out in the hole and the idea of a good night's sleep. Lorenz finally came back on. "Here's the number. Would you like me to connect you?"

Venus wrote down Eleanor Purdy's phone number. It was nearly twelve-thirty A.M. "No, thanks. I don't think Mrs. Purdy would appreciate a telephone call at this hour."

A hot shower triggered sleepiness. She pulled on a clean T-shirt and underwear and slipped between the bedsheets. Two minutes later, she drifted off into a deep sleep.

The soft turn of the doorknob jarred her awake. Someone was standing just outside her condo door. She lay still and listened as she reached for her gun.

The doorknob turned again, very softly. Turned several more times. She sat up in bed. Through the darkness she could see pale light streaming from underneath the door. And shadows. Someone moving outside. She could hear footfalls, one foot shifting to another as the ambitious intruder worked the doorknob. She slipped off the bed and moved soundlessly across the room, her back against the wall, holding the gun upright, elbow bent. With her other hand she reached out and flung the door open.

She saw his back before he dove into a stairwell and disappeared, the clattering sound of his feet on the iron stairs all that remained of him. The staircase was barely lit with a single lamp using up its last kilowatt. The stairs led down to a narrow landing, then another set of stairs to the condominium building's ground floor. Venus moved cautiously, listening. He might pounce out of the blackness. The staircase was full of shadows where a good-sized man could hide. But the intruder must have already made it to the ground and through the exit door. She moved one step at a time to the landing, paused, then down the last flight of stairs. She was reaching for the exit door when from the shadows on the stairs came a rustling sound. She felt the hair on her arms bristle. She aimed her weapon at the shadowed spot and said, "Come out of there."

It did. A rat the size of a cocker spaniel lunged straight at her. She flung herself out the exit door into the cold dark night.

The condo's exterior parking lot had about ten cars parked in it, counting the agency's vehicle. Most of the condo owners, including her, parked their cars inside the garage. The lot was reserved for visitors and service vehicles. She looked around. No sign of the animated shadow she'd seen on the stairwell. Suddenly she felt a cold breeze pass between her legs and looked down at her scanty clothing. Still, she needed to flush out the snake.

Now she wished she'd been smart enough to grab her cell phone and keys before she had chased after the intruder. In this pinch, she'd even settle for the condo manager, with whom she was not on speaking terms.

Reflections from a street lamp illuminated the parking lot enough to see inside most of the vehicles. At the far end of the parking lot, a dark purple Escort was parked parallel to the street. She thought she could make out a figure inside the car, a profile, and a spot of burning ash, like the tip of a cigarette. Other than that, there was no sign of anyone on foot. She walked five steps into the parking lot when a freezing gust of wind reminded her of her nakedness. And then it occurred to her that she'd let the exit door close behind her. She went back and tried the handle. Locked. When she returned to the parking lot, the purple car was gone.

Ten minutes later, she had managed to roust the condo's manager, a birdlike widow named Mrs. Beasley, with eggplant-colored hair wound in jumbo rollers and wearing a pink chenille bathrobe. Fortunately, Mrs. Beasley remembered Venus was not only a tenant but some variety of cop, she wasn't sure from what agency. She let Venus back into the building and handed her a duplicate copy of her condo key, wearing a vicious frown the whole time.

"Hey, thanks, Mrs. B.," said Venus gratefully. "It was freezing out there."

Mrs. Beasley could control herself no longer. "I don't care if you are some kind of cop," she declared flatly, "you're a nuisance and a pervert." The widow Beasley disappeared into her condo, shutting the door with a soft, almost reverent, gesture.

When the girl came out into the parking lot in her underwear, Crumley had spotted her instantly. He froze in position, fearing any movement from inside the Escort might catch her eye. After a while she walked back toward the building and checked the door. Crumley switched on the ignition, stepped on it, and drove half a block, turned a corner, and waited a while before circling back around to pick up Dixon. By then, the girl was nowhere in sight. He looked around for Dixon. Where the hell was he?

Crumley smoked and thought about his life and how far he'd come from the foster home where his foster dad had made a habit of tying him to a post in the basement and whipping him raw. His foster mother screaming in the background, "Hit him for me. Hit him for me." At least twice a week, once for some infraction of the SOB's rules, the second beating "for good measure." Crumley had run away at thirteen and never looked back. He managed to survive on the streets of Newark, learning all the tricks of the street trades as he grew into a hulk of a man, a little slow on the brain function, at least according to his boss, but still amazingly resourceful. One lucky afternoon, Delbert Dixon—coolest of the gangster dudes, fresh out of college and already running a big-time arms-smuggling operation—had plucked him off the streets, handpicked him for his gang. And then he learned the gunrunning business. Ever since Dixon plucked him off Euclid Avenue, what? Eighteen, twenty years ago? Ever since, Crumley's puny twinkling star had done nothing but rise. And now, in just a short space of time, if all went as planned, and Crumley got his paycheck, he'd be sitting pretty. He reckoned he'd buy a nice car and drive it around Newark, himself decked out in fine tailored clothing. Living well is the best revenge. He'd turn into the sort of man his foster mother used to refer to as, "Who d'ya think ya are? Mr. Diamond Jim Brady?" Crumley never knew who Diamond Jim Brady was, but now that he thought about it, he must've been a dude like the miner, Mister Jim Hardy, who had discovered the Lac de Lune. What they called nouveau riche. Crumley wouldn't mind one bit being a nouveau riche, and if it happened, and it seemed like it was looming right there on the near horizon, he'd remember to give something to charity. Maybe for orphaned kids. Yeah, that was it. Orphaned kids.

Crumley peered out the window and saw Dixon approaching the car, walking right out in the open through the parking lot with the street lamp shining right on his patent-leather hair, his breath puffing out of his mouth in little clouds. No doubt about it, Dixon had his faults just like any other man; he drank and doped too much, and he had that intestinal trouble that caused him to fart like a bull. Still, Dixon was the smartest goddamn feller Crumley had ever met, and he'd met his share. However zany Dixon's schemes seemed at first, Dixon always knew what he was doing, and, almost always, Dixon scored. Which was why he was the boss.

Dixon pulled open the passenger door of the car and slid inside.

"How'd it go?" Crumley inquired.

"How does it usually go?" Dixon smirked, drawing his lips back almost as far as his ears, answering Crumley's question with a show of teeth. "We got her now, see? Now all we need to do is keep on her tail. She'll take us to it, I guarantee."

"So what's next, boss?"

"Shut up. I'm trying to think."

Dixon would never admit to Crumley that he'd tried and failed to break into the chick's apartment. Still, Crumley sensed a waver in Dixon's self-aggrandizing aplomb. After all these years, Crumley could read his boss like a good book, and Crumley had read a few.

As Crumley drove, Dixon ruminated. Volpe might know immediately if the stone Dixon delivered to him was a fake. If not immediately, Volpe could always run tests on the stone to verify its authenticity. If so, Dixon could claim ignorance and demand at least a partial fee for his efforts at retrieving it. If Volpe didn't pay up, he'd be dead meat. Either way, if he could locate the diamond, Dixon was on the brink of making millions in one fell swoop. Whatever it takes, baby. Whatever it takes.

CHAPTER TWENTY-TWO

As sight man for Parecles, Gordon Volpe ranked high in international diamond-trading circles. The title "sighter" held prestige and signaled a man's arrival as an expert diamantaire, a title that, of course, Volpe richly deserved. At the young age of thirty-six, Gordon Volpe had proved his mettle in the diamond trade, having entered the trade as a sales clerk and learning it from the ground up. Now he owned a town house in Manhattan and a large home in Connecticut, where until recently he had lived happily with his pretty wife, Crystal, and their two prepubescent daughters, upon whom he doted. Gordon Volpe, in short, had reached the top. And then he blew it.

Money had been short these past two or three years. His doing. He'd made one too many trips down to Atlantic City, lost every cent of his cash assets at the roulette wheel. So far, no one outside of A.C. knew of his critical financial situation. Now the casino to which he owed over two million dollars had given Volpe six months to regurgitate the entire amount, or he'd face fraud charges from the casino's owners. They had caught him lying on his gambling loan application. Fraud, big-time fraud, and bankruptcy, and it would all come out in public, his reputation dragged through shit for all the world to see. Crystal and the girls would be reduced to poverty and the whole family disgraced. Volpe himself would surely lose his standing in the diamond trade. No client or mining company would ever trust him again. Selling his town house was out of the question. Too humiliating. And he'd have to confess to Crystal. The situation had gnawed and festered and created an unremitting feeling of dread that Volpe couldn't shake no matter how hard he tried. The feeling of dread caused his everyday work to suffer, adding to his financial woes and resulting in a lack of sleep or even relaxation of any nature. Volpe had been on the brink of either committing suicide or declaring bankruptcy and preparing himself to face the music when news broke of the discovery of the Lac de Lune diamond in the Northwest Territories. Suddenly, Volpe saw a way to save himself. If all went as he'd so meticulously plotted out, Volpe's troubles would soon be over, like waking from a bad dream, back in his ordinary world.

This morning, Volpe had received a phone call from Simon Mehta, the independent diamond courier who kept a small office in the Luxor Building, the same building as Volpe's office on Forty-seventh Street. Mehta had told Volpe he shouldn't miss a special word-of-mouth-only sighting event at the New York offices of KAM Ltd., one of Brazil's oldest diamond mines producing the finest-grade rough. Mehta told Volpe to expect a phone call from KAM Ltd., which came in not ten minutes later. The courier needn't have called. KAM Ltd. always invited Volpe to their sightings.

The event fell into the usual five-week cycle of the international diamond trade, a tradition older than Volpe himself, created by the Diamond Trading Company, a De Beers holding based in London's financial district. The five-week cycle controlled the number and quality of diamonds offered to the trade in any given time period. For no apparent reason, although surely they had a plan up their clever sleeves, KAM Ltd. was offering this one-time sighting of stones to only a select few of their regular clients. The diamonds had been recently pulled from a newly discovered Brazilian alluvial mine bed, stones of such vivid pink that KAM Ltd. guaranteed the bidding would be fierce. Volpe loved nothing more than a fierce bidding war for great stones and, now that his salvation plan had been set into motion, he felt a bit of the old competitive spirit returning. Volpe immediately made his usual preparations for the viewing, which was scheduled for the following day. The timing wasn't exactly perfect, all things considered, but at least Volpe could put in an appearance, thus giving the impression that all was normal in his world.

Of course, Volpe expected to see Yitzhak Goldman and his nephew David at the KAM bidding. The dandyish young David Goldman, tight-assed and entitled, had never matured beyond the brat nephew Yitzhak had introduced into the business when he was just twelve years old. Now at twenty-something—Volpe couldn't remember David's exact age—the Goldman boy sported a black pencil-thin moustache, shorn sideburns, and a flashy wardrobe, much to his Hassidic uncle's chagrin. And yet Yitzhak never remonstrated his nephew, for young David Goldman cleaved and cut and polished some of the world's grandest diamonds, and only for Yitzhak's clients. Uncle Yitzhak paid his nephew generously. Known in the trade as a genius cutter, David Goldman was, according to rumor, one of the three cutters Jim Hardy had chosen to compete to cleave the Lac de Lune.

Volpe wondered how Rubicon was progressing with the cleaving of the acrylic models of the Lac de Lune. Before too long, Volpe told himself, he would be carrying the real thing to Antwerp for the moment of truth, when he would ask Rubicon to cleave the Lac de Lune without shattering it. Although he hadn't told Rubicon, Volpe had settled on the Belgian diamond cutter as the best man to cut the problematic stone.

After checking for messages from Dixon (there were

none), Volpe was ready to face the fiercely competitive KAM Ltd. sighting. After that, he might call Rubicon and hint at the possibility of a big project.

The first person Volpe saw upon entering KAM Ltd. was Yitzhak Goldman, his black fedora pulled low over his forehead, sunglasses shading his eyes, exposing only the lower half of his face and the two black ringlets decorating his ears. Predictably, David Goldman stood beside his uncle, his talented hands thrust deep into his Armani pockets, Hollywood sunglasses shading his green eyes. He seemed preoccupied and, if Volpe wasn't mistaken, a trifle jittery. What did David Goldman have to worry about in life? David Goldman had a lot to live for. If drugs were making him jittery, Volpe predicted David Goldman would succumb to their lure, for David had always been the addictive type. Volpe knew this, because he recognized himself in the younger man.

Yitzhak spied Volpe as they waited for their security clearances in the lobby of KAM Ltd. The two rival diamond brokers spoke to each other as if for the first time in months, and the conversation was not unpleasant.

"So, Yitzhak, what's new at De Beers?" asked Volpe, truly interested although he didn't expect Yitzhak to level with him.

Yitzhak Goldman waved a tired hand. "Nothing much. A new pipe or two in Canada." He shrugged. "What can I say after all? A cartel's a cartel. So a new pipe or two don't matter so much. Not to De Beers."

David stuck close to his uncle's side and didn't seem to be paying any attention to the older men's conversation.

Yitzhak leaned into Volpe, so close that Volpe caught a whiff of the older man's breakfast. The King of Forty-seventh Street repeated an offer he'd already made privately to Volpe half a dozen times in the past week. "Gordon, you're sure you don't want to accept my offer of a loan? It's the quickest way out of your troubles, son, take my word. A simple nod from you and the money goes into your bank account. No interest, no payback. Only the prize, when it reaches your hands.

Think of it, my boy. Your troubles would be over. Life would be sunny again, worth living."

How the hell Yitzhak had learned about Volpe's financial crisis was a mystery, but nothing related to Forty-seventh Street and the diamond trade ever escaped Yitzhak Goldman's ears. He had his spies everywhere. Even, apparently, Atlantic City. That's what made him the king. Part of it, anyway.

Volpe shook his head.

David had obviously overheard the offer his uncle Yitzhak had just made. He sneered at Gordon Volpe and made a gesture like spitting at Volpe's feet.

Yitzhak sighed and straightened up. Volpe could see his cloudy breath as he said, "Okay then, Gordon. You've had your chance. Don't come whining to me when your life suddenly falls apart. Or worse."

The security guard was taking longer than usual checking in each of the diamantaires who had been invited to the sighting. Volpe, representing Parecles, was one of only eight diamantaires invited to the exclusive KAM Ltd. sighting. And now it occurred to him that he had first learned of the sighting from Simon Mehta, the courier who often worked for Yitzhak Goldman, and Volpe wondered about that. Mehta, though not a diamond broker, had handled enough diamonds to know good rough when he saw it. Plus, he had a reputation as a busybody.

The guard was checking in Samuel Moe from Tiffany. After the guard cleared Moe, he disappeared around a corner. Now Volpe was third in the line behind Yitzhak and David Goldman and a man he didn't recognize, who looked to be an Abkhasian Jew.

"So," said Yitzhak, just to be polite, "how goes for Parecles?"

Volpe shrugged much as Yitzhak had earlier. "I'm still only a minor stockholder," he lied—didn't everyone lie about their stock holdings?—"though I continue as their sighter, and I'll pop into the retail shop for special clients. But I'm pretty much on my own now, attracting my own clients."

Yitzhak said, "Ah. The independent broker. A bold move, Volpe, very bold."

Volpe smiled. "I'm a bold man."

"That you are," agreed Yitzhak Goldman. "And young and ambitious, might I add. By the way, I understand that the thieves were most clever."

Volpe blinked twice rapidly but otherwise showed no reaction. "I take it you're referring to the theft of the Lac de Lune," Volpe said casually. "Apparently, very clever."

Suddenly David Goldman cackled and pulled at the tip of his nose. He found something quite humorous but wasn't sharing it.

"Ah. Brilliant, these thieves," agreed Yitzhak.

"Yes, but whose thieves?" said David suddenly, jutting his chin into the conversation. "I would bet my life on it, these thieves are working for one of the big boys." He peered over the rims of his sunglasses and added, "Of course, Parecles would never do such a thing."

"Of course not," agreed Volpe, just to be polite. He had always despised David Goldman and felt certain the feeling was mutual. "Nor would AKG or Rosy Blue, for that matter. Maybe it wasn't an inside job."

Yitzhak, who by now had moved up to the front of the line, handed his and David's credentials over to a KAM Ltd. security guard. Volpe took the opportunity to address David alone. "You mean to say you think the thieves come from De Beers?"

David Goldman didn't even blink behind his sunglasses. "No, Gordon," he replied dryly, showing no respect for the older man. "What I mean is that the thieves came from outside the trade, but they were most likely hired by someone from inside. I'm willing to bet both you and I actually know the individual behind the theft of the Lac de Lune."

Once through security, the men were ushered one by one down a long corridor to a second security checkpoint.

Yitzhak and David went first, aiming their eyes up at a monitor that interpreted the pattern of their irises. A door slid open and Yitzhak stepped inside, followed by David, who peered over his shoulder at Volpe before the door shut between them.

Volpe waited a full half-hour before his turn came at the monitor. The monitor knew Volpe's iris intimately and the diamantaire was immediately granted entry into KAM's sleek lobby, where he was met by an usher who confiscated Volpe's credentials, including his U.S. passport, and then led him to a door with a window looking into a small room sparsely furnished with a plain wooden table, a straight chair, and a jeweler's lamp. The usher opened the door for Volpe, then left him alone inside.

A tall window on the far wall leaked pale winter daylight into the room. Volpe sat down in the straight chair, pulled it up to the table, and reached into his pocket for his magnifying loupe. He set the loupe on the table and then folded his hands and waited. A few silent moments passed and then Volpe looked up and glanced out the window in the door, startled to see David Goldman's face pressed up against the glass, David making a ghoulish face. Volpe turned his head. He'd be damned if he'd play cat-and-mouse games with him. But he wondered, did David suspect Volpe had something to do with the Lac de Lune murders? Volpe shivered as a cold paranoia flashed down his spine. This is stupid, he told himself. Just act normal. No one, especially David, could know of his plan.

Eventually the usher returned, this time with a box the size and shape of a shoebox, which he set on the table near Volpe.

"Enjoy," said the usher, and he left the room.

Volpe pulled up closer to the table and removed the lid from the box. What mix had KAM Ltd. put together especially for Parecles? Peering inside the box, Volpe knew almost instantly that the owners of KAM Ltd. had not chosen Parecles to receive the cream of the diamond crop. He reached into the box, rummaged through the rough diamonds until his hand felt the heaviest stone, which he removed from the box and held up to the natural light.

Indeed, the diamond, even in the rough state, was a vivid pink, the color of a gown Volpe had seen once on a woman who often came into Parecles's retail shop, a woman whom he particularly admired for her beauty and her air of self-possession. Not a very ladylike pink, more of a sensual shade, a bit shocking, a bold pink. But then, of course, the stone's color was apt to change radically after it had been cut and polished. A diamantaire is trained to gauge these potentialities, and yet one could never be completely certain that the stone would live up to its initial promise. Once the rough was cut away, and the stone gradually shrank in carat weight, anything might happen. The color might be less vivid, less interesting, browner, or, on the other hand, it could turn out even more brilliant and vivid than seen in the rough stage.

The largest pink KAM Ltd. was offering in Parecles's sight box weighed approximately sixty-eight carats in the rough. Not spectacular by any stretch of the imagination. Furthermore, the diamond contained a problematic inclusion with striations branching out into approximately one-fifth of the egg-shaped stone. Once the rough was cut away and the inclusion removed, Volpe estimated that perhaps two good stones of relatively moderate carat weight would remain.

If Volpe had to guess, he'd say a great diamond cutter could get a twenty-eight- or twenty-nine-carat pearshaped vivid pink and a twelve-carat round from the finished stone. That was an optimistic estimate, Volpe knew, but he was fairly certain of his skill. In all, Parecles might make a profit of a quarter of a million U.S. dollars from this stone. Not the best deal in the diamond world, but KAM Ltd. wasn't one of the big mining companies and, to be frank, Volpe hadn't expected much more. He wondered though what Yitzhak and David Goldman's sight box contained. Were they favored over Volpe?

Rummaging through the rough stones, Volpe pulled out

another stone, examined it, and made a mental note of its potential value. He continued appraising the rough stones and was nearly at the bottom of the sight box when he felt something odd inside the box. He pulled it out gingerly, a soft hairy object. In the same instant that Volpe saw the creature in his hand, the scorpion whipped his venomous tail at Volpe's palm. Volpe screamed and flung the deadly insect across the room. He had narrowly missed being stung. A security guard appeared almost instantly.

"Over there in the corner," Volpe said calmly, having recovered his composure.

The guard removed his gun from its holster, aimed at the scorpion, and fired, blasting the hairy arachnid into a million pieces.

"We don't have scorpions in New York," the guard said.

"No," replied Volpe, shooting his shirt cuffs. "Not anymore."

Volpe was retrieving his U.S. passport and other identification when Mr. Granger, KAM Ltd.'s general manager, rushed into the lobby and buttonholed him. Granger wore an expression of consternation, and his long fingers fawned at Volpe's sleeve.

"Terrible mistake, Gordon, just terrible."

Volpe gently removed Granger's hand from his sleeve. "I don't understand," he murmured. "What mistake?"

Now Granger wrung his hands and squeaked, "The sight box. Somehow they were switched. I would never have offered you such a dismal collection of rough stones, I swear to you, Gordon." He leaned forward and whispered into Volpe's ear. "That sight box was meant for the Goldmans, not for you."

Volpe wondered about Granger's remark all the way back to his office. Curiosity finally got the best of him, so he picked up the telephone and called Yitzhak Goldman. After pleasantries were exchanged, Volpe said, "Yitzhak, now that you've brought David into the business, who examines your sight boxes?"

"Oh, David. Always David. How else would he learn the good from the bad?"

"So you don't touch the sight boxes anymore?"

Yitzhak Goldman chortled. "Why should I when I have a nephew with a better eye than mine?"

CHAPTER TWENTY-THREE

Antwerp

When he had recovered from the shattering of the first simulated facsimile of the Lac de Lune, Rubicon went back to work and immediately broke two more simulated models. This sent the diamond cutter into a rage heard up and down Treble Lane.

Rubicon gnashed his teeth and paced the floor, fuming as much as any man would upon failing three times in a row. Several hours passed before Rubicon was able to calm himself enough to face the remaining four models of the Lac de Lune.

This gletz and its accompanying bubble presented the greatest challenge of his long and illustrious career. He had to get it right, if for no other reason than to recover his self-respect. Rubicon moved the fourth model to his cleaving bench, sat down on his cutter's stool, and placing his magnifying loupe to his eye, studied the striations in the stone. The gletz terminated about three-quarters of the way through the stone in a tiny bubble. That bubble might contain water vapors. The vapors could react to the heat generated by the cleaver's friction against the stone, bursting the bubble and causing the entire stone to shatter.

It had already happened three times: The simulated models had been made to include the bubble. So far, each time he had brought the cleaver down onto the chisel, the model's bubble had burst, that force sending shock waves through the striation, resulting in a devastating shattered mess. The floor beneath the cleaver's table was now littered with spent simulated shards and bits. This fourth model, exactly the same as the others, marked a milestone of sorts for Rubicon; in his entire career, discounting his apprenticeship, Rubicon had never had to cleave more than four models of any given stone. In fact, so great were Rubicon's skills as a diamond cutter that he rarely needed to practice on models at all.

But this Lac de Lune. What a challenge.

Rubicon sat at his bench for five uninterrupted hours, studying model number four through his loupe, occasionally running his fingers over its rough outer skin, often peering through the small window that mimicked exactly the one cut into the real Lac de Lune by a geologist at the mine where the diamond was discovered.

Toward evening, Rubicon's back gave out and the old man had to lie down for a rest. No sooner had he begun to relax, the lure of a nap having slowed his addled breathing, than a sharp bark rose up from below the window. Kors. Barking at what? Damn dog. Wearily, Rubicon rose from his bed, reached for his eyeglasses, placed them crookedly on his nose, and peered out the window and down into the street where now both Dobermans were barking and growling viciously.

Beneath a street lamp, Rubicon saw a dark-skinned man who seemed to be hanging far back from the chained beasts now straining their tethers. The man held his hands up as if to show the dogs that he was unarmed and harmless. But Kors and Krum would have none of it and continued barking until Rubicon shouted down to them. "Shut up, you two pig-headed bastards!"

The dogs ceased barking at once.

Rubicon called out to the dark-skinned man, "Whatever it is you are selling, I'm not interested."

The dark-skinned man dropped his hands to his sides and seemed to relax. He wore a heavy overcoat and a wide-brimmed hat, but still, Rubicon could see that he was a small man. Small and insignificant. When he spoke, his breath came out in a cloud.

"It's very cold out here. May I come up and speak to you inside your warm house?"

"You have a lot of nerve interrupting a man at his work," growled Rubicon.

The small man smiled, reminding Rubicon of a black-faced sheep that once belonged to Francine the tatter. She had kept it in the courtyard behind her shop. It stank up the neighborhood, and one night a certain neighbor had stolen into the courtyard with a pistol and blasted that same expression off the sheep's face, putting the neighbors out of their misery.

"Simon Mehta sent me," the man called up to Rubicon. "About the . . . you know. The rock."

Rubicon rolled his eyes. There wasn't enough time in the day for fools like this. Simon Mehta would never send an intermediary. He was himself an intermediary. And if he had important business, Mehta would have come himself. That was how Simon Mehta worked, how he had always worked. Therefore, this man down below in the lane must be an imposter with designs on the Lac de Lune. This was how Rubicon saw it anyway, as he hung out the window braving the cold evening air to glare at the unwelcome visitor.

"You think I was born yesterday?" shouted Rubicon.

"But it's true what I say—"

Rubicon did not let the man finish. For the first time in perhaps twenty years, he slammed the window shut and locked it. The little dark-skinned man in the heavy overcoat and wide-brimmed hat stood looking forlornly up at the window for a few minutes before he turned and loped down Treble Lane. As he went, Rubicon could see from the breath escaping the man's moving lips that he was talking to himself.

Rubicon went to bed early that evening, without a bite of supper and only one small pull on the bottle of cognac he kept handy for purposes of warmth. Warmth was good, inside the belly, but the room was stifling and so, before going to bed, he unlocked the window and pushed it open. He rested peacefully before falling asleep, thinking how he had run off the pesky little man, but more important, he rested peacefully because just as the little man disappeared down Treble Lane, Rubicon had hit upon a plan of attack that he felt certain would cleave the Lac de Lune with a loss of no more than approximately twenty-eight carats, and even those discarded carats might result in multicarat cut-and-polished stones.

No one ever slept more soundly than the diamond cleaver of Treble Lane slept that night. And the dogs slept, too.

New York

Volpe was elated. Already he possessed the canvas belt and its contents, a most crucial part of the plan. And now, Dixon had finally called to report that the Lac de Lune was on its way to him, traveling across the snowbound interstate highway from west to east. Dixon had estimated that he would make his delivery to Volpe in three or four days, weather permitting.

In his office on Forty-seventh Street, Volpe glanced out the window and noticed that it had started snowing. The snow fell thick and Volpe seemed to recall a weather report from that morning predicting a snowstorm over the city. He sat at his desk, bare except for a silver dagger letter opener and a small crystal ashtray into which he now tapped the ash off a Player's. Behind him, on the credenza, his computer displayed a screen-saver photo of Volpe's wife and two daughters.

He was alone for the winter, having stretched his bank

credit to bundle wife and girls off to Paris. They would stay in a small apartment he always rented for them because his wife had many Parisian friends and her sister lived there. The girls would study their French in school and Crystal would do some skiing in St. Moritz, and take the girls on little side trips to Italy and the British Isles.

He liked being alone. In fact, as much as he adored his family, he often wished that he had never married in the first place. It made it harder to think.

He might have insisted that Dixon fly back with the stone, but in the end decided it was too risky what with heightened security measures at the airports lately. No, much safer to travel overland with the gun monkeys, even though he'd have to wait a few days longer to finally hold the Lac de Lune in his hands. And Dixon had assured him that all had gone without a hitch, in spite of his having to waste Fairview and the girl.

The killings bothered Volpe, but no matter what happened, nothing evidentiary connected Volpe to the theft of the stone. If anything happened to Dixon and his driver, say, they got stopped for a speeding ticket and the stone was discovered, no one would ever know that Volpe had masterminded the operation. Unless Dixon cracked under pressure. But Volpe had enough evidence to have Dixon fried if he snitched, so he wasn't worried. Still the murders bothered him.

Eleven.

Volpe had never before committed a crime. He was deep enough into the diamond trade to know the ropes, to understand how thieves operated at all levels of the trade, how diamonds were constantly being stolen at every stage along their journey from the mines and alluvial beds to the sight boxes, to the brokers, to the cleavers, the cutters and the polishers, who used their sneaky sleeves to switch flawed stones for the flawless stones they stole. Even the wholesale jewelers could not be trusted, often switching stones their clients had selected before setting them into platinum or gold settings. So many thieves. So much deception and greed. Volpe had never succumbed to the temptation and now he enjoyed an impeccable reputation in the trade, both among his peers and with his private clients. Therefore, Volpe had reasoned when he first devised the plan to steal the Lac de Lune (during a quick trip to Canada to view the stone for himself), no one would ever suspect him. Nearly everyone in the trade had come under scrutiny since the theft of the fabulous stone. But those with spotless credentials, like himself, were the first to be crossed off the government agents' list of suspects. Now the search had apparently narrowed to known diamond thieves and smugglers. If Volpe had ever been considered a suspect, he had certainly been dismissed as a far too decent man to ever commit such a heinous crime.

He hadn't counted on murder. He'd been naïve on that score, instructing Fairview to acquire the stone by whatever means necessary. When Volpe had seen CNN's report of the assault on Zone Mine, he had nearly suffered a heart attack. He'd never really considered that blood would spill. If he were honest with himself, he would recall fleeting thoughts of potential killing for the stone. He had contacted Fairview through a third party who had assured Volpe that the job would be easy, and could likely be finessed without violence of any kind. But no guarantees had been offered, and Volpe had preferred to ignore the possibilities of violence, to forgo the hard work of being completely candid with himself, preferring to skim the surface of his otherwise clear conscience.

Eleven dead.

Suddenly Volpe felt cold and beads of sweat formed on his brow. A scorpion in his sight box. Maybe it wasn't meant for David Goldman. Maybe the scorpion had been meant for Volpe. He stubbed out his cigarette and reached into his pocket for his cell phone. Dixon answered his cell phone on the first ring.

"Someone tried to kill me," Volpe told Dixon, testing the gunrunner.

"Shit, man," Dixon came back, "you best be careful as hell."

"Problem is, I don't know who wants me dead."

"That's a problem, all right."

"I was wondering if you might have any guesses."

Dixon guffawed over the line. "That's a good one."

"I'm serious."

Dixon's voice morphed from jocular to sober. "Swear to God, I haven't got a clue."

"You're sure?"

"Chrissake, you know you can trust me. I'm a fair-and-square operator. Always have been. That's why you hired me, remember? 'Cause I don't go behind my clients' backs."

"Well, someone wants me dead, I'm fairly certain about that." Volpe recounted his experience in the KAM Ltd. sight room.

"For real? A scorpion? Shee-it, I thought they only did that in James Bond flicks."

Volpe decided to level with Dixon. They were, after all, partners in this crime. "I think that someone knows what merchandise is heading my way. I don't know how it leaked out, but I'm fairly certain that someone knows. And I have a good idea who that is."

"Another broker?" Dixon guessed.

"A courier. A diamond courier. A guy named Mehta. Simon Mehta. You ever heard of him?"

"Hell no. And I don't know how anybody could find out. Unless somebody's spying on you. So who is this Mehta anyway?"

Volpe said, "It's not important. What is important is that somebody knows about the operation and is after my merchandise. I want you to be very cautious during your journey, do you understand?"

"Not to worry, my man," Dixon came back. "Everything's under control. Just stay cool and watch your back. Maybe you should hire a bodyguard. I could recommend a couple of real dudes out of Newark."

"Maybe. I'll think it over. So you have a safe trip."

"Will do."

Volpe studied his immaculate hands, the long slender fingers, the perfectly manicured nails. In this business a man benefited from graceful hands.

The snow was falling thicker and faster now, and darkness setting in over Manhattan. He wondered if the streets were navigable and peered outside. Ten stories down, the street was invisible beneath a blanket of snow. A couple of large trucks plowed through the drifts, but he could see taxis and private cars pulled over, waiting it out. He'd probably have to walk to his town house. He hated the cold. When this was all over, Volpe thought he might move to Miami where the climate suited him. Live like a prince. Give Crystal and the girls the world on an oyster shell, as long as they'd leave him alone.

Volpe stood, reached for his cashmere overcoat hanging over a chair, pulled it around him and buttoned it up to his neck. In one pocket, he found a pair of leather gloves. He pulled them over his graceful hands. He'd forgotten his hat this morning. Damn nuisance, but he'd have to brave it. As he locked his office door behind him, Volpe wondered what Crystal and the girls were doing right now in Paris. What time was it over there? Ten-thirty P.M. A fleeting image of Crystal obliging a Frenchman sprang into Volpe's mind. He was surprised at how little it bothered him.

Johannesburg, South Africa

Dieter Haakvig was working on the sixth model of the Lac de Lune when his telephone rang. The telephone was all the way across his studio near the front windows that looked out upon Mandela Park. A bright summer sun splashed across the studio as Dieter, cursing out loud, abandoned his work and went to answer the telephone. Why was it that, almost without fail, whenever he was deeply concentrating on a difficult problem the telephone rang? More than once Dieter had considered turning off the ringer, or better yet, taking the phone out. But Alice wouldn't hear of it. Alice had to know where Dieter was at all hours of all days. Alice could best be described as a possessive wife, very jealous, and yet Dieter loved her with all his heart. The Haakvigs, already in their forties, were still trying to make a baby, and Dieter hoped, if for no other reason than to keep Alice out of his hair, the plan would be successful.

The phone rang insistently until Dieter snatched it up off its cradle.

"Haakvig."

"Mr. Haakvig," said a voice he didn't recognize, "look out your studio window."

Dieter turned and looked straight out the window. He heard a popping sound and saw the window glass shatter before he fell to the floor where, as he bled to death, a shadowy figure, an insignificant little man wearing an overcoat in spite of the summer heat, stepped inside the shop and removed the remaining model of the Lac de Lune. At dinnertime, Alice discovered her husband's body and calmly, as was her nature, called the police.

CHAPTER TWENTY-FOUR

Dixon and Crumley shared a good laugh. Dixon had finessed the phone call from Volpe. They had taken turns eating breakfast at a place called Chez Gus near the agent's condo and keeping watch for the small blond chick to come outside into the parking lot. Sooner or later, she had to come out and then they'd follow her. Now that both men had been fed and watered, they sat together in the purple Escort waiting for something to happen.

Dixon picked bacon out of his teeth. It had got stuck up between his incisor and the next tooth over. Crumley tapped out a hip-hop rhythm on the dashboard and made the mistake of opening his mouth. "You sure about this?" Crumley asked.

Dixon studied the bacon bit on the tip of his middle finger, then used his thumb to flick it into the car's stale air. He didn't bother answering Crumley's jackass question, just rolled his eyes. He reached into his jacket and pulled out the leather pouch holding the stone. He pulled the stone out of the pouch and fondled it the same way he fondled a whore's tit. Round and firm, and fake.

Crumley opened his maw again. "So the dude thinks we're delivering the genuine goods?"

Dixon grinned. "Thing is, how were we to know it's a fake? So we score twice, see? Volpe pays us for a job well done and, soon as we find it, we keep the real thing."

"Soon's we get our hands on it."

"I said that." One thing Dixon hated was a pessimist. "We'll find it. All we do is deliver her into Merle's hands. She'll take us right to it, I guaran-damn-tee you." He tilted his head, calculating. "I'd say within the next day or two."

"You sure?"

Dixon stared at Crumley like he saw Crumley as some lesser species, and barked, "I said so, didn't I?"

Crumley turned his head as if to look out the driver's side window. Dixon had cajones, all right. Still, he didn't have to treat him like a goddamn four-year-old. What was that old saw about honor among thieves?

New York

David Goldman met the courier Simon Mehta outside the Park Avenue home of Goldman's uncle Yitzhak. As he watched Simon approach through the falling snow, carrying his little black briefcase, David Goldman felt a familiar tingle creep up his spine, releasing waves of warmth at the nape of his neck, the spot where he was most sensitive.

So Simon had scored the pink marquise!

Goldman licked his pencil-thin moustache and beckoned Simon Mehta underneath the awning at the entrance to Yitzhak's apartment building. A doorman stood just inside, blowing into his cupped hands. "Come under here out of the snow, Simon," Goldman called a little louder than he'd meant to. "You'll catch your death." Goldman signaled to the doorman who stepped forward and opened the door.

"Good evening, Mr. Goldman. Going up to your uncle's penthouse?"

Goldman said, "Yes, Frederick, but not right away. My friend here"—he gestured at Simon Mehta—"and I have a little business to conduct and we wanted to get out of the weather."

A fireplace in the small luxuriously furnished lobby cast a burnished glow over the scene, a welcoming respite from the freezing weather that had chilled Simon Mehta to the bone. He'd tried to nab a taxi at JFK, finally having to settle for a share with a stout overperfumed matron from the East Side and a dissipated literary agent from Tribeca who insisted on lighting a cigarette inside the cab. With the snowstorm at its peak, travel into the city had been slow and arduous, and packed in with the rabble, extremely uncomfortable. Simon could still smell the cigarette smoke and the stout lady's perfume. They had combined into a scent so awful that he had retched several times during the trip into town, and now his clothing had taken on the noxious odor.

"Sorry about the bad smell," Simon apologized. And he recounted his harrowing trip from the airport.

Goldman, anxious to get on with business, waved Simon's apology away, taking some of the smell along. The doorman politely excused himself and went outside to stand in the cold.

"It must be very beautiful." Goldman rubbed his hands together.

"Oh, yes, indeed, my friend." Simon bent a knee, rested his briefcase on his thigh, and twirled the combination lock. "The most beautiful vivid pink you've ever seen." Opening the briefcase no more than four inches, he reached inside, brought out a simple velvet bag, and handed it to Goldman. Loosening the drawstring, he peered inside and his puzzled expression caused Simon Mehta to laugh out loud.

"Magnificent, isn't it, sir?"

"What?" cried Goldman, holding out his hand so Simon Mehta could see what had come out of the little pouch. "But this is . . ."

Mehta whispered, "Now give it back."

Aghast, Goldman nearly fainted, but he soon recovered his composure and dropped the velvet pouch into Mehta's outstretched hand. Mehta placed the pouch in his overcoat's inside pocket, its weight causing his overcoat to hang crooked.

"Simon Mehta," Goldman cried in a whisper, "from where did you rip this off?"

Mehta held up a hand. "Tut. This must remain my little secret. Of course, I will need your help, I am hardly experienced in the shady dealings of your business. You may expect an equal partnership, but just you and me. No syndicate. And your uncle Yitzhak, David, will surely agree to find a buyer in the most discreet manner. If we work quickly, we can turn it into several stones and no one will ever be able to prove anything."

Placing a hand to his heart, David Goldman exclaimed, "That my eyes should live to see it!"

"Now you sound like old Yitzhak." Simon Mehta's beady eyes twinkled mirthfully. Reaching into his overcoat, he pulled out a second velvet pouch and held it out to Goldman.

"Ah, the pink marquise. Even more beautiful than I imagined."

"I always love to see your reactions, David. You make the job of courier a worthwhile enterprise just by the expression on your face when I deliver the goods. Of course, I like being paid, too."

David Goldman paid Simon Mehta every cent he had promised and included a thousand-dollar bonus.

"For a job well done, Simon. And remember, not a word of this to anybody. Uncle Yitzhak and everyone else for that matter must think that I cut this stone. Got that?"

Mehta winked. "About the other," he said tactfully, "give some thought to my proposition and call me in the morning, but not too early. Jet lag, as usual."

"I needn't think it over, Mehta. I hereby agree."

The diamond cutter and the courier shook hands, Simon

Mehta said his goodbyes and stepped outside, waiting beneath the canvas canopy while the doorman rustled up a taxi.

David Goldman rode the elevator up to Penthouse 2, his heart barely contained in his chest. He was absolutely certain that his uncle would be overjoyed at how the pink stone had turned out. And once this transaction was completed, he could spend all his time on the purloined Lac de Lune.

Seattle

At eight o'clock in the morning, Venus reached Eleanor Purdy at her home in a Yellowknife suburb. Explaining her connection to Mackenzie and the Zone Mine investigation, Venus had hoped to put the recently widowed woman at ease, but her explanation only seemed to cause Mrs. Purdy more anxiety.

"I have nothing to say. Nothing to offer. Please leave me alone."

She had a young girl's voice. Venus had difficulty putting the voice together with Mackenzie's brief description of her. A sweet voice, the voice of an angel, or maybe a siren.

"Mrs. Purdy," Venus tried gently, "Sergeant Mackenzie has confided in me certain facts that could prove him innocent of complicity in this crime."

She came back fast, snapping, "What facts?"

"I'd rather not discuss this over the phone. I'd like to meet with you in person. But it will be a few days before I can get back to Yellowknife. I was hoping you'd contact RCMP headquarters and speak to an Officer Benton, tell her what you know to be true."

"I know nothing to be true or false. Now leave me alone."

The line went dead.

Mixx met Venus in her condo parking lot. He stood leaning against one of the agency's unmarked vehicles, a black Lexus, apparently waiting for her. She had taken the time this morning to knock on Mrs. Beasley's door and, when the widow opened it, apologized for waking her up in the middle of the night. Mrs. Beasley had sniffed and said flatly, "Next time, I'll report you to the condo committee."

She handed Mixx an overnight bag. Mixx held the door open for her. She slid into the passenger seat and Mixx slid behind the wheel. Mixx said, "Our guys are heading back to the ranch this morning."

"What about you?" She still wasn't sure if she wanted him on the case.

"I thought I'd spend the morning with you."

Venus smirked. "Then you'll have to buy a ticket to New York."

Mixx looked surprised. "What's in New York?"

She told him about Sarah's phone call in the night, about Volpe, apparently a diamond broker in New York City. "I have a hunch about this Volpe lead. But first let's hit a Starbucks."

Mixx laughed. "I'm taking you to Ancient Grounds. The coffee's way better."

"Oh, *pardonez-moi* for suggesting Starbucks. How unmetro. You know, Mixx, you're damn lucky you weren't assigned to some hellhole like Twisp, Washington. They sure as hell don't have any Ancient Grounds there."

"I can't help my inclinations," Mixx came back.

"The hell you can't."

"Don't be so goddamn obvious," Dixon snapped. "She's seen the purple car in the parking lot." He grimaced. "I should've taken the cherry pie. Much less distinctive. She sees us here, she'll know we're following her."

Crumley put the Escort in reverse and backed out of the choice parking spot he'd scored in front of Ancient Grounds. Parked in a loading zone a half-block down First Avenue. They watched the two federal agents go inside the coffeehouse, order coffee, and emerge with giant steaming cups. They returned to their vehicle, parked exactly in front of the coffeehouse, the girl sipping from her coffee cup as the man drove away.

"Follow about two cars behind," Dixon instructed.

Crumley did. Five minutes later, the Lexus turned onto State Highway 99, heading south. Crumley followed at a distance. Twelve minutes later, the black Lexus took the Sea-Tac International Airport exit.

"Shit."

Crumley glanced over at the boss. He hadn't shaved in two days, and when he frowned, he reminded Crumley of the clown pictures his aunt Sue collected.

"Keep 'em in sight. See which terminal they stop at."

The Lexus pulled over to the curb in front of the Alaska terminal. Venus stepped out of the car, reached in the back seat, and pulled out a small travel bag, then headed into the terminal.

Crumley pulled over to the curb, several cars behind, idled, waiting for instructions. Dixon opened the car door, got out, then leaned back in and said, "Circle the airport. Pick me up here in about fifteen."

Crumley circled the airport for half an hour. Finally Dixon came out of the terminal, the big clown smile even wider now. Crumley pulled over and Dixon slid into the passenger seat, rubbing his hands. "Man, I can't believe how lucky we are, I just can't fucking believe it."

Crumley glanced over. "How so?"

"She's headed to New York City." He raised a finger and shook it at Crumley. "But you know what? We're gonna beat her there. Let's find the damn Hertz lot and turn this piece of crap in."

Half an hour later, Dixon and Crumley were on a United flight to Newark, scheduled to arrive two hours ahead of Venus's Alaska flight into LaGuardia. Dixon had wangled the seats out of a counter clerk who had a thing for Brooklyn accents.

As they settled into their seats, Dixon leaned over to Crumley and said, "We need a trap, a lure of some kind. Get her on our turf fast. I could grab her and turn her over to Merle for fun and games till she talks. Merle can always make a woman talk."

Crumley came back, "I gotta get some sleep."

"Pussy."

Dixon used his cell phone to call New York. Crumley heard only Dixon's side of the conversation, but he could tell Dixon was speaking to Sabryna, his squeeze-in-residence.

"So here's what I want you to do for me, darlin'. You call this number I'm going to give you and ask for Venus Diamond. Got that? Venus as in the planet. Diamond as in a girl's best friend. Write that down. That's good. Now, it may take a while for them to locate her. Tell them you have some confidential information about the Lac de Lune diamond. You know, that diamond that was in the news. Yeah, well, someday you might just own a little piece of that rock, baby, if you play your cards right."

The operator at Seattle FBI headquarters didn't know the name Venus Diamond.

"Sounds phony to me," she declared.

"She's a federal undercover agent," Sabryna insisted. "Maybe she doesn't work for your branch, but she's a federal agent. I have some very important confidential information for her."

"Really, miss, I can't be taking time to check all the government agencies."

"It's a matter of life and death. You might lose your job if you don't find her, didja ever think of that, how someone might die because you didn't find her and let me give her this confidential information. And it would be your fault for not connecting me up with her. How're you gonna feel, then?"

The FBI operator sighed. "Hold the line, please."

Sabryna filed her nails while she waited. Outside, snow

covered the fire escape except for the top railing, which had melted and then frozen up again into thick icicles. A small bird with a fat red chest, maybe a sparrow, clung to the icy railing. Sabryna puckered her lips and made squeaky tweeting noises even though the window was shut. The little bird hadn't heard her. It seemed to shiver. Why the hell didn't it get off the ice? Sabryna reached over and tapped the window-pane. The little bird took flight.

When the operator finally came back on the line, she said, "I have located the agent, miss. Is the information you have pertinent to the Zone Mine investigation?"

"That's correct. And I can't give it to anyone but Venus Diamond."

"I'll patch you through to her cell phone."

Sabryna smiled. She'd do anything to please Dixon. Because she wanted a piece of that rock.

"This is Agent Diamond." Venus stood in line waiting to board the Alaska flight to LaGuardia.

"Hello, Agent Diamond. Are you Venus Diamond?"

"Correct," she said to the caller.

"Oh, hi then. How are you today?"

"Just dandy."

"I saw the Lac de Lune diamond. I thought you should know."

Venus looked at her caller ID. No information.

"Where are you calling from?"

"New York City. I live here. Well, actually, I live in Newark, but my, uh, office is in Manhattan? I saw that diamond that was in the newspaper here in New York."

"Can you hold on while I arrange for this call to be recorded?"

"No. I don't want to get involved, see? No recording or I'll hang up faster'n you can say Lay-A-Day."

So the caller did know something about the case.

"All right. No recording. What can you tell me? Be specific. Start with your name and address."

"No name, no address. I told you, I don't want to get involved. Too many people have already died. I don't want 'em coming after me."

Anonymous tipsters often provided the best information. Venus decided not to argue.

"Okay. Remember to be specific. Give me as much information as you can."

"I saw it, the Lac de Lune? In a diamond broker's office in Manhattan, on Forty-seventh Street. See, I work for this bigtime retail jewelry company. I can't mention any names. Let's just say I work for the cartel. And I'm the manager's PA, you know what that is?"

"Personal assistant."

"Right. So the other day, I mean two days ago, my boss sent me to this diamond broker, to pick up a package? I never know what's inside the packages, but I'm guessing it's diamonds. I mean, duh. The broker—see, most of those Forty-seventh Street diamond people are some kind of Hassidic Jew. This guy's an American. I mean, he's, well, non-Jewish. At least, he doesn't wear those little dreadlock thingies over his ears. And kinda young. Thirty-five, six. Good-looking, too, like killer looks, you know? And he was busy with another client, so I was just wandering around his little office. It's tiny, just one outer room, looks like somebody's fancy living room in miniature, with an office in back. I happened to walk by the office and the door was open just a little bit? And I saw the Lac de Lune. Sitting right on his desk."

"Describe the stone."

The caller described the stone's size and shape, information she could have gleaned from news reports. Or she might actually have seen it.

"I'm sure it was that diamond. I'd bet my kid on it, if I had one, but I don't."

"Name of the diamond broker."

"Volpe. Gordon Volpe. His office is on Forty-seventh Street. In the Luxor Building."

"Why are you reporting this?"

Silence. Then, "I understand there's a reward out for locating the Lac de Lune. Am I right?"

Venus said, "The FBI has offered a reward for information leading to the arrest of the individuals who attacked Zone Mine, murdered seven people, and stole the Lac de Lune. If the information you're providing now leads to those individuals, you may have a stake in that reward. Of course, you'll have to give your name and a contact number. Can you tell me anything else?"

"Hmmm. How much is the reward?"

"You'll have to ask the FBI directly. I work for a different federal agency. But I can have an FBI agent contact you—"

"Oh no, oh no. No, I won't fall for that trick." The woman coughed, a hacking smoker's cough from deep in the lungs. "Just give me a minute to think."

Venus waited. This could be the big lead. She couldn't afford to blow the call off as a crank report. Finally the woman spoke again.

"Okay, it's like this, see? My boyfriend? He wanted me to contact you with this information. I don't know why. But I'm thinkin' I'd like to have a share of that reward money. For helping you guys out, see? But if Delb . . . I mean, if my boyfriend finds out I'm claiming the reward money, he'll kill me. So you got to promise me immunity or whatever you call it. Then maybe I'll give you a name and a way to contact me."

They always ask for a promise of immunity. Venus said, "What else can you tell me?"

"I told you, I want immunity first."

"That has to come from the FBI."

Venus gave the caller Mixx's name and phone number, though she doubted the caller would ever make contact with the FBI. Maybe after it was all over. Maybe then she'd come out of the woodwork to claim her share.

"Oh, and one more thing, Agent."

"Go ahead. I'm listening."

"This dude, Volpe? He runs Parecles Diamond Brokers. He's got a workshop on Forty-seventh Street, right down the block from his office. Stuff moves pretty fast between his office and his workshop, and then it gets shipped out to clients. By stuff, I mean diamonds. What I mean is, if you want that big diamond, you better catch Volpe by tomorrow. Otherwise, I can almost guarantee the stone will be, what do you call it? Cleaved."

CHAPTER TWENTY-FIVE

Dixon's brain worked its wonders. Once in a while, he glanced out the window and noted the landscape twenty thousand miles below. Cold as hell down there. Cold, and dry as a goddamn bone. Talk about ugly. Some of the most desolate landscape he'd ever seen. Dixon thought if he had to live out here in the American hinterlands he'd go psycho within a few weeks. What he needed was a real city. All he'd ever known was cities. Newark and New York. His entire life revolved around those two cities and he didn't much like traveling outside his home territory. A gunrunner needn't travel so much these days, when armored tanks and surface-to-air missiles could be acquired over the Internet.

Dixon came from a long line of gunrunners; he was third generation. Dixon wondered what his grandpa would have said about buying Russian surface-to-air missiles over the Internet. Probably, "Too damn easy. Takes the fun out of it." But Delbert Dixon had a phobia about traveling abroad and so the Internet had become indispensable to his business.

But now the stakes were higher than Dixon had ever expected, the competition fierce. Higher and fiercer than ever before. And only he, Delbert Dixon, held the clue to finding the genuine Lac de Lune. Trap Venus Diamond. Hurt her bad enough and she'll lead you to it. And he intended to do that, take it at any and all costs, and then sell it on the diamond market. Dixon knew exactly where to sell the Lac de Lune for the highest profit. He'd do that, and then he'd retire from the business. Oh joy.

"Crumley."

"Yeah?"

"Put your seat light on. When the flight attendant comes, ask her for two Dewar's on the rocks. Ice side."

Crumley frowned, puzzled.

"Just do what I say."

Dixon unfolded out of the window seat and crawled over Crumley, jerking his head toward the back of the plane. Crumley got it. John.

Crumley looked up and saw an attractive brunette smiling down at him.

Venus sat beside a girl with a face like a seal pup and a gift for chatter. Venus pretended to sleep, leaning her head against the airplane's window. The girl got up and apparently changed seats, because she never returned.

Maybe Mixx was right. Maybe he should have come along to New York. Confronting Volpe might prove dicey. Still, she preferred working alone. Call it her Achilles' heel. Maybe Song. Louie could practically read her mind; they made a good team. At least professionally. But not Mixx. He might come off as slick and urbane, but she sensed Mixx was the sort of agent who followed the letter of the law unquestioningly. Who lacked imagination. She'd rather face down Dixon alone.

And Volpe. This big-time diamond broker. What was his role?

Buzz Radke had been a loner, too. When they were first assigned as partners, both Venus and Radke had balked. Soon enough they discovered their mutual dislike of partnering and that had formed a bond between them. And too, Radke had needed Venus to show him the rural ropes in eastern Washington.

Radke had been following the tube for several years when he first paired up with Venus. He knew the players, or most of them, including Victor Bout, Russia's master of the tube. Bout had made a killing smuggling arms and diamonds in his private jets. "Sockfuls of diamonds," Radke used to say. "Effing sockfuls."

Radke had been a brilliant researcher when he got assigned to NSC's top-priority case tracing the North American arm of the weapons-for-diamonds trade. Venus had taught him how to track, how to stalk the prey. Together they had come within a gnat's ear of pouncing on the enemy. But Fairview, their key link, had foiled their plans. Fairview and his Company 8.

Wait a minute. Venus sat up in her seat.

Tube. What's a tube? Sure, it's just a metaphor for the route illegal trafficking follows. A metaphor, nothing else. Drugs, and humans, and animal parts and weapons and diamonds follow the same route, known in the vernacular as the tube.

What's a tube?

Venus peered out the airplane's window and saw a pale moon rising in a blue velvet, star-studded sky. The plane banked, turned over the harbor, and she saw the lights of Ellis Island, and then of Manhattan proper. In a few minutes, they'd be on the ground, and she'd be working again, her thoughts wrapped around her job. She pulled the airline's flight magazine out of the seat pocket in front of her and started leafing through its pages. Takeoffs and landings rattled her nerves. She perused the magazine's pages, idly flipping, and then suddenly stopped on a page that caught her interest.

The background was solid black, the woman's face barely silhouetted by side lighting. One of her hands, the left hand, rested against her jawline. The nails on her long graceful fingers were perfectly manicured. On her ring finger was a large emerald-cut diamond set in a simple platinum crown on a platinum band. The ad slogan, meant to induce guilt and open wallets, read: "Prove how much you love her."

What had Radke said in the terse e-mail riddle? "Free-range chicks. New York: David Goldman. Antwerp: Rubicon. Jo-burg: Haakvig. Watch out for the Russian. Instructions to follow."

New York

David Goldman lived in the far reaches of Brooklyn Heights in a tired two-story walk-up that since 1919 had reeked of boiled cabbage. A rent-controlled apartment he'd inherited from his parents, may they rest in peace, the dwelling cost David only two hundred dollars a month. If that wasn't enough of a steal, the apartment came with its own balcony facing into an abandoned lot with southern exposure. After his parents had passed on, David had covered over the balcony with a catalog-order sunroom frame, installed lights, and cultivated one of the neighborhood's finest marijuana crops, which he shared with no one. A young man is entitled to his secrets.

Young Goldman was toking a reefer, cleaning a handgun, and watching a Monday-night football rerun when the doorbell rang. Simon Mehta, prompt, as usual. David slouched up off the couch and went to let Mehta in, still uncertain in his mind if he should allow Mehta to leave the apartment alive. Some of life's most important issues are decided spontaneously, and David supposed he'd know when the time came.

Mehta stepped inside the warm apartment, rubbing his gloved hands together. "Ah. The warmth, David, the warmth. Have you any idea how freezing cold is the night? I tell you, it was all I could do to drag myself off my own cozy couch out into the weather."

Shrugging his overcoat into David's outstretched hands, Mehta pretended not to notice the handgun on the coffee table. He sighed. "The subway was the worst, the very worst I've ever seen it. One gentleman actually shoved me to the ground in order to make his train. You can imagine my lack of balance what with carrying this extra weight. And too, I've managed to develop a horrible kink in my groin section." He reached down and demonstrated where. "I tell you, David, I am thrilled to be rid of this albatross."

"Let's have it, then."

Simon Mehta unbuckled his belt and dropped his pants. "And look how chafed I have become, just on the trip out here." He rubbed his inner left thigh before removing the plastic mesh pouch fastened with twine around his waist, dangling between his legs. As he proffered it to David, Simon Mehta's eyes twinkled when David snatched the parcel.

"David, you are such a girl, you really are."

David ignored Mehta's remark, instead making for his workshop in the rear of the apartment. His best testing equipment had been set up on his workbench awaiting the parcel's arrival. Nearby, only one model of the Lac de Lune remained after David had shattered all the rest. On this last model, he hoped to perfect his technique; otherwise, drastic measures would be called for, in the image of one Jean Claud Rubicon. And if David finally had to resort to Rubicon's talents, he'd have to kill the old diamond cutter afterward. That meant both Simon Mehta and Rubicon. Then no one else would remain who knew that David Goldman had lost his magic touch.

David turned on the halogen light above his workbench, sat down and placed the parcel in front of him on the workbench. A thrill sped along his spine as he unwrapped the plastic mesh, untied the cloth covering, and watched as the stone rolled out onto the bench's wooden surface.

It looked real enough. The weight felt right. Taking up his loupe, he peered through the stone's tiny window, the viewing slot carved into the stone's rough outer surface by the Zone Mine geologist. Inside, he saw the gletz and the tiny bubble at its deepest end. Dicey.

Mehta came up behind David and coughed. "Go away," David grumbled. "I can't work with you breathing down my neck. Go in and watch the football game or something, just leave me alone."

He smiled indulgently, although David Goldman missed the performance altogether, his one eye behind the loupe, his other squinted shut. "But David, you must see how I cannot leave you alone with the stone. Not that I don't trust you, not at all, my friend. Only that we are partners in this business, and once you have verified the stone's authenticity, you will give it back to me. I'll keep it safe until you are ready to cut it." David glanced up sharply at Mehta, but Mehta just smiled and finished. "Once we have split the stone into, shall we say, roughly, two parts? Then I will go away. We shall never speak of this again and no one will ever know."

David reached into his shirt pocket, fished out a joint and Bic lighter, lit the joint, and inhaled so deeply that Simon Mehta thought he might pop. Exhaling little bursts of air, he reminded Mehta of a car's faulty exhaust pipe. What a shame, this habit, he thought, the Goldman boy a prisoner to his dope, such a waste of good money and potential talent. Perhaps if he hadn't gone to seed, David might have finally mastered the cleaving art. But no, this was a weakling, a mere shadow of his powerful uncle Yitzhak, the King of Forty-seventh Street. No, David had lost his touch, and now he retained his reputation only through the good graces of his clever friend Simon. It had been Simon who had first suggested the solution to saving David's reputation. For a small sum, very reasonable in Simon Mehta's opinion, Simon couriered gemstones to Jean Claud Rubicon in Antwerp, who cleaved them. Mehta then returned to New York with the cleaved stones and delivered them to David, who in turn handed them over to his uncle Yitzhak, representing himself as the master cleaver.

Yes, indeed, David Goldman owed his reputation to Simon Mehta, and Simon intended that David never forget this important fact.

"All right," David relented. "Just go sit over there."

Simon crossed the little workshop, located a stool in a dark corner, and sat down to watch David from a distance. Leaning back against the wall, the courier's arm nudged something hard. Simon Mehta glanced behind him and saw a gun. A big gun, if he wasn't mistaken, a Russian Kalashnikov. Mehta frowned to himself. When had David started collecting serious guns?

The next thing Simon Mehta knew, David Goldman had attacked him and had pinned him against the wall.

"You sorry son of a bitch!" Goldman snarled into Simon Mehta's face. "This thing's a phony and I'll bet you knew it all along. You think I'm this stupid, you little weasel!"

"But David, why would I, your dear friend—"

"Get out," shouted David Goldman. "Before I kill you."

CHAPTER TWENTY-SIX

It made sense beating the girl to New York. Dixon had work to do, setting things up with his goon, Merle Tremaine, and taking care of business with Volpe before his prey showed up at Volpe's office and confiscated the fake stone Dixon would have left with Volpe. She'd take Volpe into custody as mastermind of the Zone Mine murders. Then Dixon would have it arranged with Merle to nab the girl before she left town. Maybe she'd come along nice and cooperative; maybe Merle'd have to disable her slightly. But she'd come all right. Come to Merle, baby. Because that's where she'd end up, in Merle's clever hands.

Crumley slept during most of the flight home, a blessing Dixon hadn't anticipated, extra time to work out his plan.

Transporting the fake Lac de Lune through airport security proved a snap; Dixon simply dropped the stone in its leather pouch into his pocket and walked past the wand lady without incident. He wondered: If the stone was a real diamond, would the wand catch it?

Maybe just for insurance, he should kill Volpe. Just to ensure he wouldn't name names. Volpe wasn't a regular on the smuggling circuit; he couldn't be fully trusted like his other contact, the laundry man, the diamond broker who accepted the cash for Dixon and other tube masters, the diamantaire who shall remain nameless and faceless to all but Dixon. So, yeah, maybe when the feds arrived, they should find Volpe dead. He'd have to ponder the pros and cons before reaching a final decision. Right now, he was too goddamn bushed to think any farther than Sabryna's bed.

Sabryna opened the door and gasped at the sight of Dixon, her famous simultaneous squeaking and inhaling setting Dixon off right from the start. She mauled him, purring. She laid it on real thick, like she was overjoyed to see him, like she hadn't been whoring around in his absence. Dixon didn't give a monkey's ass, he just wanted out of the cold and a soft bed to sleep on. He might poke her too, if he could get it up. The plane ride from Spokane to Chicago and from there to Newark had taken it out of him; he was exhausted and all he really wanted was sleep. Tomorrow, the poop would hit the fan and Dixon had to be fresh and alert in order to pull off his scheme.

He let Sabryna fawn over him, let her draw him a nice hot bath and afterward use her talented hands on his back, massaging and cooing in tandem. She did a lot of things in tandem. She brought him a nightcap, Stoly on ice, and slipped beneath the covers beside him, cozying up a bit more than he needed at the moment.

"Crumley work out okay?" Sabryna asked as she traced the curve of Dixon's ear. It tickled and he slapped her hand away. She recoiled but didn't complain.

"Yeah. He worked out fine."

Sabryna smiled. "I know you've been worried about him lately, him being so dense and all. But, hey, you couldn't ask for a more faithful employee."

"Oh, yeah."

It came out dull and sarcastic and Sabryna pouted. Dixon

reached over and patted her shoulder. "He's a fine employee, sugar, faithful as a damn hound. A little boneheaded is all."

"I never said he was the sharpest pencil in the box," she defended herself. "Only that he's as faithful and trustworthy as they come. I'll bet he did everything you told him to do, and did it without complaining, too."

Dixon allowed that Crumley had been cooperative. "But he asks questions, Sabryna. Ever since he started working for me, what? Twenty years ago? He always asks the stupidest questions. I don't like that in an employee. It grates. You know how impatient I am with stupidness. Worst part is, he asks the same questions over and over again, each time like it was the first time, like he doesn't remember he already asked the same thing. He might have early onset Alzheimer's for all I know."

Sabryna tittered. "I don't think so. He's just kind of dull-headed, that's all."

"C'mere, baby. Hold Daddy's pecker nice and tight."

Sabryna obliged, reaching underneath the covers and finding the needy object instantly. She had a good aim, lots of practice. That was part of her charm. Hell, most of it. But she was smart, too, smartest whore Dixon had ever known, which made her all the more desirable.

"You did a fine job, baby," Dixon murmured as she caressed the flaccid organ. "You played it out like a champ. And she fell for it, too. She's on a flight to New York even as we speak."

"Thanks, sweetie." Sabryna didn't exactly blush at the compliment, but she felt her pride swell pleasantly, and she held him a little tighter, squeezing now and then, in case it might help the process along.

"Now tomorrow, I have another job for you. Do you know the diamond district?"

"You mean Forty-seventh Street, up there?"

Dixon grunted, which Sabryna took to mean "Yes, up there."

"All's I know about that street is it's full of Hassidic Jews carrying briefcases handcuffed to their wrists. I've been on that street a few times, but to say I actually know the Diamond District would be stretching it."

Speaking of stretching it, Sabryna felt movement in the object she caressed.

"I'll need you to go up there tomorrow morning. Meet a man who's never met me but who knows my name and reputation. Meet him and deliver a message from me. First, you'll need to call him. Have him meet you at the dairy bar on Broadway and Forty-seventh."

"Honey, can we talk about this later?"

"Yeah, sure, babe. In the morning." Dixon yawned. "Okay. That's enough for now, sugar. Put your hand away. I just gotta sleep."

"But, honey, it's been so long. And I'm so horny."

"Shut the fuck up, Sabryna, and let a man sleep." Dixon turned over and immediately slipped off into dreamland.

Venus's flight arrived late after circling the airport in a holding pattern until the runway could be cleared of ice and snow. She had only carry on luggage and made it to the front of the queue at the taxi stand. She was halfway into the city in the back seat of a cab when her cell phone rang.

"You found Dixon yet?"

"Mixx, I'm in a taxi on the way into the city. Give me another fifteen minutes or so and I'll have him in custody."

"Ha, ha." Mixx's falsetto laugh.

"Anyway, I'm more interested in the diamond broker."

"Volpe?"

"I'm betting Dixon works for him."

"Maybe I should come out there, too." Mixx, being chivalrous, or perhaps envious.

"I'm okay. And it's going to take a day to set things up. Come tomorrow, if you feel the urge."

"You'll keep us apprised of developments?"

"Now you're sounding like Wexler."

"Never met the son of a bitch. I've heard he's a hard-ass boss."

"Mmm." Noncommittal.

"You be careful."

"What's to be careful? I'm in New York. Nobody knows me from Alice in Wonderland." She disconnected and sat back against the smooth vinyl seat for the rest of the ride.

Her room at the Washington Square Hotel faced onto Waverly Place with a view of Washington Square Park, now coated with snow, looking pristine beneath the soft glow of street lamps, not a dope dealer or pigeon dropping in sight, just two patrol cars, one on the north side of the park, the other on the east side, maybe waiting for action. They might have to wait a long time. Even the most hardened derelicts had fled indoors out of the cold.

The bed was a sleeper's nightmare, the mattress at once hard and lumpy, and the synthetic-fiber sheets so threadbare the frayed blanket poked through. The slick bottom sheet and the mattress cover shifted constantly underneath her like the San Andreas fault, two opposing layers sliding toward disaster, threatening to spill her out onto the floor. She lay still, thinking about Sarah Fairview and her children.

The third child not yet born. And the other women of Company 8, like Sarah, dutiful wives and mothers, meek women who had surrendered their strength to their men, the men of Company 8, who had suddenly disappeared, whose women denied knowing where they had gone. Like they'd disappeared off the face of the earth. She remembered the hatch in the meadow behind the red barn at Lay-A-Day Ranch. Sarah had said they had bought the land cheap because it was a former Defense Department radioactive materials burial site. Like Hanford, or Rocky Flats. Or might the hatch have been used as an old missile silo? No. Sarah said the Realtor had told her husband when he bought the property that the land had been a burial site for radioactive waste. They were warned to stay clear of the field. Radio-activity.

Wait a minute.

She sat up, triggering a landslide of bed linens.

When Sarah came on the line, she sounded sleepy.

"Sorry to call so late, Sarah."

"That's okay. I wasn't really asleep."

"Sarah, when you first moved onto the ranch, do you re-member seeing the hatch out in the field?"

"The old hatches? Let me think when was the first time I saw one of them."

"You mean there are more than one?"

Sarah hesitated. "As I recall, there are about five or six of them scattered around the field."

Venus waited. Beside the bed, the radiator hissed and spat. Snowflakes accumulating on the windowsill had formed a sloping drift that partly obscured her view of the park.

"I guess the first time I actually saw one of the hatches wasn't until after Jacob was born. That was almost a year af-ter we had moved onto the ranch. Ron had warned us to never go out into the field, it was dangerous, he said, we might be contaminated with radioactivity. I'd never gone closer to the field than the barn, and then only when my older son would play hide-and-seek and I'd go out to the barn to look for him. Then one day, Jonah ran into the field before I could catch him and I had to run after him. I was so terrified Ron would see us in the field, but luckily he had gone into the barn. I was able to grab Jonah and run back out of the field before Ron came outside. I remember stubbing my toe on something, looking down and seeing the hatch, a large round metal hatch, and then another one not far from the first."

"Just two?"

"Ron mentioned on several occasions that he'd found more hatches out there. I recall him saying five or six were spread around the field."

"You don't recall seeing the hatches before you actually moved onto the ranch?"

"Oh, no, certainly not. I didn't even see the ranch until after my husband bought it. And then, it was six or seven months later when we finally moved onto the property. We had to sell our house in town first."

Mixx must have been in a bar, because when he answered his cell phone she heard raucous background noise, and what sounded like a live country-and-western band.

"Where are you?"

"Alki Tavern."

"What in the hell is a cosmopolite like you doing in that dive?"

"Ever been here?"

"Negative."

"Then stop sneering. For all you know, the Alki Tavern might be a fine gentlemen's club with the music turned up a little too loud."

"I need you to go back over to the Lay-A-Day."

Mixx didn't reply right away. Venus peered out the hotel window. Snow had been falling for nearly an hour, the patrol cars had abandoned the park, and now a man or woman, she couldn't tell which, was taking up residence beside the arch on the park's north side, crawling into a cardboard box, a thin barrier from the snow. Venus shivered.

"Why?"

"Those hatches in the field behind Fairview's barn."

"What do you mean 'hatches'? I thought you said there's only one."

"I spoke with Mrs. Fairview. She remembers now her husband saying several hatches are scattered around the field. You need to open them up. Look inside. Verify Sarah Fairview's explanation of what's inside."

"You must be taking drugs. I can't believe you want me to drive all the way over to eastern Washington to commit suicide."

"Nothing will happen."

"Are you kidding? Mrs. Fairview told us the ranch land belonged to the Defense Department and was a burial ground for radioactive waste. Expose yourself. I'm not stupid enough to radiate my ass."

"Mixx, listen to me. First thing you do is check with the Department of Defense. Determine if they ever conducted nuclear testing or stored radioactive materials at the Lay-A-Day site."

"Mrs. Fairview already told us they had. That's why they got the land so cheap."

"Sarah Fairview might have been misinformed by her husband. To keep her away from those hatches. So she wouldn't know what's really down there."

Mixx snickered. The background noise had revved up another notch. "What's really down there?"

"I don't know for sure."

"What's your best guess?"

Venus wrapped the thin blanket around her shoulders. "A tunnel."

Mixx chuckled. "A tunnel, you say?"

"Just check it out, that's all I ask."

A woman's voice came on the line. "Honey, Eddie-Teddy can't talk anymore. He's busy, see?"

"Put him back on."

Venus heard little struggling sounds, then the woman squeaked. Mixx said, "Sorry about that."

"Who is she?"

"What's it to you? Some bar bunny. Very drunk. She just grabbed the phone from me. I sent her away. She's over at the bar, pouting."

"Oh, yeah? Some bar bunny? She knew your name."

"Everyone here knows my name. Lately I'm a regular."

"Since when are you a regular at that dive?"

The bar bunny might take Mixx home with her. Mixx could fool around with the bar bunny if he felt like it. She should butt out.

Mixx continued. "Hey, the poachers you busted just before they hauled you off to Canada. Ebert and what's-his-name. Up on the Peninsula."

"What about them? The case is open and shut, ready for trial. And it belongs to Interior, not you guys."

"Not quite. There's more. Drugs, too, but I can't elaborate right now."

"And how does Ms. Bar Bunny fit into the picture?"

"Look, I'm doing a favor for your pal Song. Bar Bunny may be a stool pigeon. I'll run the details by you later. I have to go now. Ms. Bunny's starting to strip."

"All I ask is that you double-check Sarah Fairview's explanation of those hatches in the field. Oh, and one more thing."

"Yeah?"

"Yitzhak Goldman. What did you find out?"

"The King of Forty-seventh Street checks out cleaner than a Maytag ad. Your hunch is off."

"Maybe."

She hung up abruptly. Remade the bed. Searched the room for more blankets. No such luck. She peered out the window. The homeless person in the cardboard box seemed to have fallen asleep, snow now coating the cardboard box. Behind her, in the hotel room, the radiator rattled, putting out dry, comforting heat. She thanked her lucky stars she had more than thin cardboard for shelter, and slipped beneath the bedcovers. A minute later, she was asleep.

CHAPTER TWENTY-SEVEN

Crumley rolled in around two A.M., noting with dismay that several of his houseplants had withered in his absence. He dropped his suitcase in the bedroom, found the watering can in the kitchen, and gave every plant food and water, the nourishment they had lacked in his absence. He'd been gone longer than he'd expected, otherwise he would have asked old Mr. Wilson down the hall to care for his houseplants. Should have. Should always have a backup plan. He put the watering can away, underneath the kitchen sink where he'd found it, ordered in a sausage-and-anchovy pizza, and foraged in the fridge for a bottle of Millers, pleased to discover an entire six-pack he'd forgotten about because he'd hidden it in the bottom crisper drawer, saving it for a desperate occasion. Like now. A man needs cold beer with his pizza. He popped a top off a High Life and guzzled the entire bottle, his Adam's apple bobbing like a Halloween game. While he waited for the pizza delivery, he went into the bedroom and unpacked his suitcase.

It had been his foster mother's suitcase, the same luggage he had packed with his few belongings when he had run away from that foster home twenty-some years ago. The suitcase had held up nicely, being an expensive Skyway, real leather, white turned ivory over the years, sturdy, with plenty of blue satin elasticized pockets inside. He set the suitcase on the foot of his bed, flicked open the two latches and raised the top, smiling at the beautiful job he'd made of packing his clothes. If nothing else, Crumley was a neat man, and he knew how to fold his clothes.

He sorted underwear and socks for the laundry and set aside shirts and trousers for the dry cleaner, then, as was his habit, he ran his hand over the suitcase's satin pockets in case he'd missed anything. And apparently he had. A side pocket bulged beneath his hand. He pulled back the elastic and reached inside. Out came a small tape recorder and some of those little microcassettes. Emptying the pocket, he counted twelve microcassettes in all. Damn Dixon had trespassed on his luggage, probably ran out of room in his own, hadn't bothered informing Crumley that he'd put the girl's tape recorder and cassettes in his luggage. What if his suitcase had been searched at the airport? What if they'd found the tapes and decided to listen to them? Crumley's ass would be busted, while Dixon would sail through security without a hitch. He thought about calling Dixon up right now at Sabryna's place and giving him the what-for, but in the end opted for job security. Dixon was the boss, after all, and could fire Crumley on the slightest whim. Crumley had seen Dixon do that to other employees.

Crumley's low-rent three-room apartment had been furnished off the street from various items people had left out on the sidewalk for just such people as himself. The living room windows faced onto a pretty tree-lined street. In winter, when the leaves had fallen and died, when like now the empty branches were coated with snow, dripping icicles, the cold sun slanted at an angle that washed the room. His plants loved this winter light and so he kept his curtains open day and night. The sofa, an old maroon chesterfield, fuzzy fabric, had faded from sun exposure, its armrests worn thin, and the seat cushions had been lumpy ever since Crumley had rescued the sofa from the street. Beside the sofa, a small Ikea end table supported a huge white ceramic lamp, its base shaped like a pair of smooth buttocks. The dusty pink shade had frayed scarlet fringe. When Crumley had plucked it off a street corner, the fringe was almost completely torn off and just hanging, but he brought it home and sewed the fringe back on, and the lamp was as good as new.

Dust had accumulated on everything during his absence but Crumley decided to wait until morning to houseclean. He sat back on the maroon chesterfield and studied the tape recorder and microcassettes. The microcassettes were numbered from one to twelve. He popped microcassette number one into the tape recorder, found the controls, and turned it on.

The girl's voice reminded him of Charlotte Rampling, his all-time favorite movie actress even though she was old enough to be his mother. A deep, throaty voice that belonged only to strong women, the kind of women who'd just as soon be on top but who would play it any way you liked it. Sexy.

Crumley had heard some of the Karen Crandall tapes when driving Dixon around out West, when Dixon would play them just for something to do. The story the girl told had saddened Crumley; her youth in Canada had been much like his own, foster home to foster home, passed around like an old shoe. But she had managed to put herself through school, more than Crumley could say for himself. She had gone to college in Canada and learned to be a geologist. Then her adventure began when she moved up to the Northwest Territories and went to work for this prospector fellow named Big Jim Hardy, as a geologist at Hardy's company, called Zone Mine.

Together, Hardy and the girl—Crumley still didn't know her name—had prospected way up north near a lake called Lac de Lune. That's where they had discovered diamonds, according to the girl, and that was where the first tape ended.

Crumley found tape number two and played it, but got only a few minutes into it when the pizza delivery interrupted him. He got up and buzzed the delivery boy into the building, then found his wallet and drew out a twenty-dollar bill. When the boy came to the door, Crumley traded the twenty for the pizza, telling the boy to keep the change. Crumley went into the kitchen and placed the pizza box on the small gate-leg table, popped another Miller, and continued listening to the girl's story. The tapes were thirty minutes long each side and he'd finished what he could eat of the pizza before tape number two ended. He was tired and the food had made him sleepy, so he carried the tape recorder and his beer into the bedroom, undressed, and went into the bathroom to shower, placing the tape recorder on pause. When he returned wearing fresh pajamas, he clicked off the pause button and crawled into bed, placing the tape recorder on his chest.

The girl spoke with a kind of reverence about her days at university, remembering a particular professor with fondness. "He was like a father to me," she said in what Crumley thought was a wistful voice. "And then one night after dinner at his home with his wife and family, he molested me on the drive home. Right then and there, I lost all faith in parental figures and I almost committed suicide that night."

A tear streaked down Crumley's cheek. He wiped it with the sleeve of his pajamas. He had so much in common with this girl. If only she'd lived. Maybe they could've become friends. Maybe even lovers. Why the hell did Dixon have to kill her? Dixon had no effing morals, no respect for human life.

He fell asleep before tape number three had ended, vowing to listen to every tape up until the end. The end being when Dixon had plugged her through the brain.

The Barrens, Northwest Territories

The polar bear stirred and slowly woke from her artificially induced torpor. She might have felt pain; she might have felt hunger. She might have thought of her cubs. In her stirrings, she struck out once or twice with her paws, as if batting at the gigantic arctic mosquitoes she had to endure in summer months. But no mosquitoes disturbed her on this freezing winter's night, only their memories. She slowly opened her eyes and gazed around. Not much to see; the bear had been caged inside a small shack. If she looked in the right direction, she would see moonlight seeping beneath the door, creeping across the bare wood floor, casting a pale light on her swollen belly. It had been shaved, invaded, and sewn up again with perfect stitches.

A scraping sound startled the bear and she rolled halfway over. The door flew open and moonlight filled the cabin.

The bear's eyes reflected the green northern lights and sheer terror.

Gordon Volpe woke as usual to his Bose radio alarm, National Public Radio news just rounding out the hour, a soft, soothing female voice reporting on a new mass gravesite found in Rwanda. The quality of the reporter's voice made the event sound like a children's Easter egg hunt.

Volpe practically bounced out of bed, so soundly had he slept during the night. He showered and shaved, scrubbed his fingernails and lotioned his hands, and, noting icicles hanging from the gargoyle outside his bedroom window, dressed in his heaviest-weight black wool suit, adding a cashmere vest underneath the jacket for extra protection against the elements.

"Winter is indeed upon us," Volpe commented out loud to himself, since he was alone. Volpe enjoyed waking up alone; he rarely brought his wife to the Manhattan town house. A distinctly manly odor permeated the apartment, and each time he stepped inside, Volpe inhaled the scent of freedom. But the place would have to go if anything went wrong in this once-in-a-lifetime commission of illegal activity, say, if he had to leave the country suddenly and never return. He had made the necessary arrangements for just such a dreaded outcome, just in case; he had a friend in Brazil, a diamond-mine owner whose *garimpeiros* drew their barges through the swampy riverbanks, skimming the alluvial beds for diamonds. He could flee to Brazil, where his friend had invited Volpe to join his business, part of which involved, Volpe suspected, a deep commitment to the De Beers cartel. Well, Volpe could grit his teeth and surrender to De Beers. De Beers wasn't going away anytime soon. In the diamond trade, De Beers, like its trademark slogan, was forever. And so he had this backup plan, including a first-class airplane ticket to Rio, just in case. Crystal and the children would have to fend for themselves, and that needled his conscience, but since he had no intention of allowing his scheme to go wrong, Volpe gave little thought to that what-if.

The snow of the previous night had turned to slush the consistency of petroleum jelly and Volpe dodged the worst of it, hopscotching onto little patches of bare sidewalk all the way to the corner of East Eighty-sixth Street and Fifth Avenue. With the languid aplomb of a lifetime New Yorker, Volpe dangled a limp Michelangelo hand and a taxi appeared instantly. Half an hour later, he was entering his office building on West Forty-seventh Street when Volpe literally bumped into Simon Mehta. Mehta, exiting the building with his eyes cast downward at the slippery sidewalk, hadn't noticed Volpe, and Volpe, moving at his usual hurried clip, couldn't avoid the collision. Simon Mehta careened sideways, skidding on the sidewalk, losing his balance and his hat, falling forward and down shoulder first into a pile of slush.

"Oops," quipped Volpe as if he'd let loose a soft fart in public, and sidestepping the fallen Mehta, he pushed open the building's door.

"You could help a man back onto his feet," grumbled Mehta, but Volpe hadn't heard him and was already inside the building heading for the elevator when his cell phone rang.

Dixon. Volpe's heart pounded in his chest.

"It's here."

"How soon can you come?"

"Give me an hour. I'm way downtown, and the snow's—"

"Fine, fine. Just come straight up to my office. Be very careful traveling to Midtown."

Dixon laughed into Volpe's ear. "Hell, I've traveled twenty-five hundred miles with this thing strapped to my groin, and never once been bothered. I doubt the last thirty blocks will present a problem."

"Well, just be careful," repeated Volpe. "You never know."

Simon Mehta found purchase against a fire hydrant and struggled to his feet, cursing Volpe as he checked for injuries. Finding nothing broken, just bruises, Mehta gathered his dignity and loped off down Forty-seventh Street. At Broadway, he turned right and walked half a block to a small dairy bar, went inside, ordered a plain keifer, and stood at the counter drinking it and marveling at Volpe's lack of common courtesy.

Mehta's brand-new overcoat, soaked through from the slush, sent damp cold through his body; almost instantly, he felt a fever coming on and the idea of going home to bed appealed to him. But no. Business before comfort. He checked his watch. Two minutes later, precisely on time, the woman who had called him that morning appeared in the entrance of the dairy, looking woefully out of context. She had told him she would be wearing a red leather jacket, that's how he would recognize her. It was a tight-fitting scarlet thing she wore over a couple of cantaloupes. She might have had a pretty face once. She looked like a streetwalker, and it was all Simon Mehta could do to gather enough courage to nod her way. She hustled inside the dairy, ignoring the sidelong glances and the palpable scorn infusing the atmosphere. She had a hard-bitten hooker's face, her jaw set tight, a world-weary expression that Mehta thought aged her about twenty years, and yet she wasn't hard to look at as long as you didn't mind focusing on the cantaloupes and lusting in your heart. Her head was bare but she had had the sense enough to wear gloves in this frigid weather, and now as she joined Mehta at the counter, she peeled them off, momentarily suggesting she might be about to perform a striptease. Mehta kept a space between them and gestured toward a booth. She walked ahead of him, past the tables of men in black hats and ringlets, their eyes downcast to avoid contact with a whore. She slid into one side of the booth, Mehta into the other.

"You're Mr. Simon Mehta?" she asked.

He nodded and squirmed slightly in the booth.

"I'm the person who spoke with you over the phone early this morning."

She had a Midwesterner accent, a bland, nondescript newscaster's voice. But she was no newscaster. Not this painted odalisque. Mehta felt a stirring in his groin. He crossed his legs and drummed his fingers on the tabletop.

"So who are you, and what do you want with a simple man such as myself?"

The woman smiled coyly, unzipped the leather jacket, revealing a low-cut sweater that barely contained the two large white perfectly matched globes that Mehta thought might actually be real. She tossed her head back and her blond hair fell over one side of her face, completely covering one eye. The other eye, the shade of a fine sapphire, Mehta noted, sparkled. She'd been gorgeous once.

"My name is Sabryna. That's all you need to know. No last names, if you please. Well, I know yours, but that doesn't matter because everybody in the business knows your name."

"What business?"

"You know."

Mehta shook his head. "Maybe. Maybe not. Tell me. To what business do you refer?"

"The tube."

Careful not to show even a glimmer of recognition of the

word and its meaning, Mehta lowered his voice slightly and lied, "I do not understand."

Sabryna feigned a yawn.

"I'm a smart girl, mister, so don't try playing games with me. You and I both know what tubing means. Every diamond dealer knows the tubes exist, whether or not he takes advantage of them. Now, I have an offer from Delbert that could make you a pile of cash."

Simon glanced around the dairy. "We shouldn't discuss such business in this place. Too many ears. Perhaps we could take a little walk?"

Sabryna left the dairy first and walked to the corner of Broadway and Forty-seventh Street where she waited. A few minutes passed and then she saw Mehta approaching. Together they turned down Forty-seventh Street and walked west, carefully avoiding icy patches on the sidewalk. Sabryna explained her relationship to Dixon. "I'm Delbert's go-between, you might say, like yourself, a courier of sorts. But what I have to deliver isn't diamonds."

He glanced up at the woman's face. She had a good six inches on him. "Then what?"

Sabryna looked around as if for eavesdroppers lurking on the bustling sidewalk. When it seemed safe, she pulled one hand out of her red leather jacket and with it a small Polaroid photograph, which she handed to him.

Mehta studied the image no longer than five seconds before thrusting the picture into his overcoat pocket.

"You recognize it of course."

He nodded.

"So you see, although I said I did not come to deliver diamonds, I have stretched the truth a tiny bit. The bottom line is, Delbert has the Lac de Lune, or else a good replica, and he wants to be certain if this stone in his possession is genuine or fake."

Mehta felt his heart race. Carefully, he queried, "Why me?"

They had reached a corner and were waiting for a chance

to cross against the traffic. Sabryna leaned down and said softly, "Because you know diamonds better than anyone in this city."

He blinked. "Why, that's not true at all. Any number of diamantaires in this city know diamonds far better than I, a simple courier."

"Delbert doesn't trust any of the diamond brokers. He's not taking any chances."

Sabryna handed Mehta a business card. "Delbert will be at the information counter in Grand Central Station at exactly noon today." She consulted a watch on her wrist. "That is exactly half an hour from now. He will have the stone with him. You will recognize him by a black patch he will wear over one eye, and a green scarf. He knows how to recognize you. When you meet, hand him this business card. He will then ask you for the photograph. Show it to him."

The light changed and Simon Mehta stepped into the crosswalk. Instead of accompanying him across the street, Sabryna turned and hurried off in the opposite direction.

He stared down at the business card, amazed.

Gordon Volpe was listed in the telephone directory under "Diamond Brokers."

GORDON VOLPE, LUXOR BUILDING, 5 W. 47TH STREET
PHONE NUMBER (212) 555–0321.

Venus wrote down the address and phone number and e-mailed the same information to Mixx in Seattle and Wexler in Washington, D.C. Before leaving the hotel, Venus loaded her gun and placed it in a holster strapped to her right side. Things might get ugly. This anonymous caller was surely a setup, but it was the best lead so far in the case, and she'd be negligent if she didn't follow it up.

Snow had begun falling again, this time a light dusting.

When she emerged from a taxi at the corner of Sixth Avenue and Forty-seventh Street, Venus looked around for the Luxor Building, easily locating it in the center of the block. Across the street was a small coffee shop. She ducked inside, found a window seat that looked out into the street in front of the Luxor's entrance, and ordered breakfast. While she waited, she sipped coffee and watched the street traffic, mostly Hassidic men dressed in dark suits and overcoats, wearing black fedoras above their ringlets and carrying briefcases. Bent over against the chill wind, they hurried intently along the cavernous streets.

The Luxor Building was nondescript, ten stories high, dwarfed by the taller buildings on either side. It was made of pink granite, its windows small but numerous, the front entrance double glass doors. Once in a while, a figure would emerge from the building, hurrying away down the street. More often, people would enter the building, usually men, usually carrying briefcases, always slightly bent over and wearing a furtive expression.

The waiter brought her breakfast; scrambled eggs, a bacon side, sourdough bread. When he returned moments later to refresh her coffee, she said, "Has Volpe been in for breakfast yet?"

The middle-aged man scowled. "How would I know? This place was packed this morning, everyone trying to get in out of the snow. Bunch o'seesees. They wanna see snow, they should be so lucky. I'll show them snow. I've seen snow in my life, real snow."

He had a Russian accent.

"Let me guess. Siberia?"

"You Americans call it Sigh-beria. Poof! It's See-bee-ria. Can you say that?"

"See-bee-ria."

"*Harascho.*" He turned to go.

"Wait a minute," said Venus. "What about Volpe? He come in here very often?"

The waiter came back to her table. "You mean Mr. Volpe from the building across the street?" He pointed. "That Mr. Volpe?"

"Yeah. That Mr. Volpe."

The waiter tilted his head and began counting silently on his fingers. "Six days," he finally replied. "Six days since he's come here. Strange, 'cause he used to come every morning promptly at seven-thirty. You one of his clients?"

"You might say that. But I've never met him in person, see? And he told me to meet him at the restaurant straight across Forty-seventh Street from the Luxor Building. I didn't see any other restaurant on this block so I came in here. Problem is, we've never met in person and I don't know what he looks like."

"Ah." The waiter nodded, understanding most of what she had said. "So he don't know what you look like and you don't know what he look like and maybe then you miss each other. Right?"

"That's what I'm thinking. In my head."

The waiter laughed. "In your head? You say 'thinking in your head'? Where else can a person think from? From his fingers?"

"It's an American expression. But yeah, that's what I was thinking. In my head."

The waiter nodded and hurried off to a table where several diners were pleading for coffee refills. On his way back to the kitchen, Venus caught his eye and jerked her head. He understood her body language and scuttled back over to the table.

"More coffee, miss?"

"Sure. And I was wondering if you could describe Mr. Volpe. So I'll recognize him when he comes in."

"Tall, very thin, very handsome young man, maybe thirty-five, thirty-six. Nice blond hair, lots of it. He won't go bald. Very, how do you say, groomed? Yes, very groomed and very elegant." The waiter smiled, proud of his English, and added,

"Of course, he will be wearing a diamond ring on his small-est finger, what you call the pinky. Yes, I think to say you will recognize him when he comes in."

"Hey, thanks. What's your name?"

"Gennady. Gennady Fedosov. Once I was famous man in USSR. I run biggest mine in Siberia." He sighed. "But now, now look at me. This is what price I pay for freedoms."

"Maybe no one's told you, Gennady. The Communists lost. Russia is a republic now."

Gennady laughed from deep in his gut. "Of course, of course. You think I don't know that? I was there when it all happened. But then, you see, came chaos. And the Mob. You know what Mob is?"

"Gotcha."

Gennady shrugged, showing her two empty palms. "So here I am, washing dishes, cleaning tables. But hey, better this than driving taxi."

Excusing himself, Gennady returned to the kitchen. Venus looked out the window. *Now,* she thought.

Taking out her cell phone, she punched in Gordon Volpe's office number. Three rings later, a man's voice answered.

"Volpe."

"Good morning, Mr. Volpe. My name is Caroline Sexton and I am looking for an engagement ring. That is, my fiancé is looking for one, but he has asked me to do the groundwork for him, you know? You were recommended to me by a friend of a friend of my mother's. I realize how silly that sounds, but six degrees of separation, you know? I am looking for some-thing in the area of four carats, and just the stone. I already have the setting."

"Miss Sexton, I am afraid you have too little knowledge of the diamond business. In the first place, you should always acquire the stone first, before the setting. Secondly, as a bro-ker, I acquire diamonds strictly for my wholesale clients. I do not, except in very special circumstances, for example, a close friend, locate and procure diamonds for retail clients. And so

I'm very sorry, but I don't think I can be of any help to you, although I do wish you luck in your search and happiness in your upcoming marriage."

"Oh, no." Venus made tiny whining sounds. "Oh, this is absolutely disastrous. You see, I need to find my diamond by this afternoon. Our engagement party is just a month away, and my jeweler has promised to place the diamond in the setting I've already picked out in time for the party. But I must deliver the stone to him before five o'clock this evening. I'm at a loss, Mr. Volpe. I need someone who knows diamonds to help me pick one out. Could you . . . would you consider an offer of a generous fee to accompany me to Parecles and help me select a stone?"

"Miss Sexton, I must tell you that I sympathize entirely with your predicament and I do wish that I were available to assist you. However, I am expecting an important client this morning and simply cannot leave my office until I have finished up my business."

"What time would that be?"

"Miss Sexton, I'm truly sorry, I just can't be of any help to you."

Sobs and sniffles. "Perhaps later this afternoon? When you've finished with your client?"

"I'm very sorry, but—"

"Mr. Volpe, let's talk turkey here. I'm going to make you an offer you can't resist."

"Really, Miss Sexton—"

"No, I'm serious. Hear me out. I belong to a national association of women attorneys. You may have heard of us—Women Esquires? We are a powerful lobby, and we represent a group of affluent women with huge amounts of disposable income. We've recently begun a buyer's club, which has proposed that every woman in our association purchase her own 'me' ring. You know, the right-hand diamond."

"Of course, I am very aware of the trend."

"Let's not kid each other, Mr. Volpe. It was a De Beers marketing device, completely created in an advertising agency.

And brilliant. We're talking a lot of diamonds here. A lot of disposable income. A lot of self-centered female attorneys who can afford to pamper themselves. I can deliver the account to you."

Volpe considered. The "me" ring business might make a nice little stash. Maybe enough to buy that apartment Crystal loved near the Champs-Elysées. More important, meeting a client at Parecles, being seen at the wholesale shop, might contribute to the appearance that nothing had changed in his life. Once he had delivered the Lac de Lune to his client, he'd be free of all the charades, but for the time being, his business affairs must appear normal and aboveboard. He sighed, letting Miss Sexton know that she had touched his heart.

"All right, then, Miss Sexton. I have to visit my workshop this afternoon in any case. This is where we show our loose stones. I can take you along. Can you come to my office at one-thirty this afternoon?"

"Oh, my God, Mr. Volpe, of course I can come. You're an angel, you truly are."

"You realize that under these circumstances I am waiving the normal security precautions. We rarely admit strangers into our facilities, for obvious reasons. I want you to come alone."

"Oh, absolutely, Mr. Volpe. Absolutely."

Gennady Fedosov had apparently gone off duty because another waiter brought the check. She had wanted to ask the Russian if the Siberian mine had dug coal or diamonds.

The worn wood floor of Rubicon's studio had all but disappeared underneath shards of zircon from shattered models of the Lac de Lune. Rubicon had somehow managed to break his own record for model shattering, having now failed to successfully cleave five out of seven of the great diamond's facsimiles. Five. What incompetence from a man of his stature! Was this damned gletz so capricious that even he, Jean Claud Rubicon, the world's greatest cleaver in the opinion of more than one diamantaire, would in the end fail to cleave the real thing successfully?

And what exactly in this instance defined success? Rubicon had set the bar high; of the 384 carats in the Lac de Lune, the cleaving should result in a loss of no more than twenty-eight carats, and those divided into no more than twelve parts, all producing magnificent gems. Twenty-eight carats. Was it too much to ask of himself? Rubicon tore at his hair and cursed every member of his family starting back with his great-grandmother and including his sister in Brussels who remained his only living relation. Cursed them all to hell. When he'd completed the family litany, he finished up by cursing himself, but alas, he felt no better than before, and now, as Rubicon sat at his cleaving bench, he reached a grave decision.

If he failed to successfully cleave these last two stones, Rubicon would hang himself from the rafters in the ceiling of his studio. If, as he was beginning to suspect, age had robbed him of his brilliant talents, had dropped a tremble into his cleaving arm and clouded his vision, if indeed this were the case, he had no reason to continue living, none whatsoever.

Francine would take care of Kors and Krum, feed and water them, and keep up his garden. His sister would arrive from Brussels to gather up his meager belongings and empty his bank account as if she deserved a farthing of his life's savings, having never once come to visit, not even at New Year's, having never once sent him a letter, not even a postcard, having telephoned him over the past twenty years perhaps five or six times, just to let him know that she was still alive and kicking, just to check on his health, and how close he might be to kicking the milk can.

He should change his will. Leave it all to Kors and Krum. Yes, that's it. Before tackling the last two models, Rubicon would summon his solicitor and arrange the necessary codicil. To hell with Marcella. Sisters are good for nothing, absolutely nothing.

Rubicon stared down at the cluttered floor. Through the window, a cold winter's sunbeam infused light into the fractured simulated shards, sending up motes of dancing light along the walls and across his cleaver's table, tiny flickers hovering there to mock his foundering talents. A man is only as good as his talent, and when that goes, so should the man.

Kors barked, a sharp sudden sound startling Rubicon out of his turgid melancholy. He stood and went to the window, looking down below for the source of Kors's agitation. Now Krum had joined in, the two Dobermans' vicious barking echoing up and down Treble Lane. And then Rubicon saw him, that same dark-skinned little man standing across the lane just out of reach of the tethered dogs, looking up at Rubicon's window.

"What in hell do you want?" shouted Rubicon through the open window. "I have already told you to get lost."

The man attempted a smile but only managed to grimace. Once he found his voice, he called up to Rubicon. "Simon Mehta sent me. You must believe this and let me come up and speak to you. It is very important."

Rubicon spat out the window. "Are you some kind of idiot? Haven't I already told you to go away?"

"But Mr. Mehta says it is vital that I deliver his message."

Rubicon considered. He could take his pistol from beneath his mattress and shoot at the man, not to strike him, only to run him off, or he could slam the window shut and ignore him, but then Kors and Krum would bark endlessly, driving him mad, or he might call the police to have the man removed, but he hated the police, such busybodies, or, and this seemed the most absurd but perhaps the most practical solution, he could invite the man up and give him the briefest of audiences before sending him tumbling back down the stairs to the ground where the Dobermans would feed on his limbs.

"Show me some proof that Mehta sent you."

The little man tilted his head as if thinking it over, then reached into his overcoat and removed a small jeweler's case, the size jewelers used for rings. Looking around as if to check that they were alone, the man slowly opened the jeweler's box and held it up at arm's length for Rubicon's benefit.

"I can't see that far," grumbled Rubicon. "Just a minute." He left the window and searched the shop until he found his binoculars. Back at the window, he peered out at the object the little man was holding at arm's length.

If Rubicon's eyes weren't deceiving him, the little man was in possession of the grand pink marquise diamond that Rubicon had cut and polished and given to the courier, Simon Mehta. It could be a fake, so many people made facsimiles these days, but something about the way the stone glittered in the sunlight told Rubicon this was the very same pink diamond he had cleaved out of rough and cut and polished into the brilliant marquise shape and then delivered into Simon Mehta's hands.

Rubicon called to the dogs, ordering them to allow the little man past and into the garden. He went downstairs and unlocked the door, opening it cautiously in case the little man pulled a gun or tried some trick. But to Rubicon's relief, the man just bowed and said, "It is a great privilege to meet the master of diamond cleavers."

"Come on up," Rubicon growled.

If the layer of shattered simulated diamond coating the floor caught the little man's attention, he didn't show it. He stood silently as Rubicon examined the pink marquise through his jeweler's loupe. Finally Rubicon looked up and said, "Why did Simon Mehta send you?"

"My name is Carlos Fontana," the man said gravely, holding out his hand for Rubicon to shake but which the older man ignored. "I represent the diamond broker whose client ordered this stone and arranged to have you cut it. A beautiful job you did, indeed. Of course"—Fontana smiled conspiratorially—"everybody thinks the work was accomplished by young Mr. Gold—"

"Stop!" cried Rubicon. "That name will not be uttered in my presence."

Fontana shifted on his feet and glanced around the studio as if looking for a place to sit down. Rubicon indicated a small easy chair that he normally reserved for Francine when she complained about her knees. Fontana unbuttoned his overcoat and sat gratefully down in the easy chair.

"If I may continue with my story: Mr. Mehta delivered this pink marquise several days ago to its owner, and of course, Mr. Mehta was paid handsomely for serving as a courier between you and my special friend."

"The name of your so-called special friend?" Rubicon was testing Fontana. He already knew the diamond broker's name.

"Goldman. Yitzhak Goldman. I have been a business associate of Mr. Goldman's for the past fifteen years. Mr. Goldman finds me completely trustworthy and reliable." Fontana lowered his eyes and added, "However, I must confess to telling one small lie. It was not Simon Mehta who sent me here, but in fact, Mr. Goldman."

Rubicon frowned. "Then why did you say Simon Mehta sent you?"

"Because I knew that you would know his name, considering that he is a courier to the trade. I wasn't so sure you would recognize Mr. Goldman's name."

"Hell, I knew Yitzhak Goldman since before you were born into this miserable world, you little lying insect."

Fontana held up a hand. "Please, allow me to go on. In time you will understand. But you must let me give you all the details before passing judgment."

Rubicon glanced over at his cleaver's bench where the remaining two models of the Lac de Lune stood on their cement pedestals. He doubted that Fontana had spied them yet. He backed up, placing himself between Fontana and the models, and as soon as he had a chance, he turned and placed a large piece of canvas over them.

Fontana said, "You needn't try hiding them from me, Mr. Rubicon. I know that you have been working on models of the Lac de Lune. It is about that very stone that I have come to speak with you."

"Well, get on with it and let me get back to work," grumbled Rubicon.

Fontana rested his elbows on the armchair, raised his hands slightly, and placed the tips of his fingers together. "Before his terrible murder, Mr. Jim Hardy, the prospector who claimed to have discovered the 384-carat blue-green diamond on his staked land, had contacted my associate, Mr. Goldman. He told Mr. Goldman that he wished to do business with him. By business, I mean, Mr. Hardy wished Mr. Goldman to broker the diamonds he claimed he discovered at his mine. Including the Lac de Lune. I believe he called it Zone Mine. Did you ever have the pleasure of meeting Mr. Hardy, Mr. Rubicon?"

Rubicon shook his head. "Only his courier."

"And that would be the same Simon Mehta."

"I am not at liberty to divulge names," said Rubicon flatly. "Now, please get to the point and let me get back to work. I don't have time for gossip."

In fact, Rubicon had not decided whether he would go to work on the remaining two models or put a rope around his neck, but that wasn't any of Fontana's business.

Fontana tapped his fingertips together, back and forth, back and forth, in little rapid gestures. "The truth of the matter is, Mr. Jim Hardy never existed. He was a pseudonym invented by an American undercover agent who has for several years been attempting to break up a certain business"—and here Fontana emitted a tiny cough—"thinly but without question connected to Mr. Goldman."

Rubicon's shoulders went limp and he stared into the near distance. "Not another smuggling tale. Please, I want nothing to do with smugglers and the rest of them. I am a simple diamond cleaver, granted, the best in the world, but I have no interest in where the gems come from or how they come into my hands. War diamonds, blood diamonds, good diamonds, bad diamonds, it's all the same to me, some larger and more beautiful than others, but all the same. I don't give a dog's tick where they came from. I do my work and I amaze my clients and that's enough for me. Spare me the offer you are about to make, Fontana."

Fontana tilted his head back and laughed. "You are quite the sharp one, Rubicon. I admire that in a man of your stature."

The sound emitted from Rubicon's throat might have been made by Kors or Krum. Fontana shifted in the easy chair, and when he reached into his overcoat pocket, Rubicon felt quite certain that the little man intended to pull a gun on him. Rubicon's own gun was under the mattress at the other end of the studio. He picked up his cleaver and aimed it at Fontana.

"Oh, dear," cried Fontana, "I'm afraid I moved too quickly and startled you. But there is no need to worry, no need at all. I am unarmed and, as you can see, small in stature and woefully out of shape." He pointed at his double chin and then reached back into his pocket. "I have a letter here somewhere, if I can just find it, addressed to you and marked 'Strictly Confidential.' " Fontana continued searching his overcoat pockets. "Ah," he said finally, "here it is, a bit wrinkled, but here now, I deliver this to you as per my instructions. Mr. Goldman, Yitzhak, that is, informed me that the contents of the letter within this envelope could not be trusted to the world's postal services." He held out the small ivory envelope.

Rubicon set the cleaver on the bench, snatched the envelope from Fontana's immaculate fingers, and reached for a cutting tool, which he used to slit the envelope open at the top. Drawing the letter out of the envelope, he detected a faint odor of men's cologne on the single sheet of paper, and as he unfolded it, the scent became somewhat stronger, as if the wearer of the cologne had only recently touched it. Rubicon went to the window to read in the daylight. Turning his back to Fontana, he studied the letter. To his surprise, it was just one sentence long:

Rubicon: First Dieter Haakvig. Who will be next?

Rubicon crumpled the note and tossed it into the air. It landed quite close to his own feet. "Mr. Fontana," Rubicon said, "please go away now and never come back."

Before he knew it, Carlos Fontana had left the studio and disappeared down Treble Lane, and if Rubicon was not mistaken, the little man had been chuckling.

Snow had begun falling, gently at first, then the brimming clouds tore apart, spilling snow thick as cream into a northerly wind, nearly blinding Dixon's one visible eye. He could barely see three feet ahead as he struggled uptown against the driving storm blanketing the city's streets in thick white drifts, snarling traffic. The subways were experiencing delays. Dixon pushed on, heading uptown on foot, a heavy green scarf wrapped around his face and neck, tucked into his overcoat. Beneath layers of wool and microfiber, the leather pouch with the stone inside hung from a nylon cord around his neck, resting against his chest where his heart throbbed against it, a constant reminder of his ambition. It was already eleven-thirty, and Dixon had no choice but to travel by foot if he were to reach Grand Central by noon. He pushed on through the snowstorm, feeling like an athlete on the last leg of a race, moments from victory.

Grand Central Station teemed with commuters rushing home before the storm trapped them in Manhattan. Simon Mehta jockeyed through the mob scene, aiming for the information booth. When he finally reached it, the queues were ten or fifteen deep at every window, desperate passengers inquiring about trains, the air thick with selfish determination, each prospective passenger living his own version of events. Mehta couldn't help thinking that had this been a genuine public emergency, these jostling, irritable citizens would be calm, civilized, and helping each other out. But since this was merely a snowstorm, everyone felt entitled to rude behavior, pushing, shoving, yelling, cursing, and displaying other boorish tendencies. Mehta kept a distance between himself and the crowded information booth, straining his neck for signs of a man wearing a black eye patch and green scarf. By twelve-fifteen, the man had not appeared, at least in Simon Mehta's range of view. He wondered if he should forgo the tantalizing mystery and head uptown to the warmth and coziness of his small apartment on the West Side. In fact, he was just turning to leave when he spied a man elbowing his way through the mob scene, coming toward him. One of his eyes was covered with a black patch and he wore a green wool scarf around his neck. Mehta stood on tiptoe, waving the business card Sabryna had given him. The man approached and Simon Mehta suddenly felt the thrill of danger lurking in his immediate future.

Dixon had recognized Mehta instantly. He knew everybody in the diamond trade, even those who didn't use the tube for illicit profit. Mehta, Dixon had observed over the years, was among the innocents, a faultless, faithful, unquestioning mensch who served his clients and never asked questions. Mehta was known around the trade as a law-abiding, upstanding independent courier. But Dixon believed that, like any other man, he could certainly be bought for the right price. Fighting a path through the crowds, Dixon finally reached Mehta, who by now was holding up the photograph of the Lac de Lune. Grabbing the courier's elbow, Dixon steered him back through the mob scene into a men's room. Mehta didn't resist, allowing himself to be led deeper into the intrigue. Once inside the toilet facility, Dixon led Mehta to a stall which both men entered. He latched the stall door before unwinding his green scarf and removing the leather pouch from around his neck. He patted his overcoat pocket. "I am armed, Mehta. If you start to run, you'll be dead before you reach the door."

Mehta nodded his understanding of the gravity of this moment. Dixon placed the leather pouch in his hands. His fingers trembled as he loosened the string and then the stone rolled gently into the courier's cupped hands. Mehta gasped.

"What do you make of it?" Dixon asked. "And hurry up, willya?"

Mehta removed a magnifying loupe from his pocket, located the little window sliced into the rough stone, and, placing the loupe to his right eye, his best eye, studied the stone. Dixon shifted from one foot to the other. "Hurry up, damn it."

Mehta held up a hand. "Please, please. I need quiet. Please."

Dixon fumed but kept his trap shut. Minutes passed and other commuters came and went in and out of the stalls. Dixon blew out an impatient breath. At that moment, Mehta looked up at him and said, "You are to be congratulated."

"So it's the real thing?"

Mehta nodded.

"That goes against everything I've been hearing," argued Dixon. "See, this stone came off the miner's dead body. Word going around is this is a fake, that the real Lac de Lune was being sent to a girl named Venus even before the miner was shot."

Mehta shrugged and murmured, "Still."

"And too, I made that scratch right there." Dixon

pointed. "With my diamond pinky ring. Diamonds can't be scratched, but glass can. So either I've been misinformed, or you're lying through your teeth."

Mehta shrugged and shook his head. "Lots of rumors are flying around. But you see, here where you managed to scratch the stone, it has a glass overlay to disguise it. So that a thief would think it was a fake. But the truth is, this is the real Lac de Lune."

"You wouldn't be playing games with me, would you, Mehta?"

Mehta shook his head firmly, adding, "I am positive. I would bet my life on it."

"In that case," Dixon came back, "if you're wrong about this, if you are lying to me, I'll hunt you down and shoot your ass dead, got that?"

Mehta shrugged lightly and, with some reluctance, placed the stone back into the leather pouch. Dixon snatched up the pouch, looped it around his neck, and wrapped the green scarf tightly over the cord. Dixon opened the stall and started for the door.

Mehta spoke up then, in a quiet voice. "We haven't finished our business, sir."

Dixon turned around and shot one finger out at Mehta. "We will, my man, we will. But first, my client must pay me. Then I'll get back to you."

Dixon left, battling his way back through the mob scene, disappearing into the street.

Mehta stood in the men's room and for a moment seemed frozen. Then he turned and caught his own image in a mirror above the washbasins. A lazy grin spread across his face. Speaking to the man in the mirror, he mimicked Dixon. "I'll get back to you." Tears welled in Mehta's eyes and a slowly rising gurgling noise moved up from his throat, escaping his mouth in waves of laughter.

Dixon reached Volpe's office at ten minutes before one o'clock. Snow had drifted up against the double glass doors of the Luxor Building and he kicked it away and scuttled inside. In the elevator, he the only passenger, he checked his overcoat pockets. First pulling out a small bottle of brandy, replacing it in the pocket, and then pulling out his gun, which he didn't plan to use, but always packed. He wouldn't need his gun, because Crumley would be waiting outside the elevator on Volpe's floor, gun ready, and Crumley would do the dirty work. Dixon preferred it that way.

Locating his cell phone, Dixon placed a call to Crumley. No answer. He left a detailed message, clicked off, slipped the phone back into his pocket, and smiled to himself. For the remainder of the ride Dixon moved his lips silently, rehearsing the last words he would ever say to Gordon Volpe. Since Dixon had met with Simon Mehta, his plans had drastically shifted from Plan A to Plan B. He had originally intended to deliver the stone to Volpe, who would immediately check it for authenticity, and declare it a fake. Dixon would plead ignorance and demand to be paid for carrying out his part of the deal by delivering the weapons to Fairview and returning with the stone. Volpe would pay up and Dixon would resume trailing Venus Diamond until she led him to the real stone. All this rested on the stone Dixon possessed being a fake.

Plan B, reserved for use only if the stone was genuine, involved a more delicate handling of the situation. Volpe would immediately recognize the stone as genuine—unless Mehta had been lying—and pay Dixon for a job well done. Dixon would then bring out a celebratory bottle of brandy and he and Volpe would drink to their mutual success. Meanwhile, Crumley would be waiting at the door to Volpe's office, gun in hand, ready to plug Volpe while Dixon grabbed the Lac de Lune. Dixon and Crumley would leave with a double bounty, his cash payment for the job and the real Lac de Lune. But he'd needed to know which way things had to go before meeting Volpe, thus Simon Mehta had served a valuable purpose.

Now that Dixon knew the stone was genuine, Plan B went into effect. When he reached Volpe's floor, he stepped out of the elevator. The corridor was empty. Most of the tenants and clients had abandoned the offices and gone home before the storm got worse. Dixon looked around. No Crumley. He paced the corridor for a few minutes, occasionally checking his watch. Volpe would be in his office around the corner and farther down the corridor, waiting. Where the hell was Crumley? Dixon found a private corner, and made a call.

Crumley wasn't happy about being awakened. He'd battled insomnia all night, ending up on the living room couch, the tape recorder running at low volume, the television set on, volume off, its soft flickering light finally lulling him into a deep sleep around ten o'clock in the morning. So when his cell phone played the William Tell Overture, Crumley sat up with a start, opened his eyes, and groaned. The tune kept on playing until Crumley answered the call.

"Where the hell are you?"

"Hey, boss, I can't hardly move, see, I had insomnia real bad last night and only just got to sleep a couple hours ago."

"I don't give a flying crap about that. Get your ass out of bed and up here to the Luxor Building. I'm going in to see Volpe in about five minutes. You're supposed to already be here. Now I'll have to drag out the business with Volpe until you get up here. And it's now officially Plan B time, so hurry your ass."

Crumley rubbed his eyes. "What about Merle? Can't Merle do the job?"

"Shut up and listen to me, Crumley. I know my business and I know who can do what job and who can't. You work for me. You don't question my decisions. Is that clear? Now get the hell out of bed and uptown."

Crumley continued to protest, but the line had gone dead. Crumley hated it when people hung up on him. Dixon frequently hung up on Crumley, but he had never complained because Dixon might fire his ass, which was as good as saying Dixon would have him killed. Probably Merle would do the job for Dixon; he couldn't imagine Dixon killing anybody if he could get someone else to do it for him.

Like Crumley, this time.

Crumley had never killed before. Even back when he lived on the streets, he had never killed. He'd never even roughed up anyone, except in self-defense. So far, while working for Dixon, Crumley had escaped the violent side of the business. Driving, hauling weapons, delivering cash and diamonds, he'd done all of that, and he even packed a gun for good measure. But he had never had to use a weapon on anyone. He attributed it to his dull but congenial personality; he didn't exude confidence and inspire fear the way Dixon could simply by dropping a tic in his eye. No, Crumley had so far in his life measured out fairly benign, and now, as he sat on the couch fighting sleep and pondering Dixon's command, Crumley decided he liked how his life was going. He had no desire to kill anyone, not even for all the money and glory in the underworld.

He stood and walked over to a small bookcase that supported the television. Crouching, he scanned the three rows of books, running his finger along their spines, searching for a particular volume. Homer, Robert Louis Stevenson, Mark Twain, Shakespeare, David Guterson, Raymond Chandler, Timothy Egan, the whole G. M. Ford collection, the *New Shorter Oxford English Dictionary*. Ah, here it was. He pulled *Roget's Thesaurus of English Words and Phrases* from the shelf. The cover was black, white, and orange, with a Penguin insignia, and it said, "Signpost to the language of the twenty-first century."

Tucking the thesaurus under his arm, Crumley loped into the kitchen and found the last of his diet Cokes in the fridge. He carried the Coke and the thesaurus back into the living room and sat down on the couch. He opened the thesaurus to

L and paged through until he came to the *lu*s. He searched the page for the word "lune," but the word wasn't listed, probably, Crumley decided, because it wasn't a real English word. But right there were similar words: "lunacy, lunar, lunatic asylum, lunatic fringe." He looked each of these words up and then paged to the *la*s.

"Lac, resin, 357, n." Crumley turned to item 357. The word "lac" had been placed among words describing resin, words like "pitch" and "tar" and "ambergris" and "tragacanth." "Lac" just dropped into the middle as if it belonged there. Well, maybe it did. Now Crumley had a hunch that the word "lac" as in "Lac de Lune" was also a non-English word. And then he suddenly remembered the word "loch," which he knew meant "lake" in Scottish. Loch, lac, lake. Okay. Reaching for the telephone directory, he looked up the phone number of the New York Public Library and placed a call to their consultant services. When a lady's voice came on the line, Crumley said, "I need to have something translated into English."

"From what language?"

"I don't know. Maybe French. I'm thinkin' in my head it's French."

A long sigh, then, "What is it exactly that you need translated from the French?"

"Lac de Lune."

Laughter. "You must be the fifteenth person who's called about that diamond since it was discovered."

"I don't care about the diamond. What does it mean?"

"It's very easy, really. 'Lac' means lake in English. 'De' means of. 'Lune' means moon. Put together it means Lake of the Moon, or Moon Lake."

"What about the term 'sight box'? You got anything on that?"

"Spell it."

"Uh, I'm not sure. I just heard the term spoken. I didn't see it spelled out."

Crumley heard the woman's impatient sigh. "Well, help me out here, sir. In what context is the term used?"

Crumley rubbed his jaw, feeling two full days of stubble. "Well, diamonds, I guess. Yeah, the context would be diamonds."

"Hold on."

While he waited, Crumley reached over and straightened up the little microcassettes he had stacked on the coffee table. Stacked them in piles of three, according to numerical order. The girl had numbered them from one to twelve. He'd fallen asleep halfway through number nine, and still had a few hours to go.

"You still there, sir?"

"Yup."

"In this context, 'sight' is spelled s-i-g-h-t. The term 'sight box' is used to identify the box into which the diamond mining companies place rough diamonds for a diamond broker's approval. A price will be set for the contents of the box, and if the broker likes the looks of what is inside, he pays the price and the contents of the sight box are then placed in a safe until the broker has time to contact his client. If the client likes the price, the broker notifies the diamond seller. The diamonds are removed from the sight box, packaged, and placed into, it says here, a dark blue briefcase. On the fifth week of the traditional diamond-trading cycle, the broker pays for the diamonds, picks up the briefcase, and delivers the stones to his client, which is often a jewelry manufacturing company. That answer your question?"

"Uh, partly. What does a sight box look like?"

"Let's see." A long pause, then the librarian spoke up. "Traditionally, a sight box is a cardboard box about the size and shape of a shoe box."

"Really?"

"Yes, sir. Really. Now is that all?"

"Hey, yeah, for now anyhow. Thanks, ma'am." Crumley hung up and stretched. He had a long day's work ahead of him and he guessed he'd better get started, in spite of a lack of sleep.

"Lack." Now, there's the word in English, only spelled differently. Crumley loped back into the kitchen and put on a pot of coffee.

CHAPTER THIRTY-ONE

A t one o'clock exactly, after being buzzed into the Luxor Building, Delbert Dixon placed a gloved hand on the brass handle of Gordon Volpe's office door and pushed it open, entering the tiny reception room—as claustrophobic as he remembered. The door to Volpe's private office was open a crack and Dixon heard Volpe in there talking on the phone.

Dixon looked around. Sleek, postmodern stuff he loathed jumped off the walls, assaulting his aesthetic sensibilities. He reached out and straightened a print hanging crooked on one wall, an abstract image of what Dixon thought might be two individuals of indeterminate gender being beaten by a horse wielding a whip. Beneath the image was the picture's title: *West African Diamond Miners*. He squinted at the picture as he eavesdropped.

"All right, Sydney, so Miss Sexton and I will arrive at the shop at two o'clock, give or take a few minutes. Have the best of your four-carat Brilliant Ds ready to show. No, she doesn't sound like the fancy type. Very bourgeois. She'll want the brightest white she can get. And most likely she'll want a round, yes, she sounds very conservative. I have to go now, Sydney. I have a client waiting."

Dixon appeared in the doorway. Volpe's heart pounded in his chest. The moment had arrived. From now on, his life would be free of financial worries; his life would be perfect.

The two men exchanged greetings and Volpe motioned Dixon inside his office, offering him the same leather chair Dixon had sat in before. Volpe peered out into the reception area to be certain that Miss Sexton hadn't arrived early in her enthusiasm, then ducked back inside his office and locked the door.

A man on the brink of success often rubs his hands together in anticipation, and this is what Volpe did while Dixon removed his gloves, unwrapped his outer clothing, and made himself at home in the deep leather chair. Volpe sat at his desk facing Dixon. Cold air wafted off Dixon's outer clothing. Volpe noticed a large bulge beneath Dixon's tattered black turtleneck sweater.

Dixon took his sweet time, making a show of it, drawing out the time as long as he thought reasonable, giving Crumley time to get up to the Luxor and into position. "It's a witch's tit out there," he complained. "No suckin' way I'd be out in that blizzard except for big goddamn business like this we got here."

Volpe, unaccustomed to such base language, smiled thinly. His hands, his graceful manicured hands, trembled like two palsied spiders as he tapped his fingertips on the desk blotter. He watched as Dixon reached beneath the black turtleneck collar, slowly withdrew a leather pouch from inside his shirt, raised it high over his head until the cord around his neck released itself, then brought the pouch back down and set it gently before Gordon Volpe.

The two spiders inched forward. Grasping the pouch, Volpe fumbled as he opened it, the heft of it already sending chills through him. When the stone rolled out of the pouch into his hands, Volpe's mouth fell open and Dixon heard a little intake of breath. Volpe fondled the stone, turning it over and over in his hands before finally picking up his loupe and examining it.

Dixon could have explained about the glass casing, but decided to wait until Volpe said something, thus giving Crumley more time.

Five minutes passed in silence, then Volpe set the stone on his desk blotter and looked up at Dixon.

"This is a fake," he declared flatly.

Dixon winced then smiled, flicking out a hand. "Mr. Volpe, my friend, what could make you think it's a fake?"

"There is no doubt that this is a replica of the stone. A fine replica indeed, but not the real thing. I am an expert diamantaire, Mr. Dixon. You have insulted my intelligence. I know what I'm talking about. This is a fake." Volpe rolled the stone across the desk toward Dixon, folded his hands, and waited for Dixon to speak.

Dixon allowed a silent moment. Placing one finger on Volpe's desk, he traced a diamond shape on the fine polished wood. "Ya see," he allowed after a pause, "it looks like a fake because it's made to look like a fake." Dixon chuckled as if at a private joke. "Allow me to explain."

Without naming names, Dixon explained. "See, I happen to know that the real stone is in there." He pointed at the stone. "Inside the glass casing. So nonetheless, Mr. Volpe, sir, you got the real thing right here."

Volpe reached out, picked up the stone, and examined it a second time. Dixon glanced at his watch. Crumley better hustle his ass. When Volpe cleared his throat, Dixon looked up at him.

"I need some time," Volpe declared. "I need special equipment in order to be sure. This means I will have to transport the stone to my shop. I'll get back to you with the results."

Dixon shrugged. "Still and all, Mr. Volpe, I did my end of the job. I'd like to have my wages now, if you don't mind."

The phone on Volpe's desk rang once. Volpe seized the receiver, his anxiety noted by Dixon. Was he expecting someone to call? Was Volpe planning a double-cross? All the possibilities circulated through Dixon's brain.

Volpe spoke gruffly into the phone, paused, and then appeared greatly relieved, his brow clearing. "Oh, hello, David. No, no, not at all. Sorry about the gruff tone of voice. It's the weather. Horrid out there. Nasty day. How can I help you?"

Dixon flicked his thumbnail and listened to Volpe's side of the conversation.

"I see. Yes, of course, I do want first bidding rights. What? Well, no, actually, that won't work, David. I am leaving my office very shortly and won't return today. I'll tell you what. Meet me at Parecles. No, not the retail shop, the workshop. I'm bringing a client over. I can take a quick look at the inventory and give you an answer on the spot. What's that? Oh, no, no. Not at all. My client won't take but a few minutes of my time. Just come on over anytime. Yes, David, see you then."

Volpe hung up the receiver. "Sorry about that. Where were we?"

"I was sayin' I'd like to be paid for my work, Mr. Volpe," Dixon drawled.

Volpe shook his head. "Not until I determine the authenticity of this stone. For all I know, Mr. Dixon, you could have switched stones on me."

"Hey, Mr. Volpe, do I look stupid? I went to college, ya know, I'm an educated man. Why would I try to pass off a fake stone on an expert diamond broker like you?" Dixon's lips quivered defensively. "No, siree, I'm not stupid, Mr. Volpe, sir."

"Nevertheless, I cannot compensate you until I verify the stone's authenticity."

Dixon wagged his head. "I ain't asking for compensation, Mr. Volpe, sir. I'm asking for cash dollars." His mouth warped through a fluid smile.

Volpe considered for a moment. "If you'd like to accompany me to my workshop, you may. Once I'm convinced the stone is authentic, I will pay you on the spot."

Dixon tilted his head. This dropped a kink in his otherwise smoothly plotted arrangement. Should Dixon be seen in public with Volpe shortly before Volpe's murder? If he didn't go along, if he waited here in Volpe's office, no one would ever have to know Dixon and Volpe had done business. But Dixon doubted Volpe would go for that plan. No, he'd better accompany Volpe to the shop so he could verify the diamond's authenticity. The courier Simon Mehta had insisted this was the authentic Lac de Lune, a fact Volpe would surely determine with his fancy equipment. Dixon didn't like it much, but he'd go along for the ride. Besides, that gave Crumley more time. Crumley could be waiting in the Luxor for Dixon and Volpe to return, and then shoot Volpe. It made sense.

"Okay." Dixon reached for his gloves. "Let's get this over and done. I need to be paid today."

Volpe glanced at his watch. "I'm expecting a client at any moment. I have agreed to accompany her to my firm's workshop. She's looking for a particular stone. Engagement ring, nothing very important. She'll be here any moment now. I want to appear at the workshop as if all is normal, so as not to raise any suspicions. You may accompany me and the girl, but you must be presented as another of my clients."

Dixon smiled. "That's easy. I can do that. What say, you introduce me as, let's see." Dixon wiggled his jaw around. "Yeah, that's good. Call me Mr. Vespucci." He grinned. "I like that. Mr. Vespucci."

"All right, then. When the girl arrives, I'll introduce you as one of my clients, a—uh—a Mr. Vespucci, and then the three of us will leave here together for the workshop. It's only a few steps from this building; we needn't travel far in this frightful weather."

Volpe slid the stone back inside the leather pouch, placed the pouch in his briefcase. From his desk drawer, he drew out a pair of handcuffs and attached one side to the briefcase handle. "Once my business with the girl is completed, we'll borrow some of the special equipment. I have a private office there. We'll authenticate the stone and then I'll pay you."

Dixon nodded. "So, uh, we come back here for the cash, right?"

"Certainly. I don't travel with that kind of cash in my pocket. We'll return to my office and I'll hand over the cash. That is, if this is truly the Lac de Lune."

"Excellent." Dixon stood up. "I need to hit the can before we go anywhere."

"Down the corridor to your left, third door on the right-hand side." Volpe handed Dixon a key to the men's room.

In the men's, Dixon used his cell phone to call Crumley. After three rings, Crumley answered.

Crumley sat in the Reading Room of the New York Public Library, several books stacked beside him, one splayed open to page twenty-one, the last page of the book's first chapter. He had placed his cell phone on vibrate and now it did, tickling his buttock. He reached back for it, got up, and dutifully walked outside the Reading Room to answer the phone.

"Plans have changed," barked Dixon. He launched into a detailed explanation, finally instructing Crumley to be waiting in the Luxor Building, on Volpe's floor, when they returned. "You got that straight, Crumley? I want this to look like a random hit."

"Uh, sure, boss. Sure, I got it."

"Okay," said Dixon, only partly satisfied that Crumley understood the change of plans. "It's one-thirty. Be in place on Volpe's floor before three-thirty. Got that?"

"Uh, yeah, sure."

"And for chrissake, be there on time."

"Uh-huh."

"And Crumley? One more thing."

"Yeah?"

"Call Sabryna and Merle. Have them waiting in Sabryna's car outside the Luxor. By then the street should be cleared. If they can't come by car, hire a taxi, or come on foot, I don't care how the hell they get here. We might need them. Tell them to wait outside the Luxor. Got that?"

"Sure. Uh-huh."

"Fer chrissake, what's the matter with you, Crumley? You in a place where you can't talk?"

"Yeah."

"How close are you? Give me a street number."

"Fortieth Street."

"Hell, you're practically here. So get over to the Luxor and sit tight, call Sab and Merle, and be ready."

"Sure."

Crumley put the phone away after turning it off altogether. He had always known he had a one-track mind; he was what they call a batch processor, could focus on only one thing at a time, everything else being so much background static. Returning to the Reading Room, he saw a young man in baggy trousers and little wire-rimmed glasses collecting the books he had left on the table.

"Whoa," he whispered. "I'm not through with them."

The young man snarled, set the books back on the table, and huffed off.

Crumley resumed his place at the table, found the page in the book he had been reading, and, resting his elbows on the desk, head in his hands, he found where he had left off.

Dixon retraced his steps along the corridor to Volpe's office. Crumley had sounded half-conscious, like his brain had numbed. He'd said he hadn't slept the night before. Hell, Crumley always sounded like his brain was soaked in Ambusol. When he entered Volpe's reception area, the door to Volpe's private office was open, and Dixon could see him and the backside of another person. Must be Volpe's client, Miss What's-her-name. Anyway, a petite blonde in a sable coat.

When she turned around, Dixon saw the woman's face. An alarm bell rang in his head but his memory failed him. He was pretty sure he'd seen her before now, but he couldn't place her or the circumstances in which they had last crossed paths.

This was some classy broad, her ruby red hair marcelled, her face painted all sophisticated, what he could see behind the dark Hollywood sunglasses, her perfume sultry and warm, the kind of scent that made Dixon want to grab her and tear off her clothes. He couldn't tell about her figure underneath the full-length sable coat, but guessed it meshed nicely with the petite face and the tiny hands encased in kid gloves. When Volpe introduced Dixon, the lady held out one gloved hand and Dixon grasped it carefully, the way he'd handled test tubes during college chemistry.

"Mr. Vespucci, allow me to introduce you to Miss Caroline Sexton, another client of mine."

Dixon saw that Volpe had handcuffed the briefcase to his wrist.

Simon Mehta, home now in his cozy apartment, heat pulsating off the rattling radiator, wasted no time spreading the word. First, he notified Yitzhak Goldman. Yitzhak at first balked, but Mehta was adamant.

"Yitzhak, I am your friend. Would a friend lie to a friend? If you go there right now, you will see for yourself. What? No, no, Yitzhak, do not take David along. He'll only make problems for you."

Next, Mehta placed a long-distance telephone call to Jean Claud Rubicon. It was six hours later in Antwerp, which put it at Rubicon's suppertime. The old man did not seem pleased at the interruption.

"I tell you, Jean Claud Rubicon, you don't want your dinner interrupted, then don't pick up your telephone. It's that easy."

"What do you want?" demanded a surly Rubicon.

And Mehta told him exactly what he wanted. When he had finished, Rubicon scoffed into the phone.

"How many times have I told you, Simon Mehta, I am

not listening to all this gossip and rumormongering. When it all comes out, the Lac de Lune will come into my hands. It was destined. I don't need you and your clever tricks." He hung up abruptly.

Mehta chuckled to himself and made another phone call. It took six or seven rings before Carlos Fontana finally picked up his telephone.

"You got caller ID?" Mehta asked Fontana.

"Who wouldn't in this business?"

"I know that you switched stones on me, Fontana. Back in Antwerp. When we first met in the train. But you made a terrible mistake, do you see it now? Yes, we were both mistaken, my friend."

Fontana listened patiently and when Mehta had finished he snapped at him.

"Simon, what does a simple courier like you know about authenticity?"

"But it's true, I swear to you, on my life, Fontana, my life. Just go there and see for yourself. If you hurry, you might beat Yitzhak to the punch, if you catch my meaning. Wouldn't that drop a nice twist in Yitzhak's plan?"

Mehta didn't need to telephone Gordon Volpe. Volpe was already neatly in place. Nor did he need to contact Dieter Haakvig in Johannesburg, now that Dieter had been permanently eliminated from the competition. And so his telephone calls completed, Mehta turned on the television and watched a game show.

Antwerp

Carlos Fontana, wearing slippers and smoking a cheroot cigar, smiled out at Antwerp's evening sky. The air was clear and cold, and the stars twinkled like little diamonds. He couldn't help chuckling to himself.

What a wonderful invention, the cell phone. One can be anywhere in the world and receive a telephone call just as if he were right down the street. Forty-seventh Street, for example. When all along, he was in Antwerp, in a lovely hotel suite, enjoying a fine cigar and preparing a most wonderful surprise for Jean Claud Rubicon's two ferocious curs. What a simpleton, that Simon Mehta. Stealing here and stealing there, always playing the little games, never smart enough to see the bigger picture. As far as Mehta's ability to recognize the real from the fake, well, Fontana could only laugh and shake his head. A small, insignificant man, that Simon Mehta.

Now Fontana rose and went into the bedroom. Half an hour later, he emerged, dressed in his finest winter gear, and went out into the streets of Antwerp.

New York

Simon Mehta didn't hear David Goldman enter the apartment, using a key Simon himself had given the young man in a flickering moment of camaraderie some months ago and had forgotten about. Didn't hear David steal up behind his chair, place the barrel of the gun to his head. Didn't know what hit him when the bullet from David's gun streaked through his head.

Didn't feel the floor when he fell onto it, dead on impact.

On the way out, David Goldman ripped Simon Mehta's overcoat off the wall hook and turned it upside down, searching the many pockets. Empty. Ripping open the coat's lining, he hit the jackpot. A freefall of glittering diamonds rained down over the floor.

"Goddamn thief," Goldman mumbled. "I told Uncle Yitzhak, didn't I?"

PART THREE

CHAPTER THIRTY-TWO

Antwerp

Snow had fallen throughout the long winter night and Treble Lane at sunrise resembled a Brueghel winter scene. In his second-story workshop Jean Claud Rubicon, cursing to himself, stoked wood in his fireplace and lit the kindling. In seconds a great blaze leaped hot orange flames, illuminating Rubicon's ravaged face and warming his hands. He hadn't slept for three days, hadn't eaten, had relied only on thick coffee and enough brandy to flood Antwerp. Rubicon's gun lay on the windowsill—prominently displayed, fully loaded, though one bullet would suffice—a reminder that if he failed in his mission, he had vowed to kill himself. Hanging, he had concluded reluctantly, though more dramatic, would have required him to climb up on a stepladder in order to secure a rope from a hook on the ceiling, a task against which his arthritic knees would surely balk. A single shot, then, clean and quick. Rubicon returned to his workbench.

As he sat at his workbench, elbows resting on the wood surface, his forehead pressed against the heels of his hands,

Rubicon's gnarly fingers tore at what was left of his hair as he alternately cursed and whined over his own inadequacies. To hell with his reputation. To hell with vainglorious pride in his heretofore brilliant accomplishments. To hell with Kors and Krum and all the neighbors on Treble Lane and with everyone he had ever met in his long and heretofore successful career. He should have listened to his mother, the sensible woman having urged her son to stick with the family's chocolate business where at least he'd find security. Now his mother's exact words came back to haunt Rubicon:

"Jean Claud Rubicon," his mother had said one morning over the din of the chocolate factory's giant truffle mixers, "of all my children, you are the only failure. How can this be, Jean Claud? Why do you persist in believing that you have one shred of talent when it is perfectly clear to everyone else in Levante that you are a fumblebum with the clumsiest fingers ever to shape a chocolate truffle? I ask you, my son, please do not speak to me again of your fancy artistic dreams. An artist you are not. Stick to running the electric mixer."

And so, in a quest to prove his mother and all of Levante wrong, a teenage Jean Claud had set out for Antwerp in search of work as an artist. What kind of artist did not concern him, only that he legitimately earn the title in order to throw it back in his mother's face, and to shame her before all the people of Levante. Before long, Jean Claud had found a job in a diamond factory, where some of the world's finest gems came for cutting and polishing. Jean Claud's first job was as janitor, cleaning up after the diamond cutters left their benches at seven P.M. every evening to return to their homes for supper and a night's rest, before returning the next morning to their workbenches beneath the tall windows that lined the walls of the diamond factory's workshop.

It was in these late hours of evening as Jean Claud swept and scrubbed for his little pay that he accidentally discovered the secret talent residing in his fingers. The master diamond cutter, Frobiche, known as the world's greatest cleaving artist, fell ill at his bench one winter afternoon just as Jean Claud was arriving for work. The two met in the employees' latrine, where Frobiche was vomiting profuse quantities of blood straight onto the latrine floor, the effects of intentional poisoning by a rival diamond cutter, he told Jean Claud between episodes. Jean Claud had turned to go for help, but the master cutter begged him to stay at his side. His time had come and he wanted a witness to his death and revenge against his rival. Jean Claud knelt on the latrine floor beside Frobiche who now dribbled red bile down his jaws. In a final gesture, the old man slipped a diamond ring off his pinky finger, a ring that Jean Claud had often admired whenever he had passed the master's bench. The ring's brilliantly faceted diamond seemed to dazzle Jean Claud nearly blind.

"Your hand," demanded the master, his weakened voice hoarse and shallow.

Jean Claud held out his left hand. The master placed his own ring on the pinky finger of Jean Claud's left hand. He stared down at it in wonder and awe.

"Go to Treble Lane," the dying Frobiche instructed Jean Claud. "There you will find my teacher. He is very old, nearly one hundred years. Show him the ring. He will teach you."

Jean Claud held the dying master's head in his hands. "But what can I do to deserve this, your dying gift to a boy you hardly know?"

The dying man held up one talented finger and pointed at Jean Claud. "I can see it in your hands. You have a master's hands." The old man turned his head and sucked in his last breath, cold air that rattled on its final exit.

Ever true to his word, young Jean Claud sought out the master's master and studied under him for many years. This was how Jean Claud Rubicon learned his art, becoming a cleaver of such extraordinary talent that his work was revered all over the world and his shop never wanted for inventory.

Now, sixty years later, Jean Claud, in the midst of cursing the memory of his mother, remembered the dying master Frobiche's words, words so powerful that he jerked himself out of his suicidal funk, rose from his workbench, and began pacing the studio floor, a sure sign that he would soon get back to work. Guns and hanging ladders had suddenly been replaced in his mind by a new idea about how to approach the troublesome gletz in the Lac de Lune.

One model of the Lac de Lune remained. It sat alone on Rubicon's workbench. Rubicon studied it, picking it up gingerly, cemented stand and all, and peering through the tiny window cut into the model's rough outer skin. Like the others, this model possessed the same gletz as the real Lac de Lune, at least according to the instructions Rubicon had received from Mr. Jim Hardy. And now, suddenly Rubicon had this inspiration to try an entirely new approach. And if his idea proved successful, Rubicon would have discovered a revolutionary new approach to cleaving diamonds.

Rubicon sat down, seized his sketchpad, and began sketching out a series of facets that he would cut into the two diamond gems he expected to carve out of the single large stone. But first, he would have to cleave the stone into exactly two pieces. The brilliant plan he had struck upon while meditating on his mentor was to first lightly polish the rough gem as one large stone, removing all the gritty encasement material until the stone was completely clear. At this point in the game, instead of presenting itself as an obstacle, if Rubicon were to use his smallest cleaver and approach the gletz broadside, the gletz would serve a purpose; two perfect diamonds would fall from the cleaver's tool on either side of the gletz. One of the gems would be slightly larger in size and weight, but both gems would finally weigh in at close to 140 carats each. A loss of 104 carats might seem excessive to the layman, but any diamantaire would thrill to the economy of a mere 104 carats lost from a 384-carat stone. Rubicon had never—ever—employed laser tools in his work. He considered laser technology anathema, a form of cheating that inevitably produced inferior results.

In place of laser technology, Rubicon would use his own steady hands and his gradually fading vision, which he still trusted far more than any X-ray device. But now Rubicon saw that the cleaving tool might in fact have been the problem all along. He had spent hours on that single problem alone, deciding which cleaver's chisel to employ with his hammer. In the end he had chosen his number two chisel and now a desperate man decided this had been his biggest error all along. Bending over his tool tray, Rubicon searched among his chisels for his least-used implement: chisel number one, the smallest of all chisels. After ten minutes searching, an exasperated Rubicon flipped the toolbox over, pouring its contents onto the floor.

In Rubicon's garden, Kors and Krum reacted to the sounds of tools crashing to the floor with impassioned barks and howls. Rubicon came to the window and, leaning out, cursed at the Dobermans, who instantly ceased their diatribe and began licking their paws, their eyes half-shut as if in torpor.

Rubicon was turning back to his work when out of his peripheral vision a figure in the street caught his attention: Carlos Fontana, scurrying up the lane, his hat pulled down over his head and one gloved hand gripping a fat snowball which no doubt he intended to use against Kors and Krum. Instinctively Kors and Krum awoke to the interloper, their howling echoing in the lane. Rubicon picked up the gun on his windowsill and aimed it at Fontana.

"Drop that damn snowball," Rubicon shouted down at Fontana. "Before I shoot it from your hand."

Fontana dropped the snowball and grinned sheepishly up at Rubicon.

"I only meant to tease them a little. How goes it, Jean Claud?"

Rubicon quieted the Dobermans. "It goes shitty. What do you want now?"

Carlos Fontana cautiously approached Rubicon's garden where Kors and Krum sniffed at the snowball, low growls still emanating from their throats. "I have a business proposition for you."

Rubicon spat out the window. "I have no time for business. I have enough business as it is."

Fontana tried his best to smile engagingly, but the dogs frightened him and he could only manage a sickly grin. "I am now in possession of the—shall we say—real thing."

"Poof," retorted Rubicon. "I don't believe you. Now you are sounding like Simon Mehta, the little squirrel. You want something from me, Carlos Fontana, I can see it in your eyes from way up here."

Now Fontana stood near Rubicon's front door, the nearest to the Dobermans he'd ever ventured, his courage bolstered by his urgent need to gain entry to the shop. "Just a piece of the action is all," he whined up at the diamond cleaver, adding, "and you'd better hurry. It's freezing cold out here. You wouldn't want a good man to freeze to death on your doorstep, would you, my friend?"

"Oh, hell, the door's unlocked. Come up then and get it over with." Rubicon disappeared from the window. Fontana reached for the door handle. Kors and Krum growled louder, showing pointed yellow bicuspids. Fontana grasped the handle, turned it, and literally fell into the foyer, slamming the door against the snarling curs. Climbing the steep stairs, he uttered a curse against all canines.

CHAPTER THIRTY-THREE

Rubicon sat at his workbench, determined antithesis of hospitality, his back to his guest, his hands sorting out tools he had plucked from the floor. Stepping into the studio, Carlos Fontana looked around. Rubicon's jeweler's tools were scattered everywhere across the shop's worn wood floor.

"What's going on here, Jean Claud?"

"What's going on is I'm busy, as you can see if you'd only use your eyes."

He smiled engagingly at Rubicon's back. "Ah, of course. You are busy. You are always busy, Jean Claud, which is why you are so successful."

Rubicon half-glanced over his shoulder. Fontana hurried to correct himself. "Of course the main reason for your success is your brilliant talent. No one cleaves a diamond like you, Jean Claud. Everyone knows you are the most gifted artist in the industry."

That was enough to satisfy Rubicon. He turned to face Fontana.

"And what do you want from me that you come at this ungodly early hour of a winter's evening? A man needs to concentrate on his work."

Carlos Fontana glanced over his own shoulder as if checking for eavesdroppers. Taking two steps in Rubicon's direction, he whispered, "Without a shade of doubt, Jean Claud, I am in possession of the genuine Lac de Lune."

Rubicon did not bother turning around to face Fontana, only rolled his eyes to scan the ceiling. Carlos Fontana continued.

"You see, Mr. Goldman's nephew, David Goldman—"

Rubicon turned beet red and yelled, "That name shall not be spoken in my shop!"

"Of course. I apologize, Jean Claud," Fontana mewled obsequiously. "What I am trying to say is that the nephew of Yitzhak Goldman has"—and here he checked his pocket watch—"how shall I put it?" He consulted his pocket watch a second time. "He has all along been a fraud of the first order."

"Get to the point."

"It has come to my attention by not unreliable sources, that, er, the nephew of Yitzhak has for the past several years been entirely incapable of successfully cleaving a diamond. He has become so enamored of drugs and, well, debauchery, that he has simply lost his edge. You are aware of the many visits Simon Mehta has paid you over the years? With business, this stone and that stone. Well, can you imagine, my dear friend, that all along, it was Yitzhak's nephew sending Simon Mehta to you? You would cleave the stones and return them to Mehta who in turn would return them to . . . well, you-know-who. You, Rubicon, have all along been preserving the young man's reputation." Fontana tapped the face of his wristwatch for emphasis. "Now what do you think about that?"

A short silence ensued and then Rubicon muttered, "I am not surprised."

Fontana scuttled over toward the cleaver. "Yes, yes, it's true. And now, my dear friend, I wish to bring you the very best of news."

"Spit it out."

"You shall be chosen to cleave the Lac de Lune. That is, as soon as it falls into my hands."

Rubicon sighed and swiveled on his stool to face Carlos Fontana. This wasn't the first time someone had tried pulling wool over Rubicon's eyes. "Correct me if I am wrong, Fontana, but didn't you say only moments ago that you in fact had possession of the stone?"

Fontana's hand shot out. "Meaning that I have direct access. I can acquire it whenever I wish. But time is of the essence, Jean Claud, as you surely understand."

"Then quit the doublespeak and spit out the point of this unannounced intrusion!" Rubicon's eyes blazed. Perhaps it was the reflection of the fire in the fireplace but still the flaming glare sent a chill through Fontana as if a hot icicle had punctured him. He steeled himself and got straight to the point.

"Jean Claud, you are the only man in the world who can successfully cleave the Lac de Lune. I believe this with all my heart. And so, I would like to acquire the stone for you, deliver it here into your talented hands."

"You mean steal it from my rival."

"Honestly—yes. That is exactly what I mean. And I can do it without anyone ever knowing how I came by the stone. Since, er, the current owner has acquired the stone illegally, he cannot report the theft to the police."

Rubicon folded his arms across his chest. "And how would you explain your coming into possession of the stone, let alone delivering it to me?"

Carlos Fontana grinned now from one ear to the other. The moment of his coup de grâce had at last arrived. Reaching into his overcoat he withdrew from an inner pocket a simple white envelope and held it out to Rubicon, who snatched it up impatiently.

"Read that and all will be revealed," intoned Fontana as he pulled up a wooden stool and made himself comfortable.

Rubicon tore open the envelope and extracted a single

sheet of white paper on which someone had written in a flowing cursive hand.

> To Whom It May Concern
>
> I, James Hardy, hereby assign possession of the blue-green diamond named Lac de Lune to my friend and colleague, Venus Diamond, on the single condition that she permit no other than Mr. Jean Claud Rubicon of Antwerp, Belgium, to cleave the stone. Should my fate be decided prematurely, I hereby assign Mr. Carlos Fontana of New York, New York, full responsibility for delivering the stone into the hands of the cleaver, Mr. Rubicon, from whence the rightful owner, Ms. Diamond, shall claim its parts once it has been cleaved. Ms. Diamond is then instructed to oversee sales of the stones derived from the Lac de Lune. All proceeds from the sales shall be freely gifted, without inquiry, to Mrs. Eleanor Purdy of No. 3 Kimberlite Road, Yellowknife, Northwest Territories, Canada.

The letter was signed "James Hardy" and dated two months ago.

Rubicon glanced up from the page. "This is a photocopy."

"The original lies in a safe-deposit box in New York."

"This might have been forged for all I know."

Carlos Fontana shrugged. "For what would I do that? You can see from the contents of Mr. Hardy's letter that he all along intended for you to cleave the stone and for me to deliver it, without either of us being compensated. Why would I forge such an unfair instruction?" Fontana shook his head. "No, Jean Claud, the photocopy represents the real thing. Mr. Hardy personally handed the original letter to me in Canada not more than a few weeks ago, really just shortly before he was so brutally murdered."

Rubicon flailed the letter at Carlos Fontana. It left his fingers and fluttered to the floor near Fontana's right foot. Fontana leaned over to pick it up. In doing so, he spied a tool very near his foot, a number one chisel, which he picked up along with the letter.

Rubicon did not miss this gesture and sprang off his workbench. "Give me that chisel," he demanded.

But Fontana drew his arm back and gripped the chisel tightly. "A moment, please, Jean Claud."

"That is my number one chisel. I have been scouring the place for it. I need it. Give it to me."

"Ah, not so fast, Jean Claud. Now just calm down and listen to me, your friend."

Rubicon dove at Fontana, knocking him off the stool onto the floor where the two men rolled around, each struggling for possession of the chisel, both cursing like guttersnipes. In the end, Fontana claimed victory, sitting on the chest of his opponent, holding the chisel aloft where flames from the fireplace transformed a simple length of steel into a red-hot Solomon's sword.

Rubicon, gasping for breath, snarled and cursed. Fontana said, "Listen to me now, Jean Claud, or I shall toss this chisel into the fire."

"You can't! There is no other number one chisel like mine. The fire will destroy its finish."

"Tut! Such a superstitious fellow. But listen, my friend, for you and I are on the brink of great fortune."

Rubicon really had no choice but to listen, pinned beneath the courier's frame. He lay still and heard Fontana's proposal.

"It has all the elements of a perfect, well, crime. First, you see, I steal the Lac de Lune from the person now in possession of the stone, and deliver it into your magnificent hands. This involves very little work on my part, for the person in question is, shall we say, a bit vulnerable to me."

"You mean he has the hots for you."

"Not at all." Fontana seemed amused. "You see, I know a little secret that this gentleman would not care to have revealed."

"You mean blackmail?"

"Crudely put, yes. Now then, once the stone is in my possession, I travel a circuitous route to deliver it to you. Once you have cleaved it in two, you and I will divide its parts fifty-fifty. You will then cut and polish the two stones into three or four large stones each. Once they have been cut down and faceted, no one can ever positively identify them as parts of the Lac de Lune. We'll sell the stones for a great fortune. And both of us, Jean Claud, will be able to retire in luxury."

He lay still and silent beneath Fontana's buttocks.

"Well?" said Fontana after a lengthy silence.

Rubicon summoned every gram of strength and in one powerful heave, bucked, sending Fontana flying toward the fireplace. Fontana howled as he hit the hard stone hearth. Rubicon scrambled to his feet.

"Now listen here, Carlos Fontana, you son of a bastard, you can't be playing tricks on Jean Claud Rubicon. Look! Look at me!"

Facedown on the hearth, Fontana raised his head and, with a mournful sheep-eyed stare, looked at Rubicon.

"That's better. Now, you nasty double-dealing first-generation American slut, you listen to Jean Claud Rubicon."

Fontana nodded.

Rubicon lectured his visitor. "You Americans are greedy pigs. All you ever care about is money. More, more, more. That is the American's creed. You should have it sewn onto your flag. Greedy and lazy. You think you can get rich using only your evil brains. It doesn't bother you even one tiny bit that you steal from others more needy than you. You put your own comforts first, and you lavish—"

"Please!" Fontana held up a pleading hand. "Get to the point, Jean Claud. Every minute is precious. We must act quickly, before the stone is mishandled, perhaps even stolen by . . . well, you-know-who."

"Shut up, you imbecile, and listen to me. I am Jean Claud Rubicon, master cleaver. I am the foremost expert and I say this not out of stupid pride but simply to state the facts as they stand. Now, if as Mr. Hardy's letter states, the Lac de Lune, once cleaved, is to be delivered to this Mrs. What's-her-name in Canada, then we must abide by Mr. Hardy's wishes. The Lac de Lune, after all, was Mr. Hardy's property, not yours or mine to profit from." Rubicon made a spitting sound. "Only an American would concoct such a despicable crime."

"But we stand to make a fortune. Think of it, Jean Claud, think of it!"

"I don't wish to participate in your sleazy schemings, Fontana. I care only about cleaving the stone. Once that is done, all is out of my hands. I can only hope to high heaven that you do the right thing."

Fontana's eyes brightened. "Ah," he purred, scrambling to his feet. "So you are willing, at least, to help me obtain the true Lac de Lune." He brushed his hands together to remove the hearth grit.

"You go to hell, Fontana. I have agreed to one thing, and one thing alone. I will cleave the Lac de Lune, as Mr. Hardy has apparently expressed his desire that I, and I alone, should cleave the stone. What happens to the stone after that— poof—that is up to you."

At this moment, Carlos Fontana edged up to the open window and rested his elbow on the sill. Jean Claud continued lecturing him about the loose morals of American society. While he appeared to pay attention, Fontana reached into his overcoat pocket and carefully palmed some jalapeño peppers laced with meat drippings. When Rubicon wasn't looking, he set the jalapeños on the windowsill and flicked them, one by one, out the window.

The jalapeños seemed to fall from the sky. Kors and Krum immediately investigated, sniffing the meat-juice scent. First Kors and then Krum gobbled up some of the jalapeños. The fiery treat burned their tongues, sending both Dobermans into peals of howling.

Jean Claud paused in his rant and rushed downstairs, cursing the canines, his rant now transferred from Americans to Dobermans. As soon as Jean Claud had left the room, Carlos Fontana sprang over to the workbench. The last of the Lac de Lune models, model number one, sat on its pedestal, cemented in place. Fontana snatched up the number one chisel, which Rubicon had placed on his workbench, and set about chiseling the number one stone from its pedestal. It didn't come easily, the jeweler's cement having taken firm hold, and Fontana began to sweat as he struggled to free the stone.

Down below, Rubicon screamed at the dogs, who howled in pain.

Fontana, cursing the cement, grabbed a larger chisel and tackled the job, frantic to free the stone. The dogs had now stopped howling; perhaps Rubicon had given them some water. Fontana worked faster. Small pieces of cement flew off the pedestal but the stone did not come free. Now Fontana heard Rubicon's heavy footfall on the stairs. Any second now . . .

Plang!

One hard blow broke the stone free from its pedestal. Fontana reached into his overcoat and fished out an identical stone, substituting it for the original, which he pocketed. Rubicon was halfway up the stairs now, reaching the landing.

Fontana grabbed a jar of jeweler's cement from the workbench and with the chisel quickly cemented the substituted stone to the pedestal. Once it held, he sprang back across the room and rested his elbow on the windowsill just as Rubicon came through the door.

"Goddamn neighbor kids," grumbled Rubicon, returning to his workbench. "Now where were we?"

Carlos Fontana smiled. "I was about to say that within twenty-four hours, Jean Claud, I shall deliver the Lac de Lune into your magnificent hands."

"Hell, you came all the way to Antwerp to say that? Why are you sweating?"

Carlos Fontana laughed nervously and swiped at his damp brow. "The fire. It makes me hot. And sleepy. I must be going, Jean Claud."

At this juncture in his despicable plot, Carlos Fontana realized that the cement would require about an hour to fix firmly.

"But before I take my leave, dearest friend, I wish you would join me as my guest for a dinner at Mongoose Tavern down in the diamond district. It is quite the divine repast."

"I am a working man, can't you see that? I have no time for lunching out. Go take yourself there." Rubicon sat down at his bench and turned to his work, his right elbow nearly bumping up against the pedestal holding the freshly cemented stone.

Fontana broke out in a profuse sweat now. Very gently, so as not to upset Rubicon and cause his elbow to make contact with the precarious pedestal, he said, "The special today, I am told, is rabbit stew." Knowing that this was Rubicon's Achilles' heel.

"Rabbit stew!" Rubicon turned to face Fontana.

"French rabbits."

Rubicon didn't even struggle with his conscience. He stood up, reached for his coat and his hat, and licking his lips, said, "We'll take a taxi. It's faster."

CHAPTER THIRTY-FOUR

He'd finessed the sleepy security guard at the lobby entrance. But when David Goldman entered Parecles's diamond workshop on the second floor, the security guards in the foyer immediately took notice. Everyone knew David Goldman, the famous diamond cleaver, worked for his uncle, a rival, and had no business entering Parecles. This snowy winter afternoon, the flashy younger Goldman wore a flowing crimson overcoat, matching dyed mink beret, and high-top Dr. Martens. Over one slumping shoulder, he carried a bulky backpack, apparently so heavy it made him lopsided.

Cold air wafted off David's overcoat and his razor-thin moustache had collected snowflakes, melting now into glistening drops of water that dripped onto his puckish lower lip as he approached the security desk. Setting down his backpack, Goldman patted his moustache neatly with his gloved hand. The first guard, Ed Jancovich, immediately recognized the famous diamond cleaver, but acted nonchalant.

"Help you, sir?"

David smiled politely. "Mr. Volpe's expecting me."

"Mr. Volpe's not in the shop today. Hardly anyone's in the shop today. Most everybody went home before the storm hit." The guard shook his head. "He ain't here."

David peeled off his hat and overcoat, slipped the beret into an overcoat pocket, and slung it over one arm, making a show of shooting his cuff and reading his diamond-faced Piaget watch. Beneath the eccentric outer gear, the young man was nattily turned out, as if to conduct serious diamond business.

"Perhaps Mr. Volpe is on his way." David smiled disingenuously. "I'm a bit early, after all. Mr. Volpe set the time for three-thirty and it's now only . . . uh . . . twenty-six past." He leered at the two officers. Neither man blinked.

"I am David Goldman."

The second security guard turned to Jancovich. "Maybe Mr. Goldman didn't understand what you told him, Ed." He turned to David, jerked a thumb toward Jancovich, and sneered. "Mr. Yanko-vick here says Mr. Volpe ain't in. What he means is, Mr. Volpe ain't in."

From the workshop's interior a disembodied voice came booming over a partition.

"Gordon's on his way now, fellows. He called in a while ago. He's bringing clients over from his office."

Jancovich raised his eyes to the ceiling. David peered over Jancovich's shoulder in the direction of the free-floating voice. "Is that Fish?" he called out.

A moment passed and then a portly figure emerged from behind a partition, an elderly gentleman dressed in a dark green three-piece suit, a gold watch chain dangling from his vest pocket, snaking across his broad belly. Fish.

"Oh, good afternoon, Mr. Fish. You remember me, don't you? David. David Goldman. Yitzhak Goldman's nephew. We met some years ago at the diamond convention in Madison Square Garden."

Mr. Fish thrust out his hand. "Of course, son, I remember you well. The talented young David Goldman. What's driven you into enemy territory?" Here Fish leaned in and gently jabbed David with his elbow. "Have you deserted your uncle to join the competition?" Mr. Fish broke into booming laughter and slapped David's back.

The security guards retreated, maintaining a cautious distance, as if they thought that any moment now David would pull a gun from his backpack and shoot the place apart. Mr. Fish ignored their obvious concern and led him around the security partition into his office. Goldman flashed a victory grin over his shoulder and followed Mr. Fish into the tiny room, no bigger than the average California closet, but unkempt and cluttered. He indicated a high wooden stool that David recognized as straight off the diamond-sorting floor.

"Sit down, my boy. Sorry for the guards' rudeness. We're not accustomed to unannounced visitors at the workshop, unless one of the brokers sends a client in to tour the facilities. And then, they always call ahead." Fish grinned jovially. "It just so happens Gordon is on his way over right now. He should arrive any moment now with two clients. I don't recall their names. Did I overhear that he's expecting to meet you here, as well?"

"That's right, sir," David lied, flashing a charming toothy smile at Fish. "My uncle has decided to sell some of his inventory. Mr. Volpe requested first sighting. I've brought the stones along, as Mr. Volpe informed me that he felt more comfortable viewing the inventory in his own workshop with his own equipment."

"Ah." Mr. Fish clasped his hands together. "So the King of Forty-seventh Street is preparing to retire, eh?"

"Not at all. My uncle is merely cleaning house, Mr. Fish." David smiled, adding another lie to his growing list. "As I said, Mr. Volpe asked for first bid on the overstock. But I don't want to disturb him while he's with clients."

Mr. Fish nodded solemnly, no doubt appreciating young Goldman's thoughtfulness. Such fine manners in today's youth were rare indeed.

"Could I wait here in your office until Mr. Volpe has finished up with the clients?"

Mr. Fish waved his hands. "Of course, of course. Please make yourself at home, son, as much as one can anyway in this discombobulated rat's nest. As you can see, I am not a very neat housekeeper." Mr. Fish chuckled and fussed with the paperwork piled on his desk.

"Thank you, sir."

On the desk, Mr. Fish's phone rang. He picked it up, spoke into it, and listened. Finally, he said, "All right, Gordon. I'll meet you here on the floor, at the elevator."

Mr. Fish leaned down and opened a small safe beside his desk, reached in, and pulled out a black velvet pouch. Goldman could hear stones rattling inside. Fish relocked the safe, slipped the bag of gems into his jacket pocket, straightened up, and went to the door.

"Gordon and his clients are just leaving his office up the street. They should be here any moment now and I'd like to meet them at the elevator. Excuse me, won't you, my boy? Some nice chocolate truffles in the tin over there. I won't be but half an hour and then you may have Gordon all to yourself."

David Goldman smiled to himself. The ruse had worked.

The sable coat's collar brushed against Venus's neck as Volpe led them through the snowstorm along a practically deserted, snow-packed Forty-seventh Street. Finally, they turned into a building at the corner. A small brass plate beside the entrance was engraved with the building number and a discreet "Parecles International, Ltd." Volpe held the door, then led them across a shabby lobby past a desk where a sleepy security guard nodded at Volpe and waved them by.

Venus followed Volpe into an elevator, Dixon on her heels.

Dixon wore the same crooked smile she'd noticed back in eastern Washington. Same lackluster glaze over his eyes, maybe drug induced, maybe just innate dullness. She'd know him anywhere, and as quickly, placed where she had seen him: a quarter mile or so up the highway from Lay-A-Day Ranch. Passenger in a semi cab that pulled a long trailer. Trailer with New Jersey plates. She recalled what the driver looked like, though she didn't know his name. But this was him, all right. Must be her lucky day.

The sable coat belonged to her sister, Echo, who lived in New York but was out of town just now, Venus had learned from their mother, reciting her experimental poetry somewhere in eastern Europe, God help the Croatians or Estonians or wherever it was. Echo's money came from the trust funds established in her name by the sister's wealthy mother. Venus had one, too. Not a sable, a trust fund, but she never touched it. At the moment, the sisters were not speaking but Echo's doorman didn't know that. Echo's doorman knew Venus by sight and let her into her sister's swank pad on Washington Square. Venus had spent the remainder of the morning in Echo's walk-in closet, reinventing her persona to jibe with the Catherine Sexton identity, starting with Echo's sable coat. It helped to have a politically incorrect sister. Echo's stiletto-heeled boots, two sizes too large for Venus, made ludicrous footgear in this foul weather, but also fit the Sexton persona. Her sister's hairdresser, Craig, tackled Venus's hair and makeup on an emergency basis. "You will feel your identity shift," Craig assured her as he applied the finishing touches on her makeup. Venus had glanced in the mirror and recognized Catherine Sexton, upper-middle-class princess, staring back at her. The transition was complete and credible. Her badge and her gun fit into the inside pocket of the sable coat, the only evidence of her true identity.

The air inside the elevator was close and warm, seeping through a ceiling vent, circulating germs and somebody's onion-bagel breath. Venus glanced up and saw the security camera recording all activity in the small square box. Volpe chatted affably and Venus tried to pay attention while at the same time observing Dixon who stood beside her, nearest to the floor buttons. How had he maneuvered himself into that checkmate position? Venus glanced at the buttons and saw that upon entering, Volpe had pressed 2.

Dixon snorted and said, "Like the ad says, 'Rock her world.'" He flashed a sarcastic smile at Venus. "Ain't that right, Miss Sexton?"

Simpering at Dixon, Venus murmured agreement. Mr. Vespucci, my ass.

When the elevator reached the second floor, Volpe turned aside and stretched out a guiding arm. Where was Fish? Irritated, Volpe said, "We exit on this side."

Dixon seemed intent on keeping to the rear, a configuration that slightly unnerved Venus. She tried falling back, letting Volpe and Dixon move ahead of her, but each time she paused, Dixon stepped aside and waved her forward. The dance of deception had commenced and it wasn't about to end anytime soon. She was sure that Dixon didn't recognize her yet, but eventually an alarm would ring somewhere inside his shellacked head.

"This isn't necessary," murmured Volpe, motioning his guests around the security entrance where an X-ray machine loomed. Waving the guards aside, he explained, "That's for employees. Never know when they might try to steal gemstones."

A bank of windows formed the north-facing wall, tall glass rectangles leaking remnants of daylight filtered through relentless snowfall so thick the flakes cast shadows across the old wood floor. The harsh winter light seeped into the space, illuminating a long wooden table where six men sat on high stools, their heads bent over their work. The men wore black short-sleeved, pocketless coveralls that zipped up the back to discourage the pilfering of gems. Five of the six men wore yarmulkes on their heads; several wore beards in various tones of salt-and-pepper. All six leaned into the table, loupes held to their eyes, their fingers working swiftly, deftly, on piles of evenly sized incandescent stones that sucked up the puny daylight and threw it back tenfold in pyramids of dazzling brilliance, piles of stars, each worker focusing on his own pyramid of light, his face awash in gemfire, and these were still diamonds in the rough.

"Geez." Dixon salivated. "So many diamonds all in one place. It's enough to make a fella weep." He walked over to the men working at the table, stood on tiptoe, watched one sorter examine a rough gem and whisk it into a pile. Dixon whistled on his way back to Volpe's side, and Volpe showed amusement at Dixon's wonderstruck awe.

"Must be twenty million bucks' worth o' rocks on that table."

"Wrong." Volpe grinned. "More like seventy million. Notice these are large-carat stones. The sorters are dividing the stones into roughly equal carat sizes. Virtually all of this shipment, which just arrived from Canada, will retail for six-figure prices each stone. That's once the stones are cut and polished, ready to be set. Since we are both the wholesaler and the retailer, we stand to profit from the maximum price at point of sale."

Dixon's salivating mouth fell slack-jawed.

"Ah, Gordon, there you are. So sorry I missed you at the elevator." A rotund gentleman, jolly as his green suit, approached Volpe, his hand outstretched. "I was with a client." Shaking Volpe's hand, he nodded at the others. "Fish is my name."

"My workshop manager," Volpe added. "Mr. Fish, meet Miss Sexton and Mr. Vespucci."

Fish's eyebrows shot up. "Vespucci, eh? Well, how do you do, sir?" Turning to Venus he added, "And this is the little affianced princess, I presume? How do you do, Miss Sexton? I have selected some glorious stones for your inspection."

Venus rattled off something appropriately princessy as Volpe and Fish led her and Dixon toward the workshop tables. "But first, you must have a tiny tour of the facilities. Mr. Volpe always insists his clients see the intense workmanship

Parecles puts into its product. Just now, my boys are working on a shipment of very exquisite rough straight from the Canadian arctic."

"I suspect that these particular stones are outside your fiancé's budget," murmured Volpe.

Venus played along. "Oh no, Mr. Volpe, no, not at all." She flashed a flirty grin.

"Ah. In that case," enthused Fish, "I would be delighted to show you some particularly unique gems."

Now Volpe made a split-second decision to reverse his plans. Gripping Dixon's elbow, he steered him toward the rear of the big room. "Miss Sexton, will you kindly excuse us for a few moments? Mr. Vespucci and I have some urgent business to transact. I'll just leave you here with Mr. Fish to watch the sorters. Solly over there on the far end is the crew leader. He'll have the finest stones on his bench." Volpe flashed a meaningful smile at Fish. "Clients always enjoy the show, don't they, Mr. Fish?"

"Oh, absolutely. Come along then, Miss Sexton, and allow me to show you around."

Fish led Venus across the warehouse toward Solly and his colleagues.

Volpe and Dixon walked to the rear of the big room. Volpe unlocked a door and the two men crossed the threshold, Volpe glancing out once at Fish and Venus before shutting the door.

Fish rubbed his hands together. "Now then, young lady, you are about to gaze upon some of the world's most amazing gems." He steered her toward Solly's bench. Solly, the lead sorter, grizzled and toothless, peered up over his magnifying loupe. A smile that started on his lips suddenly warped into a silent scream and then Solly cried, "Holy shit."

David Goldman's first shot whizzed past Venus, striking Fish in the back.

CHAPTER THIRTY-FIVE

Fish lurched forward, his eyes fixed in a death stare, knocking Venus to the floor and crumpling on top of her, his blood spraying over Solly. Next Goldman aimed the gun at Solly. The old man held his arms up as if fighting off a bad dream, but this wasn't a dream and Goldman fired. Solly went down. In a spray of bullets, Goldman picked off Solly's fellow sorters like sitting ducks in a carny game.

In the ensuing silence, Venus lay motionless beneath Fish's body, playing dead. Time slowed to what seemed an eternity. Then, footsteps sounded, tramping across the wood floor. Venus turned her head slightly and saw a pair of Dr. Marten boots, much like a pair she owned and often wore, no more than six inches from her face. The boot kicked, striking her face, and she lost consciousness.

When she came to, lying in a pool of blood, she heard the boots running across the floor. She looked up and saw the pyramid of diamonds Solly had been sorting, the stones now drenched bloodred, glittering like rubies in the fading daylight streaming from the window. She lost consciousness again.

In the office, Volpe and Dixon had heard the gunshots. Volpe opened the door a crack, peered out, then shut the door and locked it.

"Goldman," he said flatly. "He's gone mad."

Volpe had been thermal-testing the big diamond and was just about to make a pronouncement when the attack came. Now he headed straight for the rear exit door in his office. Dixon snatched the stone off Volpe's worktable and shoved it into his overcoat pocket. The two men fled through the exit door and down the fire-escape stairs, their shoes slipping and skidding in the snow. When David Goldman finally broke through the office door, he found the room deserted, the diamond nowhere in sight. Cursing, he pursued his prey down the fire escape stairs.

Across the workroom, Venus opened her eyes, saw Fish's dead body, heard the gunman cursing, heard the clattering of footsteps on the fire-escape stairs. Gently, she moved Fish's body off hers and struggled to her feet. Wiping blood from her eyes, she looked around. Dead bodies everywhere. Dead silence. From her coat pocket, she took her gun and cell phone, and called 911. Moving around the room, she checked for survivors, but they were all dead. Why hadn't the killer shot her? Had he thought she was dead? Had he lost count of the number of shots he'd fired? Why hadn't the guards come to their aid? Were they dead, too? Shedding the blood-soaked sable, gun poised, she moved across the workshop to the office and through the open door. No bodies, living or dead. Then she saw the exit door leading to the fire escape. She went through it into the snowstorm, and down the fire-escape stairs.

Below, through the falling snow, she saw Volpe and Dixon running down Forty-seventh Street, their assailant chasing them, pausing only to fire his assault rifle at his prey. So far he'd missed. Shopkeepers and the few pedestrians braving the storm now ran for cover. Venus aimed at the armed man and shouted for him to stop. Either he didn't hear her or he didn't care. He kept chasing Volpe and Dixon. Halfway down the block, Dixon turned, faced his attacker, and held up the big diamond. As if to bargain. "Let's do a deal, man," Dixon cried. "I'll make you a good deal." The attacker aimed his gun at Dixon, sighted him through its scope. Dixon tossed the big stone to Volpe who was only a few yards ahead. Volpe caught the stone just before a bullet struck Dixon in his brain, the organ he had trusted most. Dixon fell backward into the snow, splayed out like the angel he thought he was.

Volpe, grasping the stone Dixon had tossed him, ran like hell, but the attacker was gaining.

Venus, cursing the stiletto boots, struggled to catch up. Blood trickled across her forehead and flooded her eyes. She held her handgun at arm's length, aimed, and fired at the gunman, intending to injure him. The bullet struck his backpack. He spun and fired back in her direction. She leaped behind a lightpost.

Suddenly Volpe stopped running, turned around, holding his stomach.

"David," cried Volpe. "David Goldman, listen to me."

The gunman turned back to Volpe. "Give it to me," he shouted. "It's mine."

"But, David," Volpe protested. "Just put the gun down and listen to me."

Venus moved in cautiously. Goldman hadn't seen her come out from behind the post.

At the corner, Yitzhak Goldman rounded the block and turned into Forty-seventh Street, an air of anticipation adoring his cheeks. Walking beside him, a lovely blond woman, her cheeks deeply tanned, chattered excitedly.

"I tell you, Yitzhak, Gordon will be so surprised to see me. I just missed him so much, and today is his birthday. I imagine he hasn't even given it any thought; you know how preoccupied he is with his business. The girls are fine with their nanny back in Paris. You must join us for a glass of champagne."

At the suggestion of Simon Mehta, Yitzhak was on his way to Parecles when Crystal Volpe had nearly collided with him in the street. Now he couldn't shake her and only hoped her presence wouldn't complicate an already difficult plan.

Crystal Volpe took Yitzhak's arm as they turned into Forty-seventh Street. Yitzhak happened to glance up and see his nephew holding an AK-47 pointed at Gordon Volpe. Another man lay facedown in the snow in the middle of the street. A woman pointing a gun at David Goldman was moving in like a leopard stalking its prey.

"David!" shouted Yitzhak. "David!"

David Goldman fired his weapon and struck Gordon Volpe in the heart. Crystal Volpe screamed. Volpe's hands lost their grip on the stone as he slumped over onto the snow. The stone rolled sideways toward the snow-packed gutter. David Goldman dove after the stone. Venus fired, wounding him in his leg. Goldman dropped the AK-47. Staggering, he fell into a snowdrift, clutching his leg and screaming in agony. His backpack fell open and diamonds poured out, rolling into the gutter, disappearing into the sewer.

Venus checked Dixon's pulse and found none. Volpe was breathing but going fast. He looked up pleadingly into her eyes as she tried making him comfortable. He was whispering something. Venus leaned down and put her ear to the dying man's lips.

"But, David," he managed before sucking his last breath, "it's a fake."

CHAPTER THIRTY-SIX

Yitzhak Goldman hurried up the street, crying, "David, David, my boy, what is going on here? What has happened? Let me help you, my poor nephew."

David lay in the snowdrift watching his uncle approach. Things hadn't been going as he'd planned, and he was in no mood for his uncle's comforting arms. All these people getting in the way, in between him and the Lac de Lune. And now, Uncle Yitzhak had to show up. With something like bitter regret, David reached into his pocket and pulled out a handgun.

Arms outstretched, Yitzhak rushed toward his nephew.

"I'm sorry, Uncle Yitzhak," David mumbled before he shot Yitzhak through the heart. Seeing Yitzhak fall, Crystal Volpe turned to run, but Goldman fired again and she crumpled into a heap beside Yitzhak.

Rolling onto his side, David Goldman looked down the street for the girl. He'd have to take her out, too. Who was she? Why was she armed? Maybe a cop? Where had she gone?

Silence fell over Forty-seventh Street, and then the whine
of sirens in the distance, growing louder. Slowly Goldman
rose to his feet. Nothing around him stirred. The sky had
darkened and snow had stopped falling. Dragging his bloody
leg behind him, he loped through the frozen tableau. The
sirens sounded closer now, real close. It hadn't played out according to his plan.

Where was she hiding?

Back at Parecles, he'd used a silencer on the handgun to
kill the three security guards. Then he'd drawn the Uzi from
his backpack and used that to kill Fish and the sorters. He
thought he'd shot the girl then, too, killed her, too, but he
must have miscalculated. He had intended all along to kill
only the guards and Fish and anyone else who might witness him taking the stone from Volpe, and, of course, Volpe
himself. A quick hit-and-run inside Pareceles's workshop.
He hadn't counted on the sorters being at work. Hadn't
counted on Volpe's client or the girl in the fur coat. Or Uncle Yitzhak and Mrs. Volpe. He didn't intend to leave any
witnesses.

What about onlookers in the street? Peering from windows? This killing out in plain view. Screw 'em. They could
never identify him beneath his flamboyant overcoat and beret.
He could always claim someone stole his clothes, intending to
imitate him. Sure, he could finesse the street witnesses. But
not the girl. He'd kill her, too, once she showed herself. She
had seen far too much.

Three things left to do: Grab the diamond, kill the girl,
get the hell gone before the cops arrived.

And now the Lac de Lune lay just a few feet from him, in
the snow that covered the gutter. Waiting to be plucked.

He moved slowly in the soft glow of streetlamps, dragging his leg across the snow, his eyes darting sideways,
watching for the girl, for any shadow that might reveal her.
She might have run, but he doubted it. Stepping over Crystal
Volpe's body, he paused to study Uncle Yitzhak's face in

death. Poor Uncle Yitzhak. The King of Diamonds shouldn't have had to die. That had hurt. Still, even his uncle had seen too much. He stepped over Uncle Yitzhak.

Ah, there it lay, waiting for him. A street lamp shot a cold beam that glanced off the stone, creating a dazzling dance of light and color. More beautiful than any of the models. More beautiful than he had ever imagined. The one and only, ladies and gentlemen, the genuine, lovely Lac de Lune. David dragged himself up to the gutter, bent over, and reached for the stone. Come to me, baby. Come to me.

The beautiful object of his desire felt warm to his touch, as if fire emanated from within, but as he tried to grab it, the stone rolled away, following a trajectory into the gutter. He seized it just before it slid down the black hole. Snatching it up, he clutched tightly, as if the Lac de Lune might by its own powers escape his grasp.

At last. The Lac de Lune belonged to him now. The most coveted diamond in the world. Maybe the most beautiful. Certainly the most fabulous. His.

Slowly, he rose to his feet and loped down the block.

If all had gone well at KAM, when he'd placed the scorpion in Gordon Volpe's sight box, nobody would have gotten hurt. He'd only meant to frighten Volpe out of the competition for the stone. But no, Volpe had to pursue the Lac de Lune, as if he had any claim to it at all. As far as David was concerned, only three individuals had claims to the Lac de Lune: Dieter Haakvig, Jean Claud Rubicon, and himself, David Goldman. If all had gone as he'd originally planned, David would have, by process of elimination, won the right to cleave the stone.

Dieter Haakvig had been easily dispatched. David had paid Simon Mehta a fine sum to carry out that assassination. But with Rubicon something had gone wrong. Simon Mehta had failed in his attempts to kill Rubicon.

Or had Simon double-crossed David? Had he made a deal with Jean Claud Rubicon, cutting David out of the picture?

Simon had been acting weird lately, secretive and simpering, even more so than normal.

But now all that was behind him. Now, the Lac de Lune belonged to him and he would have the glory and honor of cleaving the fabulous stone. Everyone in the trade would know who had cleaved the stone. His reputation would flourish, and yet no one in the business would ever challenge how David Goldman had won the competition to cleave the Lac de Lune. No one would ever dare criticize the King of Forty-seventh Street's nephew. Yitzhak would have been, as usual, David's moral guardian. And Uncle Yitzhak would have burst with pride and rewarded him with all sorts of wonderful perks and goodies.

That is, if things had gone smoothly.

Unfortunately, things had not gone as smoothly as David Goldman had originally planned. And so, the backup plan had come into play, a quickly sketched plan to corner Volpe in the workshop at Parecles, to kill him and any witnesses, and then seize the Lac de Lune. A simple, straightforward backup plan, leaving no witnesses. But somehow things had gone wrong.

If he could just bind up this bleeding leg, he'd make a clean escape.

Here they came now. Down at the far end of the block, cops swarmed all over the place. Sirens blaring. Goldman dropped the stone into his pocket, navigated a snowdrift, and studied the street. Down the block he saw the Luxor Building, and across from it, the café. Its door open. Then he saw her.

She stood just inside the door to the shop. A café, its lights out, but he could see her in the light from the street lamps. He'd get her now.

CHAPTER THIRTY-SEVEN

The interior lights had been turned out, the normally bustling café plunged into darkness, the booths and counter vacant, illuminated only from the street lamps outside. Russian music played softly from a ceiling speaker. "Moscow Nights." Da, da, *da*-de-da. Da-da, *da* de da.

Goldman cocked his head and looked around. The tables had been wiped clean and the kitchen, which opened up into the main dining room, appeared deserted. Still, the front door was unlocked, so at least the manager must still be lurking around somewhere. Might've heard the commotion in the streets. Might have ducked for cover.

"Hello!" Goldman called out. "I know you're in here."

No response.

Goldman shut the door and glanced out the front window. Now a crowd had formed at the far end of the block and cops swarmed everywhere. He could see their patrol-car lights and hear the ambulance sirens. He moved cautiously toward the back of the café, his handgun poised, ready to fire. Passing the kitchen, he grabbed a dishtowel, started to bind his leg, and then realized that would mean setting his gun down momentarily. No way.

The music seemed to grow louder, or he might be imagining it. Louder and louder, until it hurt his ears. Faster and faster, the violins piercing his brain. Agitated now, he moved toward the rear of the café, seeking an escape route. And then he saw it.

A door in the rear of the café, below an Exit sign.

He grasped the door handle and turned it. It wouldn't open. Was it locked? How could that be? Wasn't that illegal? He fought with the door, trying to force it open. Shoving his shoulder against it, cursing. The door seemed to give a little.

"Drop the gun."

Goldman's scalp crawled. The woman. He turned around to locate her position. The café's front door stood open. The music stopped.

"I said, drop your gun. Do it now."

Goldman squinted through the darkness. Where was she? He yanked hard at the rear exit door but it didn't budge. Aiming his gun into the darkness, he fired once.

Silence. Then, "You're cornered, man. Drop the gun."

Where was she? Frantically, Goldman considered his few options. If he pulled hard, the door might open and he could escape. If she came after him, he'd shoot her. Or he could stand his ground and get rid of her once and for all right here. Then flee. Whatever, it had to happen fast.

He fired once again.

The bullet shattered a window and it rained glass. Still, he couldn't see her. Where was she hiding? And then he saw her shadow, cast long and tall against the café's service counter. She was crouched underneath the lip of the counter and now he could make out her silhouette. Goldman aimed at her head and fired.

The bullet struck the countertop, ricocheted, zinged off into the darkness. She returned fire, striking his arm. He clutched the wound and moved into the galley. Directly behind her now, on the other side of the counter, he stood up, leaned over the countertop, and aimed his gun at her head, just inches from her face.

"It's over, young lady," he said softly, placing the gun's barrel to her temple.

Venus felt the cool round tip of the gun's barrel against her skin. It had come to this. She had stalked him along the block as he made his escape, had him cornered in the café, had the upper hand until he'd eluded her only seconds ago, and now she was all his.

"Let's talk," she tried.

David Goldman laughed. "What? Like, 'let's make a deal' talk?"

"I mean, let's talk about Radke."

He should have shot her right then, but the mention of Radke's name apparently threw him off guard.

"What about Radke?" he said hoarsely.

"How Radke had fingered your uncle Yitzhak as the laundry man."

"What are you talking about?"

She could feel his breath on her face, but still couldn't see him. She'd have to move to see his face and she dared not move. The cold round spot had warmed now, from her body temperature. Still, she felt its pressure, its urgency.

"Your uncle Yitzhak laundered cash and diamonds for the tube. For his cooperation, he got paid in diamonds. African diamonds. Siberian diamonds. Canadian diamonds. Whatever. Uncle Yitzhak was the middleman for the arms smugglers. The cash and diamonds moved through his hands. What will they do now?"

"You're nuts."

"You didn't know about your uncle?" Keep him talking; buy time.

Silence. Tension oozed from him. The clamor in the street

grew louder, closer. He had only moments to escape. He'd have to shoot her soon.

He whispered, "My uncle Yitzhak was the King of Forty-seventh Street. He ruled this business. You ask anybody on Forty-seventh Street who helped them make it in the diamond business, they'll tell you it was my uncle Yitzhak. He helped folks, he even helped his competition. When they were down and out? He loaned them the capital to come back."

"You mean, he gouged them with high-interest loans. And if they didn't pay up, they were beholden to him for life. Like Volpe." A guess, anything to keep him talking.

"Gordon never got a dime from his Uncle Yitzhak. Sure, my uncle knew Gordon was in financial trouble, and he even offered to help him out. But Gordon said he didn't need anyone's help, he could bail himself out of whatever financial mess he'd got into. I hear it was gambling down in Atlantic City."

"But Yitzhak knew who Radke was. So did you."

"Radke was a cop. Everyone on Forty-seventh Street knew him and hated him."

"You knew it was Radke who mined the Lac de Lune?"

"Everybody in the business knew that. He got lucky, that's all."

"So who killed him? Your uncle?"

A pause. In the street, searchlights now flooded the block. Maybe they'd search door to door, flash lights into the café. Sweat trickled down her back.

"Uncle Yitzhak never killed a flea. He didn't believe in that."

Maybe she had piqued his curiosity. Or maybe he had lost so much blood he was losing track of time passing. Still, she'd just about run out of time.

"Hey, miss, I'm just a simple diamond cleaver. I don't involve myself in the business end of things. But I can tell you, Uncle Yitzhak never killed anyone."

"Right. Your uncle didn't kill. He hired others to kill for

him. And he hired someone to kill Radke. But the assassin failed, because Radke disappeared. Years later, he shows up as a diamond prospector in the Northwest Territories, and he's mined the most fabulous diamond ever found in Canada. Now everybody on Forty-seventh Street wants a piece of Radke, dead or alive. But mostly Uncle Yitzhak. Uncle Yitzhak knew that Radke had reached the original source of diamond smuggling in and out of Canada. Radke had all but fingered the tube master of the Northwest Territories. The laundry man was bound to protect his source of wealth."

The café's front door swung open. A head ducked inside.

"You say anything, you're dead," he whispered.

Venus nodded.

The figure in the door leaned inside the café, looked around, and ducked back outside. Venus heard a voice call out, "Over here!"

He heard it, too, and panicked.

"Okay, miss," he said and fired the gun.

The bullet would have streaked through her skull if Goldman hadn't fallen sideways as he fired, the barrel of his gun turning upward, sending the bullet into the ceiling. He heard a snarling growl as powerful arms wrapped him in a bear hug and threw him to the floor. He struggled, but his assailant was strong and his wounds had drained his energy along with his blood. Now pinned to the floor, his breath coming fast, he whimpered beneath his attacker.

Gennady Fedosov, the café waiter, held Goldman down while Venus cuffed him.

"Good work, Agent Fedosov." She set her gun on the counter while she frisked the sobbing Goldman.

Fedosov grinned. "We've been after Yitzhak for a lot of years, ever since the Soviet fell. You see, he double-crossed the Soviet people."

"You didn't make a very good waiter."

Fedosov cocked his head inquiringly.

"Too polite."

"Ah." Fedosov scratched his head.

The Lac de Lune weighed more than she had imagined. She hefted it up out of Goldman's overcoat pocket and set it on the counter. When she glanced up to see Fedosov's reaction, she saw the barrel of his gun.

"Turn around, miss," he said pleasantly. "If you want to keep the good looks. And put your hands on your head."

As Fedosov pocketed the gem, she said, "Enter the Russian."

Fedosov showed mild surprise. "So Radke warned you."

"Yep. Only I didn't expect a waiter. Anyway, the laundry man's dead, comrade."

Fedosov could only smile at this. "There are others."

"Let me guess. You supply the tube with weapons from eastern Europe. You worked with Yitzhak Goldman, got your cash for weapons directly from him. And then Volpe wanted in on the game. You delivered weapons to Volpe in exchange for the stone. But Volpe double-crossed you, tried to cut you out of the spoils."

Fedosov chuckled softly. "Something like that. You are very good."

"So who put you and Volpe together?"

"Ah. That is a private matter. In our business, we do not, how do you say, snitch."

Fedosov reached behind him and yanked the rear exit door open. "I don't wish to kill you," he said. "Besides, you will never find me." He disappeared into the night.

CHAPTER THIRTY-EIGHT

Hold on, chief." Venus glanced up from her cell phone at the Alaska Airlines ticket agent. "You got a Concorde to Yakima, Washington?"

The ticket agent studied his computer screen. "How about a nonstop 767 to Sea-Tac, change there to a crop duster?"

They settled on the 767 to Sea-Tac. Venus took her boarding pass and walked to the gate, resuming her conversation with Wexler, the NSC's director of transnational threats. "Okay, chief, I'm back. Could you repeat that last sentence?"

"I asked you what connection Ron Fairview had to Volpe and Yitzhak Goldman."

"Radke had it right. Fairview and his Company Eight were posing under that free-range chicken façade. They were smugglers, working the tube up into Canada. Fairview's death might have temporarily halted their operation, but I'm guessing his boys are back in business. Fairview's operation ties in with the East Coast smuggling routes. He met Volpe through Fedosov, who set up the plan to exchange weapons for the Lac de Lune. Mixx is looking into Fairview's New York City trips. We'll find that Fairview and Volpe met with Fedosov. I'm betting Fedosov promised the weapons in exchange for a piece of the Lac de Lune that Fairview would supply to Volpe. Volpe would have the diamond cleaved and the smaller half would go to Fedosov. I'm betting that was the agreement."

"And Yitzhak Goldman?"

"Was the laundry man. And pissed when he learned that his arms contact, Fedosov, was brokering a deal with another diamond broker. To Yitzhak Goldman, Volpe started looking like competition. And so Yitzhak offered Volpe a loan to pay off his gambling debts, with the condition that Yitzhak would receive the Lac de Lune in payment, but Volpe refused. Yitzhak decided to hell with negotiating, he'd just take Volpe out of the picture and grab the stone. But before his boys could snatch the stone from Volpe, things went goofy. Now Yitzhak's dead, and Fedosov has the stone. I'm guessing he's on his way to the Lay-A-Day Ranch."

Wexler snorted over the phone. "Why would he head out there? Why wouldn't he just hop a flight to Saint Petersburg or somewhere else in Russia?"

"Because we've put a watch on every flight leaving JFK and Newark headed to Europe and all points east."

"Still. I don't see the connection."

"Fedosov knows we'd catch him heading east. So he'll head west and try to make his exit from the U.S. at the safest possible point. That would be via Fairview's smuggling route."

"So we surround the ranch and take them all."

"Not so fast, chief. We've got women and children on the ranch and adjoining properties. We can't afford to endanger their lives. This has to be finessed."

"So we clear them out first."

"Chief, we can't have another Waco. This is a made-to-order disaster."

"I don't like you going in there alone."

"I'll take Mixx, how's that?"

"Not good enough."

"Okay, let's put a backup team together. But I go in first, with Mixx, understood? No one else moves in until I say so."

"You're endangering yourself and Mixx."

"Hey, I've paid off my karmic debts. Mixx can hang in the background."

Venus showed her boarding pass, walked onto the plane, and headed for her seat in the rear. She hated flying in the tail of the plane, but the flight was sold out and the only seat available was a jump seat near the rear exit door.

"Just trust me, Wexler. Give me twenty-four and I'll deliver what you want. Nobody hurt. No scandals. No Waco."

She maneuvered down the aisle past other passengers still fussing over their overhead baggage. She was halfway to her seat when she saw him.

Wexler said, "I want backup in position when you go in."

"Sure thing. Gotta go."

His head bent forward against the aircraft's window, he stared out at the tarmac. His thick hands rested in his lap, the fingers entwined, thumbs twiddling. He hadn't seen her. She moved back to her seat, buckled up.

Halfway into the flight, a lithe attendant handed out headphones and the movie started. *Teacher's Pet*. Passengers pulled their window shades and the cabin went dark, illuminated only by the flickering movie screens. Laughter erupted almost immediately.

Venus stood, walked forward, using her hand to shield her face as she passed Fedosov's aisle. When she reached the first class cabin, she showed the purser her badge and left a message for the pilot.

Returning to her seat, she noticed that Fedosov was watching the movie. She saw his eyes glittering though the dark, his lips tightly set. She turned sideways in the aisle as she passed his row, and when she reached her seat, she didn't leave it again until the 767 landed at Sea-Tac.

Mixx was waiting out front in the company's dark Lexus.

Venus had followed Fedosov through the airport, down to baggage claim, and had watched him retrieve a small, battered, fabric suitcase. He then stepped out onto the sidewalk and joined the taxi queue.

Mixx followed the taxi into Seattle. The cab pulled into the curved drive at the Olympic Fairmont. Fedosov got out, paid the driver, and walked into the hotel.

Mixx waited in the car while Venus went inside. Fedosov was registering at the front desk. She waited until he had entered the elevator before showing her badge to the desk clerk. Ten minutes later, she left the hotel, slid into the Lexus, and Mixx drove away.

"Just go once around the block. He's settled for the night. I've taken the room next to his."

"Oh, hell, you have all the fun."

"You can come visit."

"Dinner?"

"Sure. Room service. In fact, you can play waiter. Unless Fedosov decides to dine out. Now drop me off at the next intersection."

At eight o'clock, Fedosov called room service and ordered dinner. Mixx masqueraded as a waiter and delivered the meal.

"He's alone in there," Mixx reported. "No sign of visitors and he ordered dinner for one. Nice cut of beef and excellent champagne. Oh, and the bug's under the desk lamp. I finessed that while he was pretending to search for tip money."

"He tip?"

"Negative. Said he'd catch me later. He sure got that colloquialism down."

CHAPTER THIRTY-NINE

Vancouver, B.C.

Roland Mackenzie awoke with a start as the door to his cell clanged open. Two guards led him, half-clothed, down the provincial prison's cellblock, through a warren of halls and into a brightly lit tunnel. At the end of the tunnel, fresh air greeted Mackenzie as he was shoved into the rear of a dark van, its engine idling. The van rounded the corner past the front of the B.C. Provincial Jail. From the van's rear window, Mackenzie saw the mob. Their signs and banners bore his name. Some of the mob shouted about justice, and some scuffled with police officers. Mackenzie thought he heard his name chanted in the same singsong breath as the word "execute."

"Execute Mackenzie! Execute Mackenzie!"

So the rumors he had heard were true. The mobs had grown impatient over the past few days and now were calling for his immediate execution.

Even as the van rounded the corner into a separate cellblock unit, Mackenzie could hear the mob shouting for his execution.

"That's all for you, eh," quipped one of his guards. "Now don't you feel special, Sergeant Mackenzie?"

Some hours later, Mackenzie awoke for the second time to a guard calling his name.

"You have a visitor, Mackenzie. Up and at 'em."

"What time is it?" Mackenzie sat up and rubbed his face. He had barely slept after the transfer from solitary to protective custody, his new cell even colder and filthier than the last. His dreams had been full of mob angst and terror. Exhausted, he nonetheless felt glad to be awakened.

"It's six A.M. Let's go."

Mackenzie heard the shackles around his ankle clank as he walked sandwiched between two jailhouse guards and thought for the hundredth time how, as a Mountie, he had always found the sound comforting. A shackled inmate can't escape from custody. And now he was the shackled inmate.

The visitors' room was large and cold, painted a sallow green with fluorescent lights glaring overhead. Simple metal tables lined up in rows were bolted to the floor as were the chairs surrounding them. At one table in the far corner of the room, a slender man sat by himself, hands folded on the table, his thumbs twiddling, head bowed as if meditating on the digital motion. When the door clanked open, the man glanced up and watched as Mackenzie and a guard approached him.

Mackenzie didn't know the man, at least from this distance, he didn't recognize him. A sinister thought came to mind: What if the man were one of the mob from outside? Maybe one of the dead Zone Mine guards' relations? What if he had somehow masqueraded as Mackenzie's attorney to gain entry into the prison? What if he had smuggled in a weapon and would attempt to kill Mackenzie?

"Who is the visitor?" Mackenzie asked the guard as they approached the man.

The guard shrugged. "All I know is I'm supposed to bring you in here and supervise a fifteen-minute visit. I don't know who the hell comes to see you."

The man stood now as Mackenzie reached the opposite

side of the table. This close, Mackenzie was certain he had never seen the man before in his life. He was tall, slender, and had a stooping posture. His hair had thinned at the crown. He had sallow skin and round, coal button eyes. He wore a tentative expression and when he smiled his lips merely twitched. He waited until Mackenzie had sat down before he sat back down on the opposite side of the table.

"You don't know me," the man began, his voice wavering nervously. "But I think I can help you beat this rap."

He had a New York accent. Mackenzie recognized it because, some years ago, he had attended special joint border-patrol training in New York City.

"Go on," said Mackenzie suspiciously.

"Name's Crumley," said the man. He squirmed in his chair, placed his hands up on the table, and refolded them. "It's a long story, but I can tell you, Sergeant, I've got proof you didn't do the crime. See." Crumley reached up and ran a big hand across his lean face. "I've got some tape recordings. Made by a girl. Her name was Crandall. Karen Crandall."

Mackenzie leaned forward. "What? What are you saying? What do you know? What tapes?"

Crumley raised his bony hand. "I wouldn't raise your voice, if I were you, Sergeant. Let's just keep this between you and me. That guard over there? Who knows what side he's on, y'know what I mean?"

"Yes, yes, of course." Mackenzie lowered his voice. "Go on, please, sir."

Crumley grimaced. "It's a long tale," he said quietly. "I'll try to tell it fast. We don't have too much time. They say we've only got fifteen minutes. Well, it's like this, see. I got mixed up in this racket back in Jersey." And he told Sergeant Mackenzie the whole story. Weapons smuggling. The Lay-A-Day Ranch. Ron Fairview. The little tiny tape recorder, and the girl, Karen Crandall.

"She told her story, beginning to end. She told how she went up to Yellowknife to work for a guy called himself Big Jim Hardy. And how she found kimberlite on the shores of

Lac de Lune last summer, and how she and this guy Hardy brought a rig out onto the lake earlier this winter and drilled down into the craton, and how they discovered the Lac de Lune diamond in the first sample bore." Crumley went on, "You know what I mean when I say 'tube,' Sergeant?"

"Of course. Go on. Hurry. We haven't much time left."

Crumley glanced around. The guard stood at a distance, his watchful eyes aimed at them but his brain obviously trained on an interior movie. Crumley continued his story, how Hardy had just about enough evidence against Ron Fairview and his men to indict them on international arms and diamond smuggling, but that he wanted more. He was tracing Fairview's diamond smuggling back to the source.

Crumley grinned.

"I can see it in your eyes, Sergeant, you know what I'm talking about. Purdy. The security guard Radke, posing as Big Jim Hardy, hired at Zone Mine. Purdy was one of the guards killed during the assault on Zone, when Radke and his security guards were murdered and Miss Crandall was taken hostage. According to her tapes—I've listened to all of them—Purdy worked as a security guard at several of the Canadian diamond mines. He owned his own small stake, but he had never hit a lode. Rumor was, Purdy made big money, real big money, and his security guard job was how he did it. See, Purdy was Ron Fairview's source for smuggled Canadian diamonds. He stole them from the mines. In their place, he mixed in African diamonds of equal or lesser value supplied by Fairview. The mixes were all made in the rough, before the little polar bears and such were lasered onto the stones. So some of the stones sold as Canadian diamonds, certified with the little polar bear symbols and so forth, were actually what they call blood diamonds from Africa. Diamonds traded to Ron Fairview in exchange for weapons of war that Fairview acquired from the East Coast. From my boss, Dixon, in Jersey. Miss Crandall had always suspected Purdy was a thief and smuggler, but she couldn't talk Radke out of hiring Purdy. My guess is, Radke was planning to catch Purdy and his pals redhanded. And Dixon, he was working for the tube masters. Only Dixon's dead now. Has been since yesterday evening. I knew one man he worked for, a diamond broker in New York named Volpe. According to Miss Crandall's tapes, Volpe visited Purdy in Yellowknife just before the attack on Zone Mine. Karen says on her tapes that she took pictures of them together in a bar. She had no idea, I'm thinkin', that her boss was a federal agent who was setting Purdy up for a fall.

Mackenzie nodded. "It's all coming together now."

"And I can tell you Volpe was a novice to the tube. You ever hear of a diamond broker name of Yitzhak Goldman, Sergeant?"

"I—no. Please, go on. Our time's almost up."

"Yitzhak Goldman—he died too yesterday—he was called the King of Forty-seventh Street in New York City. Yitzhak Goldman was Purdy's main contact. Yitzhak was the tube's laundry man. He laundered the cash that flowed between the arms and diamond smugglers, and he set up the deliveries, when arms and diamonds were exchanged for cash.

"But then, just recently, the Lac de Lune diamond caused a kind of rupture in the East Coast tube. People getting greedy, know what I mean? And a neophyte butted in on Yitzhak's contacts and set up the big Zone heist, cutting Yitzhak out of the picture. That got Yitzhak right where it hurt most, and he tried driving a bargain with Volpe, but Volpe was too greedy. He didn't want Yitzhak's money. He wanted the Lac de Lune, a greater source of wealth.

"Well, Sergeant, they're all dead now, or most of them anyhow. My boss, Dixon, Yitzhak Goldman, his courier Simon Mehta, Gordon Volpe, and a bunch of innocent folks, too. See, Yitzhak's nephew, the cleaver, David Goldman, he went nuts and killed them all. Still, the tube masters back East, they've never been caught, and I guess that's because they have some special arrangement with the federal government, like how they have it in Russia, you know? My guess is they'll always have that conduit to run diamonds and weapons and drugs and humans and such. The government needs the tube, or I should say, some corrupted government officials in our country's national security agencies need the tube.

"I'm no genius, Sergeant, no political analyst. I can't explain it up at that level. But all's I know for sure is that you were never involved in the tube, East or West, that you didn't commit these crimes at Zone Mine, that you're being framed. And I even know who's framing you."

Mackenzie whispered, "Where are the tapes? Have you got them with you?"

"Hell, no. I wouldn't risk that. First thing I did, see, after I conducted my own independent research, I made duplicates of all the tapes and stashed them in a safe place. Then I carried the originals with me out here to Vancouver. I have them locked up in my hotel room safe, Sergeant. I wanted to turn them over to the proper authorities, but I'm guessing that's not a wise idea."

Here Crumley winked.

"No, no. Under no circumstances should you give those tapes to the RCMP."

"You want they should go to your attorneys?"

"No, no. I can't trust them, either. They were appointed by the RCMP. No, here's what I want you to do. Are you listening carefully, Mr. Crumley?"

Crumley grinned and leaned a little forward.

"I want you to deliver those tapes to a U.S. federal agent named Venus Diamond."

"I figured as much. But see, there's one problem with that, Sergeant. She might want to take me into custody. I mean, I guess I played a role in this whole mess. But I'm not fit for prison, Sergeant. Prison scares the hell outta me. No, I'd rather deliver the tapes to someone you trust, up here in Canada. That person can turn them over to Agent Diamond."

"In that case, Mr. Crumley, listen to me carefully."

The prison guard came out of his mental movie theater and called out, "Time's up, lads."

"Just give me a name, Sergeant. And an address."

"Eleanor Purdy. Number Three Kimberlite Road, Yellowknife."

Crumley stood up.

"Wait."

Crumley said, "Yeah? What else?"

Mackenzie said, "Why, Mr. Crumley? Why are you helping me?"

Crumley studied his bony hands. "All my life, Sergeant, I've been looking for a chance to do good. This is my chance. Karen Crandall gave me this chance by saying what she did on those tapes."

Mackenzie nodded.

"And, too," Crumley added, "I guess I sort of fell in love with her. With Karen Crandall. She won my heart, Sergeant. Nobody's ever did that before."

"Thank you, Mr. Crumley."

"Thank Karen, Sergeant. She's the hero."

In the morning, Fedosov, wearing a brown sports coat and dark trousers, carrying the small suitcase, emerged from his hotel room. Riding the elevator to the lobby, he walked to the reception desk and arranged for a rental car. When it arrived, he checked out of the hotel, paying cash, placed the suitcase onto the passenger seat, and slid behind the wheel of the late-model sedan. He spent fifteen minutes studying a roadmap before driving off.

During the night, Fedosov had not left his hotel room. He had not placed any telephone calls. He went to bed after watching the ten o'clock news and apparently slept through the night. He snored, excessively. The bug Mixx had placed underneath the table picked up and transmitted every sound in Fedosov's room, some less pleasing than others. Venus slept only intermittently, she and Mixx taking turns listening to Fedosov's irritating snore.

The morning air carried a light wind with only a hint

of snow. Venus and Mixx followed Fedosov's rental car at a cautious distance. Fedosov had difficulty negotiating the downtown streets but finally found the entrance to the I–5 Interstate. He drove the speed limit, negotiated the tricky express lanes and the Mercer Street Mess all the way north to Burlington, found the exit for State Highway 20, drove eastward. He got lucky: Highway 20 was open due to unusual springlike weather. On Highway 20, he stopped at Twisp for coffee and once again at Omak for gas and to use the restroom. He carried the suitcase into the restroom with him. When he emerged from the restroom, he was folding his cell phone and smiling to himself.

"He's made contact."

Venus and Mixx watched from across the road as Fedosov turned north onto Highway 97. An hour later, Fedosov turned into the county road leading to Lay-A-Day Ranch.

"Backup in place?"

Mixx nodded. "All set."

"How many?"

"They promised me twenty-five federal agents and another thirty or so military personnel. They're answering to me." Mixx paused, then added, "And, of course, I'm answering to you."

"Okay. We'll give him a ten-minute lead, then move in behind him. You're in charge of communication with the team."

Mixx glanced over at Venus. She hadn't slept much and he saw dusky circles under her eyes. She had spooky eyes, wide green, crazed eyes that he found disconcerting. He'd never told her that, afraid she'd take it wrong.

"You okay?"

Venus shrugged. "Sure."

"Want me to take the lead here?"

"Go to hell, Mixx."

No guards patrolled the gate and, as they approached the compound, nothing moved except for the ravenous chickens plying the hard ochre ground and a thin cold wind across the tall grass in the distant field.

The rental car sat idling in front of the Fairview home. Fedosov had abandoned it in a hurry, leaving the driver-side door ajar, the engine running. And then it exploded into flames. He wasn't leaving any clues behind.

The chickens squawked and scattered in the flare of flames. The rental car quickly burned down to a hot metal skeleton.

No one answered the door at the Fairview house. If Fedosov was inside, he wasn't telling. Venus tried the front door. Locked. She kicked glass out of a living room window and entered the house. Mixx stood watch on the porch, gun drawn.

The living room and kitchen had recently been cleaned. An unfinished meal sat on the table. Breakfast, a bowl of oatmeal on the tray of a child's high chair. The bowl still warm to the touch. A cup of milk spilled on the tray. The kettle still on simmer. Venus turned it off.

The children's bedroom was neat, Jonah's bed made, clothing neatly hanging in closets, children's toys in a toy box. Over the crib, a penguin mobile hung still in the silence. A stack of cloth diapers piled on a layette wafted a freshly laundered scent.

Fedosov hadn't been here.

Nor had he visited the parents' bedroom. A tracker knows the scent of her prey and Venus had Fedosov's scent memorized. The one advantage of tracking poachers for so many years was how the senses sharpen acutely. Still, sometimes they failed her. Like back in New York. She should have sensed him in the café. And instinct goes only so far. She couldn't have known the waiter was another servant of the tube. Yitzhak Goldman's Russian counterpart. Still, Radke had warned her of a Russian, and she'd missed her cue.

She came out onto the porch where Mixx was smoking a cigarette. He quickly doused it, wearing a guilty, sheepish expression. As if she cared.

"He never went in."

Mixx nodded. "What about the barn?"

"Let's go."

The barn too appeared deserted. No sign of life, even of the family dog. In the rear of the barn, the makeshift cell where Karen Crandall had spent the last days of her young life now hosted nothing more dangerous than a few barn spiders.

Stepping outdoors through the barn entrance, Venus saw him first as a flash of brown out in the field on the waving winter wheat. Then he was gone.

"The field."

They ran across the dusty yard, chickens flapping and squawking, their feathers flying. Before they reached the field, Fedosov had disappeared. Of course, Mixx had failed to check out the silos as she'd requested. Too rural for a city slicker. Venus pulled her gun and motioned Mixx to follow her into the center of the field. Another advantage of tracking poachers for years is memory. She had retained a physical memory of where the silo doors were laid into the ground.

The first iron door didn't budge. She moved to the next and saw that it was wide open, a gaping hole in the ground twenty feet in diameter, opening into a concrete tube, a steep sloping paved tunnel.

"Down there."

"Hell, no," protested Mixx. "You won't get me down there."

"Well then, stay the hell up here and pay attention. When I call for help, you call in the troops. Got it?"

"Right-o." Mixx was about as brave as a trapped Christmas turkey at this point.

She stepped on the first rung of the ladder. Caught Mixx's flickering eye. "You'll do better, Mixx, if you acknowledge the fear, ride with it, let it energize you."

He laughed nervously. "Hell, I hate the rurals. Gives me the creeps. And it's too damn quiet. I can't think when it's this quiet."

"I'll talk to you on the radio. Fair enough?"

"Go on."

"I'll need light."

Mixx brightened. "I've got a flashlight in the car."

He ran to the car, returning in less than two minutes with a small Eveready flashlight.

"It's powerful," he offered feebly, "for its size."

She tucked the flashlight into her belt and went down into the darkness.

CHAPTER FORTY-ONE

Darkness enveloped her. A cold draft blew from below, but warmer than the near freezing ground-surface temperatures. Venus reached into her belt for the flashlight. Its beam traveled about fifty feet downward, now on a more gradual slope, pooling light on a hard surface. She walked forward, keeping the light beam on what appeared to be the bottom of the concrete hole. But it wasn't the bottom, only a curve in the hole, and now as she rounded the corner, she realized that she was entering a wide concrete tunnel, twenty feet wide by fifteen feet tall, an oblong tube.

Ah. That was the other word for tube.

Tunnel.

She had never thought to take it literally. To her, the tube had been a metaphor for the smuggling operation. Now the metaphor had morphed into the literal; a tunnel for smugglers who operated a section of the international smuggling trade.

Like the ancient warriors of Samarkand, the builders of this tunnel had been excellent engineers. The concrete walls were finished smooth, an air-conditioning system ran through an overhead duct. The floor of the tunnel had been made wide enough to accommodate military tanks. A lighting system ran along the upper edges of the walls, now extinguished, she guessed, to confuse her, disorient her, perhaps to scare her back to the surface. A video camera was attached to the ceiling, its lens aiming downward. At her.

Fedosov must have moved quickly through the tunnel. She shone her beam ahead of her, illuminating about thirty feet clearly, another twenty feet just barely. She attached a headphone to her radio and contacted Mixx. His voice came back clearly.

"Mixx, you need to contact the joint border unit. We need agents on the other side of the border."

"Mackenzie's unit? You don't really trust them, do you?"

"Contact them. Have the Canadian unit meet me on the exact opposite side of the border from the Fairview ranch."

"How do I describe that?"

"Figure it out, Mixx. I've got my own problems."

As she moved forward, the cold draft blew against her face. Again, her tracking experience came into play. She had developed an internal compass. The tunnel curved slightly on occasion but for the most part ran in a northerly direction. The floor of the tunnel followed an incline. She walked for half a mile, counting off her distance as she went. Every time the tunnel turned a corner, a new video camera appeared on the ceiling. Now the floor slanted downward, a shallow but distinct declination. Ahead of her, she thought she heard a rumbling sound and prayed it wasn't a cave-in. She could still feel the floor of the tunnel rising and falling, as if following the contours of granite underpinnings formed naturally beneath the surface soil. Now rising again, gradually rising. Suddenly, her flashlight beam pooled wide, this time on another obstacle, but not a corner. Something else.

A door. Ten feet by ten feet, a great steel plate set on runners. She approached it cautiously, running her hand along the wall. No switch. Had Fedosov gone through that door? The sound should have carried clearly in the confines of the tunnel. Must have been the rumbling she had heard moments ago.

Fedosov was on the other side.

She ran the flashlight's beam around the perimeter of the steel door and then she saw the controls. A single metal button flush against the concrete wall. Okay, here goes. She put her index finger against it and pushed. The giant steel door groaned, rumbled up along its runners, and doing so, revealed blinding light.

Daylight.

When her eyes adjusted, she stepped out into a field of wheat grass, identical to the field where the tunnel had begun. Maybe five acres of wheat grass bending in the cold dry wind. When straight and unbending, the grass stood five feet tall, her height. When it bent against the wind, she was able to glimpse around her. The first thing she saw was the security camera bolted on the exterior of the tunnel. Her every move had been tracked.

She turned to face south and in the distance saw Lay-A-Day Ranch, a spot on the horizon. The tunnel had taken her underneath Fairview's wheat field, underneath the international border zone, and onto farmland on the opposite side of the border.

Welcome to Canada.

Turning north again, she moved cautiously through the high grass. The wind blew against her face, chafing cold. And then she saw him, maybe a hundred yards ahead of her, emerging from the grass heading toward a red farmhouse, carrying the suitcase. Running like a bat out of hell.

She ran, keeping her eyes on Fedosov. Saw him head across a green pasture where horses grazed. Saw him cross a small bridge over a pond, saw him reach the porch of the farmhouse. Saw someone open the door. Saw Fedosov go inside and the door shut.

Venus spoke into the radio. "We've got him now."

"One slight glitch," Mixx came back.

"What?"

"The joint border patrol unit is on a training assignment up in Calgary. Shit, Venus, I'm sorry as hell. Want me to contact the local Mounties?"

"I'm going in after him. You do whatever works."

The old farmhouse and small barn made a sweet pastoral scene amid cultivated green pastures dotted with grazing sheep, Guernsey cows, and, in their own corral, sleek stallions. The farmhouse sat on the banks of the pond, where a small dinghy was tied up to a wooden pier. Behind the farmhouse, a neatly manicured narrow dirt road led out to the main highway.

The old Victorian farmhouse and barn were both freshly painted red with white trim. The house's multipaned windows were covered in neat white curtains and a thin line of smoke rose from the chimney. A few chickens roamed in the near field, fat glossy birds with multicolored feathers, yellow legs, and great red wattles. Behind the farmhouse, the small red barn stood with its door slid open, a stack of milk cans loaded into the back of a small pickup truck. Inside the barn, several cows grazed on hay, emitting the occasional moo, the loudest sound Venus heard as she approached the farmhouse.

How long until the Mounties arrived? Five minutes? Five hours? Fedosov knew she had followed him. Even if he hadn't seen her leave the tunnel, the security cameras had tracked her and even now they were watching her. From her waist pack, she removed her Glock and slipped in a magazine. She flicked off the safety and carried it as she walked up to the farmhouse, took the steps two at a time, crossed the porch, and stood at the front door. Raising a fisted hand, she knocked twice, waited twenty seconds before the door opened.

"You'd better come in," said Sarah Fairview.

She looked wan and haggard, as if she hadn't slept in days, maybe weeks. Her belly showed now, even underneath her heavy winter cape. She held the infant in her arms.

Venus stepped inside the farmhouse, the warmth strangely welcoming.

"Where's Jonah?"

"They have him upstairs in a bedroom. He's all right, I think, so far. They promised not to hurt him if I cooperate with them."

She led Venus into a spacious country living room. A fire blazed in a large stone fireplace at the east end of the room.

"How many are there?"

Obviously terrified, Sarah smiled helplessly as she looked over Venus's shoulder. Venus turned around. Fedosov had appeared in the doorway, holding an AK-47, maybe courtesy of his former government.

His thick hair fell across his forehead, partly covering one blazing blue eye. Two bright red spots colored his cheeks. He was still panting for breath from the long run through the tunnel, the field, and the pasture. A second weapon, a long knife in a leather sheath, was tucked into his belt. He turned suddenly and aimed the Kalashnikov at Sarah Fairview.

"Drop your weapon or she and the baby, I shoot them."

Venus placed her gun on a small pine table. Fedosov stepped forward and snatched it up, added it to his waist belt.

"Move over there and sit down. Both of you."

Venus and Sarah moved to the couch Fedosov had indicated on one side of the fireplace. The infant fussed in Sarah's arms. Fedosov sat in a wing chair opposite them. The small suitcase sat beside the wing chair. Between the woman and Fedosov, a low leather trunk covered with a hand-crocheted tablecloth served as a coffee table. An arrangement of miniature winter squash formed a centerpiece. Nothing else cluttered the table. Neat as a pin, like the rest of the room, like the rest of the tidy little farm. Venus had the impression of having stepped into a children's storybook. Then Fedosov aimed the gun at the fireplace and fired.

The sound frightened the baby. He began wailing. Sarah

held the baby against her breast and crooned into his ear. Venus realized she didn't know the younger boy's name.

"What's his name?"

"Noel. He was born Christmas Eve."

"Hey, Noel."

"You ladies don't speak, understand?" Fedosov demanded.

He was deciding what to do with them. The fire crackled and spit. From upstairs came the sounds of footsteps shuffling across the floors and then down a staircase. Then a voice called from somewhere on the ground floor.

"Let's go, Gennady."

Where were the Mounties? They should have been here by now. Had they located the right farm? Where in the hell were they?

"Okay, just a minute," Fedosov yelled back. "I am doing it now."

"Oh, God," Sarah cried. "Please don't hurt my babies. I beg you, don't hurt them."

"Shut up!"

Fedosov motioned with the gun for the women to move. "Over there. In that corner."

Venus and Sarah stood and moved into a corner of the living room. Sarah began crying softly, pressing the infant Noel to her breast. Two glass windows met at the corner beam. The women stood facing the outdoors. Outside one of the windows, the fishpond came nearly up to the edge of the house. Outside the other window, more of the pond and a little patch of ground, hard now, its grass brown and matted.

Fedosov said, "Open up that window."

Venus opened the window nearest Sarah. So he was planning to shoot them and dump them out into the fishpond.

Venus whispered, "Can you swim?"

Sarah nodded.

"Get ready."

"I tell you to shut up!"

From behind them came sounds of Fedosov rising from

the wing chair, and now Venus could make out his reflection in the window. He had set down the AK-47 and had drawn one of the Glocks. He was going to do this close-up, execution style. Why? Maybe he didn't trust his aim from a distance. Maybe he had never killed before. Could be.

He came forward toward the women. He seemed undecided as to which to shoot first. Little Noel began fussing. That seemed to unnerve him. He coughed lightly and raised the gun to Sarah Fairview's head. He stood to the rear and to the right of Venus, directly behind Sarah. He inhaled deeply, the gun poised. Then Noel sneezed.

Venus lurched sideways, whirled around, and knocked the gun from Fedosov's hand. Her right leg bent at the knee slammed into his groin and sent him tumbling backward. The Glock flew across the room. She dove at Fedosov, a groaning pile of jelly on the carpet, and jerked the other weapon out of his belt. Still, Fedosov struggled. The knife came out of his belt and he flailed it at her face and chest, and his comrade rushed to his aid.

"Run, Sarah. Take the boat."

"But Jonah—"

"I'll get him. Go!"

Fedosov held the knife at her chest. Sarah climbed out the window, dove into the pond, and swam toward the boat, Noel clutching her neck.

The second man was twice Fedosov's size and powerful. One steely arm wrapped around Venus and sent her flying across the floor. When she landed, the second man was standing over her, holding the AK-47 pointed at her head.

Somewhere behind her, Fedosov was groaning and cursing. The larger man walked around her, running his eyes over her body. She could see Sarah through the window, swimming toward the little boat. Now someone was running along the pier. Holding a gun. Trapping Sarah and the baby in the water.

The goon with the AK-47 growled. She saw his bloodshot eyes, his beastly yellow teeth. He reached out one leg and flipped her over onto the floor. He placed one large foot on her stomach, pointing the gun's barrel downward. His mouth opened into a great maw and he drooled. The pressure of his boot on her chest crushed her lungs. She gasped for air. The gun's barrel was now inches from her face. She heard herself pleading for her life but couldn't tell if her words were spoken aloud or only in her head. The barrel touched the tip of her nose and then moved up slightly to rest on her forehead. Jesus, oh, good Jesus. She shut her eyes. And then gunfire. A barrage of gunfire. She opened her eyes and saw him bite his tongue in half as he crumpled. She rolled over just in time to avoid being crushed beneath his falling body.

The Mountie standing in the doorway came forward.

"Well, now," he said calmly. "Just aboot teatime, eh?"

She heard another gunshot. Through the window she saw the man on the pier fall into the pond. Two Mounties ran down the pier to help Sarah out of the water.

"There's a young boy upstairs."

The Mountie shook his head. "The boy's fine. We got him first. And another suspect." The Mountie shrugged. "Unfortunately, he's dead."

Fedosov lay on the floor, a weak whimper leaking from his lips. Still, his fierce blue eyes held their fire and he was staring at the suitcase. Venus removed the suitcase's key from Fedosov's coat pocket, unlocked the suitcase. Inside, a foam pad cradled the stone Fedosov had taken from David Goldman. She plucked it out, held it up to the fire. The rough octahedron-shaped stone caught the firelight, shone luminescent. She heard Fedosov catch his breath.

They pulled Sarah and Noel out of the pond, loaded them and Jonah into an ambulance chopper, and headed for Vancouver. The gunman shot by the Mounties on the pier would be dredged out of the pond later. Fedosov got to ride in the RCMP chopper along with a couple of unfriendly Mounties, and the corpse of the last survivor of Fairview's Company 8, who had been holding Jonah upstairs. Venus led an RCMP officer, Mackenzie's replacement, back through the tunnel where Mixx stood in the field of grass on the Lay-A-Day Ranch, smoking and watching the chickens pecking futilely at the frozen ground. Snow began to fall.

CHAPTER FORTY-TWO

Bud had just opened for business when the stranger ambled into his bar. Bud had never seen a man with quite so large a head compared with the rest of his lanky body. The man was dressed for the weather except for his hands, large bony hands that the cold had turned bright pink, the color of rhubarb. The man glanced around nervously at Bud's other patrons, and then approached the bar where Bud held court before a magnificent hand-carved antique mahogany and mirror-back bar.

"I'll have a greenie," the man said, his voice wavering anxiously.

"What the hell's a greenie, bub?" Bud looked around. Must be some stumblebum newcomer up here after a prospecting job. Hell, who'd ever heard of a "greenie"?

"I mean, a Heineken."

Bud rolled his eyes, slid over to the fridge, and fished out a greenie. So that's what the lad meant by a "greenie." Bud slid back over to the bar and laid the greenie down on the counter.

"You want a glass?"

"Nope."

The man wrapped one rhubarb-colored hand around the green bottle, tipped it, and swallowed about half in one long pull. He set the bottle down, looked Bud in the eye, and said, "What I want is what Karen gave to you before they kidnapped her."

Bud felt all the blood drain from his head. He felt dizzy, as if he might faint. He gripped the bar and his eyes darted around. No one else seemed to have heard the stranger say Karen Crandall's name. Bud leaned up close to the stranger's face.

"Who in the goddamn hell are you, buster?"

"Who I am don't matter. Just say I'm Karen's emissary. She wanted you to know she appreciated all you did for her. How you looked out for her and all when she first came up here to Yellowknife. She was real fond of you, and she asked me, indirectly, to thank you for being her friend when she didn't have a friend or a job or anything but a wide-eyed city girl's vision of prospecting for diamonds in the far north. She wanted me to thank you for introducing her to Big Jim."

Bud's eyes grew wide and round as saucers and he white-knuckled the bar counter. "You saw her? You saw Karen?"

The stranger bowed his head. "Afraid not, sir. Had I seen her, she'd still be around. I got to her too late, you might say. But she left me a message. And part of that message was to thank you for being her friend." He tilted the greenie again. "Another part of her message was that she wanted me to retrieve what you were holding for her. You know what I'm talking about?"

"Yeah. Yeah, I know."

"You got it handy?"

"It's back in my office. Locked up in the safe."

The stranger nodded. "Maybe we better go back there

now. Get it out of the safe, out in the fresh air where it might do some good."

Bud looked around. None of the local crowd seemed to notice him speaking to this stranger. He straightened up, jerked his head. The stranger came around behind the bar counter and followed him into his office.

"I never touched it," Bud swore, "except to take it from Karen's hand and place it right here in the safe. Even when things went down, I never touched it. She made me promise. I was only to give it to her when she asked for it. Now I guess she'd say it was okay, you being her friend."

Five minutes later, Crumley walked out of Bud's bar carrying the small camera Karen Crandall had entrusted to him. The images recorded on the camera would add credence to Sergeant Mackenzie's case for innocence.

Eleanor Purdy was setting the kettle on to boil when she heard the rumble of an engine coming from the ice road leading to her cabin. Wiping her hands on her apron, she moved to the kitchen window, pushed back its lace curtains, and looked out. The stark white sky fused into the barren white ground; no horizon offered perspective on this bleak winter's morning. Sound carried far across the frozen landscape; the vehicle she had heard was still nearly a mile distant, an RCMP vehicle heading toward her cabin. Then she saw it; the black Hummer stood out like a fly in a bowl of buttermilk, still a speck, though she recognized it as a police vehicle. Roland had driven a similar vehicle whenever he came out to the cabin.

No more than a mile off, still, she had time enough to prepare for their arrival. Eleanor went to the china cupboard, removed her best teapot, sugar, and creamer, and several cups and saucers. The men would be cold when they arrived; they would welcome a cup of tea and some nourishment. Carefully, Eleanor set out the tea things, shook dried black tea from a tin into the teapot, and placed a fresh-baked ham and a loaf of homemade bread on the kitchen table. The kettle whistled and Eleanor turned to the stove, turned off the burner, and carried the kettle back to the table, where she poured it over the tea leaves into the pot. Placing the cover on the teapot, she peered once more out the window and saw the RCMP vehicle slowing to a stop in front of her garden gate.

No garden this time of year, but come summer, when the ice had melted and the snow retreated to the northern hinterlands, the rich soil would burst with life, sending up great shoots in a hurry to mature, colossal cabbage heads and turnips the size of basketballs, pumpkins as big as Cinderella's carriage, sunflowers measured in meters instead of centimeters. Everything up north grew fast and fat beneath the midnight sun, or else it died when the short summer suddenly lost its nocturnal hold to the slanting horizon. And the days grew dim and dreary, like this morning's sorrowful excuse for daylight, this horizonless ice desert inviting living things to slumber beneath thick mantles, to dream of a brighter time, the white nights of youth, when life pierces the fecund defrosted soil and life creates life in such a big hurry and the softened earth bears fruit. Such a time would come again soon, and Eleanor Purdy expected to live long enough to greet it.

The RCMP Hummer had parked just outside the front gate, and now as Eleanor moved quickly toward her bedroom, she heard voices. She could not understand what they were saying, only understood they were human voices, a sound that rarely penetrated her world, a sound that had almost always brought her pain and terror.

Up a tiny staircase and into her bedroom, Eleanor moved swiftly to the bedside table where she kept her gun. Removing it from the small drawer, she glanced up at a framed photograph on the table.

Roland Mackenzie wore his RCMP uniform for this formal photograph he had had taken just for Eleanor soon after they had met and fallen irrevocably in love. Roland had come home to Yellowknife on holiday that sweet summer, two former high school sweethearts reunited as two adults in the autumn of their lives. They rediscovered the unspeakable joy of true love freely given, the ripe passion only known to the wise. Now Eleanor raised the photograph and held it to her breast and a soft heaving sob escaped from her lips. Then, placing the gun on the table, she said, "Just in case," and left the bedroom, closing the door only partway behind her.

The RCMP, two of them, had come around to the kitchen door. She recognized both of them and opened the door immediately. The officers doffed their hats and outer garments in the gear room and stepped into the warmth of Eleanor Purdy's kitchen.

"Thank you," said Officer Benton, at first declining Eleanor's offer of tea and biscuits. "We just had our tea from a thermos on the way out here."

Eleanor nodded as Officer Benton and her new superior, Officer Landis, held their hands up to the woodstove. She knew why they had come. Still, she smiled hospitably and said to Officer Benton, "I thought you had gone on holiday, Sandra."

"Bad timing," Officer Benton answered glibly. She moved away from the fire, stood facing Eleanor.

"Eleanor, do you recall that immediately after the Zone murders, we had the unfortunate duty of interviewing all the widows and other family members of the victims?"

Eleanor nodded.

"The case, as you know, is still open. Sergeant Mackenzie will go to trial next month. At this point, we're just wrapping up a few loose ends." Here Officer Benton exchanged a glance with Officer Landis. He had been gracious in allowing Benton to take the lead, seeing as how he was the superior officer. But Benton knew the case against Mackenzie more intimately.

"The information you may be able to provide, Eleanor, is crucial to the central argument of the prosecution."

Eleanor folded her arms across her generous bosom. As she did so, she glanced down and noticed that a spot of blackberry jam had stained the bib of her white apron. The hell with it. She wished the Mounties would just get it over with and get out.

"Having been called out here on numerous occasions to intervene in domestic disputes—"

"No disputes. My husband was beating me."

Benton grimaced. "Quite right, Eleanor. I was being delicate. In any case, I'm keenly aware that you were a victim of domestic violence. Jack was a violent man and you're better off without him in your life. Still, he was your husband and the father of your only child."

"My son died in Iraq. I have no family left."

Both Benton and Landis murmured sympathetically.

"You've had a lot of suffering for one human being, Eleanor. A lot of suffering." Benton inclined her head. "May we sit down now?"

"Of course, both of you, please."

The Mounties sat at Eleanor's table. Now she took the kettle off the stove and poured more hot water into the teapot. Both officers partook of Eleanor's hospitality, hungrily consuming ham sandwiches and biscuits with jam. Eleanor sat opposite the officers, watching them eat, waiting for the punch line. Get it the hell over with.

Now Officer Benton drew a napkin across her mouth and got straight to the point. "Jack Purdy was my friend, as you know. Even so, I never excused his treatment of you. Everyone knew that he was a violent man, that he had no control over his temper. I had no sympathy for him, and to be frank, Eleanor, when he died I didn't shed a tear."

Eleanor poured tea and handed each of the Mounties a cup. Benton added sugar to hers and began stirring the hot brew.

"Even so, I am an officer of the law, and therefore compelled to defend victims of violent crimes. Such as the crime of murder. Jack Purdy was a victim just like the others. Just like Lamar Atkins and Nathan Mwangi. And the rest of them, and their families. But Jack, now, he was my friend. Folks around here knew that. You might say that was cause for me to recuse myself from this investigation. But Sergeant Landis has permitted me to remain on the case, in a minor capacity, since it was my initial intuition and investigation that resulted in the findings against Sergeant Mackenzie."

Sergeant Landis spoke up. "We have full confidence in Officer Benton's qualifications to assist in this case."

Eleanor could do no more than paste a saccharine smile across her face.

"I'll come right to the point, Eleanor."

Finally.

"We are aware of your relationship to Sergeant Roland Mackenzie."

Eleanor's face lit up in a sort of pleasant inquiry.

"We know that you have been lovers for over a year now, and that you were planning to divorce your husband in order to marry Sergeant Mackenzie. It would be useless, even foolish, to deny this fact."

Eleanor shrugged. "Why deny something that brought joy into my life?"

"Then you admit to the affair?"

Eleanor laughed. "Call it whatever you want. Roland and I are in love. That's a rare enough condition these days, especially for old fogies like us. We plan to be married, and when this nightmare is over, once Roland is exonerated, we shall be married."

Officer Landis set down his teacup and said, "We don't expect Sergeant Mackenzie to ever walk free, ma'am. The evidence against him speaks volumes about his guilt."

"Which brings us right to the point." Officer Benton reached inside her jacket and brought out a folded sheet of paper. She handed this to Eleanor, saying, "Hard as this is for me to do, I have to serve you with this subpoena to appear before the grand jury investigating the Zone murders."

Eleanor unfolded the paper and read the subpoena, her heart racing. So this was it? This was the only reason they had come? This puny excuse for a visit? And all along, Eleanor had expected something far more serious. Looking up at Sergeant Landis and Officer Benton, Eleanor spoke calmly, with dignity.

"Of course," she told them. "I shall be happy to testify."

As they were leaving, stepping out of the gear room into the cold, Officer Benton noticed a snowmobile parked directly behind a four-wheel-drive Jeep. Benton recognized the Jeep as Eleanor Purdy's. She said, "That new, Eleanor?" And indicated the snowmobile.

Eleanor looked Benton straight in the eye and said, "Yes. Yes, I bought it just after Jack passed."

Benton stared at Eleanor, but the woman didn't blink.

"Well, it's a good idea to have a vehicle like that way out here in the suburbs," said Benton finally.

The RCMPs tipped their hats. Eleanor stood at the kitchen window and watched the black Hummer weave across the ice toward Yellowknife. She watched until their Hummer disappeared around a bend. Then she took the tiny staircase up to the second story of her cottage. In her bedroom, a man sat in a chair, looking out the window from behind the ruffled curtains.

"They are gone, Mr. Crumley," said Eleanor, smiling at her guest. "Now, which of us will make the telephone call?"

CHAPTER FORTY-THREE

International Peace Arch,
U.S.–Canada Border

At sunrise, a thick lavender mist rolled across the marshlands and settled over Semiahmoo Bay. Where the marshland met the shore, the International Peace Arch rose out of the mist to mark, in case anyone questioned it, the border between British Columbia and Washington State, USA. In spite of rigorous border patrols and unusually tenacious customs officials, both Canadian and American, a few criminals still manage to finesse the border checks and slip into the country of choice; some heading north, running from U.S. marshals, others heading south, fleeing the Royal Canadian Mounted Police, still others evading the IBET patrols with their sophisticated data banks containing the names and descriptions of the world's most dangerous criminals. Terrorists, smugglers, and human slavers who tried crossing these borders feared IBET patrols most of all.

A cold sun pierced the lavender mist, shooting golden beams that lit up the Peace Arch and perhaps dropped a ray of good cheer into the morning routine in the little buildings housing border officials. Already, vehicles had lined up on both sides of the border, waiting for passport inspection, vehicle searches, and the occasional sniffing from the resident drug hound. The Canadian side had been fairly quiet during the night and the sudden accumulation of vehicles wanting to cross into the United States might have puzzled the border officers were it not for the huge sale advertised at the Costco store in Blaine, Washington. Spring was just around the corner, after all, the loonie was gaining strength against the greenback, and Costco had a half-price sale on women's dresses and fishing gear. In spite of the long line, the guards worked deliberately, thoroughly, checking each of the randomly selected vehicles. Nothing out of the ordinary jumped out at them this morning, that is, until the polar bear appeared.

A dirty white pickup truck drove up to the gate on the Canada side, the pickup pulling a trailer upon which sat a large cage. Inside the cage, an adult polar bear paced restlessly, its breath flowing out in great clouds, its nose sniffing the air. Iron shackles around the polar bear's legs hinged on chains fastened to the cage. The animal had been safely secured and presented no obvious danger to the curious crowds now forming around its cage. Two Canadian border guards approached the driver's side of the pickup and spoke to the driver, who stepped out of the vehicle and accompanied them during a thorough inspection of the cage. The spectacle caused great excitement, including a spate of controversy, easing the dullness of the long wait in line, and when the border patrol finally waved the pickup and the caged polar bear through into the United States, one disgruntled Canadian border guard grumbled, "Sonsabitches even want our polar bears."

A half hour passed, the mist burned off and a clear blue sky appeared over the Peace Arch. The same border guard who had cursed greedy Americans happened to look up from his work and notice a Royal Canadian Mounted Police vehicle approaching, its siren whining. "Now what?" he remarked to his partner. He was the chief duty officer this morning, and so when the RCMP vehicle squealed to a stop near the immigration checkpoint, he approached the Mounties wearing a quizzical expression.

"Did a polar bear pass through here this morning?"

The border officer looked surprised at first, and then nodded. "Checked out fine. Circus bear."

"Headed for?"

The border officer remembered the bear's destination. "San Diego. Vehicle operator had papers. They looked to be in order."

The Mountie grunted and made a call on his radio, then swung his vehicle around and sped back north. The border guard shrugged and went back to work.

U.S. Interstate 5 runs south from Blaine, Washington, the northernmost Washington town before the Canadian border. The interstate passes through low-lying flatland fields carpeted in early March with a thin layer of dead grasses, interrupted occasionally by shallow screens of skeletal deciduous trees, a seasonally barren wasteland providing little shelter for wild animals or desperado immigrants on the run. A few back roads lead off the interstate into rural farmlands that in springtime explode into fecund lushness, but now lay stark and bare and hesitant, God's abandoned backwater. Travelers don't stop along this section of the interstate, not in winter, unless misfortune blows out a tire or sucks the fuel from the gas tank. Even then, travelers do their business and get out fast, before the landscape permeates their psyches.

The white pickup truck pulling the caged polar bear made it fifteen miles into the United States before the pickup's left rear tire blew. The driver expertly negotiated an exit off the interstate onto Semiahmoo Spit Road, drove onto the shoulder, stopped the vehicle, and got out to fix the tire. Back in the cage, the polar bear, which had been dozing, raised its head and sniffed the air, then stood up and began pacing restlessly.

The phone call from the Mounties had wakened Venus from a deep sleep. She'd been expecting the call, but not so soon and certainly not at this hour of the morning. She reached across the armrest and poked Mixx.

"Let's go, Sandman."

Mixx groaned and sat up, smoothing his nice hairdo. "Where the heck are we anyway?"

Venus started the ignition. "Ferndale."

"Where the heck is Ferndale?"

"South of Blaine."

Mixx shook his head, maybe trying to reorganize the nuts and bolts. He reached into the back seat and found the thermos. He poured Venus a cup, handed it over. He drank directly from the thermos. "Lukewarm doesn't do it for me. Let's find a Starbucks."

Venus grinned. "We're a long way from the nearest Starbucks, city boy. Like about fifty miles."

The cassette tapes Crumley had given to Eleanor Purdy for safekeeping had been turned over to the Canadian prime minister. Wexler, representing the U.S. National Security Council, had flown to Ottawa to meet with the prime minister and officers from the joint border patrol unit. Mackenzie would be exonerated, based on Karen Crandall's recounting of the events that had occurred at Zone Mine and at Lay-A-Day Ranch. Though he hadn't confided everything to Crandall, events following the assault on the mine proved Radke's theories had been on target, his instincts about the West Coast smuggling route and its handlers correct. Following the trail Radke had suggested in his terse e-mail opened up a can of worms Venus hadn't counted on. Still, she guessed that had Radke survived the assault on Zone Mine, he would not have been at all surprised at the smugglers' connections.

The surprise came with Eleanor Purdy's telephone call to Venus. Crumley had come on the line and, recounting Crandall's taped narrative, detailed how the same person who had murdered Radke had stolen the real Lac de Lune diamond in a fast-switch motion. And Crandall had identified Radke's killer. Timing couldn't have been better.

Venus turned on the Lexus's flashing light and slammed the throttle to the floor.

"Take it easy, Venus."

"You want to drive?"

"No, I just—"

"Then can it and get on the radio. We'll need the border patrol out here and roadblocks put up from Sedro Woolley northward. When you're finished doing that, phone Wexler in Ottawa. Tell him we're about to pick up Radke's killer. That will make his day."

"Why don' you make the calls and I'll drive?"

"Do it, Mixx. And don't worry. We won't crash."

The pickup truck pulling the cage appeared suddenly on the horizon.

"Eleven o'clock on the entry ramp, Mixx."

Mixx looked across the highway. "Bingo."

Venus shut off the flashing light, screeched onto the right-hand lane, and exited at Semiahmoo Spit Road. The road passed underneath the interstate, a left-hand lane leading to the southward entry ramp. Venus swerved left and was headed onto the ramp when she noticed that the pickup had reversed direction and pulled off the ramp into a clump of scrub brush. She slammed the Lexus into reverse and screeched backward onto the shoulder. She was out of the car and running into the scrub before Mixx had buttoned his overcoat.

The scrub made poor cover and Venus could see even before she caught up with the pickup that the driver's side door was open and yellow smoke poured out of the exhaust pipe. The cage's right side wheels had slid into a ditch, the cage now tilted precariously. Inside, the polar bear struggled for purchase, and when Venus ran past, it bared its pointed teeth and growled.

The driver had fled into a field and was running now

across the scrubland toward a marshy inlet. Abruptly trapped on a soggy wedge of ground, the driver searched frantically for an escape route. But the marsh surrounded now; the only option was to go back toward the pursuer whose gun was drawn, who had gained ground and was only a few yards distant.

The driver pulled out a weapon and fired at Venus. Venus drove into the scrub. A flock of wild geese took flight, honking. More gunfire. Venus crawled forward on her belly, gun drawn, hoping the shallow scrub would camouflage her for just a few more yards. Sometimes being small is an asset.

Silence fell across the scrubland. Venus could see her prey's boots, could see how the boots struggled to stay balanced in the soggy ground.

"It's over, Officer. Put down your weapon and place your hands on your head."

"Venus, is that you?"

"Drop your weapon. You're under arrest for murder."

"I don't understand. I'm on holiday. Doing a little side job. Hauling this polar bear down to San Diego."

"This is your last warning. Drop your weapon and place your hands on your head. Now!"

Sandra Benton raised her gun and, preparing to fire, took one ill-fated step backward, falling into the marsh. Venus scrambled to her feet and moved in. Benton, struggling to her feet, lost her grasp on her weapon. The gun sank into the muddy water.

Overhead, a helicopter clattered into view. Finally. They'd have to land on the interstate, the only solid ground. Hurry the hell up.

Still, Benton wouldn't come gracefully. She came up out of the marsh water charging like a mad rhino, knocking Venus to the ground. Placing one heavy boot on Venus's wrist, Benton bore down until Venus's hand involuntarily opened and the gun fell out. Benton grabbed it, her laughter riding the wind. Venus raised her head and found Benton's calf muscle, bit down hard. Benton hollered and leaned over.

Venus flipped the larger woman onto the ground. But Benton had the weapon and thus the advantage. She pointed the gun at Venus.

"Now you're my prey," Benton snarled. "So run for your life, baby doll."

Benton fired once at the ground beside Venus's foot. She could shoot her now, if she wanted. But she wanted some fun. She wanted a chase. She wanted prey.

She fired again. "Run," she yelled.

Venus ran helter-skelter through the scrubland, a moving target teasing her pursuer. As Benton chased her, she moved gradually closer to the marsh. Once, she reached into her waist pack for her second weapon, but Benton fired a shot that grazed her arm. The second shot zinged past Venus's head. Now Benton was racing toward her, holding the gun at arm's length, aiming for Venus's head.

"Right between the eyes," Benton yelled, and then she tripped.

It seemed the oddest of obstacles. A scared rabbit runs. This scared rabbit hadn't run, though, when it heard the gunfire. It had frozen in place, confused and frightened, unsure which direction was safe, in what direction it should run. It froze, and when Benton's boot tip brushed up against its tiny body, it shivered and Benton's natural instinct was to jerk her foot away from the object. She lost balance and fell forward on her face. The rabbit leaped out of the scrub and bounded off.

Benton wasn't a quitter. When Venus attempted to handcuff her, Benton bucked backward, shoving Venus into the marsh. But it was all over for the RCMP officer, and when the border patrol moved in, Benton broke into a sob.

Venus drove the pickup pulling the caged polar bear. Mixx followed in the Lexus. When they reached the border at

Blaine, border guards searched Benton's pickup and the trailer. Nothing. Venus placed a call to a local veterinarian. When the vet arrived, Venus assisted as he tranquilized the polar bear.

The polar bear's X-ray revealed a healthy bone structure, and in a pouch surgically inserted inside her womb, the exact outline of the fabulous Lac de Lune.

CHAPTER FORTY-FOUR

Antwerp

Jean Claud Rubicon sat at his workbench, his number one cleaving chisel balanced atop Lac de Lune model number one, the last of the test models left to cleave, his cleaver's hammer poised above the chisel. The moment of truth had arrived, at least for Rubicon, who believed that if in the final attempt to successfully cleave a model of the real thing he failed, then he was unworthy of cleaving the genuine stone. And anyway, he had begun lately to wonder if the Lac de Lune actually existed at all, or if the letter from Mr. Hardy, the prospector in Canada's northern diamond country, actually was a hoax, perpetrated by one of Rubicon's rivals. Could that be?

Or perhaps that scoundrel Fontana had invented the ploy, including manufacturing all these models of a stone that never existed? Fontana was certainly not above playing such a scurrilous joke. After all, hadn't it been Fontana who just last week had plied Rubicon with stewed French rabbit and fine violet liqueur after switching models on Rubicon behind his back? Well, that little maneuver had failed just as soon as Fontana got so drunk he fell off his chair at the tavern, landing with a suspiciously loud thud. Rubicon had immediately investigated, discovering the model in Fontana's overcoat pocket. Upon close inspection with a magnifying glass, Rubicon had ascertained that the stone in Fontana's pocket bore specks of jeweler's cement on its surface, indicating that it had been ripped off its pedestal on Rubicon's workbench. Sure enough, when Rubicon had arrived home that evening, another stone model stood in its place and it hadn't even set into the cement. So Fontana had tried tricking Rubicon, perhaps believing that he possessed the real thing when all along both these stones were absolute fakes, mere practice models. And Rubicon had a strong hunch that Fontana had obtained his facsimile, by hook or by crook, from that two-faced scoundrel Simon Mehta. Well, Fontana must have been sorely disappointed when he awoke on the tavern floor only to discover that Rubicon had fled, leaving him the dinner bill and an empty coat pocket.

The model Fontana had substituted shattered on the first blow. And now Rubicon was down to the very last practice stone, model number one.

He thought he had the correct angle, and the pressure on his chisel felt almost right, his hammer poised just the exact distance from the chisel's foot to gain energy with the motion of the first blow. Rubicon squirmed on his bench, feeling for the proper stance. Ah, there it was. And now, for the proper pressure from the chisel before the life-or-death moment arrived.

That morning, he had decided that for the sake of practicality, a gun to the head was the preferred method of suicide. The gun lay ready now, loaded, the safety latch off, on the windowsill beside two fresh, raw sirloin steaks. His workbench and the floor surrounding were littered with shattered shards of the last model of the Lac de Lune. Should this last attempt fail, Rubicon simply had to rise, walk over to the windowsill, toss the sirloins down to Kors and Krum, place the gun to his head, and fire.

Ah. There was the correct pressure. Rubicon sucked in one deep breath and let the hammer down fast and hard.

Chink.

Chink?

Ca-chink.

Ca-chink?

The stone divided into two nearly equal pieces that fell apart and rolled to rest on the worktable.

Rubicon stared. Could it be true? Then, refusing to believe his eyes, he jumped up and ran across the room to the windowsill. Opening the window, he grasped the sirloin steaks and flung them down to Kors and Krum. The Dobermans caught the meat in their jaws and set about savaging the bloody gifts. Next, Rubicon picked up his gun, turned the barrel until a single bullet entered the chamber, and held the gun to his head, the barrel resting against his right temple, his trigger finger poised. Just as he was about to pull the trigger, Carlos Fontana materialized as if out of thin air, standing across the street from Rubicon's studio.

"I'll be goddamned if that's the last thing I see before hell," he grumbled. Setting the gun down on the windowsill, Rubicon leaned out and shouted, "What do you want now, you deceitful American pus? Can't you see I have things to do?"

Fontana smiled sheepishly and called up to Rubicon. "Forgive the interruption, my friend. I have come to share the morning newspaper with you." He held up an issue of the *Antwerp Daily Mail*.

"What in hell do I want with newspapers, Fontana? I am in the process of committing suicide. A man on the brink of eternal damnation hardly needs to read tomorrow's weather report. Why don't you go back where you came from. Go on, now, shoo. Go. Get away."

Kors and Krum, enraptured by the raw meat, ignored the scene.

Seeing his chance, Fontana scuttled across the street and past the dogs. Holding the newspaper aloft, he pleaded, "Quickly, Jean Claud, open the door before the curs attack me. I beg you. I have such wonderful news. It will surely convince you not to end your days on earth. I beg you, my friend, let me in, just for a few moments of your time."

"Oh, hell. What does it matter, anyway?"

Rubicon, gun in hand, went downstairs, let Fontana into the building and into his studio. Fontana quickly made himself at home in the one comfortable guest chair, unfolded the newspaper.

"You have exactly five minutes of my time, Fontana, during which I expect a sincere and remorseful apology for attempting to rip me off."

Fontana bowed his head. "Oh, what a pity," he complained. "How often my benevolence is mistaken for deceit. I do apologize, my friend, for any misunderstanding that might have occurred between us the other night at the tavern. But now, pay close attention. I am about to change your gloomy outlook on life. Ahem." Fontana cleared his throat and began reading from the *Antwerp Daily Mail*.

" 'The Lac de Lune Mystery Is Solved.' That's the headline. This, now, is the story. 'U.S. federal agents reported early this morning that the mysterious disappearance of the famous Lac de Lune diamond has been solved and that the last of the gang members who carried out the murderous assault on the Canadian mine where the diamond was discovered has been taken into custody. Officer Sandra Benton, of the Royal Canadian Mounted Police, was charged late yesterday with the murder of Zone Mine owner and prospector James Hardy, otherwise known as Buzz Radke, an American undercover agent employed by the U.S. federal authorities to investigate arms and diamond smuggling between the U.S. and Canada. Radke had uncovered evidence that Benton and her uncle, Jack Purdy, were smuggling African diamonds through his unproductive Canadian diamond mine.' "

Rubicon tore at what little hair remained on his head.

"Damn it, Fontana, I have no time for this nonsense. Get to the point of all this or get out of my shop."

Fontana held up a delicate hand. "I'll skip the details and get down to the bottom line, my friend. Listen carefully. 'The Lac de Lune diamond has been placed in the custody of an American federal agent for delivery to a prominent Belgian diamond cleaver sometime this week. A source close to the investigation, who prefers to remain unnamed, reports that the fabulous diamond will arrive in Antwerp sometime this week in the hands of the U.S. federal agent, whose name is not being released for reasons of security.

" 'The diamond will be cleaved, its parts then delivered to Mr. Radke's heir, Eleanor Purdy, a Yellowknife widow whose husband was killed in the assault on Zone Mine. Mrs. Purdy, herself a former prospector, had originally led Mr. Radke to the site at Lac de Lune where Mr. Radke and his geologist, Canadian Karen Crandall, also a victim of the murderers, eventually discovered a diamond craton. Mr. Radke's last will and testament stated that, upon his death, all Zone diamonds, including the Lac de Lune, would become the property in equal parts of Mrs. Purdy and Miss Crandall. What Mrs. Purdy will do with her inheritance is unknown at this time. What is known for certain is that Antwerp's own Jean Claud Rubicon, son of simple local candy makers, has won the right to cleave the world's most famous gem.' "

Fontana looked up from the newspaper. "Now, my friend, what do you have to say?"

Rubicon looked down at the last model of the Lac de Lune, divided now into two near perfect halves. Could it be true? Might his mother have been wrong?

Acknowledgments

Sincerest thanks to my editor, Kelley Ragland, for unremitting patience, support, and encouragement over the years.

Thanks to Ragnhild Hagen, who taught me that cabbages and turnips do *not* grow on vines, that Highway SR20 through the Cascades is closed during most of winter, and that Yakima, Washington, is not served by Greyhound Bus Lines.

The efforts on my behalf of my literary agent, Tony Outhwaite, have enriched both this work and my life, for which I am eternally grateful.

Thanks to Captain Dave Williams for his hospitality aboard *Salt Heart,* for berth, blaster, booze, and crab fishing, and for not dropping anchor at Quilcene. Writing aboard *Salt Heart* is pure magic.

Special thanks to diamond broker Earl Allen. Thanks to the men and women who shared their "diamond" stories, and most especially to novelist and nonfiction author Matthew Hart, whose extraordinary book *Diamond: The History of a Cold-Blooded Love Affair* informed, enthralled, and sharpened my senses about the mysterious world of diamond trading.

Finally, thanks to the inimitable G. M. Ford, master storyteller and raconteur, collaborator in all things, and the love of my life.